CHRISTMAS AT THE *Inn* ON MAIN STREET

from The Authors of Main Street

Christmas at the Inn on Main Street
An Anthology
First Edition
© 2016 The Authors of Main Street
ISBN: 978-1-62522-087-5
All rights reserved.
November 2016

This is a work of fiction. Names, places, businesses, characters, and incidents are either the product of the author's imagination or are used in a fictitious manner. Any resemblance to actual persons living or dead, actual events or locales is purely coincidental.

Box Set Cover Image: Designed by Kjpargeter / Freepik
Box Set Cover Designed by Henry Bright and B. A. Brown

Indie Artist Press; Romania Books
Pleasant Grove, Utah

FOREWARD

The Authors of Main Street write stories about people like you. We are the writers you'll run into on your own Main Street, strolling around the farmer's market, coming out of the local salon, or dashing into the post office. Now, our small-town authors have come together again to provide their readers with another tasty holiday treat. Each of the following stories contains just the right amount of heart to warm you up on the inside on the coldest day. Some of their characters might even have you believing in the magic of the season!

I hope you'll enjoy these holiday tales from the talented pens of our members. For more information about the Authors of Main Street, be sure to follow our blog and Facebook page and subscribe to our newsletter. Wishing you the warmest of holiday seasons.

Gina Ardito
Award-winning author of The Calendar Girls series

Chelsea's Christmas

E. Ayers

CHELSEA'S CHRISTMAS
BY E. AYERS

Leaving behind an unhealthy relationship, Chelsea Montgomery has come home to lick her wounds. Working in her father's law firm gives her the perfect place to hide as she avoids men and relationships. Until she meets a charming man with a beautiful son.

Keefe Assam is a successful attorney with a great life. Then, his ex-girlfriend suddenly drops off a toddler she claims belongs to him, and he is faced with the possibility, and the responsibility, of raising the boy alone.

Christmas might just herald the start of something wonderful for Chelsea, except for one problem. Her ex-boyfriend has decided if he can't her...nobody can.

ONE

Chelsea Montgomery pulled into the driveway of her childhood home and directly into the garage. Her vehicle's clock glowed 2:47 a.m. She opened the door to the kitchen and flew into the awaiting arms of her dad. "Oh, Daddy!"

It was almost noon when Chelsea opened her eyes and looked around her old bedroom. Home cocooned her in its warm embrace. Her life as she knew it was over and her dreams shattered. She got up and looked in the bathroom mirror. Her right eye was still swollen and colorful. She had bruises on both arms, her hip sported his boot print, and the thigh below it looked horrible. But the hardest part was taking a deep breath. He must have kicked her in the ribcage. She had two broken ribs. He had caught her off guard with his fist, sending her backwards until she hit the floor. As she ran her fingers through her hair, she felt the goose egg on the back of her head, probably from that fall. The doctor said to stay quiet and not lift anything.

She had failed to see the warning signs of Jason's constant demands, his desire to control everything, and that jealousy. She had chalked it up to male ego and had thought it was cute how he constantly hovered over her, so protective of her and everything she did.

Staying with him was totally different from her childhood home. Her father almost never raised his voice to his children. Instead, he put them in a protective bubble. Bad things happened to other people but not to her family. No matter how hard she tried, something always seemed to be wrong.

She remembered the first time she had attempted to fix a meal for her family and had burned it. She probably was ten at the time. Her father never fussed. He thanked her for trying so hard as he scraped the burnt contents of casserole into the garbage disposal and left the pan to soak. He told everyone to eat the salad, and then he was taking everyone out for banana splits.

Her dad had done everything he could to protect his children from his less than stellar clientele. He had devoted his entire law practice to finding convicts who had been unfairly accused, which meant digging through court files of frequently heinous crimes. Finding the innocent within that group was like looking for that proverbial needle in the haystack. She was following in her father's footsteps and had gone to work for the same agency when she graduated from Baylor.

Okay, I can stand here and feel sorry for myself or pick up the pieces and face life. She turned on the water in the shower. *That's a no brainer. Licking my wounds isn't going to get me very far.*

Feeling refreshed, dressed in jeans and a tee shirt, she made her way to the kitchen and fixed a cup of coffee.

"Want me to make something for you? Or would you rather go out to eat?" Cody Montgomery opened the refrigerator. "I have eggs, if you want breakfast, plus there are salad fixings and plenty of lunchmeat."

"I don't want to go anyplace looking like this."

He tipped her chin upwards. "It's not too bad. A little makeup, a pair of sunglasses, and no one will know."

She shook her head. "I have no desire to do anything at the moment." She looked at her dad as he sat across from her at the kitchen table. "I don't want to talk about it."

"I understand. But if and when you do, you know I'm here for you."

She nodded. "Still have that opening at your law office?"

"For you? Always. I don't think I could have a better partner. But you do understand that the job doesn't pay much."

Chelsea shook her head as a slight giggle escaped. "I know, a whole dollar a year to make the work legal. When do you want me to start?"

"The day you graduated would have been nice. But you may start whenever you are ready to come back."

"Do you have a real desk for me?"

"I have that conference room table. Why don't you stop by the furniture store when you feel up to it and choose whatever you want? Until then, there's the table."

She nodded. "When I'm ready."

The following Monday she started working. It was as though she'd never left. In all the years of her being away at college and a year of working in Texas, nothing had changed except for her father's computer, and she wondered if he had routinely kept up with all the software changes and updates. *Probably not.*

The first three days, she spent updating things and creating spreadsheets to track all work. Not that there was much. Most of it was usually research that led to a guilty man. The agency did send them a list of names and the cases, but habitually her father spent his time checking court records online for possible innocents. Every name he had checked was in a document with notes typed beside it.

His secretary Carlie was partially responsible for his lack of more modern methods, because she was not very good on a computer. She even refused to use a smart phone for anything other than a phone. Why Cody kept the woman was almost beyond Chelsea's comprehension. But Carlie did show up for work every day, was loyal, and didn't talk about cases. And Carlie needed the money. Chelsea was determined that Carlie would learn to use the computer for more than typing a document. The woman needed to learn to handle a spreadsheet and learn to use a simple computerized accounting system.

When Chelsea was certain she had everything the way it should be, she went to the furniture store for a desk. She found exactly what she wanted, and it seemed as though it had been designed just for her. The U-shaped desk was perfect for the kind of work she did. Then she bought a new computer and several printers with the idea that she could set up each one for specific jobs. Satisfied with what she had done, she went back to the office.

"Did you find everything you wanted?" Cody asked as he stood in the doorway to her small office.

"Yes. But I want to ditch my car. I don't want him to find me."

Cody nodded. "I think the entire family is breathing a sigh of relief that you are home and away from him." He stuck his hands into his pockets and leaned against the doorframe. "I agree with the idea of getting another vehicle. Does he know where you grew up?"

She shrugged. "I don't think so. Maybe the town, but I doubt it. I've never said much about my family other than I worked for my father."

"Montgomery is a common name. And I've kept a low profile."

"Dad, thank you for being the best father anyone could ever have."

Cody beamed. "I've done my best to give all of my children a good foundation and support them. I've tried hard to recognize that you are all different and have different needs."

"As far as I am concerned, you are the best."

"And after that, I hate to tell you that I have to leave tomorrow for Norfolk, Virginia. I need to interview a few people there."

"You found something?"

He nodded. "Seems one of the kids from a law school near there found something and contacted the agency when they hit a dead end. But this young student..." Cody paused. "Gut feelings are often worth a closer look. Are you going to be okay if I leave?"

Chelsea nodded. "Go, Dad. I'm a grown woman. I don't have to have my daddy to get through my problems." She looked up at him and smiled. "It's just nice to know he's there for me. Besides, you've got a great alarm system on the house and here in the office. I think I'm quite safe."

"If anything happens and you need me, I'm a phone call away. It will only take a few hours to get back here. DeeDee is here, and you know she will do anything for you."

"I'm glad you found her. I've never seen you so happy."

It was Friday afternoon, twenty-five minutes before they closed, when Carlie pressed the button on the intercom of their old phone system. "Line two. Oldham, Gleason, Assam, and Sharp."

"Thanks." Chelsea opened Notepad on her computer and punched the flashing light on her desk phone. "Chelsea Montgomery."

"Um, I *asked* for *Cody* Montgomery."

His tone got to her, but she tried to remain polite.

"Well, you got me. He's out of the office. What can I do for you?" She opened her desk drawer and looked for a bottle of water.

"Um, nothing. When's the best time to reach *him?*"

When hell freezes over. She withdrew the bottle and uncapped it. "What's the problem?"

"Look, I'm sorry to bother you. I'll call back."

"Wait! Who are you?"

"Keefe Assam. Tell him I called."

The line went dead and began to play that horrible screeching beep that was supposed to attract your attention so that you would hang up the phone.

Chelsea punched her finger on the disconnect button and then redialed the law office. "Keefe Assam, please. This is the Cody Montgomery office."

A few clicks and Keefe Assam picked up the line.

"Now just what was it that you wanted?"

"Excuse me?"

"You asked for Cody and you've got me. What's the problem?" She hated when everyone treated her like a little kid who still worked for her dad because she refused to have a babysitter, and her father refused to allow her to stay home by herself at the end of each school day.

"I need to speak to Cody about a case."

"Well, you got me. Spit it out."

"I stumbled upon something that Cody Montgomery might be interested in."

"Meaning?" The face came to her. He'd been a year ahead of her at Baylor's law school. Tall, dark, and handsome with vibrant green eyes, he had a reputation for being aloof and haughty.

"I don't have time to tell you and then tell him. Once is enough."

"No problem. Tell me and it's done."

"Fine. It's not my problem." Keefe rattled off the case.

Chelsea kept up with his fast pace and noted everything. "Thanks." She pulled up her calendar. "May I treat you to lunch next Friday? Mr. Montgomery will be back by then."

"Sorry, I'm busy." He disconnected the line once again.

No problem, hotshot! I'll get you. She saved the file and

began to look up the two cases. *Oh, did you ever stumble onto something.*

It was well after five o'clock when she turned the lights out in the office and left. She was used to doing the preliminary legwork on cases for her dad. She'd been doing it since she was a kid and her dad offered to pay her to work for him. *I used to think he just couldn't stand the idea of my being alone after school.* That thought made her laugh. *Following in your footsteps, Dad, is that what you had hoped for all along?*

She walked past Main Street Bridal in time to see her oldest sister walk out the door. "Hey, Julia, want to grab some coffee?"

Julia turned and grinned. "Sounds like a plan." She scurried across the street. "How's it going?"

"You mean at the office?"

"Yeah."

"It was monotonous until today."

"What do you mean?"

"Another law office called for Dad. Someone stumbled upon a very thin case."

"Oh, sounds...ah...boring."

"No. Bridal dresses are boring."

"How's your eye?"

Chelsea waved her hand as if to brush off the injury. "Dad told you?"

"No, DeeDee did."

Chelsea lifted her sunglasses. "Well aside from the fact that the whites of my eye still look yellow, I'd say that I've covered what's left of the bruising with makeup."

"I know you don't want to hear this, but none of us liked him. I'm just sorry you didn't get out before he almost killed you."

"So am I. And I don't need a lecture. My e-reader is filled with books about toxic relationships. Thinking back, I can see all the warning signs. I just failed to recognize them. I kept chalking it up to the stress of school. I figured it would get better once we graduated and I passed the Bar. But it was always something. After he calmed down, he'd make love to me and tell me how wonderful I was."

"No lectures from me. You're the smart one." Julia took a

few more steps and then stopped. "Do me one favor, let me set you up with a better wardrobe. I'm sick of seeing you in black pants and a jacket. They do nothing for you. Nothing!"

"Oh! I don't even have to think about what I'm going to wear. I just grab and get dressed."

"And that's what you look like!"

Chelsea pulled open the door to Elizabeth's coffee shop on Main Street. The place was filled with the after-work crowd. She looked around and when she spotted Keefe Assam, she yanked on her sister as she fled out the door.

"What?" Julia followed her sister. "What is wrong? Slow down. I'm in sky-high heels!"

"I'm not going in there if he's in there."

"If who is in there?"

"Keefe Assam. He's Harcourt Assam's son."

"The lawyer?"

"Yeah, Keefe has gone in with his dad."

"So?"

Chelsea scrunched up her nose and rubbed her forehead. "I virtually asked him out this afternoon, and he turned me down."

Julia put her hands on her hips. "There's no virtually about it. Either you asked him out or you didn't."

She let out a sigh. "I offered to buy him lunch Friday, and he said he couldn't do it."

"Did you give him another day or ask him what day would be better for him?"

"No. He said he was busy and hung up on me."

"Chelsea Montgomery, do you need lessons on how to get a date?" She grabbed her sister's arm and turned her around. "We're going back in there because I want a cup of Elizabeth's yummy, frosty, iced coffee with raspberry chocolate mixed in it."

"You're joking, right? Two minutes ago you were complaining that I looked like hell, and now you want me to go in there?"

Keefe grabbed his cup of coffee and waited for a moment until a seat became vacant. He couldn't get that one case out of his head. He had stumbled on it accidentally when a client of his father's was the victim of a man with a similar name. It had left him with questions as to who the perp really was. He was looking up a rap sheet of the perpetrator when he stumbled on the other man's. As he searched the court records of the man serving a life sentence for murder, he realized that the whole case was insubstantial. He discussed it with his father, who suggested he turn it over to Cody Montgomery. But his father also warned him not to stick his nose into things and to stop chasing rabbits.

Keefe sipped at his coffee and savored the espresso laden with sweet coconut milk. Shaking the feeling that they had the wrong man in that old murder case wasn't going to be easy. The assaulted victim of this latest burglary probably had found the true perpetrator of the murder two years prior. There were too many similarities in the cases.

He worried that Cody Montgomery would never get his message. He didn't need some assistant or incompetent paralegal playing around with the case and botching it. He knew he had something and it bothered him. His dad dealt mostly with personal injury cases because he claimed it paid the bills and was lucrative work.

Keefe had graduated with high hopes of doing more for society. Lawsuits over fender benders were not his idea of protecting the people. But here he was doing what his father did, because it paid the bills.

He looked up and a familiar face put an end to his personal deliberation. He was a long way from Texas, but he could have sworn she had been an underclassman. He couldn't remember her name, however he was certain he'd seen her on campus. Even the way she had pulled her hair into a knot at the back of her neck looked familiar. He went back to staring into his coffee. He swirled the drink and then took a sip.

But when she walked to the table where Elizabeth kept the sugar and cream, he got a good look at her. He could have sworn she was doing everything possible not to look at him, which was quite different from most women. He was tired of being the poster boy for tall, dark, and handsome. That was not who he was.

Maybe she's gay. He went back to his thoughts about the cases the firm was handling and one simple one that had been dropped in his lap as if it were a super prize with which they were entrusting him. *I've been practicing for two years. I'm not green and fresh out of college. I know what I'm doing.*

He finished his drink and ordered another. His parents had expected him to move home after he graduated. Instead, he found an apartment over an antique shop. It had been newly renovated and was quite nice. The shop stayed open until eight p.m. on Friday and Saturday, but the rest of the time, by six o'clock it was closed. That meant almost no noise. Maybe his favorite thing about the apartment was being two doors from Elizabeth's coffee shop. After work, he'd park his car in the alleyway behind his apartment and walk to Elizabeth's. First thing in the morning, he'd grab that cup of java before heading into work. He didn't even own a coffeepot.

He muttered to himself as he removed his suit jacket. "It's too warm for this time of year."

His phone rang. "Hi, Mom. What's up?" "Dinner tonight?" He looked at the young woman who had captured his attention. She now sat at a table on the far side of the room with her back to him. "Ah, tonight is not a good night." He hated to turn her offer down when she had cooked one of his favorite meals. "Maybe if you have some left over, I'll have it for lunch tomorrow." He listened to his mother's concerns. "No, Mom, nothing such as that. I'm just busy. I ran into an old schoolmate from college, and we're hoping to catch up this evening." He decided that wasn't lying. "Thanks, Mom, for the offer. It's much appreciated, but maybe another night."

He could barely take his eyes off the woman across from him. He just wished he could remember her name. She was dressed very plainly in pants and a jacket. The woman she was with was a total knockout. It was obvious that the women were quite chummy. After watching them for another few minutes, he made a decision. Even if she was gay, he figured it wouldn't matter. They'd just be catching up on their lives since school—a little shoptalk, and maybe those were the best evenings.

With his cup in his hand, he started across the room to where the two women sat. About two strides into his stroll, it hit him that the women might be a couple.

Too late. The other woman looked up at him and smiled. His gut clenched, and that was something that never happened to him. It was as though the wall of confidence that he had carefully built around him crumbled. "Hello, if you don't mind my interruption, I'm Keefe Assam." He nodded at the one woman and held his hand out to the one whose face was familiar. "If I remember correctly, I think I went to school with you."

The woman's smile looked more like the sneer of a wild animal going for the kill. But he was already beside her, and he wasn't about to back down.

She raised her eyebrows. "Is that all you remember, Keefe?"

"I'll be honest, I don't remember your name, but I was hoping you'd join me Friday for lunch. Just a friendly lunch—catch up on things—"

She crossed her arms over her chest. "If you remember, I asked you first, and you turned me down."

"Excuse me?"

She frowned. "I thought you said you were busy. I guess it is true, you can't trust an ambulance chaser. They have forked tongues."

"Chelsea Montgomery! What is wrong with you?" The other woman looked horrified.

Keefe swallowed as the name sunk into his head. "Chelsea Montgomery? As in Cody Montgomery Law Office?"

She rolled her eyes. "Yes. Were you expecting Montgomery, Alabama? And this is my sister Julia."

Keefe clenched his teeth together and politely nodded to Julia before answering Chelsea, "I'd love to discuss the case with you and what I've found. I had no idea we were in school together or that you lived here. I don't remember you from Grayson Academy."

"My father believes in public schools. He thinks they do a better job of preparing us for real life."

It was Keefe's turn to raise his eyebrows. "Does that mean that he thinks private education teaches children to be snobs?"

"No. They learn that on their own. Elitism is quite common even among the lowest classes of the world." She smiled and picked up her cup of coffee. "Do you feel extra privileged because you attended a private school?"

"No. But I know I received an excellent education."

"Well, so did I. And I also learned quite a bit about people along the way, including those who live with very different financial backgrounds, or are from other ethnic groups or have different religious beliefs."

Keefe knew it was pointless to argue with her, especially if he was hoping for a date. She wasn't wearing any rings on her fingers, and he was taking that as a good sign. He needed to quickly change the subject. "I'd really like the chance to talk to you about the case I sent over. I'll be tied up in court all this coming week." He smiled. "Except for Friday. I found out as I was getting ready to leave that we were granted a continuance."

Chelsea rolled her eyes. "How convenient."

Keefe swallowed. "I had considered calling your office back. But on a Friday afternoon, I assumed if you could leave a few minutes early, you would."

"We might not seem busy, but we utilize every moment on the clock. My father believes in working hard and playing hard. We don't mix the two."

"Excellent philosophy, but often difficult to embrace."

"It's our values - what we believe."

"But how do you make money on convicts?"

Chelsea laughed. "We don't take a penny from them. We are strictly *pro bono*."

"Then you survive on grants and gifts?"

"How we manage is not public knowledge." She stood and carried her cup to the return counter. "Are you ready, Julia?"

Julia looked at Chelsea, frowned, and then turned to him as she held out her hand. "It was lovely to meet you. I think we all know your father. He's worked hard for the Downtown Business Association."

Keefe stood there, feeling as though he'd been punched in

the gut. Women didn't turn down dates with him. He didn't like losing.

TWO

Chelsea had barely stepped out the door when Julia verbally assaulted her.

"You'll never get a date acting that way. You can't treat him like that."

"Like what? Do you think I care about a date? I wanted to talk to him about the case. It's not as though I'm pining for a chance to go out. I think I need some time to recover. I'm not ready for another man in my life."

"You certainly can't be wallowing in grief over losing such a jerk. You need to be dancing in the aisles that you found out before you had children or he killed you."

Chelsea rolled her eyes. "I don't give a damn. I'm not like you. I don't need a man to make my life complete. I have a complete life. I enjoy my work. I like having time to myself." She raised her hands from her sides and held them wide. "Why does everyone think we *all* want to settle down, have children, and wipe snotty noses for the next twelve years?"

"You don't want children?"

"NO!" She glared at her sister. Then she saw the look of horror on her sister's face. "I love all my nieces and nephews and I love visiting with them, but after a few hours, I get to give them back and go on with my own life. I'd rather have a horse than a child."

She rolled her eyes at Julia, and without waiting for her sister's reply she took off for the home where she had grown up. *Why? Just because she loves having babies doesn't mean I want them. My life is complicated enough.*

Keefe looked around his apartment. He liked the place. Large and open, it was exactly what he wanted. The wall facing the alley was made of large blocks of glass that spanned the entire back portion of his apartment. Windows facing the street went almost from the floor to the ceiling. He had chosen expensive blinds for those street-side windows. The blinds looked old-fashioned but were mechanized so that with a few clicks on a remote control, each could be adjusted perfectly together or individually. That same remote would handle the large ceiling fans and a half dozen other items including the thermostats. He loved it. But what he really liked was his own rather unusual sense of style. He enjoyed finding all sorts of unique pieces of copper sculpture and colorful glass items. He paired it all with a sofa and several chairs covered in a soft cotton corduroy fabric in a light blue color and then added pillows and a throw done in metallic-colored fabrics. He loved the look and was pleased with what he had done. It was his style. Bold yet understated, it matched the old look of the apartment with its wide moldings and plank floors. He flopped into the deep cushions of the sofa and mentally reviewed the day.

The case he had stumbled upon was haunting him. But it was Chelsea Montgomery's attitude and demeanor that got to him more. She had left the coffee shop with her sister and seemed to have an argument with her before storming off at a pace that appeared to dare anyone to follow her. He had walked to the coffee shop's window and watched her vanish at an intersection that led to an older neighborhood of well-kept brick homes.

Memories of seeing Chelsea in the law library at school and other places around campus came to him and then quickly vanished. She was always the same. Hair in a bun, black pants, plain shirt. She was plain. She was also naturally pretty.

He knew someone who worked for a nonprofit legal group and the guy barely made enough to cover his school loans. There had to be something more to Cody Montgomery's law firm. *Maybe he's just making money on his rental properties around here.*

Pulling himself from his comfortable spot, he went to his kitchen and whipped up a meal using two small lamb chops he'd bought at the market the other day. He cubed the meat he'd cut from the bone, added spices, and mixed it with rice. Then he wrapped the whole thing in toasted nori seaweed and baked it in a sweet wine sauce while he sliced up several veggies and prepared to stir-fry them. He cleaned up the mess he had made and when he was done, he checked on the lamb before starting his stir-fry. He sat at his high bar to eat his creation and stared out the living room window. When he finished, he immediately washed and wiped until everything in the kitchen was returned to its former pristine shine.

He loved keeping his place clean and neat. He had shared a dorm in college and then an apartment. Each time, he had a slob for a roommate. Saturday was his day for thoroughly cleaning the place and, on Sunday, he liked to relax. With the weather still warm, he thought about canoeing. He thought about several places where he'd canoed as a kid and hadn't been back. It seemed like a fun thing to do. His thoughts were interrupted by the sound of the doorbell.

He punched the button on the wall. "Yes."

"Oh, thank God, it's you. Let me in."

"Who is this?"

"Oh, Keefe, it's Leighayn. Let me in."

He buzzed her in as his mind did a series of somersaults through their rocky relationship. It ended when he discovered she was seeing another guy. That's not what he wanted in a partner. He wanted a lifetime commitment. Someone to actually share his life, someone who enjoyed doing what he did. Leighayn was not that person. He realized she was too self-centered.

She knocked on his upper door.

Smile. Be nice. He opened the door. "What brings you here?"

He stared at the child she held on her hip. From her opposite shoulder hung two straps that supported two bulging bags.

"Oh, how could you choose such a horrid place to live? Uh! I'm totally out of breath. All those steps."

She dropped the bags at his feet and he moved them so he could close the door.

"Walking all those steps was bad enough, but this place is like some sterile environment. It's so typical of you. Neat

23

freak. What's this crap?" She picked up his prized piece of dichroic glass.

"It's a Jack Storms sculpture. It's called *Viviolo*. Please don't handle it like that."

She held it up as though she intended to drop it. "Well, if it's so precious, you'd better remove it. By the way, this is your son, in case you haven't figured that out. He was born on December twenty-seventh. He's yours, look at him. You walked out on me the end of May. Now I have a chance at happiness, and I'm not going to miss it." She went to the bar that separated the kitchen from the rest of the room and placed the egg-shaped piece of glass there. Then dug through one of the bags. "It's here someplace. I listed you as the father. Anyway, he's yours now." She slipped the child down her side to his feet. "He'll be two on his birthday. It's your turn. I already signed the custody papers in front of a notary. So do whatever mumbo-jumbo lawyers do to make everything legal... Happy fatherhood. I'm leaving the country."

Keefe had to force his mouth closed as his mind tried to process what she was saying. "You are dumping me with a child?"

"I'm not dumping him. He's your child. Look at him!"

He wanted to say DNA test, but the little boy before him was a carbon copy of photos of Keefe at the same age.

She laughed. "Get over it." She turned, yanked his apartment door open and walked out. "Potty train him. He's old enough."

His heart thumped against his chest and it wasn't a good feeling. The child began to cry.

Keefe went to his door and called down the steps. "What's his name?"

"Rage. Rage Assam. It's in the paperwork." She held her fingers by her shoulder and wiggled them. "Deal with it."

Chelsea walked to her old room and flopped across her bed. *Why am I here? I need my own place. But this is so easy.*

She kicked her shoes off and heard them thump as they

hit the carpeted floor. DeeDee had redone the rooms as each sibling moved away. Gone were her pink walls and the frilly bedspread. She liked the new look.

The soft peach color on the walls blended perfectly with the wood of the hand-carved furniture. The room was filled with tiny details such as the decorative scrolling that DeeDee had painted near the sills of the windows and doors. It looked unique and very sophisticated. Bright decorative throw pillows and interesting paintings added vibrancy to what could have been a monotonous monochromatic room.

Compared to Julia and Melissa, Chelsea knew she was the more artistic, but she wasn't creative. DeeDee had the eye for things, and that's what made her so successful as a bridal fashion designer. Chelsea knew what she liked, but she had no idea how to explain it or make it happen. But when her room was to be redone, she was asked a few simple questions. DeeDee took those answers and made the most tranquil oasis in a few square feet.

Chelsea forced herself from her bed and shed her work clothes for an old pair of baggy pants with an elastic waist and a faded tee shirt. She took her hair down, brushed it, and pulled it into a ponytail. Standing with her back to the mirror, she looked over her shoulder. *Gosh, it's gotten long. Maybe I should get it cut. Why can't I be like my sisters? They just give it a twist or whatever and it looks perfect.* She sighed, finished washing up, and headed for the kitchen.

As she stepped into her father's newly renovated kitchen, she looked around and began to open cabinets. Everything was in different places. Even the sink and stove had been moved. She loved the new look, and it allowed for several people to work in the kitchen without tripping over one another. *If we only had this when all of us were at home.*

She started supper using a package of chicken she found in the refrigerator. Her dad always managed to put good meals on the table for them, but his cooking was always plain and simple. She had learned to cook as he had, but loved foods that were fancier and had been made with various herbs and spices. The pantry contained several sweet potatoes. A smile tugged at her cheeks with the thought that someone had bought them knowing they were one of Chelsea's favorite root veggies. After prepping them for baking, she placed the potatoes in the oven and then added the chicken. *I'll do the other veggies last.* She looked in the pantry, hoping to find a few cans of creamed corn and some limas for succotash. But the ring of the house phone interrupted her search.

Without looking at the caller ID she picked up the line. "Hello."

"Well, that was easy." The line went dead.

Chelsea shivered. She knew who it was. Punching a few buttons on the old landline revealed the number of his cell phone. She picked up the cordless phone and called her father.

"He's found me."

"Whatever you do, don't run. You are safer in that house than you are anyplace else. Where's DeeDee?"

She looked at the clock on the wall. "I'm going to assume she's picking up the children. I'm here by myself."

"Just keep the security system on all the time. I'll call DeeDee."

"Okay. Dad, I love you."

She heard him disconnect the line. She turned and stared at the small security panel by the back door. Everything was fine. But the feeling inside her wasn't going away. How many times had her father said to trust her instincts? But was the feeling of panic an unfounded fear? Just because he called didn't mean he was lurking around the corner, waiting for her. *He's nearby. I know he is.*

The memory of that last day with Jason struck her as though she were reliving it. Even the aroma of popcorn seemed to linger in the air just as it had at the police station. The pictures and questions from the police... The questioning had started at the local emergency department. When the doctor released her, she was taken to the police station.

Chelsea answered all the questions she could. She also listened carefully to what the female officer told her. A delivery driver was about to knock on the door but spotted the altercation in the house and called the police instead. An officer had been in the area and had just passed the ranch.

He turned around and flew up the hard-pack drive to the house in time to see Jason hit her. That was the blow that knocked her unconscious.

She'd had enough for one day. Her head was killing her. After having refused the pain pills the doctor had offered her, she now coped with the most horrendous headache she'd ever had in her life. "Please will someone take me home long enough to grab my purse and a few belongings?"

The female police officer nodded. "You don't have to worry about him. He's not getting out anytime soon."

She willed herself back to reality in the middle of her father's kitchen. *He's out. I know he is. He's got friends and connections. He's out. He's found me.*

She shuddered. From her injuries and what she had been told, knocking her unconscious was not enough. He was kicking her when the police officer pulled him off her. *He would have killed me.*

She heard the garage door open and turned on the monitor. It was DeeDee. A moment later, Charley burst through the door with her pigtails a little askew. Then DeeDee followed with CJ. The smile on Cody's youngest child was identical to his father's. In fact, both children looked exactly like their dad. He never said a word about their paternity, but Chelsea knew he was thrilled to finally have two children that were truly his. Chelsea also knew DeeDee had made certain she wasn't having any more.

"Oh, Chelsea, I can smell dinner. Having you around is a wonderful treat."

"You might change your mind after I tell you what just happened."

"CJ, Charley, I want you both to wash for dinner." DeeDee turned her attention back to Chelsea. "Why would you say such a thing?"

"I've already called Dad. Jason is out and he's found me."

"How do you know that?"

"He called this house from his cell phone. I didn't look at the caller ID; I simply answered the phone."

"Oh, no. I'm so sorry. Did he give any clue as to where he was?"

She shook her head. "He's probably here in town. This phone is unlisted. How else would he get the number? He's here, and someone who knows us probably gave it to him."

"What did your father tell you to do?" She held up one finger. "Charley, CJ. Hurry up."

Chelsea put the limas and corn together in a pan and placed them on a burner. She stirred the vegetables and then added a few drops of cream and stirred them some more. "I'm scared, DeeDee. Really scared. I know I'm reasonably safe in this house, but I don't trust him."

"So somehow, someone has bailed him out, right?"

Chelsea nodded. "I can check online tonight after dinner. I'll use Dad's computer if you don't mind."

"Not at all."

Both children appeared and took their places at the table. They were well-mannered children and were growing up surrounded with lots of love. Chelsea adored both of them with all her heart. She loved children, but couldn't imagine ever having one in her life. Now Julia was furious because she took Chelsea's preference as a slur against all those who embraced motherhood. *Somehow, I've got to get her to understand from my point of view. I don't want this family torn apart. We've all had enough.*

THREE

Keefe walked to the child who was wailing and stooped to the level of his tiny face. "I'd like to cry, too. I know exactly how you feel."

The child twisted away and wound up on the floor on his belly. His little feet pounded the floor. Keefe sat next to him and patted the little boy's back. "Go right ahead and cry. When you're done, we'll figure out how we'll manage."

Eventually the little boy ran out of tears and when he did, he fell asleep. Keefe breathed a deep sigh and went to the two bags that Leighayn had dropped. He found the folder with the papers. Leighayn had named the boy Rage Assam. *Was it your rage that caused you to give him such a name? And why didn't you call me? Why didn't you tell me you were pregnant – why did you wait until now to tell me? Why didn't you come looking for child support?*

He shook his head as if it would help to clear his mind from all the questions that circulated. There were no answers to any of them. No one other than Leighayn would know the answers, and she was gone. He spent a few minutes carefully going over the paperwork that gave him custody. She'd not only given him custody; she gave up all rights to the child. Custody papers were easily overturned, but he was satisfied with the wording. Now he faced a larger problem – babysitting. Maybe with a little forewarning, he could have been prepared. Maybe with a little forewarning he wouldn't have a child sleeping on his floor.

He had to face up to what he'd done and swallow his pride. His parents were going to be furious with him. Unclipping his phone from his belt, he called his mom. "Hi, Mom. I have some news and it's going to be a bit of a shock. I have a son. He'll be two this Christmas."

"What? Who?"

"Leighayn. She brought him by tonight and left him with

me. I have full custody of him." He looked over at the child who was still asleep.

"Did you know about this?"

"Of course not."

"How do you know he's yours?"

"Mom, wait until you see him. I'll do the DNA testing, but he looks like me."

"You had better do that test. You don't want to be saddled with a child that's not yours. And you obviously never listened to me when I taught you to abstain."

He was glad his mom couldn't see the smirk on his face. "Mom, I need some help. I need to find a babysitter. Do you know anyone who would be willing to keep him?"

"Do you intend to keep my grandchild from me?"

What? "Of course not! I'll bring him over tomorrow and let you meet him."

Rage began to stir.

"Um, Mom, he's waking up. I think I need to spend some time with him. Leighayn dropped him and his belongings off and then left. He cried until he fell asleep. Let me call you back."

He went to where the child was lying on the floor and sat beside him.

Rage rolled over, rubbed his eyes, made little fists, and stretched his arms over his head.

"Hello, do you remember me?"

The boy sat up and nodded. "When is Mommy coming back?"

"According to the papers she gave me, she has no intention of returning. We're stuck with each other."

The little boy grabbed at himself.

"Do you need to go tinkle in the bathroom?"

"Huh?"

"Um, tinkle, pee, pee-pee, urinate—whatever you call it."

"Pee-pee." Rage made a face.

Keefe jumped to his feet, picked the boy up, and carried him to the nearest bathroom. But they were too late. "Okay, we tried. Um, stand here and let me get your clothes."

A few minutes later, he had the little boy cleaned up. "Let's go through your things and organize everything so we can find things when we need them."

He emptied a lower shelf in his big walk-in closet and used it for Rage's clothes. He knew small children grew quickly and often outgrew things at the speed of light. But everything Rage owned, except for the outfit he was wearing when he arrived, looked old and stained. He didn't know if they were hand-me-downs or thrift store finds. It surprised him, and yet it didn't. Leighayn always dressed to kill, and she only wore the best brands in clothing. At least the child had a toothbrush and a comb amid his things.

"Have you eaten anything lately?"

The boy shook his head.

"Okay, let's get you some food while I try to figure out how you can sleep without falling out of the bed." He put his hand out to the child and the little boy took it.

In the kitchen, Keefe rummaged around in the refrigerator and kept asking if the child wanted a variety of items.

Rage looked as though Keefe had lost his mind.

"Okay, I need help. What does Mommy feed you? Do you know?"

"Fish sticks and Hot Pockets!"

"We have a problem. I don't have either one. But that gives me an idea." He took a tomato and sliced it. He toasted an English muffin, added a tomato slice to it, covered it with some Swiss cheese, and found some pepperoni. He diced a few slices of pepperoni and sprinkled it on top of his creation and popped the whole thing in the oven. As soon as the cheese was melted, he took it out, and placed his pizza-like creation on a plate. He added a lettuce wrap he had made out of lettuce, cream cheese, and a thin slice of cucumber.

The boy watched him the entire time. His eyes weren't exactly the same green as Keefe's. Rage's eyes were more golden green, but they shared the same eye shape and long lashes.

Keefe put the plate of food in front of the boy and waited.

The child poked at it with his fingers.

"Am I supposed to cut it up in little pieces for you?"

The little boy rolled out his lower lip and poked at the food some more. "I'm not a baby. Mommy says I'm a big boy."

"Um, yes, you are. So you know how to pick that up and eat it?"

31

"What's this?" He pointed to the lettuce.

"Well, my mom calls it a lettuce wrap. I used to have it as a snack when I came home from school, but it also worked well for me when I was in college. It's cheap and easy. It tastes good."

"I want Hot Pockets."

"If you can find Hot Pockets in my apartment, I will make them. But that round thing in front of you is as close as I can come."

The child picked the English muffin up and took a bite, then devoured it. He still poked at the lettuce.

"Try it. If you don't like it, I understand. No one wants to eat something they don't like. But sometimes you have to try things." He looked at the boy who picked it up and studied the wrap as though it were a never-before-seen specimen of something horrible.

The child took a bite.

Keefe waited for a reaction. It was as though the child sucked on it rather than chewing it. But Keefe knew to wait silently.

The boy pulled the lettuce from his mouth, then unrolled what was left and ate the cream cheese and cucumber.

Keefe figured that was progress. "Are you done? Do you want more?"

The boy wiggled until he had slid off the chair to the floor. He picked up the remote and began to push buttons.

Keefe slapped his forehead as his blinds began to move and fans turned on and off. He sucked in a deep breath and went to Rage. "Are you looking to turn on the TV?"

"Mommy lets me watch TV after I eat."

"Well, you are going to have to learn how to use my remote." He sat next to Rage, then slipped him onto his lap and showed him how to turn the TV on and off and how to find a channel. He found what he thought was a suitable channel, and Rage instantly changed it to a sports channel. He laughed to himself as he put his son back on the sofa. *Well, at least we share the same taste in TV. But I need to figure out how to keep you from falling onto the floor tonight.*

Chelsea picked up her phone and touched the icon for sister. "Julia, please, I'm sorry. I didn't mean to offend you."

"Well, motherhood is more than snotty noses."

"I know that. But please understand that I don't want to be responsible for a child. I love my job."

"Well, so do I."

Chelsea frowned. "Oh, we're about to go down that same path. Please, I love you, and I love my nieces and nephews. I don't want us to argue."

"You'll change your mind one day when the right guy comes along. You just haven't found the right guy."

Chelsea listened to her oldest sister ramble on about the joy of finding a really great man. But Chelsea knew she needed to figure out how she could have made such a horrible mistake, because she didn't want to ever repeat it. What mental flaw did she harbor that blinded her to the type of man Jason was? "Thanks for the pep talk, Julia. But for now, it's probably best for me to focus on my job. As you said, when the right one comes along and the fireworks start, I'll know it."

Not with my luck. Mr. Wonderful isn't going to fall from heaven and land on my doorstep.

The following morning, she looked at the coffeepot and headed to Elizabeth's for that morning cup. The walk felt good as she looked at the houses in the neighborhood. Several homes now had new owners. But Lucille Woodbridge, in spite of her age, was still tending her gardens. Her red roses were blooming in one bed and another bed was filled with flowers that bloomed in hot pink, purple, and orange. Somehow that wild color combination worked.

Several of the trees already showed signs of changing. Acorns and other nuts littered the ground, forcing her to pay attention as she walked. The slight nip to the morning air made the walk even more pleasant.

She figured after she drank her coffee, she'd go to the dealership and look at cars. She wanted to ditch her car and those Texas license plates. They were both neon signs saying she was in town. There was no point in making it easy for *him* to find her. *I don't need a confrontation with him.*

Keefe managed to get Rage dressed and out the door. Keefe wanted to laugh at the little guy because he was quite talkative. As they crossed Maple Street, Keefe spotted Chelsea also walking towards the coffee shop. She looked once in his direction and Keefe raised his hand in greeting.

The look on her face was almost priceless. It was a cross between shock and total disdain. But she might be the perfect person to help him. If she had younger siblings or friends with children, she would most likely know what he needed for a toddler. He leaned down. "This is Miss Chelsea. We went to school together."

He figured parading through town was going to create a stir with the local gossips, but he didn't care. He was responsible for Rage, and the circumstance of his birth was no one's business. Keefe gave the child's hand a little squeeze and Rage looked up and smiled. Keefe could feel that fatherly pride running through his system.

He managed to beat Chelsea to the coffee shop. Grabbing the door, he held it for her. "Good morning."

Chelsea's gaze swept from him to Rage and back up again. "Good morning to you, and thank you. Amazing, chivalry is not dead."

He chuckled. "My mother would have my hide if I didn't hold the door for a woman, especially for a..." He smiled broadly. "For a fellow J D. If we fail to respect the members of the Bar, then we are degrading our own accomplishments."

She looked at him with her forehead knitted. "It's much too early in the morning for horse manure."

"Okay, I was going to say, 'pretty woman,' but I figured you might kill me."

"You aren't worth killing. Very few people are."

"May I buy your coffee?"

She plastered a fake smile on her face. "I have money. You seem to think I'm some starving lawyer. Maybe I should buy yours, but I don't go near married men."

"Then I'm fair game, for I'm not married and never was. I had a little surprise waiting for me when I got home last night. I obtained full custody of Rage Assam last night. Actually, all the paperwork will be completed Monday morning. I still need to file some documents with the court."

"Is he family? He certainly looks like you."

Oh that's a good way to say it. "Yes. He's family. And now he's one hundred percent mine."

"That's very kind of you to take on a child. He's cute as a button."

"Chelsea, I could use a little help. I have no idea what I need for him. I guess he needs a crib. I have a room for him, but no furniture in it. I pushed my bed against the wall last night, but I was scared to death I'd roll over on him or something. I need to set up his room, and quite honestly, he needs clothing, too. Would you be willing to help me?"

"I have a few errands I need to run today. All right, I'll help you this morning, but I need this afternoon to myself. And he's way too old for a crib. He'd try to climb out and kill himself."

She stepped up to the counter. "Dark roast with a red eye."

Keefe swiped his card in the auto-pay machine. "Make that two dark roasts. And an orange protein for this little one."

"Plain orange?" The young woman pointed to the board behind her.

"Okay, the orange tropical. That's made with all natural fruit?"

"Yes, all real fruit and organically grown."

"Great. And add three of those pumpkin muffins to the order." He looked at Chelsea. "A red eye? You didn't sleep last night?"

"I slept fine. From what you've told me, I would think you are missing sleep."

He lifted his shoulders and let them drop. Then he returned his card to his wallet. "I've had better nights."

Chelsea took her cup and went to the bar where she added some cream. The little shop was filled, but there was a table outside. She grabbed that one.

It took him a moment to catch up to her. With Rage in his lap, Keefe took the second seat and gave all three of them the still-warm muffins. The boy practically inhaled his pumpkin treat and his drink.

"I don't think this child has had many choices in food. He tends to be skeptical of foods, but so far he's eaten everything I've given him except for his lettuce last night."

"Oh gosh. I don't know what I would do with a child who didn't eat lettuce. Does he have all of his teeth?"

"All? He's got a mouthful including some molars. How many is all?"

Chelsea raised her hands palms up. "I have no idea, but it's got to be on the web. I know that children have a few less teeth than adults."

"That's a good idea. I'll look it up. How do you know so much about children?"

"My dad has a set of twins that are quite a few years younger than I am, and now my stepmother has had two children. I was still at home when Charley was born and CJ isn't much older than Rage. My dad has grandchildren older than CJ."

Keefe cocked his head. "CJ? Is that Cody Junior?"

"Not quite but close enough." She laughed.

Her laughter went straight to his heart and his heart responded with a skipped beat. There was something about her that he found engaging, and he wanted more. "No, Rage, don't make that slurping noise with your drink."

Rage pointed to Chelsea. "I like her."

"So do I."

Chelsea rolled her eyes. "You are seriously training him to sling...cow muffins?"

"Not at all! He decided that on his own. But I must say I like Rage's taste in women. What's the expression - you can't fool a child or a dog?"

"Something such as that." She grabbed the napkin that was in front of the boy and handed it to him. "Here, wipe your mouth."

Rage wiped at his nose.

"Your mouth." She pointed.

Keefe took the napkin from him and wiped the crumbs from the child's face. "You are going to require more than a napkin."

He hefted the child to his hip and went to the small men's bathroom in the coffee shop. He was almost afraid that

Chelsea would escape if he left her, but when he returned she was still sitting there waiting for him. "Ready?"

She nodded and smiled at him.

Oh, please let this go well. He smiled back, but watched her expression change to ice, and she wasn't looking at him.

FOUR

A pickup truck rode past the coffee shop, and Chelsea knew it was Jason, but he had failed to see her. *Probably not looking for me to be with a man and a child.* "Let's do it. Byrum's is just down the street. We can walk there."

Rage held out his arms to Chelsea and practically dove off Keefe to her.

"I'll carry him." She took the child who was now twisted in Keefe's arms.

The little guy instantly snuggled to her shoulder and laid his head down. She tickled his ribcage and made him laugh. "What are you going to do with him while you work?"

"I have no clue. I've got to find a babysitter."

"Donna, she's here in town. She keeps the children for my family. She's great. The only problem is that she does take a break around Christmastime for two weeks and then for a month in the summer. But we manage to work around that. My one sister usually takes the children for that month. She loves having them all there. Julia says it's hard trying to pry her children away from Melissa." Chelsea giggled with the vision of Julia attempting to get her brood loaded into the SUV. "We all take off over the holidays."

"Great. Can you find out if Donna will take Rage?"

"No problem. I'll call her later today." She quickened her steps and reached for the door of Byrum's Furniture.

Keefe's hand beat her to it. "Do you have something against my opening a door for you?"

She smirked. "I didn't realize there was some competition to see which one of us could grab the door first."

Jason constantly wanted to get the door for her and threw a fit if she touched a door when he was around. She turned to Keefe. "I'll be honest. I've had one controlling male in my life and I don't want another. Besides, I'm quite capable of opening a door."

"I'll keep that in mind."

They stepped inside and Keefe blinked several times. "I've never been in here. I always went to the big furniture store outside of town."

"That place might be larger, but there are several floors here and the furniture is all high quality." She raised her hand in a wave at Mike Byrum, the owners' grandson. "We went to school together."

She walked to the elevator, and Rage wanted to push the buttons. She leaned him down. "Push the three."

The child was about to push the button for the second floor.

"No, this one." She showed him which button to push. "You need to start to teach him his numbers."

Keefe grinned. "I think I'm going to be very busy teaching him all sorts of things. What should I teach him?"

"His name, to count to ten, the basic shapes, oh and his phone number and where he lives. Always answer his questions, give him the opportunity to do things with you, and don't baby talk to him." She smiled at Rage and then tickled him, making him squeal as they stepped out of the elevator onto the floor with bedroom furniture. "This way."

A little while later, they had found the perfect furniture for Rage and even purchased a special chair that looked more like a barstool that would fit to Keefe's table and provide better seating for the little guy. Mike Byrum promised they would deliver everything that afternoon after three o'clock. It was obvious that Rage was wearing out. "He needs a snack and then a nap before he gets so tired that he melts down. Once that happens, children become so miserable that they are almost impossible to handle."

"You are full of information about children."

She laughed at him. "You haven't met my family. You should see Thanksgiving dinner at my grandparents'. It's wall-to-wall kids. I have eight siblings, and Julia already has eight children."

The look of shock on Keefe's face made her laugh.

"That many children in this day and age?"

"Yes. My father collected us from his various marriages."

"Various marriages?"

"He married young the first time and that wife walked out on him and left us behind, then he remarried several years later and she died. Now he's married again and he's never been happier."

"Will you join me at the little café for lun—"

"Well, look who it is! I knew I'd find you if I walked around long enough."

Chelsea didn't need to turn around to know who it was. "Go away, Jason."

"When I'm talking to you, you need to look at me."

He grabbed her ponytail and almost pulled her off her feet. She reached for Keefe's arm to stay upright. "Let go! Don't you dare touch me!"

Keefe turned and faced the aggressor. "Let go of her this instant!"

"Shut your mouth before I shut it for you."

Keefe raised his eyebrows. "Are you threatening me?"

"She ain't yours. She's my woman."

"Let go of my hair...now!"

"I said to take your hands off her."

She saw the punch coming. "Keefe! No!"

It was too late. Jason's fist connected with Keefe's face.

Jason also let go of her hair.

She grabbed Rage and took off running. Cutting down a back alley, she slipped over to the back door of Elizabeth's coffee shop and stopped long enough to pound on the door. It opened immediately.

"Chelsea, what's wrong?" Elizabeth held the door open.

Sucking in a deep breath, she answered, "Jason just punched Keefe Assam."

"Jason who?"

Rage let out a blood-curdling scream and began to wail.

"Where are the men?" Elizabeth asked.

"Down the street. We had just walked out of Byrum's. Oh, what a mess. Jason is after me. He's my ex-boyfriend. Please, Rage, don't cry." She looked at Elizabeth. "He's tired and he needs food."

Elizabeth took the child from Chelsea's arms. And that was when Chelsea realized he'd wet his pants.

"What's his name?"

40

"Rage."

"You go check on the men and I'll take care of this one. I'll take him back to my place. I think I might have something from one of my grandbabies."

"I love you, Elizabeth." She leaned over and kissed the boy's cheek. "Rage, be good for Elizabeth, and we'll come get you in a little while. Okay?"

Rage let out another wail.

Chelsea walked to the front of the coffee shop and peeked down the street. She didn't see either man, and that really scared her. *What's happened?*

Keefe heard Chelsea scream and felt her rip Rage from him. But the second blow doubled him over and knocked the wind out of him. Suddenly his eyes began to burn and he heard another female screaming. There were footsteps and the guy cursed a bloody storm as he seemed to stagger back.

A woman took Keefe's arm and led him into her shop with the most sickening scents. He rubbed at his eyes and that seemed to make it worse. He could feel his nose starting to run and he began to cough.

"No, don't touch your face. Let me get you to the sink. I'm so sorry. I was trying to get him, not you, too."

He flushed his eyes by cupping his hands under the water and bringing the liquid to his face. The burning began to subside, but he didn't want to quit flushing them. He knew he'd been sprayed with mace.

"Are you okay?"

"I guess. My eyes still burn." He stood at the sink and continued to flush for what seemed like a piece of forever.

"I'm so sorry. I was trying to spray your attacker but there was that little gust of air and it must have hit you. Please don't be angry with me."

"I'm not. Do you know where Chelsea and my son are?"

"Chelsea grabbed that toddler and took off running. I'm

sure she's safe someplace. What on earth happened out there? What did you do to provoke that?"

He put the towel to his wet face and tried to at least turn in the direction of whoever was talking to him. "I have no idea who or what."

Slowly his vision came back, but his skin, nose, mouth, and eyes still burned. He could barely ascertain that she was young, black, and wearing a pink top over black pants. She took his hand and led him to a chair. He realized he was looking at himself in a mirror and his face was *blue*! He didn't even have Chelsea's phone number. He had intended to get it before they parted but he hadn't gotten that far.

He sat there trying to piece the last twenty-four hours of his life together. He'd just met one of the most intriguing women in the area. He'd gained a son he didn't know about, been attacked for no reason by a guy who threw two very hard punches, gotten pepper spray in his face, and now he sat in a beauty salon with a blue face wondering where Chelsea and Rage were. *And I've got to be home in time to catch that furniture delivery!*

"I'm sorry, I had to rinse my client." The woman smiled. "I'm Francine Henderson. Let me get something for your face. It might help."

She opened a drawer and removed a tube of cream. After squirting some on her hand, she began to coat his face in it. It felt good. A little slimy, but her delicate touch and the feel of the cream were soothing. It was also floral scented, and he wondered if that would linger on him or wash away.

"Is this going to take the blue off?"

"It might help. I don't know. But it's worth trying." She laughed. "You'll have wonderful renewed skin when you are done."

She left him and now he could see that whatever she had put on him was quite pink. It reminded him of that cream that his mother used to use on him when they vacationed at the beach.

A few minutes later, a female police officer stepped into the shop. "I'm looking for Keefe Assam."

He wanted to melt into the chair and vanish. He raised his hand. "I'm here."

"Keefe? Seriously? I never figured you to be the kind of man to come to a beauty shop."

"Now, don't you start that! He's not one of my normal clients. For your information, Amanda Randolph, I have lots of men who come in here." Francine was still holding a comb and scissors in her hands as she strode to where he was sitting. "I'm trying to remove the blue from his face. I didn't mean to spray him."

"Spray him? What did you spray and when?"

"I bought a thing of mace last year to protect myself."

"May I see it?"

Francine went to her desk and removed the tiny canister.

"Do you have the box from it?"

"No. Why would I keep that?"

"It lists the ingredients." The officer turned to Keefe. "It probably has tracer in it." She turned and walked to Francine. "Who was doing what that made you grab that can of pepper spray?"

He listened to what the black woman said and wished he could see Amanda's face. He knew the station's joking and figured his name would be used way too often.

"Can you give a description of the attacker?"

Francine described the man as tall and handsome. That's not the way Keefe would have described him.

Officer Amanda Randolph turned back to him. "Where is the child you had? And since when did you have a child?"

"I gained custody of him last night. Long story."

"So where is he?"

Chelsea handed a very tired little boy to her sister, Melissa. "Thank you. He needs attention. He's in Elizabeth's grandson's clothes. His are in the bag and need to be washed."

"Don't worry about a thing. I've got a closet full of children's clothes. He'll be just fine."

"I just took him to the bathroom, but I have no idea beyond that. He's wearing little boy underpants, not disposable pull-up kind."

"So I guess he doesn't always give a warning that he needs to go. He'll learn." She finished strapping him into the car seat. "He'll be fine. Call me and let me know when Keefe can get him."

Chelsea waved goodbye. It was obvious that Rage would be sound asleep before Melissa pulled out of Elizabeth's driveway. Now she had to find Keefe and she wanted to cut her hair. If Jason remained in town maybe he wouldn't be so quick to recognize her. All she knew was that the cops were looking for Jason and Keefe. At least the cops knew Keefe.

She walked with Elizabeth as they returned to the coffee shop and went in through the back door. Elizabeth was known for running a tight ship, and she was not happy with the pans from the morning's baked offerings still sitting in the sink.

Chelsea thanked Elizabeth profusely and then headed down the street. She wanted to get her hair cut and restyled.

She called Julia and told her what had happened. "New clothes, today. Last night would have been better. I don't want him to recognize me."

"Okay. Let me see what I can find for you. Go get your haircut, and I'll pick you up. I'll also see if Drexel has a car you can use. He's got a few cheap cars he uses when he's running to his greenhouses."

Feeling a little better, Chelsea swore to herself that she'd be fine to walk down the street to Nu Image. It was the downtown's only hairdresser, and it had belonged to the present owners' mothers since the late 1970's when apparently they bought the whole building for virtually nothing. It was a fun sort of place.

Francine and Synde kept up on the latest trends and the place was a pleasant mix of beauty treatments, from hairstyling and nails to facials and waxing. Maybe she'd do her eyebrows in some dramatic new style. Maybe Julia was right. Maybe she needed a complete makeover. Maybe straight-laced-lawyer-and-plain-Jane- part-time-rancher was not really who she was.

She opened the door and realized there were two police officers standing there. Beyond them was a man with a facial mask, and it took a second for her to realize she was staring at Keefe.

"What is going on?" She stomped past the two officers to where Keefe was sitting. "I just stood on my head to find a babysitter for Rage because I had no idea where you were or what had happened, and you're sitting here getting a facial—"

Synde came flying out of the back. "Don't go getting angry with him. It was Francine who maced him. We're just trying to figure out how to get rid of the blue dye from the mace that's all over his face."

"What?"

FIVE

The police left and Keefe endured several more treatments which left him with only a slight blue tinge in a few places on his face. Francine tried one more product on his face. But he was getting a kick out of watching Chelsea.

Synde divided Chelsea's hair into small sections. "Are you absolutely certain you want to do this?"

"Yes."

"Then at least let's donate all this hair to Locks of Love."

"Great idea." *I completely forgot about that non-profit organization that makes wigs for children with cancer.*

"Your hair is perfect because you've never bleached it. Some little girl is going to get a wonderful wig."

Synde finished dividing Chelsea's hair and asked one more time if she was certain that she wanted to cut it. Apparently she had not had a haircut since she was a little girl, and Keefe was surprised when he saw how long her hair really was. Saying it was long was an understatement. But what really surprised him was that the salon took pictures of Chelsea with her hair still in a bun, when it was down, and again when it was divided for cutting.

Keefe wanted to wince when he saw Synde put the scissors to those long tresses. Synde measured the cut hair and declared Chelsea as the record holder for twenty-three and three-quarters inches donated length from their shop. But through it all, he could only sit and watch. He wasn't allowed to move, and he figured if he even smiled, something strange might happen to the gunk on his face. So he sat and watched, fascinated with this girly world within a beauty salon.

Francine even offered to do his nails.

"Do what to them?"

"I'll treat your cuticles, properly trim your nails, and buff them. Nails get scratched and dirt and germs are hiding in those minute crevasses. I promise you'll like the way they look when you are done. Chelsea's dad comes in here once a week when he's in town. He knows how important it is for men to take care of themselves." She pulled a table in front of Keefe and placed a white towel on it and then a bowl of warm water. "Put your hands in the bowl and keep them there."

He was being held prisoner in a beauty salon. But Francine felt so bad about the spray hitting him that she was doing everything she could to make it up to him. She even offered to buy him a new shirt, as the one he was wearing was probably also stained in blue. From what Amanda said, the blue stain was made worse by washing. It didn't matter to him. He'd toss it. It was a cheap polo shirt he'd purchased years ago from a local department store.

Synde snipped away and mounds of Chelsea's hair still fell to the floor. Keefe watched as Synde lifted a few locks and cut them. She'd lift more and do the same thing. Then after all that precision, she had Chelsea shake her head, and Synde put the tips of the scissors into the cut edge like a child who didn't know how to cut on a straight line.

That thought brought him back to Rage. *Is he safe?*

Synde reached into a drawer with one hand and pulled out a hairbrush. With her other hand, she picked up a hair dryer.

Francine came to him, blocking his view. She peeled the last bit of mask off his face, then painted something else on it that burned and wiped that off with cotton balls that had been doused in another liquid. Finally, she put a few drops of what appeared to be oil in a tiny dish and applied that liquid to his skin. After feeling as though he'd been burned, he was grateful for this soothing step. "How do I look? Is the blue gone?"

"You tell me."

He took the mirror from her and realized it was one that magnified. His skin was pink and almost glistened. But pink was better than blue, and the blue was only in the deeper crevasses by his eyes.

Francine must have realized he was looking very closely at his eyes because she said, "I can't put these stronger products close to your eyes. The skin there is very delicate."

She swiveled the chair and he now faced a large wall mirror. He no longer looked blue, and when he touched his face, it was extremely soft. "Wow. I'm surprised."

"I was checking on the web. They refer to that blue as a tracer and it gets into your skin. Under certain lights, you're going to still look blue, but I think we've gotten the worst of it."

"My eyes don't look as red."

"Be glad you weren't wearing contacts. But I'm truly sorry. I promise I pointed that spray at him."

"I believe you. I also know how dangerous these sprays can be. It's not unusual for the victim to be hit as well as the attacker." He smiled at her in the mirror. "You did what you thought was best. And you stopped the attacker, that's the most important thing. I can't imagine what might have happened to me if you hadn't come along." He clenched his teeth for a moment as he remembered the confrontation. "Or if Chelsea hadn't grabbed Rage. Apparently he's with her sister. But I'm worried about him."

"What for? Melissa is wonderful with children." Francine shook her head. "With all the children Julia's had, I'm surprised Melissa hasn't had any."

"Still, I'll be happier when he's back in my possession." He looked at his watch. "Yikes, it's almost three, and I'm supposed to have furniture coming this afternoon."

"Well, go! Chelsea will call you."

He had watched Chelsea from the far end of the beauty salon. Now he didn't see her. He didn't have her phone number, nor did she have his. Her sister had his child. How could he lose a child? He flew out of the shop. *Where is my son?*

Chelsea saw Keefe leave the shop when she was in the back room. She wondered why he'd left without saying goodbye, but she was somewhat hidden while she was getting her eyebrows done. "Ouch!"

Synde ripped the special cloth from another spot and

Chelsea sucked in a breath this time. "Oh, that hurts!"

"It's always hurts more the first time."

"What are you doing to them?"

"I'm doing what you should have done ages ago. I have no idea how a Montgomery could be so lax with her appearance. Your sisters are so different in style, but they are always immaculately dressed. But even when you were little you were the one in jeans and a tee shirt."

Chelsea wanted to say something in her defense, but she was afraid to even move. Instead she gripped the arms of the reclined chair and prayed that she wouldn't wrench the armrests off as Synde started on the other eyebrow.

As Synde finished Chelsea's brows, Julia came into the small back room. "Hiya! It's about time you tamed those caterpillars."

"Thanks a lot! You make it sound as though I had some wild, wooly eyebrows instead of natural brows."

"This looks so much better. I'm sorry I took so long, but when I started to go through everything in my closet, I realized I needed to go shopping. I also raided Melissa's closet for a few things."

"How's the baby?"

"Sound asleep when I was there, but from what..." Julia looked at her watch. "He should be awake by now."

"I promised Melissa that Keefe would pick him up as soon as he woke up. She's got company coming and Keefe's got furniture coming for Rage." *Oh, that's why he left so fast.* "I don't know how to get a hold of Keefe."

Julia rolled her eyes. "And you're the smart one? Where did he buy the furniture?"

"Byrum's."

"Well, call them. No. I have a better idea. I'll call them." Julia pulled her phone from her purse. A moment later, she smiled as she said hello. "This is Julia. Chelsea and Keefe were in this morning and bought furniture for that adorable little boy of Keefe's. Well, Chelsea seems to have lost Keefe's phone number and she's got to get a hold of Keefe..." Julia held her thumb up. "Yes, 555-3269. Oh, thank you so much!"

Chelsea pulled her phone from her belt and began to call. "I can't believe you just did that."

"You get dressed, and we'll go get Rage. Drexel is going to lend you a car. You can stop by the supermarket and buy some chicken or something for dinner. Then you can call Keefe and offer to at least make dinner for him after what he's been through today. Problem solved. You have a new hot look. Jason won't recognize you. Plus, you get to surprise Keefe. Problems solved!"

Chelsea didn't know whether to laugh or choke her sister, but she was grateful for everything Julia had done. She pulled off her plain white tee and pulled on the colorful shirt her sister had brought. It scooped a little lower in the front than she was used to wearing. Then she coiled the snake belt around her waist and hooked it.

Julia walked over and redid the belt. "I guess I must dress you, too." Julia put the matching bracelet on Chelsea's arm. "Here are the earrings that match, but don't wear them around Rage. You don't want him to grab them either accidentally or on purpose and tear your ears."

She looked at the long dangles and wondered whose jewelry it was. She held the earrings up to her ears and looked at herself in the big mirror.

"One more thing." Julia handed her a lipstick and eyeliner. "No powders. I remembered. Do you remember how to use this stuff?"

Chelsea made a face at her sister and used both.

Julia grinned. "Try the mascara, but not now. You don't need to be red-eyed when you are about to fix a hot guy some dinner. It's a shame you didn't get Melissa's eyelashes, but at least with eyeliner you have eyes that show."

"I'm not so sure about the lipstick."

"You look great. What do you think of your haircut?"

"Um, different. It's going to take some getting used to. Let's just say, I'm not comfortable with any of this."

"I'm going to cross my fingers that Jason won't recognize you, because I barely recognize you."

As Keefe opened the front door of his apartment, the truck from the furniture store pulled to the front curb. He waved them in and dashed up the front steps. It took him only a moment to grab the boxes that he had shoved in the room, and move them to a corner of the main room. Now he'd be forced to sort through the boxes. He either had to find a place in his apartment to store the stuff or he'd have to take it to his parents'.

A few minutes later, all the furniture was in his apartment and the men were assembling the bed. He needed to hang the metal wall train he'd bought to go with all of it. He tipped the men and began to look around. *Now he has a room, but I don't have him.*

When he opened the package of linens, he knew exactly why Chelsea had him buy them. They were smooth as glass and very soft. She also said no to the baby blue bedspread. She pointed out others, and eventually they choose the steel gray one. She added colorful, decorative pillows in various shapes and sizes that matched the train's colors. Now the room looked as though it belonged to a little boy, but it also looked sturdy.

He liked the bookcase that would be repurposed as a toy box for the next few years. The lower cabinet would hide many of his toys. The small table and chair set would be perfect for many activities.

Chelsea warned him that children want to be near the adults, so not to expect Rage to stay in his room and play. The alcove off the living room was where Keefe kept his computer, so putting that table set in there made sense. *Quiet play, he needs to do more than watch TV.*

Pulled from his reverie by the buzz of his phone, he answered the call. "Hello."

"Keefe, it's Amanda. I wanted to let you know that we have scoured the area for Jason Mayer. We know what vehicle he's driving, including the plates, but we can't find that vehicle. We feel fairly certain that he's left town. But we have every officer on the lookout. Furthermore, we do have the warrant for his arrest."

"So are you saying it's safe for me to walk the streets?" He smirked as he said it, for he already knew the answer, and silently mouthed her response.

"We can never make that guarantee. Just be assured that we are doing everything we possibly can to keep you and everyone else safe." She softly laughed. "So what's up between you and Chelsea?"

"Friends. We attended Baylor together, and we're peers. We're also working on a project. She's got brains and plenty of common sense. It's an enjoyable combination."

"I never imagined you with someone as straight-laced and plain as she is."

Jealous, Amanda? "You'll find someone who likes playing with handcuffs."

His phone went dead and he chuckled. *Give me a woman who knows the basic joy of being with a man on all levels. Is that you, Chelsea?*

Melissa loaned Chelsea a car seat and a stroller that was perfect for Rage. Drexel put the car seat in a Toyota hatchback that he had, and showed Chelsea how the seat was mounted so that it could be used in any vehicle. "Just keep him in the back seats, not the front seats with airbags."

Chelsea nodded. "I'm not stupid. Car seats haven't changed much over the years."

"Well, make certain Keefe knows."

"I will."

Drexel placed the child in the seat and adjusted the straps to him. "There you go, big boy. The next time you come for a visit, try not to sleep so much. How am I going to teach you to ride a horse if you keep sleeping?"

Rage laughed.

Drexel made a funny face and Rage laughed even more.

Melissa smiled. "I love your new look. It's dramatic. I haven't seen you ever look this wonderful." Melissa's smile turned to a giggle. "Even Rage didn't recognize you until you talked to him. He's adorable." She raised her eyebrows. "Any chance he'll be my nephew?"

Chelsea rolled her eyes. "I spend a part of a day with a fellow lawyer and you've got me married to him. You are as crazy as Julia."

Melissa shrugged. "I think I know when my little sis is in love. She just needs to realize it. You not only adore Rage, you are head over heels for his daddy, or you wouldn't have done what you've done. You would have laughed and walked away from the whole situation. You are the tough no-nonsense sister."

"Great! I put on a fancy blouse so that Jason doesn't recognize me, and you've got me falling in love and wiping snotty noses. Thanks but no thanks." She wrinkled her nose at her sister. "And where is your brood of sixteen children?"

"We occasionally talk about it." Melissa laughed. "Don't tell Dad. When we decide, we'll tell him."

"Really?"

Melissa nodded. "Things are coming together for us."

"That's wonderful!"

"It's also a little scary." Drexel gave Chelsea a little hug. "He was loads of fun, and he's welcome back here anytime!"

"Thanks, you guys have been great." She got into the car and drove off, but once she passed through the gates of the estate, she stopped long enough to call Keefe. "Hi. Want your son back?"

"Oh, please! I've been frantic for hours."

"I need to know where to bring him."

"Do you know where the antique shop is near the coffee shop downtown?"

"Of course."

"I have the apartment above that. Do you need the exact address?"

"No."

"Okay, when should I expect you?"

"In about twenty minutes. By the way, I have all the fixings for dinner. I thought maybe I could make it up to you for ruining your day."

"You didn't ruin it. But I was worried about Rage."

"Don't be. Melissa had him and he slept for over three and a half hours. She thinks he might have missed a morning nap. She says not all children give up that morning nap. Let me drive. I'll tell you more when I get there."

Rage was a total angel in the car and that made the ride easier for Chelsea. She wasn't certain what she was going to do if he decided to kick up a fuss while she was behind the wheel. She tried to remember simple songs. As each one came to her mind, she tossed them. One little, two little, three little Indians—that certainly wasn't politically correct. She finally settled on "The Ants Go Marching" because it didn't involve an ethnic group, nor was it religious based, and it would help him with his numbers.

By the time she had sung it for the third time, Rage was catching on and singing it with her. When she reached the number ten, Rage would yell, "The end!"

She wished life could be that simple.

Jason was out there and it was obvious that he wanted her dead. She'd grown up more than aware of her father's clients, but this was different. She might have escaped the relationship, but she had not escaped from him. *He's going to kill me.*

SIX

Keefe was waiting outside his apartment for Chelsea. She jumped out and opened the back passenger door. "Good news. You may borrow the car seat until you can buy one for him."

"Great. I was thinking about that and wondering how he was being transported since he didn't have one. And I didn't recognize you. You look wonderful."

"Thanks, that's the idea." She ducked inside the car. "Everyone knows that children must be in a car seat." She unhooked Rage and passed him to his father. "We can get the car seat later. Let me grab the groceries from the cooler in the back."

Keefe took several bags from her. "Did you buy enough for a whole week?"

"I wasn't certain what you might have on your pantry shelves, so I picked up anything that I thought we might need, including a casserole dish."

"You should have called me. My pantry is well stocked." He held his outside door for her.

"I didn't have your phone number until my sister stepped in and got it for me." She couldn't see inside the apartment until she was near the top of the flight. *Omigosh!*

Her gaze swept the main room and she was taken aback. The place looked phenomenal.

Keefe stepped past her. "Put your bags on this counter. The sink is there, and if you need something, ask. I'm taking him to the bathroom before he has an accident."

She unloaded everything, and then washed her hands.

Rage ran to the kitchen with a big smile on his face. "I did it just like Auntie Missa said."

"That's wonderful! You are such a big boy."

Rage climbed onto a tall stool.

"Rage, come back here. I have something to show you. And bring Chelsea with you."

Chelsea wiped her hands and went with Rage. Keefe had Rage's room ready for him. "It's adorable! But what did you do with his table and chair set?"

Keefe held up a finger to Chelsea. "Look, Rage. Your very own big boy bed."

The child scrambled up on it. "All mine?"

Keefe grinned. "All yours. The whole room is yours. Can you open your drawers?"

Rage checked everything in his room and pulled out the few toys that had come with him that were sitting on the shelves. But when he opened the cabinet, he squealed with delight over the yellow plastic dump truck. He put his old stuffed duck in the truck's bed and began to push it around.

Keefe motioned for Chelsea to follow him. "I found that truck at the little store about a block away. I figured he'd like it."

"What little boy doesn't like playing with a dump truck?"

Keefe grinned. "And I took your advice. I put his table and chair set in my computer space."

"Great idea. You can work together." She turned at the sound of a little boy with his plastic dump truck.

He had followed them to the little alcove. He picked up his truck and began to push it on the table.

"No, Rage. Keep your truck on the floor. It doesn't go on the table."

She nudged Keefe and whispered, "You are being negative."

"No, I'm not. He has to learn to keep toys off the furniture."

She nodded. "Oh, you have much to learn. Constantly saying no or not will come back and bite you. Wait until he turns and says no to you over something. The better way would be for you to say that the truck stays on the floor because real trucks have to stay on the roads. You can say your truck needs to stay on the floor. You don't need to preface it with the word no. Save that word for when you really need to use it. If everything is one big no, he will never understand what he can do. The word no needs to be important."

"Okay, I get it. I thought this was going to be a breeze."

She laughed. "Rage, bring your truck into the living room and you may play with it on the floor while I fix dinner for us."

Keefe followed her. "What are you fixing?"

"My famous chicken and rice. It's very easy, but I need to get it made and in the oven if we want to eat at a normal hour."

"If you want cooked rice, I'll make it. It only takes about eight minutes."

"It's brown rice. It takes longer and I have wild rice for it."

She watched as Keefe pulled out a steamer.

"Oh, wonderful! Here." She handed him a box of wild rice. "Rinse it and check it. And then add about one fourth of this box to it."

She began to prepare the other items.

Keefe held up the head of bib lettuce. "Shall I make the salad?"

"Go right ahead."

Rage started to push his truck to the kitchen.

"Keep your truck on the carpet. We want to keep you and your truck safe while we are fixing meals." Keefe looked over his shoulder at her. "Is that better?"

"Much." *You are going to do just fine.* "Even though I'm not a mom, I know being a parent isn't easy. It requires lots of patience. And it gets really tough when a child is sick and you have to get up or stay up with them all night. And if you think that's bad, try doing it when you are sick, too."

"Never thought of that."

"Bet you never thought of a lot of things when you opted for custody."

"There are a few things you don't know."

Keefe swallowed as he tried to figure out what he could say. "I'm assuming that you think I was married and fought for custody. I had no idea I even had a child. An ex-girlfriend stopped in last night and dropped Rage off with me. To say I'm dumbfounded is an understatement."

"And you didn't know a thing about having a child? Who does that in this day and age?" She raised her eyebrows. "Most women want child support."

"I have no idea. She left paperwork giving me full custody."

"So you really don't know if he's yours."

"He's got to be. Look at him."

"Everyone thinks I look like my father, but I'm not his child. You need to talk to him. You have some decisions to make, but make them knowing all the facts."

"So you are not his child, and he still kept you. What's the difference with Rage? His mother doesn't want him, and I'd have no way of ever finding his real father if he's not mine. At least I have the financial wherewithal to take care of him."

"Very noble of you, but remember my father had all of us for years when he discovered our paternity. He already loved us."

"You said that as though more than one sibling did not belong to him."

"Talk to him."

The oven buzzer sounded and Chelsea went to the kitchen and took the casserole from the oven. "It needs to cool for a few minutes before we serve it. Why don't you help Rage wash his hands?"

"Come, Rage. It's time for us to prepare to eat. Grab your truck."

Rage followed him, but when Keefe asked Rage to put his truck in the cabinet, he threw himself to the floor and wailed.

"Hey, come on. There's no reason to be that upset. Trucks can't eat dinner with us, but it will patiently wait until we are done eating and then you can come back and get it."

Chelsea walked into the room, winked, and smiled at him. Then she turned her attention to the child. "Rage. Why are you crying? All trucks have to go into their garages."

Rage looked at her with his bottom lip rolled out. His eyes were still washed in tears and droplets clung to his long dark lashes.

"Are you hungry?"

Rage nodded.

"Well, if you are hungry, then your truck must be hungry." She smiled at Rage. "They need refueling just like you do. So leave your truck to be refueled while you get your fuel. When you are done eating I'm certain your truck will be waiting for you."

Rage nodded.

"Are you hungry?"

Rage nodded again.

"Then let your truck eat while you eat."

She motioned for Keefe to follow her. "Let him make his decision. We've given him the reason."

"How do you know so much?"

She rolled her eyes. "Little siblings and nieces and nephews. Give children two choices, and only two. Then have them pick. It teaches them to make decisions."

"Two?"

"Yes. You are trying to get him to put away his toys. I understand that and you understand that, but he doesn't. Keep things simple and positive at all times. Children want to please and they want praise."

"You make it sound as though I'm training a dog."

Chelsea nodded. "Same exact psychology. Just try not to say sit and stay, or you'll realize what you've said and start laughing."

He groaned to himself. "I'll never learn all of this. I'm doomed to be a complete failure, and Social Services will take him away."

"They won't do that. In all honesty, Social Services often gets a bad rap when they do so much. Did you know they have parenting classes?"

"Really?"

She nodded. "And they have lots of pamphlets on parenting, and they maintain a list of reading material available in the library that helps families." She prepared the plates, including a small one for Rage. "The office where I used to work while I was in school often handled families that needed more than legal help."

Rage toddled out of his room sans his truck.

"Did you put your—"

"Keefe, don't give him another command. He's left his truck and he's coming to the table. He's done very well. Praise him for doing a good job."

Rage smiled at Chelsea as he climbed into his new chair. Once he was seated, Keefe slipped the chair tight to the table.

Parenting might be a bigger challenge than I realized.

The evening went well and Chelsea seemed to know how to keep Rage occupied and happy. He watched what she did and tried to learn what she seemed to do naturally. She stopped once for a brief phone call and promised whomever it was that she'd call later. Then she helped get Rage bathed and ready for bed. She even helped find a few good books for bedtime reading that Keefe could download. Then she left.

He didn't want her to go. And when she left, it felt as though she had taken the sparkle out of his evening. The feeling of family dissolved, leaving him with the sensation of inadequacy. Rage had closed his eyes and from the rhythm of his little chest rising and falling, Keefe knew the boy was asleep.

Light filtered through the wavy glass blocks from the streetlight in the alleyway, adding just enough illumination to the room to keep it from being totally black. Cautiously, he stood and snapped the side rail into place, making a louder click than he intended, but Rage never stirred. Keefe tried to imagine himself as a Buddhist monk not making a sound as he left the room, but no matter how hard he tried, each step created a noise. Then there was a slight hinge squeal as he closed the bedroom door. His heart pounded in his chest. It also echoed in his temples and above his eyes. It had been a very long day.

He sat and reviewed the events of the last twenty-four hours as though they had belonged to someone else. Nothing made any sense, including the feelings he was harboring towards Chelsea.

Maybe Leighayn really had left him jaded when it came to women, but he had no desire to trust another female. He definitely enjoyed an evening with a pretty female, but he no longer looked at women the same way. But that's not what he saw in Chelsea.

There was something else about her. It was something painful, as though she was a woman who had been betrayed. Her fear of Jason was abnormal, but what that man had done that morning verged on insanity.

Keefe laughed to himself. He had attempted to act like the macho hero for Chelsea's sake, and instead he wound up being saved by a woman after she maced him. He shook his head as though trying to clear the events from his mind.

He checked on Rage one more time, and then took a shower. The warm water sluicing his body turned his thoughts instantly to Chelsea. He imagined her beside him and his arms wrapping her naked body. He moved the temperature dial to cold and shuddered as the water hit his skin. It was enough to put an end to his mind wandering where it didn't need to go. *Oh if I only knew if she is worth pursuing.* But a little part of him knew that answer, except now he had a child who needed him more.

He dried his body and realized he still had blue tracer on him. It was in his dark hair, and on parts of his neck. Under the strong bathroom lights, he could see the blue cast of his skin. *I look like I'm related to a Smurf. I really don't need this.*

Chelsea went home where she was met by her stepmother.

DeeDee's face instantly brightened. "You look fabulous! Julia told me what you were doing and why."

"Thanks. I don't feel like me. I feel as though I'm trying to be something that I'm not."

"Oh, I always thought you looked very pretty with or without makeup, but when you wore it, you looked extraordinarily arresting. This gives you a Cleopatra look that very few women can pull off."

Chelsea shrugged. "I feel like I'm dressed for Halloween."

"Never! Give yourself a chance to get used to the look."

Chelsea made a face and went to the kitchen. She rummaged around and finally settled on ice cream. *Butter Brickle with whipped cream and maraschino cherries.* She placed the ingredients on the counter, found a bowl and the ice cream scoop. She wasn't even hungry, she thought as she piled several scoops into the bowl. It was comfort food, and she knew that was dangerous. *I don't care.*

If she had been in her own place, she would have been tempted to leave the mess she had made. But this was her father's house. From the time she was old enough to reach the kitchen sink, she was taught to clean up after herself. When she returned the kitchen to pristine, she took her bowl and went to her room. She scanned the TV channels for the sappiest movie she could find, but decided most of them ended on a sad note. Giving up, she turned the TV off and found her e-reader. She found a favorite author's newest book and began to read.

When morning broke, she opened her eyes and realized she had fallen asleep, but where was her bowl? Her e-reader was sitting on the table by her bed. Slightly confused she made her way to her bathroom and took a quick shower. Now she was forced to flat iron her hair. Julia had explained the settings when she handed the appliance to Chelsea.

It took a moment to remember what her sister had said. It wasn't quite as difficult as Chelsea imagined it would be, but it did take time. She used her foundation, lined her eyes, and enhanced her eyebrows with a special eyebrow pencil. Then she lined her mouth with a lip pencil and filled her lips with color. She loved the color. It wasn't a bright red, it was more like a brown plum color. She pulled on a pair of dark brown slacks and a plum tunic that flowed down her body. She wrapped her waist with a gold belt and wore the oversized gold hoop earrings Melissa had given her.

She used to shower, dry her hair, pull it into a bun or ponytail, and be dressed in less than thirty minutes. This new routine had taken more than an hour. But whoever that was staring at her in the mirror, she looked hot. *Maybe I really do need to change things up.*

The rest of her weekend was uneventful and she had been grateful. But she had only been in her office for a few minutes on Monday when her cell phone rang.

"Hey, Chelsea, it's Keefe. I'm sitting in the courthouse parking lot and court starts in ten minutes, but I was wondering if you'd like to come over tonight for dinner. I'm cooking."

"What's for dinner, pizza?"

"My dough tossing skills suck. Most of the time it ends up on the floor. I was thinking about something else. I picked up a recipe on the web that looked really good. Do you eat seafood?"

"Yes."

"If you are willing to try something new, be at my place at six."

The line went dead. She giggled. *You'll never make it through security. You are going to be in trouble with the judge for being tardy.*

Ten minutes later, Carlie announced, "Line one, a personal call."

She was certain it was Keefe. So she was surprised when it was a woman's voice.

"Chelsea Montgomery, I understand your father is not in the office. I'm sure you don't remember me, but you probably know who I am. I'm Jenna Montgomery Sheller. I'm your mother."

Seven

Chelsea swallowed and found her authoritative voice. "How may I help you?"

"I was hoping to meet you and your sisters while I was in town."

Chelsea's head spun. *Bide time.* She forced herself to smile because everyone says it comes through in the voice. "Where are you staying and how long will you be here?"

"I'm hoping to leave by Wednesday. I need to see your father, but I want to see my beautiful daughters. I've lived for so long without you. I'm certain that you've been brainwashed with some sort of story about me, but I never wanted to leave you."

Chelsea noted the desperation in the woman's voice.

"Chelsea, believe me when I say your father tossed me out and threatened me to stay out of your lives. He paid me off."

The woman began to cry. Chelsea looked at the blue button on the phone that said the conversation was being recorded. If Chelsea didn't tell the woman, it was considered an illegal recording. "Ma'am, this conversation is being recorded, there's a device on our phone system that does it automatically."

"Ma'am? Is that what I get? I bring you into this world and I get *ma'am*? I'm your mother. Omigod, I know he's turned you against me. Who knows what he's said about me. I had to leave my beautiful daughters, my babies."

Another round of tears, and sniffling, along with a few wails came through loud and clear. Chelsea leaned her head into her fingertips as she placed her elbows on the desk.

Pictures that her father had kept of Jenna showed a young pretty woman. Of the three of them, Julia probably grew up to look the most like her birth mother. Chelsea wanted to hang up on the woman who had abandoned her father. But another part of her was curious about who this woman was, and why she wanted back into their lives after so many years.

She let the woman ramble, but some of what she said was

disturbing. Could there be another side that her father had failed to tell them? When the woman paused, Chelsea took that as her chance to slide in a comment and see how the woman responded. "I've been told I look so much like my father."

"Oh, you do! You did. You were his little clone when you were born. You are your father's child, there's no doubt about that!"

Chelsea wanted to ask who her father really was, but she kept her mouth closed and listened.

"When's the best time to catch up to your father?"

"I have no idea. Where are you?"

"The hotel here in the downtown."

Chelsea smiled. "I'll be sure to tell him."

"What about catching up with you and your sisters tonight?"

"Tonight is impossible on such sort notice. I'll call them. Maybe we can do it tomorrow night. Let me have your phone number."

"I'm in room 126. I'm so excited, darling. I've been waiting for years to see my daughters again."

I'll bet you have! "I'll call you later." Chelsea disconnected the line. She was on some sort of psychological trip and none of it was pleasant. Using her cell phone, she called her dad and left a message. Her second phone call was to Julia, and when that conversation ended, she called Melissa. They all had the same feelings. They were curious about this woman, but it was obvious that she never suspected that their father had the children's DNA tested.

Chelsea pressed the intercom to connect with Carlie. "I'm taking this afternoon off. I have some family obligations to handle. I'll be here in the morning."

A few hours later, three sisters sat in Melissa's house.

"Let's do it!" Melissa was enthusiastic about the meeting. "Three cats and one mouse. She has no clue."

"But what if some of what she's said is true?" Chelsea protested.

Julia shook her head. "If she had wanted back into our lives, she would have done it before now. Dad said she went through the money in a few years. Something has happened and she's looking for more money."

Melissa nodded. "Sorry, Chels, but I think Julia is right."

65

Chelsea told her sisters about Keefe's situation with Rage. "I guess you could be right. Why would a mother abandon her child? Because she figures that child will have a better life with the father. Is that what happened to Jenna? It is possible that Dad had paid her to go away?"

Julia raised her hand, palm out, as far as her shoulder. "Dad isn't going to admit he did something such as that."

Melissa shook her head. "I disagree. Dad is the first to admit that he's not perfect, and that he's made mistakes along the way."

Julia shrugged.

Melissa smiled. "But she can't refute the DNA testing."

Chelsea swallowed. "I know it's expensive, but it's been quite a few years since that was done. Maybe we should all be retested. Or at least Melissa and I should."

Julia shrugged. "No matter what, she's our mother."

Chelsea put her cup down. "DNA testing is often brought up in court. There's some doubt that early testing was as accurate as we have been led to believe. There are the chimeras. These are people who have two distinct sets of DNA."

Melissa frowned. "I was what...fourteen when we were all tested? That was a long time ago if you look at medical progress..."

"I don't give a flip if she is my mother. She's made no attempt to contact us until now? I'm with Chelsea. She's after something and my bets are on money!" Julia polished off her cup of coffee. "She's fishing."

"You are darn right she's fishing," Drexel said as he joined the women. "From everything that has ever been said about her, she's ripped through money as though it were grass clippings. She's after money, and she's looking for a way to sink in her claws. Tread with caution. You don't want to inadvertently give something away."

Julia pressed her lips into a tight line.

Melissa placed her hand on her husband's arm. "Drexel, remember she is our mother. I think we at least owe her the opportunity to meet with us. But there's no warm fuzzy feelings towards her from me."

Julia shook her head. "Drexel is right. I don't even want

her to know I have children. She's our mother, and that's putting us in a very awkward position. We are all curious about her. Of the three of us, I'm the only one with a vague memory of her. So it's natural to want to see her. But let's not forget the man who loved us and took care of us." She stood and poured another cup of coffee. "She thinks she can just bop into our lives and have us run with open arms to meet her. That should be a big warning sign right there." She returned to her seat. "Dad has never lied to us. If he had paid her off to get rid of her, he would have told us. And he would have told us why."

"You're right." Melissa stood. "Anyone else want another cup of coffee?"

"I'll take one." Chelsea handed her sister the coffee cup. "So what do we do?"

Drexel leaned back in his chair. "She's no kin to me so I probably don't belong in this discussion, but if I were you, Chelsea, I'd call her and tell her that the soonest anyone can clear their schedule will be Friday or Saturday. Saturday might be the better day, because then none of you have to work. And whatever you do, don't meet her for dinner! Don't even offer to take her out. Make certain Cody is there. Then meet her at two o'clock on Saturday someplace very neutral such as the fountain by the courthouse."

Chelsea couldn't stop her giggles. "So we're near the police station when Julia kills her?"

Drexel snorted. "Something such as that. Maybe I had better go to this meeting because the person who has the biggest reason to go after her is your dad."

Julia nodded. "We're all being way too emotional about this. Dad would want to be there. If she's after money, let him handle her. Plus, we are making assumptions about things when we don't know who she is or why she wants to see us."

"Or why she's waited until now." Chelsea couldn't stop the tide of emotion that was flooding her system. "We don't know her, but Dad does. People do change for a variety of reasons, and maybe she has. But we need to be extremely cautious because she's not been the perfect mother. She walked out of our lives about twenty-four years ago."

Melissa looked at Julia and then turned her attention to Chelsea. "Call Dad. Tell him what we're doing, and be certain to tell him that we're stalling until he gets here. Then call Jenna and give her the sad news that it will be Saturday before she can see us. If Dad says he's coming right home, we can do it the following day."

Chelsea held up her finger. "I'm calling him now while we are all in the room."

Court concluded early. Keefe picked up his son from Donna's and went to his parents' home so that Rage could meet his grandparents. Keefe's mom went into instant grandmother mode of trying to spoil the child non-stop. At first he found it laughable, but soon he realized that her idea of spoiling meant the child ran wild with no boundaries. His father looked at the boy as though he were a squirrel burying nuts on the greens.

After two hours of the craziness, Keefe used naptime as an excuse to leave.

"But you'll miss having dinner with us."

"Sorry, Mom, but he needs his nap."

"But I was going to make him—"

"No, Mom. I'm taking him home. And so far the only thing he hasn't eaten is lettuce and I think that's because it's a new food to him."

"But—"

Keefe shook his head and gathered his son into his arms. "Wave goodbye to everyone and throw them kisses."

Rage arched his back and Keefe knew Rage was about to protest. Quickly Keefe made his way to his car and as he strapped the child into the car seat, Rage let loose with his objection.

"Go right ahead and complain, but it's not changing a thing."

Keefe figured Rage would fall asleep, but he didn't. He

screamed the whole way home and continued to throw a temper tantrum in the apartment. Keefe couldn't get the child to cooperate long enough to use the toilet or wash his hands. And when the boy tossed himself on the floor and screamed at the top of his lungs, Keefe simply walked away and closed the bedroom door.

He turned the monitor on and watched the child from the kitchen.

When Rage realized his father was not coming back, he quieted, and then took off for the door. He turned the handle, pushed and tugged. But the door was not budging. It had been Chelsea's idea to swap the handles so that the child couldn't lock himself into his room. It also made it easy to contain the child.

After another bout of anger, Rage went to his toy box and grabbed a stuffed animal. The thing barely resembled a gray elephant. Rage stuck his pinky and ring fingers into his mouth and promptly fell asleep on the floor. Keefe let out a sigh of relief.

He's got to learn. Boundaries. The word echoed in his mind. He remembered Chelsea saying that children will seek attention, and they don't care if it's good attention or bad attention. *This parenting thing is a tough job.*

Certain the child was sound asleep, Keefe unlocked the bedroom door and dropped a sofa pillow in front of Rage's door. It didn't take but a moment for Keefe to find that same slumber. When the sound of the doorknob turning awakened him, he rolled over and smiled at Rage. "Hi, kiddo, did you have a good nap?"

Rage wiggled next to Keefe and closed his eyes again. That was when it dawned on Keefe why the child probably awakened. "Let's get you to the toilet before you go back to sleep."

A few minutes later, a very groggy little boy climbed into his bed and was fast asleep before Keefe had even left the room. This time, a wonderful sensation passed through Keefe. It was as though his life suddenly had purpose. He was no longer responsible for himself, he had a child who needed him and needed direction.

He started to look up sites devoted to parenting on his computer. Much of what Chelsea had said was reiterated on the various sites. The general theme was to stay positive and allow children to make decisions. He began to make a list of things that he felt were important. After looking at his own life and what his parents had done, he could see the mistakes they had made. College had been an eye-opener to him. He'd never done a load of laundry or even made his bed until he went to college. Someone had always done these things for him. His first year, he almost flunked out. His idea of fun was getting drunk every night even though he was under the drinking age. He later discovered that his dorm was considered the party dorm. His second year, he improved considerably. He dropped the fraternity. Slowly life changed as he took responsibility for his own actions. And by the time he entered Baylor, he was not that same person as the spoiled brat who had been sent off to college.

He thought about what Chelsea had said about public schools and realized he had missed that street education. Chelsea was the epitome of a lady. Yet she had the aplomb of someone much older who ran a Fortune 500 company. *How does she do it?*

I must have come off as a total wimp. No wonder she rolls her eyes at me. How, Chelsea? How did you learn all the things that you know? And how do you survive on grant money?

He knew he wanted Rage to play sports, but he worried about heavy contact sports such as football. Keefe's mom never allowed him to do more than play tennis or golf, but Rage was too young for both sports. *Soccer! All he needs is a good kickball to start. If I can teach him to kick, I've done something.*

He picked up the phone and dialed Chelsea.

Chelsea left her sister's house, but instead of getting off the bypass, she kept going until she reached the exit for the large shopping center on the north side of town. She wanted to do some shopping for herself. Black suits with mannish white shirts were prohibited according to Julia.

She found several things that she thought would work well. She also found a jacket that she really liked. With the coloring to pull off almost any jewel-tone outfit, spicing up her black suits with something other than white shirts, she liked the look. *It just might work.* The dark green jacket when paired with a variety of autumn colors was perfect. She found several things in various stores that she liked.

But when she walked past the children's store, she was instantly drawn into the shop. Most of Rage's clothes looked like they had been used hard before he acquired them. She found several adorable outfits in a toddler two size. The eighteen-month things looked much too small and the toddler two looked almost too big. *Side on bigger. He'll grow into them and then out of them.*

She had just finished her transactions at the counter when her phone alerted her of an incoming call.

"Hello."

"Chelsea, this is Keefe. I have another favor to ask. Is there someplace around town where I can buy a kickball for Rage?"

"A kickball?"

"He needs something light and not too big. I figured I'll take him to the park and eventually teach him to play soccer, but for now kicking a ball should be fun."

"You are lucky that you caught me because I'm shopping. There's a toy store. I'll see what they have."

"Thanks, I really owe you for all your help. I know I asked you earlier about dinner tonight, but I changed the menu. I promise not to poison you. I actually like to cook."

"I'll take you up on that offer. Let me scoot and find Rage a ball."

She stepped out of the large store, and sucked in a deep breath as fall's first blast of arctic cold swept into the area. She went back inside and found a coat for Rage. Then she bought a coat for herself.

The tag said eggplant but she would have called it dark purple. And as she walked past the jewelry counter, she noticed their fall jewelry had been marked down. A brooch caught her attention. It was silly and only a few dollars but she decided to do it. She could wear it on her coat. *I've lost my mind. No one wears this stuff except for old ladies.* As she took it to the counter to pay for it, she spotted another that would work on her coat for the Christmas holidays.

It was crazy and she knew it. She hadn't worn anything so silly since she was a little girl and her father had given her a Santa pin and a red Santa cap trimmed in white. But since these pins were exactly the opposite of her normal taste, she figured she should do it.

It was more than two hours later when she pulled into a parking space near Keefe's apartment. She opened the car's trunk and found the things she had bought for Rage. Keefe buzzed her in, and with her arms full of packages, she met Keefe at the top of the stairs.

"Don't tell me I'm spoiling him, because I'm not. He needs this stuff." She put the packages on a kitchen counter. "And please tell me that you have coffee."

"Sorry. I don't even own a coffeepot. But I can make tea."

"That's better than nothing." She didn't mean to snap at him.

"You sound as though you've had a rough day."

"Let's just say it was a roller coaster. How was yours?"

"My first mistake was taking Rage over to my parents' without setting some guidelines with them. By the time I got him home, he had a complete meltdown. That's something I don't want to face again."

"Oh my. My father is strict in a good way and DeeDee is more relaxed. But I swear CJ gets away with ten times more than we did. Check the packages out and tell me what you think."

Keefe's face drained of color as he peered into the bags.

"What's wrong?"

EIGHT

Keefe tried to calm his frazzled nervous system. "Chelsea, I just maxed out my credit cards buying Rage's furniture. I asked for a ball."

"I had already purchased the clothes when you asked. You don't owe me a dime. I had fun doing it."

He lifted the navy pea coat from its bag and spotted the sales tag that hung from the sleeve. His heart skipped a few beats. "I saved for months to buy that piece of dichroic glass from Jack Storms. Now I have a child and expenses that I never dreamed I'd have. My budget is shot to pieces."

"I said not to worry about it. It's my gift to the little guy. Take a few of those older outfits to Donna and leave them there. That way he has a change or two. At his age, an accident or a good spill requires fresh clothing."

"Why, Chelsea? Why are you doing this for me?"

"Because it was fun."

He pulled out a bag with black and brown chunks in it. "What is this?"

"Foam rocks for his dump truck. I'm sorry, but when I saw them, I knew he'd love them. I know they will be a mess to clean up." She smiled so brightly that his heart melted.

He wasn't certain what to think. After fixing her cup of tea, he checked on the food in the oven. Everything was doing well.

"Yum. Whatever you are making smells good."

"I hope you like it." He removed the undersized kick ball from the bag. "I think this will be perfect. It's very light. What do I owe you for the toys?"

"Nothing. They are for Rage." She laughed. "Everyone thinks lawyers make huge money, but they forget about starting salaries, student loans, and everything else. I just happened to get lucky."

"You mean because you live at home and work for your dad?"

She shook her head. "Living there has its perks, and its less than stellar conditions. But for now, it's good. With Jason out there someplace, it's probably safer for me to live at home. No one is going to tell me what to do or when to do it. It's a mutual respect thing. I get home first, so I fix supper. When Dad is there, we do it together."

He watched as she spoke. She was slender and very graceful. When he first knew her, she had a look about her that said stay away. But sitting in his kitchen looking the way she did, she looked more like a woman that men would trip over themselves to hold the door for.

He had done some checking and realized she had graduated top in her class. She was smart. There was something else about her, but he didn't quite know what it was.

He took the broccoli from the refrigerator and washed it. After filling his steamer with the correct amount of water, he added the broccoli to the top tier. "Let me wake Rage. I don't want him oversleeping."

"May I do something?"

"No. I've got it. Relax."

Rage awakened as soon as his door opened. "Did you sleep well? Let's go potty!"

A few minutes later, Rage had his truck and followed Keefe out of the room.

"Look who is awake and went pee-pee in the toilet."

Chelsea held out her arms to Rage. "You are so big! I'm so proud of you."

Rage wrapped his arms around her neck. "You play with me?"

"Not in these clothes. I need play clothes to get on the floor, but I brought something for my big boy who went pee-pee in the toilet." She handed him the now-open package of rocks. "They are for your dump truck."

Immediately, Rage spilled the rocks onto the floor and began to have his truck go to each one.

She giggled at his antics.

Watching her with the son that he believed was his wrapped him in a comfortable blanket. He approved of the way she talked to Rage. It was as though she recognized him as a person, except he was still learning about the world that surrounded him. She seemed to keep that in mind as she spoke to him, challenging him, and giving him permission to explore. The more he thought about it, the more he realized how much he liked her.

He stirred the creamy white sauce he'd made for the broccoli, pulled the tiny lamb chops from the oven, and put the kale and thinly sliced sweet potato into the microwave. Placing one chop on his plate, he cut it into bite-sized pieces and arranged them on a lunch-sized plate. Then he added several soft florets of broccoli beside them and a small ramekin filled with the white sauce. On the other side of the lamb bites, he added a dollop of the chutney he had made with fresh mint. Then he took some gravy and drizzled the meat with it. The microwave beeped and he took out the crisped vegetables and added a chip of each to the plate. He fixed the other adult plates and called for Rage to come eat.

The child scrambled into his chair and looked at his plate. He wrinkled his nose and poked his finger into everything.

Chelsea reached over and took his hand. "Polite boys use their forks for most foods." She picked up the green chip. "Try this one. But use your fork on everything else."

He took the kale chip and bit into it. He made a face and removed it from his mouth.

"Try this one." She smiled at the boy and then looked directly at Keefe. "This looks amazing. Thank you for inviting me." She picked up a kale chip. "I've heard of people making these in the microwave, but I've never attempted it. We do something similar in the oven."

She bit into the chip and gave the thumbs up before devouring the rest of it.

"I picked up the recipe on the Net." Pride filled him and he encouraged Rage to try everything.

The boy liked dipping the florets into the sauce before eating them. And he ate every floret on his plate.

No matter what Keefe did, he couldn't get Rage to eat the chutney and the lamb together. The boy would eat his bite of meat and then take a bite, or two, or three of chutney.

For dessert he had stewed apricots over a crumble with real whipped cream on top. The meal had turned out to be delicious and Rage ate almost everything except the kale chip. He pleaded with Rage to eat his chip before giving the boy dessert, but Chelsea shook her head no to Keefe's insistent demand. Giving up, Keefe served his son dessert. At least the child had eaten everything else. When Rage was done and was properly excused from the table, Keefe began to clean up.

"Please let me help you," Chelsea begged.

"It only takes me a few minutes, and it's easier for me not to have help. And why were you trying to stop me from making Rage eat his kale? I don't want him growing up thinking he can turn his nose up at the meals I serve. From what I can tell his nutrition has been limited to Hot Pockets and fish sticks."

Chelsea laughed. "Come to my dad's house and you will find both in the freezer. They are great foods in a pinch or for a snack, but don't ever coerce a child into eating something. A child will automatically eat what they need as long as their little digestive system isn't poisoned with a bunch of sugary carbs. You said the other night that he wouldn't eat lettuce, and tonight he turned his nose up at the kale. Try another leafy green or a different version of lettuce. It might be a texture thing or he could be allergic to it. He ate his broccoli, which was good for him, and he ate the sweet potato chip. It was obvious that he loved the chutney and he did eat the lamb. Children often rebel at the taste of lamb, because it is strong-tasting meat. They aren't used to so much flavor. But he seems to enjoy lots of flavors."

"What's Donna going to feed him for lunch?"

She shrugged. "My twin brothers never complained about the meals. She does all the normal things from soup and sandwiches to fish sticks with macaroni and cheese. Rage will be well fed and diligently watched. He will be fine. She doesn't give them a bunch of junk. And don't panic if Rage is given an Oreo with a glass of milk. He will learn to eat well."

"She's going to feed him a bunch of cookies?"

Chelsea rolled her eyes. "No. He's going to eat like any normal child. Having two cookies or some other little sweet tidbit is just a treat—a little energy boost before going outside to play. Don't worry about him."

"You are the one who just told me that a child will eat proper nutrition if they are not fed a bunch of sugar. Now you are telling me he's going to eat cookies."

"I'm not going to argue with you. If you don't want him to have a cookie, take it up with Donna. But I can tell you that she will laugh at you. Yet you made a crumble and that contains sugar. He probably had more carbs in tonight's dessert than he will get from an occasional cookie treat." She shook her head. "I know my brothers often ate celery that had been filled with peanut butter. It was a favorite snack for them. They also liked the apple slices with almond butter. And while we are on the subject of snack foods, beware of raisins. Those sticky things really coat their teeth and children often don't have the ability to properly brush it away. Buy him a child-sized electric toothbrush. It will help."

Keefe knew he was attempting to parent with no skills. Chelsea wasn't a parent but seemed to know exactly what to do. He found himself feeling jealous of that built-in female mothering thing. "Damn. If I weren't a man..."

"Huh? What's wrong with being a man?"

"I didn't think I said that aloud."

She laughed. Then raised her eyebrows. "Remember I was raised by a very macho man who also managed as a single father, doing jobs that are normally relegated to females. And he had a large brood of children. He never doubted his masculinity or worried too much about his shortcomings. He did just fine and so will you."

He wanted to believe her, but at the moment he felt swamped in the mire where Leighayn had tossed him.

Chelsea came over to him and put her hand on his arm. "Chill. You are doing fine. Look what you have managed to do in a few days. There are plenty of single dads who wish they had it as easy. I doubt you are in any danger of being evicted or walking into a dark apartment tomorrow."

His neck prickled. "Of course not!"

"You've got probably the best darn babysitter around, parents who love you and would do anything for you or Rage, even if you don't want it." She smiled. "And you have me if you run into any snags. I'll answer my phone at any hour. And you've got a good job and some job security." Her smile broadened, showing off her very straight and very white teeth. "And you've got one more thing that is probably the most important asset... You are taking this job seriously and you really care about the little guy."

"He's my son."

Chelsea raised her eyebrows. "You hope. And what if he's not? Are you going to quit caring about that darling child who is dependent on you?"

Chelsea drove home and into the garage. A little part of her wanted her daddy, but his car was still gone. Yet she was the one who told him that she was fine, and that she could handle her own problems. *I'm doubting myself, just as Keefe is doubting his parenting skills.*

"Are you okay?" DeeDee asked as Chelsea stepped into the kitchen.

"I'm fine. I had a lovely evening after a rather long day."

"I heard about that. And I completely understand how Jenna's appearance after all these years is upsetting. If I never knew my mother, I'd want to at least meet her."

"I'm not a child anymore, and I can't imagine walking away from one."

"You have plenty on your plate with Jason. You didn't need this situation, too. But it seems things never happen in a logical way. When you are down, that is when you will get kicked in the gut. Happens every time."

"I know."

"You are also a product of Cody Montgomery. Don't forget it."

Chelsea grinned. "How could I? He cloned me."

DeeDee grinned. "I don't think stuffing his DNA in you would have made a penny's difference. You have the exact same attitudes."

Chelsea rolled her eyes. "Want to see what clothes I bought?" She rolled a shoulder forward, batted her eyes, and struck a pose. "It's for the new me."

She emptied her bags onto the kitchen table.

"Chelsea, I *love* this jacket." She searched for the tags. "Washable wool. It's perfect. The color is fabulous. I want to see it on you."

"No more black jackets in court? It won't happen. I have too many nice ones and to some extent it is expected in the male-dominated world of courts."

"Don't let Judge Ackermann hear you say that or she'll have your hide!"

Chelsea laughed. "She wears black suits under her robe. And enough bracelets that if she ever fell into deep water, she'd drown. I love her!"

Chelsea showed off her purchases and DeeDee was impressed.

"Stop by the shop and let Julia grab some measurements from you. I have some ideas."

"What?"

"Don't worry about it." DeeDee showed off her best Cheshire cat smile. "It's my job to make women look wonderful."

Chelsea grabbed up her things and went to her room. Alone in her nightclothes, she reviewed the day's events and knew she was ready for a better day tomorrow and the steady routine of work. She was only half Rage's age when her mother had left. Trying to imagine life without her father was next to impossible.

She knew her trust fund from SunWest Oil would have kicked in no matter what had happened. But would she have been as prepared to handle the money? It was a rhetorical question that had no answer. But it made her think about her grandparents. *They didn't know. They didn't need to know. It's our family secret.*

How do I earn enough money to live off my tiny practice, Keefe? I don't. I don't need a dime! What I do is pure pro bono.

Tuesday morning's cold snap had left ice in places, and the ground had frosted. At noon, she checked with Keefe and he was headed over to Donna's to check on Rage. No matter what she said to him, he wasn't about to listen to her. He was determined to be certain that his child was safe.

At six o'clock, she texted Keefe, and he immediately answered. And so it went for the next several days. It was Thursday late afternoon when her father returned.

"I almost didn't recognize you, Chelsea. What's up?" He stood in her office doorway.

She motioned for him to come in and sit, but he shook his head.

"I've been sitting for almost four hours. The interstate was a darn parking lot. Tell me what all has happened in my absence."

"I told you that on Friday we are meeting Jenna at two o'clock in the hotel lobby."

"We being?"

"Julia, Melissa, and I. Jenna's very enthusiastic about meeting us."

"What about Jason?"

"No one knows where he is. And we are meeting Keefe at Trabeck's Bar and Grill at eleven. It's close to Keefe's office."

Cody grimaced.

"I know Keefe did the same thing when I suggested it, but it makes it easier on him."

"Think you can reach him?"

Chelsea nodded.

"Pick someplace other than Trebeck's."

She raised her eyebrows. "The only other restaurant I can think of near there where we could sit and talk is Daphne's Tea House."

"Yes! It's perfect. Request a small room. We'll have privacy there to discuss the case."

Chelsea picked up the phone and made the reservation. Then she called Keefe. She could tell from his voice that she had pushed him into what he considered a frou-frou restaurant for women. She turned her attention to her father. "Done."

Cody grinned and walked away, but called over his shoulder. "I can't wait to meet Keefe."

"He has plenty to discuss with you beyond the case."

Keefe was glad he had requested the entire day off. He took Rage to Donna's and came back to his apartment. He had laundry to do and several other things. Already last weekend was fading into a distant memory.

If the meeting hadn't been changed to Daphne's Tea House, he could have worn something more casual to Trebeck's. He finally decided on a plain navy suit with a lighter blue pin stripe. He donned a blue tie and checked his appearance in the mirror.

He didn't remember meeting Cody Montgomery, but Keefe's dad swore that the man had even been to their house on several occasions. Nothing jogged any memory of the man or his name. All he knew was that Chelsea had said she resembled her father.

The drive to the tea house was uneventful, but Keefe's insides were strung together into a tight coil. The closer he got to the destination the tighter his nerves knotted. He wasn't certain why. Maybe just liking Chelsea was enough to trigger the anxiety.

He remembered asking Allison Clark to the prom, and how his parents made him ask her parents first. His protest had been that he wasn't going to marry her; it was just a date. Had something in his mind triggered marriage when it came to Chelsea?

He knew that might have been the convoluted link to his case of nervous tension. The feelings that came to him when he was around Chelsea were different from what he'd felt with other women. There had been a time when a pretty woman triggered one reaction in him. But Chelsea was like that piece of glass from Jack Storms. She sparkled, and lit with vibrant colors. Every time he looked at her, he saw something different. *Could she be the one for me?*

He tried to dwell on the positive, but the undercurrent in his system just spun his guts into a tighter ball.

NINE

Keefe pulled into the parking space next to Chelsea's car. He was fifteen minutes early and she had beaten him. After heaving a few deep breaths, he got out of his car. He had expected some Victorian house, but instead he stood in front of what appeared to be a very Colonial farmhouse made with brick. Pansies in Virginia Tech colors of burgundy and yellow lined the walkway and filled several urns.

There were several cars in the parking lot, so he had no idea if Cody Montgomery had already arrived. As he walked to the steps he realized that ramps were hidden behind several large boxwoods that flanked the front of the house. From the parking lot, the ramps were not visible, but from where he stood, he could see the lovely addition that made the place accessible to those who couldn't or didn't want to walk up the stairs.

He took another deep breath and opened the door.

A woman greeted him. "Good day. Do you have reservations?"

"Maybe. I'm to meet with the Montgomerys."

"Yes, Chelsea is here. Follow me."

He walked though the house to a small room that contained one table and several chairs. The décor was an odd blend of Colonial and Victorian periods. But the smile on Chelsea's face warmed his heart. "Hello. You are here early."

"I slipped out of the office a few minutes early."

He nodded and took a seat at the table. "I took a personal day. I have quite a bit to do. Plus first thing this morning, I filed the custody paperwork with the court."

There was noise behind him and Chelsea's face brightened with another smile.

"Hi, Dad. I'd like you to meet Keefe Assam."

Keefe rose to his feet and turned to face the man. He swallowed and attempted to form the correct words. "Pleased to meet you, sir."

He held out his hand to a man who looked like he was in his early forties except for the amount of gray in his dark hair. His suit was fitted and accented in silver. The clasp on his bolo tie was a bull's head that had been beaded in red and black.

"Nice to see you again, Keefe. Your dad and I have worked together on quite a few occasions. What do you have for me?" He went to his daughter and kissed her cheek before taking a seat next to her. Then he reached under his jacket, revealing a silvery-grey vest, and withdrew a small notebook and a pen.

Keefe felt a slight tremble run down his back and hoped that it didn't show. A waitress brought menus and goblets filled with icy water. He looked at the sandwiches and had no clue what to order. *What exactly is watercress?*

Fortunately, Chelsea ordered first, and he said he'd take the same.

Chelsea grinned as though she knew he was lost.

Cody placed his menu in front of the waitress. "I'll have the goat cheese salad, with the dilled cucumber plate. Bring a pot of the house tea for everyone. And we'll all have today's dessert." Somehow Cody Montgomery looked totally at ease in this restaurant, as though he'd eaten here often.

Cody picked up his pen and again asked, "What do you have?"

Chelsea answered.

Keefe finished her dissertation. "It's a two-bit case, but I stumbled on this situation. My gut tells me they have the wrong man."

"Gut feelings are important. But even when you don't get those feelings, our job is to check everything very carefully."

Cody continued to talk, and Keefe was fascinated with this man who had devoted his practice to freeing those who had been wrongly convicted. He also found inmates who had had their rights violated. And occasionally he worked dead-end cases.

Cody Montgomery ended the meeting by apologizing over Keefe's accidental macing and involvement with Jason Mayer. He also thanked Keefe for his attempt to protect

Chelsea. "My children are the world to me."

Keefe found himself with more questions than ever. And before they left the table, he blurted, "I just obtained custody of a child that I didn't know I had."

Cody leaned back in his seat. "How do you feel about that?"

"He looks like me. I have no reason not to believe he's mine."

Cody smiled. "If you had DNA testing on the child, would it change the way you feel about him?"

Keefe shook his head. "I don't think so. I wasn't prepared for a child, but I have him. He has no one, and there's no way to locate the biological father if it's not me."

Cody smiled. "Then have him tested or you will always wonder. If he's not yours, remember that you've made the decision to raise him as your child. He's not responsible for what his mother did. But the moment you accepted him, he was yours." Cody wrapped his arm around Chelsea's shoulder. "She is my daughter and I love her. I will always love her."

"I'm certain there are plenty of children being raised without love. Rage will be raised with love. Thank you."

Cody rose and so did Keefe. There was something about Cody Montgomery. He had a commanding air about him. It was as though he owned everything around him, including the air that Keefe was breathing.

"Sir, I'm glad you are taking this case seriously."

Cody smiled. "You will never make a few million a year chasing these cases, but knowing that you've done the right thing allows you to put your head on your pillow and sleep peacefully."

Keefe extended his hand to this man. In the short visit they had, he admired Cody Montgomery's actions. Was this not what he had wanted to do when he graduated? Wasn't he looking for a way to make a difference? Instead he was dealing with boring accidents, the kind of things that should have been handled by insurance companies. Probably only one out of every couple hundred seriously required a lawyer. But people were greedy, and they wanted not just more money, they wanted revenge.

Cody picked up the tab for the meals and Keefe offered to at least pay the tip.

"Don't worry about it. It's only a few dollars."

But it wasn't.

Cody tossed two large bills onto the table and picked up his credit card from the pretty silver tray.

Keefe swallowed.

"Chelsea, would you consider dinner with me tonight?" Keefe hoped for the affirmative.

Chelsea smiled sweetly. "Ah, I have to leave here for another meeting."

"May I call you after that meeting ends?"

Cody broke into the conversation. "I spoke to her this morning. There's no ulterior motive, just enjoy your meeting. I'll text your sisters."

Keefe's curiosity was piqued, but he didn't probe. The three of them excused themselves, said their goodbyes, and left for their cars.

Keefe held Chelsea's car door for her. "Please call me after your meeting. I'd really love to have you come over tonight. I promise it'll be delicious. It will be seafood, and you did say that you eat it."

"Yes. Some things I like better than others. Scallops and other mollusks are a favorite. Lobster is so-so." She rocked her hand in front of her. "I do eat fish and shrimp, but I've never been one for cooking it. It's as though it's a foreign item at the grocery stores where I used to live." She giggled. "Most of the bars I used to frequent carried Rocky Mountain oysters, and they have nothing to do with the ocean."

Keefe swallowed. He had no desire to eat such a thing. "No problem. A seafood dinner is on the menu, and I mean things that come from the sea."

Chelsea laughed as he closed her door. Then he watched her back out. His heart beat a little harder. *Do you feel anything when we are together?*

Chelsea drove to the hotel where she was to meet her biological mother. She wondered what the woman had said to her father. *What kind of a woman walks away from her family and never looks back?*

Questions ran through her mind but she knew she'd never ask more than one or two. Melissa was there first and soon Julia joined them. It was obvious that Julia had come straight from work. Her high heels and pencil skirt screamed Main Street Bridal. Melissa was dressed more causally in a pair of brown slacks and a pretty cream-colored, three-quarter sleeve knitted top.

Chelsea was still trying to get comfortable with her new look. Her plain black slacks were topped with a purple geometric blouse and she wore large gold earrings. Chelsea looked at her sisters and wondered how they all managed to be so very different. As young teens they had played with makeup as though it were a box of crayons and their faces were empty canvases. Now they were all minimal with their use of makeup. Even after almost a week of trying to get used to her new look, she still had to force herself to wear makeup. Life was easier without it.

"Ready?" Julia asked.

Melissa nodded and Chelsea stood. Together they walked to the dining room. Chelsea never had butterflies. She'd faced many a courtroom and watched her peers falter when butterflies took flight. But at this moment, the butterflies were flapping in her stomach and tension had tightened her neck and shoulders. *How will we even recognize her?*

There was barely anyone in the dining room, and the hostess said they were expected. She pointed to a far corner. A lone woman sat at a table set for four.

Her hair was a mousy brown well mixed with gray. She smiled and stood as they approached the table.

"Jenna? I'm Julia." She extended her hand.

Chelsea introduced herself and then Melissa.

Butterflies still flittered, but they were settling. Maybe it was from watching the woman's eyes gathering moisture, but Chelsea knew she had to tug on that hard exterior that she used in the courtroom. Chelsea turned and spotted a waiter. He immediately came to the table.

"Hot tea, with milk and sugar."

Melissa ordered coffee and Julia asked for tonic water with lemon. Jenna ordered coffee.

Chelsea felt a slight chill as though something were amiss. *Trust your gut.* Her father's words echoed in her mind. Melissa wasn't saying much, and Julia so far had only mentioned the lovely weather.

Chelsea couldn't stand another second of the awkwardness. "What brings you here now? And why did you wait all these years without making contact?"

The woman grimaced. "Staying away was in the divorce papers. I received a lump sum of money and signed away all my rights to my beautiful children."

Chelsea pushed her shoulders against the chair back and waited for the woman to continue.

"I screwed up and made a mess of my life. Being married to your father was fun. I'd never had anything growing up. Suddenly I had money to buy clothes and do things. Your father constantly had his nose in his books. If he wasn't in a class, he was studying. I hated the fact that I never saw him." Her hands made tiny constant movements as though she were conducting an orchestra made up of mice. "I thought it would get better when he graduated, but it didn't. It only got worse." She wiped at the corners of her eyes. "His hours were long, and then he took on a case... We both knew where it was going, and he wanted me to do things to protect our little family, except it never felt like a family."

The waiter brought their drinks, which immediately put an end to Jenna's words.

Chelsea asked the waiter if they could have the large plate of mixed hors d'oeuvres so they could nibble. The man nodded and left.

"I told your father. I got into drugs. I was only trying to stay calm, but it seemed the whirlwind around your father kept escalating. I hated being home day after day with no break. Everything I did—I had three children to lug along

87

with me. We never even went out to eat. I felt as though I'd been imprisoned."

With trembling hands, she sipped at her coffee. "We had a neighbor two houses away who had a little girl Julia's age. She'd bring the child over to visit, and one day while we were chatting... It was so long ago. She went home and brought me a few pills, said they would help me. Those pills were my undoing. I was hooked."

She rolled her palms upward. "I left and the next few years are a big blur. Cody found me one day and sent me to a rehab center." She let out a single chuckle. "It was the first of many such places. I managed to get clean seven years and three months ago." She stopped and smiled. "I'm remarried. Joe works in a warehouse, and I have an office job working for a trucking company."

Chelsea knew that she should feel sorry for the woman, but there were no feelings there to be found. Was Jenna really any different from all the other drug cases that ran through the court systems? There were blood ties to this biological mother, but that was all there was. At least she'd gotten clean and was staying that way.

The waiter put the plate of food in front of them and Julia immediately took a stuffed celery stick.

Chelsea raised her eyebrows. "Are you happy?"

"Oh, yes. Maybe this was all I ever wanted. We both work, but we have each other."

They all munched silently and only talked about the foods for a few minutes. Then Chelsea found the need to say more. "I don't know what our father has said about any of us. So I will tell you. I'm a lawyer and I recently came back to work with my dad. I'm not married."

Julia swallowed. "I'm married to a wonderful man, and I manage a large company. I also have eight children." She giggled. "I told you he was wonderful."

Melissa laughed. "I'm married, and I have horses. Lots of them."

Julia looked at her watch and inhaled. "I had no idea it was this late. It was lovely to meet you."

Chelsea called the waiter to the table. "Check, please." She turned to the table. "I've got this. Yes. It was nice to meet you. I'm sorry you've been through so much. But I'm glad to hear you've made it through, and you've found peace in your new life. That is all our father has ever asked of us; to find our own contentment."

Chelsea signed the receipt and then stood, as did her sisters.

A few more goodbyes were said and the three siblings decided they would all head to Melissa's for a little chat after Julia picked up her children.

Chelsea walked outside and slipped her phone from her purse. She called Keefe. "Hi, I need a rain check. I'm getting together with my sisters. We have some things to discuss."

"I was looking forward to seeing you. I was hoping we could go someplace after Rage went to bed. Elizabeth gave me the name of a teen who babysits."

"That sounds lovely. I'm not certain when I'll be free. But I'm willing to do something even if it's just a long walk. I probably could use the exercise. I think I've sat too much today." *I really need to unwind.*

Keefe called the sitter and offered to pay her even if he didn't actually need her. She readily accepted and stopped by his place about a half hour later. She looked so young, but she assured him that she had done plenty of babysitting in the community and even showed him some certificate she had earned stating she had passed a babysitting class that included first aid. It was good enough for him. But he still crossed his fingers.

After fixing a meal for him and Rage, he played with his son before sending him for his bath.

Rage loved taking a bath and splashing around. His antics were quite cute. After this short while of living with Keefe, Rage seemed to have settled into the routine of daily life with ease.

Keefe lifted a slippery wet boy from the tub and wrapped

him in his hooded towel. A sharp little toenail caught Keefe's attention, so he checked the child's toes. They all needed to be trimmed. As soon as the boy was in his pajamas, Keefe offered a snack of mixed melons that he found in the grocery store. Then he scooped the boy into his arms and carried him back to the bathroom to brush his teeth and wash his hands.

Christmas wasn't that far away, and after the other night's cold snap, it felt more like autumn. Even the colors in the trees brightened after that frost. Keefe wondered what he'd do for Christmas. He imagined a fireplace with stockings hung for Santa, and Chelsea snuggled next to him while Rage slept in his bed. The little vision instantly burst. *I guess I need a tree. Maybe a train set? What am I going to give him for Christmas?*

Cody Montgomery's words went through his head. *Have him tested or you will always wonder.*

TEN

Chelsea pulled into Melissa's driveway and drove to the main house. She let herself in through the back door.

Melissa called to her, "What if I just make a salad for dinner? I'm not the least bit hungry for a big meal after nibbling at the hotel."

"That's plenty for me. I was at the tea house with Dad before I went to the hotel." Chelsea followed her sister's voice to the kitchen.

"Give me a sec, and I'll fix a salad for us."

Chelsea washed her hands and figured she could poke around in Melissa's refrigerator. She had just withdrawn a container of fresh lettuce, probably from their garden, when Drexel came through the door with one of Julia's older boys upside down in his arms. Drexel and the six-year-old were laughing. Soon a whole herd of children stampeded into the house, thrilled to be visiting with their aunt and uncle.

Melissa appeared with a wide grin. She gave out lots of hugs and kisses.

"Where's the baby?" Chelsea asked.

"Dad's got him." Julia chased after her youngest daughter who squealed and took off for the far end of the house.

"Huh?" She looked out the window and spotted her dad with DeeDee. *Family reunion time. I'll never get out of here tonight.*

Melissa soon joined them and told Chelsea to use whatever she wanted in the salad. "There's lots of tomatoes in the pantry. Drexel picked them before that frost hit the other night."

Chelsea watched as Melissa opened the freezer door and grabbed a bunch of hamburger patties.

"Drex, want to light the grill?" Melissa called.

Chaos soon settled into a low din, and Chelsea tossed the salad. Then she made certain the macaroni was well drained before stirring in the four cheeses and returning it to low heat. Melissa was the better cook. She liked staying at home and enjoyed her rather organic lifestyle with Drexel.

Chelsea wondered why her sister wasn't pregnant. Of the three of them, Melissa was the mothering one. She had mentioned adoption a few times but almost jokingly. Chelsea figured there might be a problem, and she didn't want to place her sister in a position to explain or defend.

"Don't bother with the china. We'll use paper plates. No one wants to clean up." Melissa pointed to a far cabinet. "I think I have pretty paper ones in there."

Chelsea found everything and stacked the paper items on a sideboard. It was obvious that they were all eating in the newly renovated kitchen. Drexel brought in the cooked hamburgers, and Cody arranged the juvenile chairs around the big country table.

Fortunately, dinner went well. And then DeeDee took the children for a long walk, giving the rest of the family a chance to talk.

The girls chatted and decided they all felt it was an odd meeting, but in a way they were happy that Jenna had found some stability and joy in life.

Julia pulled her hair from the confines of its bun. "I don't understand why she wanted to meet with us. Why now?"

Cody finally spoke up. "She had reached the point in her life where she felt she could meet with you. She figured you were all old enough to understand that people make mistakes. Horrible mistakes. And then spend years trying to undo whatever they did." He folded his hands in front of him. "The fact that you all got through the meeting without falling apart or freaking over her wanting to see you says that her waiting until now was probably a very good idea. If she had stepped back into your lives when you were teens when she had first kicked her drug habit, you would have never believed she was clean, and you might have truly hated her."

Cody smiled. "Now, you've met her, had a chance to talk to her. If you want further contact, she asked that I pass her information along to you."

Chelsea looked at her father and her mind spun as she

assembled the right words. "How old was I when she left?"

Cody shrugged. "I have the dates written down. I'm going to say eight months."

"She's a stranger to me. I know that sounds cold, but she was never my mother. I still can't fathom a woman walking away from her children." She looked at her sisters. "Keefe just was handed a son he didn't know he had, and that mother gave up everything. That child is precious!" Chelsea rolled her palms up. "Dad, I'm sorry. I just don't have any warm fuzzy feelings."

Melissa nodded. "I'm with Chelsea. It was an interesting afternoon. But she is not my *mother*. You are my father. As far as I am concerned, she was merely an egg donor. You were the one who raised me, cheered me on, and held my hair when I vomited because I was sick."

"Oh gross!" Julia grimaced. "We just ate. Where is your sense of decorum?"

Melissa turned to her sister and stuck her tongue out. "Decorum, *deshmorum*. I couldn't give a f...flip! It's true. Dad was our father. We never had a mother. Face it, the closest we ever came to a mother was Aunt Barbara." Melissa rolled her eyes. "And now DeeDee, except I'd call her a friend. At least both those women actually care about us."

"Well, I remember her, and to me, she looks old. I don't remember her ever being mean, but I'll be honest, I don't remember that much about her." Julia walked to the window and looked outside. "I worry because I work, so maybe I go overboard to spend quality time with my children." She turned her attention to her father and sisters. "If something happened to me tonight, will you please let them know how much I love them? Because they aren't going to remember that."

Cody smiled. "Relax, Julia, DeeDee has them. Aaron and I would never let them forget how much you love them."

Chelsea couldn't hold back her thoughts. "That's just it. I can't remember a single time when you said how much our mother loved us, and it's not like she died. She walked away from us. She chose pills over children—"

Cody shook his head. "I'm partly to blame. I was so involved with that one case that I neglected her. And then I was so angry when she left. All I had were my three little girls. I wasn't prepared to become a mother and father. What happened was between us as the adults, but it affected you." Cody pressed his lips into a thin line for a moment. "Don't blame her for what I did or didn't do."

Chelsea frowned. "And it will be the same with Rage one day."

"Possibly. Or maybe he will go looking for his birth mother. Most people seem to want to know. Now you know."

But nothing would ever make Chelsea feel sorry for the woman who walked away. Yet there was something about the visit that brought some kind of end to a child-like fantasy of a wonderful mother. Now that vision was left smashed and lying on the floor.

Chelsea stood. "Melissa, thank you for the lovely meal. I wish I'd had more room in my tummy to eat more."

Melissa laughed. "I know. I feel the same way."

Chelsea hugged her dad. "Thanks for trying. But my family is right here. She did what she did." Chelsea smiled at her dad. "And a very special thank you for being a super dad. I'm so glad you never abandoned us."

She stepped out of the old house where Melissa lived and into her car. She swiped the screen a few times on her phone and called Keefe. "Still want to meet? I want to change my clothes if you do."

Keefe sat at his computer going over some notes on his latest court case, but his mind kept drifting to Christmas. His thoughts were interrupted by Chelsea's phone call. When he hung up the phone he called the babysitter and she came right over.

"Rage is sleeping. If he wakes up, take him to the bathroom."

The young girl nodded. "No need to worry. I know what I'm doing."

"You have my phone number. I'm not really going any further than the park down the street."

The young gal made a face. "Think again. That is not going to happen. The park closes at sunset."

He blew out a breath. "Then we'll just be on the streets."

He watched out his front windows, and when he was certain he saw Chelsea's car, he flew down his steps and onto the sidewalk.

Chelsea stepped out of the car dressed in jeans and sneakers, looking a little worn around the edges.

"Are you okay? You look as though you've been crying."

"It's been a long day."

"I think we all have days like that. Are you sure you feel like walking?"

"The exercise might do me some good."

He took her hand and they walked as far as the park. Keefe pointed to the sign that said the park closes as sunset and reopens at dawn.

She nodded. "That doesn't surprise me. I know they've had a few problems over the years."

"It's not as romantic to walk the town's streets."

She giggled. "Since when did men think of romance? Furthermore, if this is supposed to be romantic, maybe you should have warned me sooner. I thought we were just friends."

He didn't like her tone. "I hope we *are* friends because friendship is important. Chelsea, I've been burned. And when Leighayn showed up with Rage, it opened all the old pain. How are we ever supposed to know when the right one comes along? So friendship is a good place to start." He lightly gave her hand a squeeze. "I know when I'm around you I feel more than friendship. I'm hoping you feel it, too."

She stopped dead in her tracks. "It's going to take me time. Your wounds are two years old, but mine are fresh. I'm not done sorting all the pieces of my life."

She looked up at him and in the streetlight he could see the tears that washed her eyes. She sniffled. "So far, the only thing I've managed to do is to make a mess of my life and sail full force into a storm."

"Maybe you need a co-captain, someone who can navigate while you explore."

"No thanks. I've had one man steering my ship into deeper, dark waters until he thought he controlled me. Well, he did, but not all of me. And when I didn't obey, the powder keg exploded. So like a wimp, I ran home to my daddy." Two tears slipped down her cheeks.

His heart pounded against his chest. He reached over and wiped her tears from her cheeks with the gentlest touch he could muster. "I thought my heart had broken when I discovered Leighayn's infidelity. I walked away. But Jason has done deeper damage. He got to your spirit."

More tears spilled over her cheeks.

He leaned over and touched his lips to hers.

She gripped his hand as though it were in a vice.

His free hand found her other hand and he clasped it. She didn't kiss back, but she seemed to accept his kiss.

"Don't ever be afraid of me. I never want to control another human being. But I do want a woman who can be my equal partner. Someone I can trust—someone who will love me as much as I love her."

"And you think I'm that person? I don't even know who I am anymore."

Chelsea and Keefe walked slowly to his apartment. She made a dive for the bathroom to try to escape being discovered in disarray. She recognized the young babysitter's name and she didn't want any gossip floating around town. Behind the closed door she softly called to Keefe. "Why don't you walk her home? It's very late."

"It's okay. I'm going to call my mom while I make that dash. It's so quiet at night around here you can hear anything that moves. I live right back there."

"Okay, then instead of going out the front door, do you want to use the back door? It will save you from walking around the block."

"Yeah, that'll be great."

Chelsea heard the back door open and Keefe saying

goodbye to the young teen. She took that as a good omen that it was safe to come out. At least her nose had stopped running, but she brought the tissue box with her just in case. A moment later, he stepped back inside, peeked at Rage, and then she watched as Keefe started to heat water for tea.

"When she said she lives right back there, she was right. I could see her almost the whole way."

"That's good. Ninety-nine percent of the time this area has no problems, but something can happen anyplace at any time." She walked to where Keefe stood in the kitchen. "I'm sorry. I look horrible."

He smiled broadly. "No. You look like a woman who is sorting out her life and has suffered a few losses along the way. Think of it this way, you are alive. You have a great big family who loves you and welcomes you back. That's a safety net that so many people do not have. And you have one more thing. You have me. I really want us to have a chance." He took the kettle from the stove. "I have a good feeling about us. There's a spark between us, a sizzling undercurrent."

"There's more." She raised her eyebrows at him. "You have a child, and I've never wanted children. That's a big red flag to me."

"I can respect your feelings and accept them, but don't let Rage become the factor keeping us apart. Problems become problems because we allow them to be. Talking about things does make a difference. Communication is the key to many things. I'm still learning to cope with the idea that I've become a single father to a child I didn't know I had."

"Are you going to have him tested?"

Keefe nodded. "Your dad is right about the question that will always linger. I need to find out and come to grips with it if he's not mine."

"You don't have to keep him if he's not yours. There are plenty of people who would love to adopt him."

"I'm keeping him. I can't explain the feelings inside of me. I have no parenting skills. I have no idea what I'm doing, but he brings me total happiness. He fills in this little part of me and makes living so worthwhile."

"Oh, do you sound like a parent. I think I heard those very

words out of Julia's mouth when she had her first one."

"Okay, let's agree that Rage is going to be a big factor in this relationship."

"That's a good place to start." She sipped her herbal tea. "This is yummy."

She talked and cried some more. Instead of criticism, she found comforting words. He sided with her, making her feel better. And he seemed to understand her need to try harder.

Keefe told of his situation with Leighayn. The hurt she had inflicted on him made him just as apprehensive of being in another relationship. Pain was pain, and he'd had his fair share of it, too.

She opened her eyes to the scent of coffee and morning light streaming between the blinds of Keefe's apartment. At first, she was guarded, but soon realized she was snuggled under a big comforter with a wonderful downy soft pillow for her head. She sat up and there was a big cup of coffee from Elizabeth's sitting on the table in front of her. She touched the cup and realized it was still hot. She looked around but didn't see Keefe. Then she heard Rage and Keefe talking in Rage's bedroom. In the small bathroom that she used, there was a brand new toothbrush and a small tube of toothpaste sitting by the sink. It hadn't been there last night. *That is so thoughtful of him.*

When she was finished, she went to Rage's bedroom door and lightly rapped.

"She's awake!"

"Yes, my boy, she's awake. Come in."

She slowly opened the door and discovered Rage was sitting in the middle of his bed. Keefe was on the edge.

"Good morning." She smiled at the two guys and then joined them. "What are you doing so quietly behind closed doors? Or is it a big secret?"

"Daddy is going to buy me a train."

"A train? You already have a train." She pointed to the one on the wall.

"No, a real train. Woo-woo! Show her, Daddy."

Keefe moved his small computer so that Chelsea could see

the picture. I'm trying to decide on the gauge. I want something he will grow into and not out of."

"I have no idea."

"For now a simple set of tracks that will circle the base of the Christmas tree."

"Woo-woo!"

Chelsea laughed at Rage. He was obviously a good child, but he had plenty of energy. "Since we didn't have a chance to walk in the park last night... why don't we pack a picnic lunch and go today. I think Rage would love to have some freedom to run, and there's a nice play area there."

"Sounds like a plan to me." Keefe stood. "I'll make breakfast for us."

"I have a better idea. Come to my dad's, and I'll make breakfast. I'd like to change before we go."

"I don't want to intrude."

"Not with my family. Dad and DeeDee will welcome you with open arms. To my dad, the house is empty."

"Are you sure? Rage didn't do well at my parents' home."

ELEVEN

A few minutes later, Chelsea, Keefe, and Rage walked through the front door of the Montgomery household.

"Hello. Anyone home?" Chelsea called.

Cody Montgomery came around the corner, holding his youngest.

Rage instantly brightened. "CJ!"

Chelsea grinned. "I forgot that they played together at Donna's."

CJ wiggled from his dad arms. "Want to play with my new X-wing fighters?"

Rage nodded and followed CJ.

"Is that okay? Do you mind, sir?" Keefe held his breath.

"Kids in this house are part of the décor. Make yourself at home. This place is child proofed. May I offer you a cup of coffee?"

"Thank you, sir. I'd appreciate that."

They chatted about the boys until guilt assaulted Keefe. Inwardly he cringed. *Certainly, he must know that Chelsea spent the night with me.*

The subject hung in the air as an unseen force until Keefe knew he needed to address it. "Chelsea and I spent most of the night talking. I promise I was a gentleman."

Cody laughed. "You're no longer children. What you do or don't do is between the two of you."

"I wish my parents were as understanding. They'd have my hide if they knew Chelsea had spent the night."

"How did they handle the news of Rage?"

Keefe chuckled. "My mother adores him. My father ignores him, and I'm sure they think he was conceived magically."

"We all know how they get here."

"What's here?" Chelsea asked as she breezed into the kitchen with her hair still slightly damp from her shower.

Cody grinned at his daughter.

Keefe hoped his awkwardness didn't show on his face. "Children."

She furrowed her brow.

Cody poured another cup of coffee and handed it to Chelsea. "Don't forget. We leave here Wednesday for your grandparents'."

Chelsea frowned. "I guess you already have our tickets, so saying I forgot to buy one won't work."

"That's right." He kissed his daughter's cheek. "The kitchen is yours. I already made French toast for everyone once this morning."

"Any bread left?"

"Of course."

Keefe instantly felt a feeling of loss sucking a piece of him away. "You won't be here for Thanksgiving?"

Chelsea shook her head. "Do you like French toast?"

"Of course. I don't think I've ever made it."

"Oh, it's so simple." She removed a bowl from a cabinet. "Watch."

"Where are you going?"

"My grandparents live in Utah. Want to come? The more the merrier." She broke several eggs into the bowl and began to whip them. "Everyone has an opinion about this. Some people like to add water, while others like to add milk. I've seen it made with yogurt, or heavy cream, or a dash of mayonnaise mixed into cream. Pick your poison."

He watched her add a dash of half and half, and the tiniest pinch of salt.

"Don't expect healthy. That would be a poached egg on dry whole wheat for breakfast."

"I like whole grain breads."

"You do? Shall I make our French toast with some?"

"I don't want to put you to any extra trouble."

Chelsea rolled her eyes at him and swapped the plain white for another loaf that must have come from the bakery shop in town. "I love this stuff. But what about Rage?"

He rolled his hands up. "So far he's eaten anything I've fed him except for leafy green things."

"Think about coming to Utah with us. Rage would have a blast. It's a great big ranch and tons of children. It's chaos on steroids out there. But my grandparents wouldn't have it any other way. They demand that we all go home for Thanksgiving and that we come over the Christmas holiday. We usually leave here on the twenty-sixth and fly out."

She soaked the bread slices in the egg mixture and placed them on a sheet of waxed paper. When she was done, she placed a pan on the stove and added a small dollop of butter. Then she ladled what was left of the egg mixture in the bowl over the slices.

"It looks easy enough."

"Oh, it is. And you can freeze whatever is left over and toast it the next day. I've actually spread peanut butter on it and left for work. It's a great breakfast sandwich."

"Peanut butter?"

"Ah-huh."

He wasn't so sure of that combination. "I've heard peanut butter isn't supposed to be given to children."

She shrugged. "We would have been in big trouble if there was a peanut allergy around here. We were raised on it. Dad learned to cook simple meals and I learned from him."

"My mom doesn't do much cooking. But she does cook. I love her peanut soup."

Chelsea turned around and stared at him. "Peanut soup?"

He nodded. "You need a good chicken-based stock. Never, and I mean never, substitute turkey stock. It's awful!"

"That bad?"

He nodded. "Horrible. Turkey noodle is fine, just don't ever use that base for peanut soup."

"Other than my dad, I've never known a guy who could cook."

"It's called learn or starve."

Chelsea laughed, then turned solemn. "I probably told you too many things last night. I'm sorry."

"I'm glad you were open with me. I understand what you went through, and I hope I've learned from it. I still cannot imagine imposing such control on someone you truly love or care about. It makes no sense to me." He drank the last of his coffee. "May I pour another?"

She turned away from the stove long enough to hand him the bag of coffee beans. "The grinder is there. Better make another pot."

With a fresh pot brewing, he heard the sounds of Rage and CJ someplace above him. "Maybe I should check on the boys."

"Good idea. Tell Rage it's time to eat. There's plenty if CJ wants more." She poured orange juice into a pan with butter, and then added cinnamon along with several other spices.

"What are you making now?"

She scrunched her nose. "A reduced orange—I don't know. It's for the toast and it tastes good."

He knew how he felt about Chelsea, but watching her was like watching a flower blossom in timed-released photography.

An hour later, they left for the park. They took CJ with them, and he and Rage played.

"I guess I could come to your grandparents'. I was hoping you'd come to my parents'."

"My grandparents laid down the law years ago. We all go there for Thanksgiving. We feed only the littlest ones first, and then the rest of us eat together. My grandmother loves it and my grandfather is so proud of his family. But really, it's insanity."

Holidays for him were quiet, boring affairs, just he and a much older sister with her husband and two boys, who would stop by his mom and dad's house for a few hours. He couldn't imagine a big family with all those children running around.

"Might be fun. I'll see if I can get a flight."

Chelsea took a tired CJ home and Keefe tucked Rage in for an early nap, being he'd missed his morning one. While the boy slept, Keefe went online and attempted to buy airfare for him and Rage. After several hours, he knew it was hopeless. The only way he'd get there was by land.

Rage had played from the moment they had walked through the Montgomery door until they left the park. But it had been fun. Chelsea brought a Frisbee, and the adults worked hard to teach the boys to throw. The little guys weren't great, but they caught on fairly quickly. The memory of the pride Rage took in himself, when he managed to actually make the plastic disk sail several feet, spread to Keefe and warmed that little place inside him that Rage now possessed.

His phone rang, bringing him back to the present. "Hi."

"Did you buy tickets?" Chelsea's voice came through the tiny speaker.

"I'm sorry. I won't make it. There's not a ticket to be had."

"Pack your bags anyway. You aren't the only one without a flight. Would you believe my super organized sister forgot to get them for her family? How could she forget to buy ten tickets?"

She subconsciously doesn't want to go? "Guess she was busy with other things."

"Well, Dad made a few phone calls, and we are all going by, um, a private jet. Guess it pays to know someone." Her laugh sounded wonderful.

"Private jet?"

"Yes."

"Wow. What can I say? That'll be a first. When and where?"

"I'm not certain yet. Someone has to call my dad back when they work out some flight plan thing. Apparently, you don't just take these things out for a Saturday afternoon drive."

Now it was his turn to laugh. When their conversation ended, he called his dad and gave him the news that he and Rage would not be there for Thanksgiving. They had been invited to a big Montgomery family gathering in Utah.

His father approved of the new friendship with Cody Montgomery. "Don't know how that man has the money he does. He does all those *pro bono* cases. Yet sometimes it seems as though he owns half this town."

"He's extremely nice. I truly like him." *And I'm in love with his daughter.*

"Good man to have on your side."

"I hear Rage waking from his nap."

"Your mom wants to talk to you."

"Tell her I'll call her back. Rage needs me." He ended the connection before his father could say another word and went to Rage. "Good afternoon, my big boy. Did you have a nice nap?"

Rage began to cry.

Chelsea met Keefe and Rage at the walk-in clinic by the north end of town. This was the other reason she didn't want to be a mother. Rage was crying, and it seemed as though every child in the place was part of the same nerve-racking cacophony. By the time she had got there, Rage had already been diagnosed with a sore throat and a double ear infection.

"What did I do wrong?" Keefe tucked his son's head under his chin as he held the child in his lap.

Chelsea shook her head. "Probably nothing. He's a child and children get sick." She looked around. "I hate doctors and hospitals."

"I can tell you are uncomfortable. You don't have to stay. I'm waiting for them to give me the prescription, and then we can check out. I added him to my insurance, but I'm not certain he's covered yet." He pressed his lips together into a hard line. "That's probably what is taking them so long. And they are having fits because I don't have his shot records with me. I made a general appointment with the pediatrician in December. What am I doing? I shouldn't be a parent."

Chelsea started to giggle. "Well, we all know that a few moments of pleasure can add up to a lifetime of heartaches."

Rage looked up and reached for her.

"Oh, wonderful. A germy little kid. You really think I want you?" She took Rage from his dad. "I'll take him into the fresh air. Where's his coat?"

"I wrapped him in his blanket."

She shook her head and snuggled the blanket around the little guy. "Coats do work better most of the time. Come on, Rage, we'll wait for your daddy outside."

She took Rage and walked away from the modern building. At least it was pleasant in the sunshine. Brown leaves swirled on the ground, while others still clung to their colors and the tree. She liked this time of year. Nights were chilly, but the days were warm enough for a light jacket or sweater. She walked under a tree that stood off to the side of the big clinic and shuffled through the leaves, making Rage laugh.

"You feel better out here, don't you?"

"They gave me a shot right here."

He reached behind him.

"Did it hurt?"

He nodded.

"Oh, you will begin to feel better real soon. That's why they gave you a shot. But the good thing about that shot is it only hurts for a moment and I bet your ears hurt much more."

"Do you have earaches?"

"I haven't had one for a very long time. And I don't want one, so you have to keep your germs to yourself. Okay?"

She tickled him and made him giggle, but his giggle quickly turned into tears as he pulled at his right ear.

"Oh, baby, I'm sorry. I didn't mean to make your ears hurt." She snuggled Rage against her and hugged him. "Keep your blanket around your ears so the cool air doesn't get to them."

She held him, rocked him, and the little guy snuggled tight to her and smiled at her. *Stop melting my heart. I'm having enough trouble trying not to fall in love with your dad.*

But when he planted a little kiss on her cheek, she could feel her eyes filling with tears.

"I love you. You're the best. When will you be my mommy? Daddy said I need a mommy. He already told me he wants you to be my mommy. He said he loves you."

She slammed her eyes closed and that squeezed the tear droplets onto her cheeks. She wiped them away, and Rage hugged her tight. *Oh why?*

Keefe paid the bill and found Chelsea and Rage near the parking lot.

"Hi. We are free to go home, except I must stop by the pharmacy and pick up a few things for him." He showed her the list of recommended items.

"No problem. Do you want me to take your list and pick

up these items for you?"

"That would be great. I don't even know what half these things look like."

She took the list and handed Rage to Keefe. "I'll see you back at your place."

Keefe strapped his son into his car seat, and then drove to his apartment. Once inside, he let Rage watch cartoons on the TV. Keefe wanted Rage to stay quiet, but the child turned the channel and found a football game. *How do you know about football? I probably don't want to know the answer to that one.*

Keefe took Monday off and stayed home with the little guy who was obviously feeling much better. By turning his desk around so he could keep an eye on Rage while he played, Keefe managed to work from home.

Chelsea stopped by Monday after work and brought coffee from Elizabeth's. After sharing some coffee, she left for her own home, claiming she had promised to fix dinner for the family.

He hated to see her leave. If there had been a way to keep her near, he would have utilized it. But he also didn't want her to think he was controlling her. She needed freedom. *She'll always need it. The need to be loved is there, but on her terms.*

Wednesday morning was bright and clear as he packed Rage into his car seat. He rode to the small airport outside of town and met with the rest of the family. This was the first time he'd met Julia's husband Aaron. Never in a million years would he have thought to put those two together.

Deep inside, he wondered what a flight would be like with eleven children aboard. From the energy level that he saw around him, the feeling of stress began to build in him. After they were in the air, the pilot told them they could move around some, but that he preferred them to remain seated as much as possible. When they ran into some turbulence through the midwest, everyone sat quietly. Julia's tote contained everything from fresh packages of crayons and all sorts of papers and coloring projects, to puzzles and travel games. It was a wee bit noisy at times, but Julia kept the children well controlled. Charley acted as though Rage was her special project. She sat beside him and helped him color.

The pilot announced, "We'll be approaching the ranch in approximately thirty minutes. I will alert you about ten minutes before we land. Please take your seats and keep your seatbelts fastened until the plane comes to a complete stop."

Julia checked two sets of diapers and changed both. Then Keefe took Rage to the lavatory.

The flight itself was fairly smooth, except for those few minutes midway. He had no idea they'd be landing at the ranch, and wondered if they would be landing in a field someplace. Then he worried if that was safe.

A well-marked landing strip could be seen in the middle of nothing. The landing was smooth as glass and the pilot asked them to remain seated until he gave word.

Cody opened the door as stairs rolled up and seemed to snap into place from the sounds Keefe heard. Cody told everyone to gather their things and leave. He helped everyone off and then took a few moments before he reappeared holding someone's doll. He seemed to know exactly which little girl owned it.

"Emily, you left Cara on the plane." He handed Julia's daughter the doll. "Mothers must be very careful with their children. You would be very upset if Cara was lost."

An older man walked to Cody and handed him a set of keys. Then Cody pointed to the various members of the family as he spoke to the older man.

The man walked over to Chelsea. "Your dad said that you get the red truck."

"Thank you." She took the keys, and then turned to Keefe. "Ready? There's no car seat for Rage, but we're on the ranch so it's not required by law."

He held the passenger door for her and she ignored him.

She raised her eyebrows. "Do you know how to drive a stick?"

"Ah, I think I can."

She rolled her eyes. "I'm driving."

He climbed in and watched her hoist herself into the cab. With Rage in his lap, they headed across a field.

"We'll beat everyone. This is a little bumpier, but it's loads of fun. Want to see the cattle, Rage?"

They drove to another field and rode close to where the animals were grazing. Then they took off and went onto a well-traveled path.

"I doubt there's a square inch out here that I don't know." She stopped several times to open or close some gates and several other times they rode over steel pipes. "Hang on tight, we've got some rough road ahead."

Rage laughed and looked out the windows. He was obviously excited and having fun.

A few minutes later, she pulled onto a paved road. "Almost there. I promise they are all well behind us. We're grabbing the guesthouse, if my aunt doesn't already have it."

Chelsea's grandmother met them and warmly welcomed them.

"Is the guesthouse available?"

"Well, yes, if you want to stay out there, you are welcomed to it. You know my policy of first here gets their pick."

"It's ours!" She turned to Keefe. "Let's go."

Visions of them sharing a private area sent his mind in another direction. *Are you sharing my bed?*

TWELVE

He picked up several bags and Chelsea grabbed the others. They headed across the big foyer and then outside. Tucked to one side was the guesthouse with a small living room and open kitchen. Then there were two bedrooms and a somewhat shared bathroom. They would each have their own toilet and sink, but the shower and bathtub were shared. That thought made him smile. It was a huge tub and he would love to share it with her.

"Awesome. The place has been redecorated. I love it!" Chelsea held her arms out and spun full circle in the living room. "What do you think, Rage? Did you see that little tub just for you?"

"I guess I missed it." Keefe doubled back to the bathroom and looked again. There in the corner was a tub-like basin with what appeared to be whirlpool jets. The whole thing wasn't six inches deep, and it appeared to have a built-in overflow system.

He realized Chelsea was standing beside him.

"What sort of tub is this?"

"With this beside it," she said, pointing to the built-in seat, "I think it's supposed to be a foot tub. I'm sure it feels wonderful after being on your feet all day." She reached into a cubicle and withdrew a remote control. "I'm willing to bet this turns it on and off and adjusts the temperature and jets."

"Works for me." He pointed to the large tub. "It's big enough for two. Think we can find a few candles?"

"Forget it. That's not going to happen anytime soon. Just kill those thoughts. I'm not ready for another relationship."

"Isn't there a saying that if you fall off the horse, you're supposed to get back in the saddle?"

She waved her hand in front of his face. "I asked for this place because it's quieter than the main house. And in case you didn't notice, there are two bedrooms. You and Rage get one, and I get the other. My grandmother will send us one of those inflatable mattresses. I think the maids are still doing chores and handling my family. As I said, it's quieter out here. We get last service, but it's worth it for the peace." She turned away and then turned back. "We also make our own beds out here."

She walked away, but her scent lingered.

Rage tugged at Keefe's pants. "Is Chelsea angry?"

He picked Rage up. "She's not angry. She was teasing me."

"Miz Donna says that teasing is not nice."

"Well, I guess between children, it's not nice. But sometimes adults do it, and it's fun."

"I told Chelsea that I want her to be my mommy, and I told her that you love her."

His stomach instantly knotted. "When did you tell her that?"

"The other day when I was sick."

His mind raced through the last few days. He hadn't seen her as much as he had wanted. She had stayed away on Sunday, and only stopped by the apartment for a few minutes on Monday. Then he hadn't seen her until today. *She's been avoiding me, and I thought it was because Rage was ill.* "Okay, son. Let's go see what we are doing today."

"Milk, orange juice, apple juice, half and half, and what do you have for cereal?" Chelsea listened. "Oh, that's perfect. Yes, a twin is fine for him. It'll go on the floor. Thanks so much. We really appreciate it." She put down the phone and smiled. "I called the kitchen to bring a few items for this refrigerator."

"Oh, I didn't know this place was run like a hotel."

She laughed. "Almost! Let's go get some lunch."

A few minutes later, they were in the main house and he met Cody Montgomery's father. Cody did not resemble his mother or his father, other than his dark hair was turning silver like his father's. But when Cody's younger brother came into the house, the resemblance between Cody and his brother was apparent, and his brother looked more like his father in build. Two more young men joined them and were introduced as Chelsea's older brothers. Suddenly Keefe felt very much apart from this big family.

Chelsea said the place was a madhouse and as more

family arrived it got worse. Keefe started to leave the main house to put Rage down for a nap when another couple arrived. As Keefe's hand touched the latch for the back door he could hear a female wail, "They took the guesthouse? Where is she? Everyone knows *I* take the guesthouse!"

"Barbara, calm down. Chelsea is here with a lovely young man and his son. She asked and I gave it to her. If you want that guesthouse, then come on Tuesday. Don't wait until your brother arrives with his family."

Not wanting to hear more, Keefe slipped out the door with his son and into the small guesthouse. The twin mattress must have arrived while they were eating lunch. It was sitting in the middle of the living room and the small bed was made. He carried it into his bedroom and re-tucked the sheets and blankets.

He put Rage down for a nap and hoped that the place had Wi-Fi, but it must have been secured. That ended his idea of how to spend the next two hours.

Chelsea came in and smiled. "Oh, you missed all the fun. Aunt Barbara is furious that we have the guesthouse, but my grandmother stood up for us."

"I think I overheard part of it as I was coming out here with Rage."

"Is he asleep?"

"Yes. He's had lots of excitement today. He was worn out."

"I'm worn out. Maybe it's jet lag, but I feel like I want a nap."

"Well take one. What's stopping you?"

"I don't know. Family? I love seeing everyone. I really do."

"Well, go visit with them, but before you do, is there Internet in this place? I can't seem to even get a signal on my phone."

"Ah, here. My stuff automatically connects. So I forget about it." She wrote the code on a notepad and handed him the little square slip of paper with the SunWest logo at the top.

He looked at it. "SunWest?"

"My grandfather works there. That's whose jet we used to get out here." She grinned. "Perks."

"So your dad calls his dad and suddenly there's a jet?"

"Something such as that." She smiled widely. "Connections always help."

"Whatever."

"I'll leave you and go back to my family. We do dress for dinner."

"Is that why you said to bring a suit?"

She nodded. "Did you hang it? Does it need steaming or anything?"

"No. It's fine."

He watched her vanish and wished she had stayed. *What am I going to have to do to make you realize how much I want you with me?*

Chelsea enjoyed her afternoon with her family. And at one point, she and her dad took a long walk. "There's something wonderful about walking with you out here."

Cody wrapped his arm around her. "I know. It is special. One of these days, I'm going to be here more than I want. Being on the board takes up time."

"What does DeeDee think about that?"

"She knows and she's fine with it. We accept each other's obligations."

They walked a little further.

"Dad, I really like Keefe."

"I know you do, and I'm aware that you've said that you didn't want children, but he has a child. How do you feel about that?"

She shrugged. "He's adorable. But I feel the same way towards him as I do Julia's children. I don't want to be a mother. I don't want that responsibility. I watch her and wonder how she has all that energy."

"How do you think I felt when your mom walked away or when Patty died? I was overwhelmed. All I knew was that I loved the children that I was given. It doesn't matter how they come to us. They are placed in our hands."

She nodded. "So you think I should accept Rage and just keep going?"

"I think you already have accepted him. You are very good with him and he adores you. Don't forget he's lost his mother. He was dumped with a stranger and you've become his adult female. That's huge."

"I have no idea what I'm doing."

"How's Keefe feeling about his new position as father?"

"Apparently totally confused. He was pitiful when Rage was at the walk-in clinic."

Cody laughed. "I know how he feels. Your mom left and two days later I was in the hospital ER because you had ear infections. I had no clue. I had a screaming baby and your two sisters. I was beside myself."

She took a few more steps. "Dad, I'm tired. Let's go back."

"No problem. By the way, that case he sent to me is interesting. Did you look over those court documents?"

"Yes, I agree it's all fishy." Her breath formed a puff in front of her face as she spoke. "But what happened to your Norfolk case?"

"Total dead end. I believe he's guilty, and the evidence is pointing to that. Even the witnesses are convinced he's guilty." He walked for another few paces. "We only get lucky part of the time, but it's so worth it when we find an innocent. Darn, it's cold out here."

It took everything she had to dress for dinner, and when the hayride was announced, she told Keefe to take Rage. For some odd reason, she was super tired.

"There's plenty to do here." She smiled. "Let Rage have fun and toast marshmallows."

She went to the guesthouse and looked around. Part of her wanted to snuggle against Keefe and feel his arms around her. To sink into that warm cocoon that a man provided held so much appeal, yet she wasn't ready to let go and open herself to another man. She thought about how he was doing with Rage and had been slightly shocked at Keefe's self-doubt when it came to parenting.

She pulled off her clothes and stepped into the shower. The warm water slid over her body from the rain heads and relaxed her to the point that she thought she'd fall asleep on her feet. She forced herself from the shower, dried her hair, and put on her pajamas. *I don't even own anything sexy. I'm about as attractive in this as a stray dog. I wonder how my guys are faring?*

Keefe tried to hold Rage in his lap during the hayride, but the little guy wanted no parts of it. Rage wanted to sit with the other kids. Keefe was worried that Rage would bounce out, or something would happen.

Aaron nudged Keefe with his elbow. "They go very slowly. The kids think it's wonderful. It's the bigger ones they worry about. These little ones stay put. They're thrilled to be on a hayride. The older ones are the daredevils."

"Really? I would think the older ones would mind."

Aaron chuckled. "What would you have done at ten or twelve on a hayride? I know I'd be goofing around."

Keefe chuckled. "You're right."

He sat back and relaxed as they started. Rage was being good and clinging to the sides of the cart as it drove across the fields. There was barely a sliver of moon. Clouds kept obscuring it, making the night even darker. But Keefe's eyes had adjusted and it seemed as though he could see for miles. Off to one side were some mountains and here and there was a glow from civilization.

Julia pointed in the direction of a larger area of light. "There's our nearest town."

A plaintive moo could be heard in the distance. And soon Keefe realized that they had begun to circle back. A few of the children were tossing hay at each other and another parent put an end to it. But when the ride came to an end, he realized they were not near the house. Instead they were looking at a cornfield with old stalks still standing. They handed out flashlights that only glowed and told everyone they would see them on the other side.

They only allowed a few people into the maze at a time, and Aaron and Keefe were next to the last to enter. He and Aaron were so twisted up inside this puzzle that they were certain they would never get out. Then Aaron spotted a marker and realized they were doing nothing other than retracing their steps.

"Are we lost, Daddy?" Rage asked with his eyes filled with tears.

"That's what we're supposed to do is get lost. This is the fun kind of lost. They call it a maze."

Rage plopped his bottom on the ground, and crossed his arms over his chest. "I don't want to be lost."

Rage's eyes grew wide as he was scooped and placed on Aaron's shoulders.

"Come on, Rage. Pretend you are on a ship at sea and you're in the bird's nest at the very top of the mast. What do you see? It's your job to tell the captain!" Aaron motioned to Keefe to watch for the markers.

A voice in the distance called, "Is everyone okay?"

Aaron answered, "Yes, sir. Best darn maze I've ever visited."

Whatever they had done to get lost, they were the last ones out of the maze.

They dropped the children onto the hay cart and jumped on the back, allowing their feet to dangle as they rode.

"Hold on tight. You've got the roughest ride." The driver tilted his cowboy hat at them and jumped on the tractor that pulled the cart.

Keefe almost fell off as it started and when he got bounced hard again. He inched his way back, as did Aaron. Now they stopped in a plowed field not far from the house. There were benches set up and a table filled with marshmallows, chocolate, graham crackers, and a variety of sweet treats that could be toasted. There was also hot apple cider and a spicy orange cranberry drink to warm them.

Keefe had never done anything like this in his life, and to share it with his son made him feel on top of the world. Melissa and Drexel joined them, as did the grandparents and several other family members. He also noticed there was no beer or alcohol anywhere. It was a bit odd, but he realized that many families didn't drink.

After a few dropped marshmallows, Keefe managed to get the hang of toasting them. Soon the next batch of hay riders joined them and eventually the place was overflowing with family having a grand time. Then several of the cowboys dumped a huge load of twigs and other brush along with a few logs into the big pit. Flames roared and everyone cheered.

All he could think of was danger from an open fire. Then it dawned on him that he was standing on a plowed field, and when he looked away from the fire, quite a few cowboys circled the area, prepared to kill any stray ember that floated in the air.

The little kid in him surfaced and he envied the children who had grown up with this sort of open freedom to just run and play. He watched Rage chasing the other boys. Twice he fell, but instead of crying, he got to his feet and ran some more. No one said, "That's too far," or, "You'll get lost." These children were free.

Julia walked over to him. "We're going to take the little ones back and tuck them into bed. We've got a monitor and I'll alert the maid. We're coming back out here." She looked around. "Once our grandparents go to bed, the flasks come out."

It took him a moment to process what she was saying. "It's been a long day. It's going to take me a while to settle Rage down for the night. Besides, I'm concerned about Chelsea. She's not been herself all day."

He gathered Rage and walked back to the house with Julia, Aaron and the children. Rage was a limp doll by the time they made it all the way to the guesthouse. A bath was a useless thought, as the child could no longer hold his eyes open. Keefe slipped the boy into his pajamas and placed him on the air mattress. Then Keefe took a shower and pulled on his pajamas and a clean long-sleeved tee.

He went in search of Chelsea, and found her in her room. She was sound asleep. He looked out all the windows and realized there was a pool not far from the guesthouse. Panic hit him like a blast of cold water. He shuddered at the thought of Rage getting out and going near the pool. As the chill flowed through him, he looked around and worried about Rage. Walking to the guesthouse door to be certain it really was locked, he spotted a small lever that said security bar.

After studying it for a moment, he pulled the bar downward and a small red light glowed. He also noticed that a tiny red dot appeared on the door handle that he had never noticed. If the bar went up the door handle dot went away. He pulled the lever down and tried the door. It was locked, but when he unlocked the door, an alarm sounded. He pushed the lever upwards as fast as he could but a phone rang in the kitchen. He grabbed for the phone.

"Is everything okay?"

He could hear Rage. "Um, stay on the line a moment. I think I awakened Rage."

He went to the boy who had already drifted back to sleep.

"Keefe, what happened?" A sleepy Chelsea stumbled from her room.

He rubbed his temples. "It's fine, I think. Go back to bed. I accidentally set off an alarm."

She vanished into her room and he went back to the phone. "What the heck did I do, other than just wake everyone? And who are you?"

Thirteen

Thanksgiving morning Rage woke up and, after giving the boy a bath in the little tub, Keefe took his son over to the main house in search of coffee. DeeDee found him and dragged him into a small side kitchen. "There's a pot of real coffee in here."

"What's in the other room?"

"Decaf."

"Oh. I thought I'd grab a cup for me and one for Chelsea, so it's there when she wakes up."

"That's sweet of you." She handed him the extra cup.

Back in the guesthouse, he fixed a little bowl of cereal for Rage and left him at the tiny table. Then Keefe took Chelsea's coffee to her.

"Hey, sleepyhead, are you that jet-lagged?" As he approached her bed, he realized she was lying in a pool of wet sheets. When he touched her out-stretched arm, she was burning hot.

Now he was glad he'd read the pamphlet the clinic had given him on fevers. And when he didn't reappear for breakfast, Chelsea's grandmother came to check. Apparently the females in Chelsea's family had noticed her behavior and were concerned.

Drexel took Rage riding with him, and Keefe refused to leave Chelsea's side. A tea was sent over to Chelsea that she was to drink. He decided it must have been some sort of herbal medicine.

Family members came and went around him. Rage would appear filled with exciting tales of what he'd done and then vanish again.

Drexel stopped at the guesthouse around two thirty and asked for Rage's dress clothes. "And you might as well dress for dinner, because Mrs. Montgomery is sending someone out to stay with Chelsea. You are expected for the craziest meal of the year."

Keefe dressed for dinner and waited. Chelsea tried to assure him that he didn't need to stare at her every single minute. But she was the one who held his hand most of the time or called his name if he walked away for some reason.

Dinner went as Drexel had said. Everyone gathered at a huge table. Children whined, a few drinks were spilled, but the family kept going. There was more food than anyone needed.

He thought about the solemn family dinners his family had and the parties where everyone was drunk. This place was so different. And when dinner ended, Cody pulled Keefe to a room away from the crowd. It was an office unlike any he'd ever seen. Taxidermy heads protruded from the walls. A jackalope sat on top of a bookcase that held everything except books. Cody reached into a cabinet and withdrew a bottle and two glasses.

"Here. You look like a man who needs to unwind and talk."

"Thank you, sir." He sniffed the contents and wondered why he was really in this office.

Cody took a seat in a large leather chair and motioned at the other one.

Keefe took it and watched Cody sip his drink. Keefe tasted the golden liquid that warmed his throat. "It's different out here."

Cody chuckled. "It was overwhelming to DeeDee the first few times, but she's gotten used to it. The little ones always love it. Drexel and Aaron have taken to it, and I believe they truly enjoy it here. Of course, my children seem to go through phases of loving and hating it. It's the only real commitment they must make to the family."

"It's a big contrast to my family's quiet meals."

"Tomorrow most everyone will head home. I'm going to suggest you stay until Chelsea is ready to fly. Don't worry. You are welcome to stay as long as you need. I think someone made a doctor's appointment for Chelsea, just to be certain it's not strep. Did the doctor mention that Rage had strep?"

Keefe shook his head. "No one said strep. All I know is they gave him a shot of antibiotics."

Cody nodded. "It probably was strep. It's been going around lately. Charley's had a few classmates with it this fall."

"I feel so bad to think that Rage passed those germs to Chelsea."

Cody put his hand up as if to say stop. "If she caught it from him, it's her own fault for touching her face or not washing her hands enough. I already know she told you to wash everything, including his toys, and to keep them washed until he was better." He smiled. "And she's usually always the first one to catch anything."

Cody refilled his glass and offered to refill Keefe's. "There's never much alcohol around here, but it's here. Dad keeps it mostly for company. He doesn't believe in drinking. I've seen him drink, but never drunk." Cody sat again. "I wanted to talk to you. Being a single father is a tough job. How are you holding up?"

Keefe shrugged. "All I can say is that I'm trying."

"That's all we can do. As long as you keep doing your best... It's hard. I made mistakes and kicked myself afterwards. I've admitted my mistakes to my children, and they know I'm not perfect. But they also know they can come to me anytime about anything."

Keefe nodded.

"But as a man, you walk a fine line. Half the time you've got to pull upon all those feminine things you didn't think you had inside you. Then you have to be a man. You've got to protect your family and set a good example for your son."

Keefe thanked Cody and went back to Chelsea who was still sick and feverish. On Friday, he took her to the doctor, and by Sunday, she was feeling better.

But Cody didn't want her flying. "Keefe, if you need to go back, go. I'll stay with her. If she gets on that plane with her sinuses, she'll be miserable."

Keefe looked at Cody and then at Chelsea. "What do you want, Chelsea?"

She smiled at him. "What's on your schedule?"

"I have to be in court on Tuesday morning. But I could probably prepare from here, if you think twenty-four hours is enough. Otherwise I'd have to turn the case over to someone else in the office or get a continuance."

Chelsea looked at her dad and then at Keefe. "Go back without me. It's easier for us to miss work than for you. Rage needs to return to his schedule, and not be constantly spoiled. Honestly, no one has to stay with me. I certainly can manage by myself."

Cody shook his head and grinned. "I'll stay. Besides, I already told DeeDee I was staying with you."

A slight giggle escaped from Chelsea as she motioned with her thumb. "He's the biggest mother hen there ever was. You'd think I was still four years old."

"I'm your father, and I've known you all your life."

Keefe chuckled. "If you are willing to put up with him, I'll go back. It's the most sensible thing to do. But I promise to call as often as I can to check on you."

Cody kissed his daughter's cheek. "See what a great job I did raising you. Good common sense to go with being a wonderful law partner. I'll leave you two alone. Keefe, be ready at one thirty, and they'll take you to your flight."

Keefe didn't want to say goodbye to Chelsea. He didn't want to leave her behind. The feeling of loss when she was not near tugged at his heart. "I feel guilty for not staying."

"Don't. I'll be fine. Dad doesn't have to stay, but he's being his normal overprotective self. But you have to consider Rage. He's too little to make his own decisions, so you have to make them for him. Get him back to his normal schedule."

He looked at the child who was playing on the floor with a set of blocks someone had found. Then he went to where Chelsea was standing. "I hate being apart from you, especially when I know you don't feel well."

He ran his finger down her cheek. "I've fallen in love with you."

"I know."

He leaned down and kissed her cheek. This time she put her arms over his shoulders and kissed his shoulder. Warm and sweet, the feeling enveloped him. He held her tight.

Rage wiggled his way between them. "Kiss! I want a kiss!"

Chelsea giggled as Keefe picked his son up and kissed him, but the child wanted Chelsea's kiss, too.

Keefe chuckled. "Chelsea, I think we're becoming a family."

Two hours later and more kissing with their goodbyes, Keefe and Rage left Chelsea on the ranch and headed home.

It was Wednesday evening before he saw Chelsea again. He and Rage met her and Cody at the airport outside of town. Rage ran to Chelsea and she hugged him tight. Keefe smiled and waited patiently until Chelsea made her way to him.

She put her arm around his waist and leaned into him. "I missed you."

"I missed you."

"Good to see you again, sir." Keefe held out his hand to Cody.

"I told you I wasn't going to bring her back until she was well enough to actually make the trip."

They walked from the small building at the municipal airport to the parking lot.

"Everyone is riding with me. DeeDee called me about a half hour ago and said she wasn't getting away in time to be here. She asked if I'd bring you home."

Cody grinned. "Not a problem. Thanks for giving me... Isn't that Jason's truck parked over there?"

Chelsea inhaled a breath as she recognized the truck.

Rage screamed.

Keefe turned and went wide-eyed.

She turned and realized Rage was missing. He'd only been one step behind her, helping her with her rolling suitcase. "Where's—"

Jason stepped from between two parked SUVs with Rage in his arms. The child's mouth had been taped, as had his little wrists. "Resist and I'll kill him."

Chelsea forgot to breathe. Finally she forced herself to ask, "What do you want?"

"You. I want you. And if you don't come, I'll kill this brat first, lover-boy second, and then I'll take out your darling daddy. So start walking to the truck."

She knew not to turn her back on a wild animal and that

was what Jason had become. He didn't want to kill anyone but her. It was basic. If he couldn't have her, no one was going to have her.

She stepped slowly backwards and slightly to the side, hoping her father would do something. He wouldn't let anything happen to her, and she knew it.

Jason circled with Rage in his arms.

She couldn't see anything other than the fire flickering in Jason's eyes. Yet it felt as though she was under Jason's total control. Each exhaled breath sounded like a whoosh in her ears. She would do anything she had to do to protect her family from Jason.

Another backwards step and another. She shut out everything except for Jason's penetrating stare.

Blood splattered.

Jason yelped.

Gunshots rang out.

A scream radiated in her ears.

Shouting.

She ran.

She kept running.

Someone grabbed her.

She screamed.

Her father wrapped her in a protective embrace. "It's over. Calm down. It's over."

She gasped for air.

She turned her face into his chest and allowed him to walk her to the airport's building.

"Sit, my darling. Coffee. Decaf for all of us."

"It's over, Chelsea."

Rage snuggled into her lap. "Are you okay? He said he was going to kill you, too."

She kissed his little head. "I'm still shaking."

Keefe lifted Rage from her lap. "Sit with Daddy until Chelsea feels better."

Cody reached into his suitcase and withdrew a flask and poured some in the adults' coffees. "For medicinal purposes."

Chelsea wrapped her fingers around the cup but she couldn't hold it as she was still shaking too much. Her father lifted it to her lips.

She sipped the hot liquid and shuddered.

Then her father pulled out his cell phone and made a call. "Drexel, I need you to go pick up DeeDee at the bridal shop and come to the airport. No questions—just do it."

She attempted to lift the cup one more time.

"Come on, baby girl. Calm down. It's over, and we are all okay."

"I couldn't let him hurt my family." She reached out to Keefe and took his hand.

Two hours later, they were still sitting there talking to the police.

Slowly Chelsea began to put the pieces together and realized something distracted Jason, and as soon as that happened, the security team at the airport fired at Jason. "Is he alive?"

Keefe answered, "He was still alive when the ambulance took him away."

She saw Rage across the way, playing with Drexel. "How's Rage?"

"For now, he's fine. To him, it was probably nothing more than a scene from some TV show." Keefe looked at his son playing. "The police have carefully questioned him and gently kept him away from us while they questioned us, until the rest of your family got here."

"They are supposedly collecting the video from the security cameras. We'll get a copy of that video." Cody motioned for more coffee.

A policewoman that Chelsea didn't recognize walked over to where they were sitting. "Excuse me, but I thought you'd want to know. We just received word from the hospital that Jason Mayer did not survive."

Chelsea burst into tears as all the emotions raced through her. Both her father and Keefe tried to comfort her, but she didn't want their comfort. These were her tears, and she didn't want to have to explain to them. "Leave me alone!"

Keefe planned Christmas very carefully. He searched the

Internet until he found the perfect place and then he checked it out the following afternoon. Elf Towne Inn was everything he wanted. A magical getaway geared to children and adults. It was run by a family, and was complete with a wooden train that ran on tracks around a large playground, pond, and petting zoo. Darling cabins were set all around the edges, but the inn itself was charming.

"We are taking reservations for next year. When would you like to come?"

"This December twenty-fifth for the night."

"I'm sorry, we close our doors December twenty-fifth at two o'clock. The twenty-fourth is our most popular evening and we don't reopen until Spring."

Keefe knew he wanted to stay on the twenty-fifth and he wasn't about to take no for an answer. He looked at the young woman standing before him. "Let me speak to the owner."

An hour later and a whole lot poorer, Keefe walked away with his reservation. He had a son, and a very fragile Chelsea who needed a very special Christmas gift. There was no question in his mind that Chelsea loved him. But she'd been through plenty of pain and was trying to come to grips with her own feelings.

She didn't want to go home and sleep in her own bed after the incident at the airport so he took her to his place. She didn't need to tell him a thing, for he knew how she had felt about Jason and all the tangled emotions bottled inside her. Even after being battered, she still loved Jason. The love and the hate were intertwined. No one could straighten out her emotions for her. She needed to work through her problems and come to terms with her feelings.

Keefe had gently held her and provided the comfort that she needed. He didn't really understand how she could love someone who had hurt her. But since Rage had come into his life, he understood the heart's infinite capacity.

Chelsea was far more sensitive than most people would have ever imagined. She was somewhat introverted and living in an extroverted world. And the damage Jason had inflicted on her went beyond physical bruising.

126

Since that night, she divided her nights between her childhood home and his place, depending on their schedules. He allowed her to decide where she'd be. It was all part of her healing process and learning to stand on her own.

She routinely visited a therapist and so did he. He wanted to be certain he was doing the right things for the right reasons, and he was still learning to be a parent.

Rage asked about the bad man on several occasions, and then it slipped far from his mind as the excitement of Christmas took over. Keefe bought an O Gauge Train Set. It was just a small starter kit. Anything smaller in size would have been too delicate for Rage and there was no way to know if his interest in trains would continue. Keefe and Rage bought a Christmas tree and set it up in the living room. Then they decorated it with Chelsea's help. And when everything was done, Keefe pulled out the train set and set it up with Rage helping him every step of the way.

Chelsea breezed through the door with her arms wrapped around a brown grocery bag. "Hi. That only took a few minutes." She placed the bag on the counter and waved a recipe card in the air. "My great-grandmother's butter cookies. They are *so* good!"

"Wouldn't it have been easier to call and just get the recipe that way?"

"I called my grandmother, and she was out of the house. I called my dad's house and no one picked up the phone. So I went over and found my dad's box of recipes and copied it onto a blank card. Besides, I figured I'd have to stop and buy a *few* ingredients."

"From the looks of that bag, I'd say you bought more than a few."

She laughed. "I didn't know how much flour or butter you had. So, to be on the safe side, I bought everything." She withdrew two cookie pans from the bag. "And just in case, I bought the pans."

She came to the tree and looked at the train set. "Oh, you did it. I thought it would be bigger than that."

"I could have gotten a bigger set, but he'd probably outgrow it. This set he will grow into, and it will be perfect

127

until he's much older."

"Did you have trains as a child?"

He shook his head as the doorbell rang. "Are you expecting anyone?"

She indicated that she was not.

Keefe went to the wall and pressed the intercom. "Who is it?"

"Cody. I have something for you."

He buzzed him in and looked at Chelsea who shrugged.

Cody came through the door with a large grin. "Hi."

Rage scampered from his spot by the tree. "Look what Daddy bought me!"

"Hello, Rage." Cody drew the boy into a big hug. "Is that a train?"

"Yes, we were just getting ready to try it."

Cody put his tablet on the table and went to the tree. "When does Rage take his afternoon nap?"

Keefe chuckled. "He should have gone down a half hour ago, but we've been very busy setting up the train under the tree. Are you prepared for a demo?"

Rage handed his father the little remote control device.

"On the count of three." Keefe smiled at his son. "One..."

"Two! Three!" Rage pumped his fist into the air.

Keefe pressed the start button and the train began to move. Once around the tree at the slow speed and Keefe increased the speed twice before allowing Rage to try the horn.

Rage glowed with his excitement. He ran to the kitchen and pulled Chelsea into the living room to watch the train.

Keefe directed his attention to Cody. "You said you have something for me."

Cody nodded, looked at Rage, and then smiled. "Naptime, right?"

Whatever it was, Keefe knew Cody didn't want to say a thing in front of the child. He slowed the train down. "Okay, Rage, blow the whistle so everyone knows the train is coming to a stop. Blow the whistle again and count down from ten."

Keefe listened to Rage count backwards, and when he reached the number one, Keefe pushed stop and the train came to a slow halt. "Okay, one last whistle. Then you must give out kisses because it's past your naptime."

Fourteen

Chelsea watched Keefe take his son to his room. "He's really trying very hard to be a good dad. He started with nothing. He never had younger siblings or was ever around too many young children."

Cody grinned. "It's a tough job raising the best law partner a man could have."

"Dad…"

"It's true. I'm leaving Sunday evening for Tennessee. I think she found an innocent man. She's definitely found something because that man's trial was a total mess."

"It was Keefe who found him, and his father recommended you, not me."

"But you did the hard part. I'd send you, but not this close to Christmas."

She frowned. "So you can go, but I can't?"

"Do you want to come?"

"No. I've got too much to do between now and Christmas."

Cody laughed. "You can go on the next one. I figure that will happen when I take DeeDee to see Karina in Spain next fall."

"You're going to do it?"

He nodded. "Melissa has offered to take the children. It will only be the two of us. I've already booked the cruise to get there." He held up three fingers. "Three months. All the big cities. DeeDee is going to be so excited. It will be my Christmas gift to her."

"So you haven't told her?"

Cody shook his head. "Keep my secret."

Keefe returned to the living room. "He was exhausted. But I promised he could run the train after his nap."

"Is he asleep?"

"Yes. I think he was sound asleep three seconds after his head hit his pillow. What's up?"

Cody retrieved his tablet. "I was finally allowed to download the video from the airport's security cameras. I thought you'd like to see it. I've seen the video from each camera, and I'm going to suggest we start by using the P8 camera."

A few seconds later, the video began to play. Chelsea watched the harrowing ordeal unfold on the small screen. No matter how hard she tried to stay objective, she couldn't. The whole thing set her pulse racing.

Keefe reached over and took her hand.

She squeezed his tightly as terror reigned inside her.

Cody stopped the video. "Chelsea, I want you to watch very carefully. Follow my finger. If I have to play it a dozen times I will."

Cody's finger went from Jason to Keefe and back to Jason. "Do it again."

He smiled at her. "You caught it, didn't you?"

This time she saw how Jason had turned. He was watching her and Rage had slid well to the left side of Jason's body and the gun was no longer pointing at Rage's head. It was aimed at her. She followed her father's finger to Keefe and saw him reach into his pocket. He withdrew something, manipulating it in his fingers and then like a kid skipping stones on a pond, he let whatever he was holding fly through the air.

"Stop! Back up."

Cody backed the video up a few frames and then she watched the object smack Jason near the temple.

"What was it?"

Keefe shrugged. "Just a stone. A weird thing I started to do as a kid when we went someplace. If I liked something or something impressed me, I always brought home a little piece of it as a reminder. A shell or a stone, or a leaf that I could press...nothing big...nothing that would get me into trouble. I thought of these objects as a memory bank. As though they would always keep me connected to that wonderful place. As we got ready to leave the ranch, there was a stone by the front door. I picked it up and pocketed it. It was my memory collector. I had wondered if it had rolled all the way from the mountains or was it pushed there by a million years of hooves."

He grinned at Chelsea. "I know it sounds stupid and very childish, but it's become a habit. I enjoyed that craziness of people, and children, and food, and what I hope will one day be my future family, and the most beautiful, intelligent woman who I hope will be a permanent part of my life."

He blinked his eyes several times, but she could see the moisture that was filling them. His gaze went to Cody and then returned to her.

"I never dreamed a small rock might save my son's life and the life of the woman I love."

Cody put the tablet down. "You have no idea how many times I kicked myself for not carrying a gun that day. I never saw you toss that stone, and I had no idea that you were even involved. Much less that you had tossed something, until I watched the video this morning."

Cody sat for a moment, without saying anything, watching her with a smile on his face. It was as though he knew she needed time to process what she had seen.

She took her gaze from her father to Keefe. "I don't know how you did that, nor do I want to imagine what would have happened if you had missed. But I swear I heard gunshots."

"You did." He picked up the tablet. "I'm going to skip those frames for now. They are frightful, and to think Rage was in Jason's arms the whole time..." Cody shook his head and went back to the various cameras. "I'm going to pick up using the P14 camera. I'm so proud of my daughter."

He tapped the screen a few times and moved the video forward to a bookmarked spot. "Watch."

The camera must have been mounted on top of the airport's single-story building known as the Welcome Center. Cody placed his hand over the bottom half of the screen, blocking out everyone except Chelsea.

She watched as she went from slowly backing up to stopping for a split second, into a backflip that she must have done a million times as a child who loved gymnastics, and took off running in an erratic zigzag pattern. Then she saw her father grab her.

Cody pressed pause. "You learned well, Chelsea. The odds

of being hit with a bullet grow slimmer with distance and the zigzag made you a very difficult target."

She looked from the screen to her dad and then to Keefe. Cody moved his hand. In the frozen frame, she could see the airport security had swarmed Keefe as well as Jason.

She squeezed Keefe's hand. "Because they knew you had thrown something?"

Keefe nodded. "I'm still not totally cleared. I was told not to leave town over the holidays, but I went to the courts and begged. I'm going to be bonded. With luck, I'll know on Monday afternoon what that's going to cost."

Cody waved his hand in such a way as to indicate it was nothing. "I'll put up the money for you. The Commonwealth Attorney has already seen these videos. It's just a matter of dotting *i*'s and crossing *t*'s."

Chelsea wanted to go back to baking cookies. She wanted to put everything that had happened behind her, but her heart was still racing from the video.

She heard the chair and was surprised when she realized it was Keefe who gripped her shoulders.

"I had to do something."

She nodded.

"He had Rage and he had you. I wasn't going to stand there and allow him to take the two most important people in my life from me."

Tears began to spill over her cheeks. "You did what you did to protect me. We all did what we did to survive. It's basic psychology. He couldn't have me. He no longer wanted me. In his mind, I was tainted, because he thought I'd slept with you. And he was determined no one would ever have me."

She heard her father's footfalls and watched him wordlessly leave Keefe's apartment.

Keefe placed a kiss on her neck. "It's a shame because he never knew the woman I know. He never really got to know her. He was too busy trying to make her into something that she wasn't." He placed another kiss on her neck. "He never saw the free spirit of a woman who is determined to set things right in the world. A woman who will tackle what must be the most grinding job to save someone, yet will smile, play, and have fun making the best-tasting butter cookies *ever* for a little boy who no longer has a mother. Jason had no idea who you really were, because he never allowed you to be Chelsea Montgomery."

Another kiss tickled her neck in that little spot just under her ear. The kind of kiss that reverberated to another area of her body and made her tingle.

"You didn't need a man to control you. You're Chelsea Montgomery, your father's clone in more ways than you'll probably ever realize. You needed to be set free."

She leaned against him, soaking in his strength and his scent. "How much longer will Rage sleep?"

"If we get lucky, we'll have enough time."

Christmas was gray, drizzly, and bitter cold. Chelsea slipped out of Keefe's bed. She was going to her father's long enough to see her younger siblings open their presents, but she'd be back. It was a thought that comforted him as he watched her shower and dress. Not a single word passed between them. There was no need for them.

A half hour later, Rage began to stir. Keefe stood in the doorway of his son's bedroom and watched the child slowly awaken. *My first Christmas with my son—a child I didn't know I had two and a half months ago.*

The DNA testing had been returned and the pediatrician had placed the findings in an envelope. She smiled as she handed Keefe the long white envelope. "I think you'll find everything you wanted to know about your son in these pages. There's the raw data and the final evaluation by the DNA specialist. It's not difficult to understand."

He took the envelope and slipped it into his breast pocket. "It was probably a big waste of money. I know the answer."

He thought about Cody and how much he loved his children. He thought about all the children who had been adopted. It didn't matter. He already knew. It was in the curl of his son's ears and the length of his little fingers compared to the other longer fingers. The way their toes snuggled to each other. Even the shape of their nostrils matched. Rage was his son. There had been no need for an expensive test.

Rage opened his eyes. "Did Santa come?"

Keefe nodded. "Bathroom first!"

Rage ran to his small bathroom and Keefe listened. Then Rage ran out and Keefe pointed to the bathroom. "You forgot to wash your hands. And brush your teeth while you are there. I don't want stinky morning breath on Christmas."

Rage returned holding up his damp hands and showing off his freshly brushed teeth. "Now?"

Keefe nodded and allowed the child to enter the living room. "Remember you must wait for Chelsea before you may open your presents that have been wrapped."

Keefe knew Christmas with Chelsea's family, who looked at Rage as though he was already a member of the Montgomery clan, meant Christmas was going to last forever. When Keefe was little, Christmas was unwrapping a half-dozen packages and then it was over.

Chelsea raced up the stairs.

When everything was unwrapped at Keefe's house, they went to Cody's where more packages were awaiting Rage. Next they went to Drexel and Melissa's house where Rage was given a pair of riding boots and a helmet, along with a few small toys. Then everyone went to Julia and Aaron's house for more presents and more food.

The next stop was his parents'. He crossed his fingers, for they had no idea Chelsea was going to be with him.

Keefe's mom almost squealed as Keefe came through the front door with Rage, and then she glared at Chelsea.

"Mom and Dad, I'd like you to meet Chelsea Montgomery."

Keefe's father snapped to attention and extended his hand to Chelsea who graciously took it.

"Pleased to meet you, Mr. Assam. I've heard so many nice things about you. I know we've met before, but I'm being honest when I say that I never paid much attention to my father's friends when I was growing up." She turned and smiled at his mother. "You've raised such a wonderful son. Thank you."

Mrs. Assam ignored Chelsea. "Come hug your grandmommy! Did anyone feed you? Do you want a drinkie?"

Keefe bit his tongue. It was Christmas, and he wasn't going to say what he wanted to say to his mother.

He had a gift for each of his parents, and he had helped Chelsea choose gifts that he was certain would please them. She had a large box of very expensive golf balls with his father's moniker on them. The price of such a box made him gasp and then she paid to have them specially engraved. She had decided to buy his mother a vase, and Keefe had helped Chelsea find a style that would suit his mom. But he almost died at the price of the sterling silver urn.

His mom had bought an excessive number of toys, more than any child needed, even though he had begged her to simply choose a few good children's books.

At exactly two o'clock, his cell phone rang, alerting him to the time. "Tell your grandmother and grandfather goodbye."

"You can't go. Your sister will be here in another hour."

"Sorry, Mom. We've got a big day still ahead of us. Tell Sis I said Merry Christmas and I'll see her around New Year's."

Rage wanted to take all his new toys with him. Keefe looked at the pile of things mostly from the local dollar store in town. He told Rage to pick two things; he could leave the rest for when he came to play.

Once on the road, he looked at Chelsea and took her hand in his. "I'm sorry they were so... horrible to you. I have no idea what my mother is thinking."

She shrugged. "It doesn't matter."

She looked at him and he caught her intense gaze. "Yes, it does matter. I can see the wheels turning in your head."

"They think I'm Rage's mother. Some little nothing of a gal from that little downtown neighborhood of older brick homes on cul-de-sacs."

She gave his hand a little squeeze. "My father wants me to tell you, because you've made your intentions to me clear. You are going to be asked to sign a palimony agreement. If someday we decide to consider marriage, there will be a pre-nup."

"Sounds like Cody is being a little too protective. But in a way, I can understand."

She tightened her grip on him. "You don't know a thing."

"I wouldn't take a penny from you."

"You say that because you think I'm just surviving off grant money as though we are a legal aid organization. I have a hefty trust fund."

"I'll assume from your grandparents who appear to be well-off."

She giggled. "My grandfather doesn't just work for SunWest; he's retired from SunWest. But he still sits on the board."

"Oh, that's comfy."

"My father now owns SunWest."

Keefe put his foot on the brakes and pulled to the side of the road. "What?"

Chelsea watched the ribbon of road in front of Keefe's car. Then pointed. "The airport is that way. You just missed the road."

He shook his head and smiled. "I took the liberty to do something very special for you and Rage for Christmas. Please trust me to give you both this surprise. We'll join your family tomorrow. I'm not telling you what it is, but if you don't want to believe me, call your dad. He knows where you are going and he approves."

She slipped her phone from her coat pocket and stared at it. "I don't think I need to call my dad. I wouldn't want to spoil your surprise. You've never given me a reason to ever doubt your intentions."

He grinned and continued driving. They drove until the mountains came into view, and then drove to a sign that said Elf Towne Inn, Main Street, Elf Towne, USA. Keefe slowed and pulled through the front gates. After a few thousand feet, an inn came into view. It took a few minutes to register and make their way to a large suite of rooms in the back corner of the inn.

"They have officially closed for Christmas, but they allowed me to bring you and Rage. There's a little place in the town not far from here that is open for meals. The inn has closed their dining room so that the family that owns this place can have their holiday. But we must be back here by seven. So wash up and let's get going."

They quickly changed into warmer clothing and got back into the car. The small restaurant had turkey dinner on the menu with all the fixings. Then they returned to the inn. They walked onto the back patio. In the far corner, there was a street sign marked Main Street and Jingle Bell Lane. The whistle of a locomotive greeted them.

"Well, hop on board, Rage." Keefe's broad smile matched his son's.

"All aboard?" The conductor called, wearing an overly stuffed pair of striped overalls with a matching cap that said Mistletoe Railway.

"All aboard!" Keefe answered.

The clackety train began to pull away from the inn. The whole trip took almost an hour as the train drove them all around the farm. As they approached a wooded area, the place lit up with thousands of Christmas lights and music began to play.

Rage was so excited he barely knew where to look before the next set of lights grabbed his attention. Then the lights began to dim and they entered a field filled with miniature reindeer grazing. The conductor slowed and eventually stopped.

"I have reindeer food if your son would like to feed them."

"Oh, please, Daddy? Please?"

Chelsea hopped out first and thanked the conductor who was probably her age. She showed Rage how to hold his hand and feed the little animals that now gathered around her, pushing and shoving for the treat of cracked corn, oats, and what appeared to be dried fruit mixed in.

"These are the young ones who were born this past spring. They have a better nature than some of the parents, who can be a little more forceful about getting what they want."

"So you raise them for fun?"

"Actually, we breed them. They are for sale."

"Who buys them?" Keefe asked as he helped his son keep his hand flat so a reindeer didn't accidentally nip at a finger.

"People who like to have an unusual pet or places such as ours who want that Christmas atmosphere."

Chelsea smiled at the young man. "I have a brother-in-law who would probably be very interested in your breeding program. He breeds Tennessee Walking Horses."

The guy laughed. "He's into highs and lows?"

Chelsea grinned and nudged one reindeer that was pushing a wee bit too much. "Drexel Cunningham."

"He's been here. I met him and his wife this past spring."

Chelsea smiled. "Small world. Melissa is my sister."

The little pail of reindeer food was empty. They climbed aboard the train and went back to the inn. This time Rage got to sit with the conductor and blow the whistle the entire way.

Keefe thanked the young man profusely as he lifted Rage from the high perch on the engine. His little cheeks glowed red in the cold wintry air.

Quietly they stepped into the empty inn and made their way to their suite. When they arrived there was a fire roaring in the big old-fashioned stone fireplace. Lanterns were lit on the mantel. The whole room glowed in a yellow light.

It took awhile to settle Rage down for the night. Julia's gift of an e-reader filled with children's books that was enclosed in a protective case made the perfect gift for Rage. Chelsea and Keefe took turns reading to Rage until it was apparent that he needed to close his eyes.

In the total quiet of the Christmas evening, Keefe took Chelsea's hand, and they curled onto the sofa. The fire was already showing signs of dimming. Keefe swiped his phone's screen and the soft sounds of an orchestra played softly in the background. Then he fiddled in his pocket.

Chelsea couldn't hold back her giggle. "I hope you weren't picking up little round pebbles in the fields where the deer and the antelope play."

He looked at her and grimaced. "I was a Boy Scout for a few years. They did teach me a few things. Besides, we're supposed to always be prepared."

"Condom?"

"Check."

"Sounds like we're going to have a very nice night."

"Glad you find that possibility to your liking. But I have something else in mind." He kneeled before her. "I want tonight to be your very best Christmas evening." He slipped an impressive diamond ring from his pocket. "In lieu of what you told me this afternoon, I'm feeling a little concerned that I will never be able to give you more than my love. You have more money than I could ever dream of owning. But what I have could never be bought. I am who I am."

He looked at the ring in his hand. Then cleared his throat. "I love you, Chelsea. I think I fell in love with you that day in the coffee shop. You have that no-nonsense way about you, and your beauty doesn't need to be painted on. You are earthy and sweet. Your scent sends my mind and body into overdrive."

He looked into her eyes. "I will never demand and always ask. So I'm asking you now if you will marry me."

"I—"

He held up his hand to stop her. "Please, may I finish? I know you don't feel ready to marry. But I want you to know I will wait however long it takes. Until then, I'm asking that you share my life and be part of my son's life, because he adores you. I'm also asking that you accept my ring not as a shackle to some medieval concept of marriage, but as my token of commitment to you and my promise to treat you always as an equal partner who is capable of making choices and decisions that not just affect you, but us as a family."

Chelsea started to laugh, and she laughed until the tears ran down her cheeks. "Did you tell my father you were bringing me here to ask me to marry you?"

He nodded. "I did everything properly. I asked him if he would consent and give us his blessing if you accepted my ring."

She slipped off the sofa, vanished into a room for a moment, and then returned carrying a small white bag. "This morning he called me into his home office where he gave me this. He said it was for the two of us. Open it."

He took the bag and looked inside of it. There at the bottom of the bag was a pregnancy test kit. "But..."

She nodded. "I know, but he said it was a reminder that no matter how careful we might be..." She smiled. "His words were if you play, be prepared to pay with your hearts for the rest of your life."

Keefe looked towards his son's room. "My heart has no boundaries when it comes to love. But the decision to have a child has to be yours."

She shook her head. "I could never put an end to a pregnancy because I didn't want to be a mother. That's who I am. But that doesn't mean I want to be a mother."

She snatched the bag back from him. "Now, lets get back to this whole marriage-proposal case that you've dropped in my lap. I'm going to accept this ring as your down payment, but in all fairness, I must warn you that I am a Montgomery and eloping is not an option. And with DeeDee and her Main Street Bridal designs, there will be an elaborate wedding."

She watched his face. He wore that perfect courtroom countenance – emotionless yet confident.

Slowly the corners of his lips turned upwards. "Do I dare to ask when?"

She shrugged. "I'll be certain to let you know before anyone else. This isn't a simple case. We need to be prepared. You know I'm going to have a long list of demands."

"Such as?"

"Being kissed daily and I'm not talking about a little peck on the cheek."

"We could start with lip nibbling." His lips found hers. "Then a move to this little spot under your ear."

Her whole body tingled.

"And slowly work my way lower until you beg for more than my lips."

"I think you are on to something very important. We need to spend a lot of time hammering those hidden..."

Keefe chuckled. "There are some things that need to be explored in depth. And I can't wait to get started."

Waking Up for Christmas

JILL JAMES

WAKING UP FOR CHRISTMAS
BY JILL JAMES

Christmas is the time for wishes to come true. All Chase Thanos wants for the holidays is for his comatose wife to awaken. Darcy Bennett Thanos has been his life since they were in college. Now, twenty years later, their marriage and their lives have fallen apart and the only thing that can put it back together is Darcy coming out of her coma and remembering all they had and could have. Just as soon as she wakes up for Christmas.

ONE

His whole life was summed up in hands. Just ten fingers wrapped in skin and supported by bones and tendons. His and hers, fingers entwined. All the differences in their lives and marriage summed up by the hand cradled in his. Lifeless and cold, like the hand of a sleeping princess in a forest glen. Wax-figure pale from six weeks of shadows and darkness. Chase Thanos rubbed his thumb across her glistening fingernails, manicured in the midst of a coma in a hospital. He grimaced. Her mother's work to be sure.

His wife, Darcy might never wake up, but she would look damned good doing it.

Wetness clouded his vision. He leaned down and touched his lips to her cool hand. "I didn't mean it, honey," he whispered in a room filled with the beeps and chirps of medical equipment, none of which could answer the most important question on his mind.

Would his soon-to-be ex-wife ever wake up?

On his good days, he prayed to God, to the gods, to karma, to the fates. Anyone, anywhere who would bring his Darcy back to him.

On his bad days, he prayed she stayed asleep. She couldn't divorce him while she was in a coma. On those days, he cursed himself and drank himself to sleep, waking up with remorse and a hangover, each vying for which was the biggest.

He gazed at their hands together, marveling again at the softness of her skin against his rough, tanned flesh. His mind strung together memories of their love-making, her back arching as his rough palms swept across her lush, smooth torso, bringing cries of passion and heat to his ears. When their differences were exciting and pulse-pounding.

Chase sighed. When had it all gone so wrong? Was it the last few years when complacency replaced racing hearts and raging hormones? Was it the early years of struggling to make ends meet and arguing over every expenditure, struggling with their meager budget? Was it the beginning when an orphan on scholarship met the girl from the heights of fortune and fame who he was never supposed to have?

If someone had said this is where it will end would he still have gone along for the ride? He laid his forehead on their joined hands. Yes. A million times yes. In the darkness behind his closed eyelids and in the depths of his mind, he relived every moment he'd shared with Darcy Bennett Thanos and wouldn't have changed a one. Each moment led to the next. Each memory made up the fabric of their twenty years together. The bad, tattered threads of regrets and remorse were still part of who they were today.

The gentle glide of the sliding glass door into the ICU room interrupted his thoughts like the abrupt ending of a dream.

He didn't need to open his eyes. The heavy undertones of her perfume and the quiet, hushed tones proclaimed louder than a herald that Darcy's parents have arrived for their nightly visit. He sat up and pushed his chair back from the bed. Rising, he turned to make way for Steven and Margaret Bennett.

"I'll be in the chapel if anything happens," he said in passing.

"Of course, Thanos," Steven Bennett mumbled, unable to look him in the eye.

Chase swallowed his anger and slid the door shut before heading down the hall to the chapel, his refuge from the nightly visits. More than one argument had ensued in their home from Darcy's hovering parents. As an orphan, he'd thought it was wonderful her parents called her each night to say they loved her. In the early years of their marriage he'd tolerated it, knowing he hadn't been their choice for Darcy and they worried. Once they'd been married ten years he'd tried to put his foot down. That had led to yelling, crying, and their first separation. After that, he didn't try anymore, just simmered inside until the bubbling anger gave him an ulcer. Now, they were too busy during the day, but they interrupted each evening with their visits that lasted exactly thirty minutes; no more, no less.

The serene quiet of the small chapel calmed him as it did

each night. He hadn't been a very religious man before his wife's car accident, but he'd found a peace sitting on the hard, wooden pew and gazing at the patterns of color and light from the stained-glass windows, the tones dancing across the deep-blue carpet from the flickering of the light behind the opaque surface in simulated sunshine.

All his worries faded in the newly-acquired knowledge he was just one small piece in the puzzle of life. The arguments, the failed marriage, his business he'd worked so hard to build, all took a back seat to the idea he was where he was supposed to be right now. He'd fought it every step of the way, but the tranquility had been worth the struggle.

His marriage vows had been words he hadn't given much thought to over the years until the accident. Until he sat in this small, calm room; night after night. Sometimes with just the company of his mind and sometimes with the company of others, searching for the answers just as he was.

In sickness and health.

Just words to repeat until you were forced to put up or shut up in a situation you never dreamed would happen.

His gaze swept the snowy white cloth on the altar until he turned back in a double-take. Red poinsettias and white lilies sat in shining brass holders. Green ferns stood tall in iron stands.

What day was it?

His mind raced as he counted the days since he'd received the call and rushed to the hospital to find Darcy barely alive. The first day had been a nightmare of fear of her dying and arguing with her parents. His days had been taken up with fighting her parents in court for the right to be in charge of his wife's care and his nights at her side in the hospital. When Steven and Margaret had been unable to prove Darcy had wanted a divorce with any papers filed, he'd been allowed to be responsible for the medical decisions. A move guaranteed to not make them like him anymore than they ever had.

He pulled his cell phone out of his pocket and stared at the date.

It was a week until Christmas.

Two

Chase opened the door of the quaint Victorian to be greeted by a tinkling bell and a mouth-watering scent of cinnamon and spice. Coming back to Macgregor's Inn on Main Street was like coming home. Humming and singing filtered out from the kitchen in the back. He followed the sounds and scents to the doorway.

White flour dotted her cheeks to match her snowy-white hair. He smiled when she wiped her cheeks and put more flour on them instead of getting rid of what was there. Her smile widened when she spotted him in the doorway.

"Mr. Thanos, you are back early this morning," she said in her gentle Scottish lilt.

"They are running some tests. I'm catching a quick shower and I'll go back."

She shook her finger at him. "You'll do no such thing. Breakfast will be ready by the time you come back down. We don't need you in the hospital too."

"Yes, ma'am," he intoned in a serious voice. "I'll be right down."

"See that you are," she added in just as serious a voice but with a twinkle in her eyes. "You need a good, hot meal. Get some meat on your bones."

She turned back to rolling out dough for a waiting apple pie as he headed upstairs to his room. He hummed along with the Christmas tune filling the Inn. His steps slowed as he reached the second floor and his room.

He opened the door to be greeted with an impersonal guest room. It had all the touches Mrs. Macgregor had undoubtedly added to all the rooms; the handmade quilt on the bed and the watercolors on the walls. A bowl of camellia blooms sat on the dresser. All the home-like touches were there, but it wasn't his home. He'd been here for over a month and it still looked like a hotel room. He had never planned to be here for six weeks.

Chase sighed. He shouldn't complain. Mrs. Macgregor opened her Inn to the families with ICU patients at the hospital for free. Without that perk he would have been traveling two hours one way from home to Darcy's bedside each day. Macgregor's Inn was a blessing he'd been foolish to overlook.

He stripped on the way to the bathroom and a shower. The hot water pounded on his back as he finally let the tears loose. His sobs racked his body. He leaned his forehead against the cold tile and pressed his hands into the wall. He stayed that way until the water turned cool and then cold.

Stepping out of the shower, the tantalizing odor of apple pie and sausage traveled through the vents. He dressed hurriedly, running a comb through his wet hair. Time for sorrow wasn't a luxury he could afford.

He would have spent the past weeks eating hospital cafeteria food and fast food on the go if not for Mrs. Macgregor and her home cooking. He stepped into the empty dining room as Mrs. Macgregor's grandson Nick came out of the kitchen with platters of food.

The young man had a permanent smile on his freckle-covered face, as if sadness was unknown for Nick Macgregor. He had the bright-red hair to go along with those freckles, as well. "Just in time, Mr. Thanos. Get it while it's hot."

"I've told you, you can call me Chase."

"No, sir. Nana would take me out to the woodshed," he said, his smile growing wider to let him know Nick was kidding. "If we had a woodshed."

Chase looked around the room. "Where is everyone?"

Nick rubbed his chin. "Well, the Peterson's left yesterday afternoon."

Chase sighed in relief. The Peterson twins had been running up and down the hallways and yelling at the top of their lungs the last few days. He wouldn't miss them at all.

"Mr. and Mrs. Johnson had to leave in the middle of the night and head home for an emergency," Nick continued. "And Mr. Olivera is packing now and leaving shortly."

"So that just leaves me?"

"Yep." Nick smiled at him. "Just you through Christmas."

Another reminder the holidays were right around the corner. His attention was snagged by the little touches of red and green around the room. A set of lighted houses sat across the buffet behind the platters of food. The same set Darcy had collected during the years of their marriage; a new house for each Christmas they'd spent together. The same set he'd found in the trash the last Christmas they'd spent together.

A clear spot sat in front of the bay window. Chase pointed. "For the tree?"

Nick nodded, his thick hair sweeping across his forehead. "I'm getting it tonight. Nana makes a big production out of decorating it. Tells a story for each ornament we put on the tree."

All he could do was nod. He didn't trust his voice not to crack with emotion. Darcy did the same thing. A story of getting an ornament. She remembered where and when they'd gotten each one. This one on a trip. This one from a relative. That one from a friend.

He moved over to the buffet and placed a spoonful of each item on his plate. His chest ached at the thought of shoveling food into his mouth. Telling himself he had to eat to stay healthy for Darcy helped, but not enough.

As if Nick could read his thoughts, the young man grabbed a plate, filled it and sat down beside him. "Hope is a powerful thing."

"What?" Chase said, his fork halfway to his mouth with scrambled eggs.

"Hope. With hope, anything is possible. Your wife is still there. You just have to reach her and give her a reason to come back."

"She's in a coma."

"Doesn't mean she can't hear you." Nick said, wiping his plate clean and pushing his chair back.

He reached over and placed a hand on Chase's shoulder and squeezed. "Tell her why she needs to come back."

Gathering his plate, Nick walked across the room and disappeared into the kitchen. He heard mumblings as he talked to his grandmother and then the clink of dishes being washed. Chase forced himself to finish eating even though the delicious food was tasteless as he was lost in thought.

Give her a reason to come back.

He straightened in his seat. He could do that.

THREE

He moved his chair in closer to Darcy's bed, the squeak of the legs on linoleum loud in the silent room. The scent of strawberries wafted up from her clean hair. Her pale hands rested on the covers. Leaning over, he placed his hand on hers. His tanned skin even darker against her winter-white skin.

"Darcy," he whispered. "Can you hear me?"

He grimaced. This was more awkward than talking to yourself. She wasn't going to reply. His shoulders slumped. She might never reply. A pit opened in his stomach that he feared falling into.

Nick's words came back to him. He sat up straighter. He could do this. He had to try. Even if it didn't work, he'd hate himself if he didn't at least try.

"Darcy," he said, closing his eyes. "We've been through so much together. Don't throw away twenty years of our love. You want to divorce me? Fine. Come back and tell me to my face. Come back and argue with me. Just come back."

She heard a voice in the dark. Who's there? Where is here? Why am I lost? She should know that voice. Why was it so familiar? Why did she think of hot kisses and warm hugs? Why did she think of anger and yelling?

She didn't want to come back. Why was he so demanding? Why didn't he understand? Safe was here. No decisions to make. Nothing to do.

He jumped as her eyelashes flickered on her cheeks. His racing heartbeat slowed. He'd been excited the first time it had happened, weeks ago. Until the doctor explained it was an involuntary reflex. He'd shone a light in Darcy's eyes and found nothing.

His fingers trembled as he swept hair back from her face. Memories assaulted him like a hammer against a nail. Sunday mornings they'd lie in bed and he'd watch her sleep. Run his fingertips over her smooth cheek and along her neck.

He'd reach the spot between her neck and shoulder. She'd smile in her sleep and open her beautiful brown eyes and look at him with love and passion in her gaze.

As if no will of his own, his fingers traveled down her cheek to her neck. Her low pulse throbbed beneath his fingertips, with no rapid blips on the screen. His palm cupped her neck and his thumb slid over the ticklish spot. She didn't move. She didn't breathe faster. She didn't awake.

"What were you expecting? A damned Christmas miracle? Are you a child, still believing in fairy tales?"

He sighed and hung his head low. The last time he'd touched her like that she'd slapped his hand away and turned over in bed, her back to him. At what point did the magic leave your marriage? When did all the little private rituals become meaningless and unnecessary?

He placed her hands back together on the covers. Although it had been years, his hands folded in prayer. His thoughts were jumbled and tangled with wants and needs. What he wanted may not be possible. What Darcy may need the most may not be him.

Nick's words over breakfast thundered into his brain. *Give her something to come back for.*

Every moment for the past twenty years was wrapped up in Darcy, like a present under the tree. More good moments than bad. Some amazing moments. Tough moments they'd weathered together. But they'd always faced everything together.

The odds of them meeting at all had been astronomical. The only thing that made it possible for him to go to the prestigious Bennett College in Central California was a last-minute, anonymous scholarship. Darcy had been set to go there from kindergarten due to the Bennett family name and that family's trust of the college for more than a hundred years.

The idea he could win over the golden girl with the silver spoon in her mouth was someone's twisted fairy-tale story. He laughed. She'd fallen into his lap. Literally.

"Must be a pleasant dream," a soft voice echoed in the hospital room.

His eyes shot open to find a male nurse at the bedside,

taking Darcy's heart rate.

"Sorry. I didn't know anyone was in here."

"I should have let you know I was working," the man replied, putting Darcy's hand back on top of the other. "You just looked like you were having some happy thoughts."

"I was," he mumbled.

"You should share them with your lady there." The man wrote on a pad and put it and the pen back in his pocket. "They can hear us, you know."

Chase stared as the man left the room and slid the glass door shut. He was the second person today to tell him to talk to Darcy. Someone was trying to tell him something. Maybe for once in his life, he should start listening.

He grasped his wife's hands and leaned over to whisper in her ear.

"Darcy, do you remember the day we first met?"

FOUR

"I need to take a picture of this for Uncle Dimitri," Chase murmured to himself. He glanced around the quad at the golden kids born with silver spoons in their mouths. *Maybe on the weekend when the space was empty. Unless he wanted to look like the hick he was.*

Sure, he'd seen the brochures, but if the dictionary had a photo next to the definition for ivy-league school, it would be Bennett College. It looked almost too good to be true. Everywhere he looked he saw well-dressed, well-fed bodies. No grunge fans in sight. No goth girls rebelling against the establishment. It looked as if an Abercrombie & Fitch catalog was doing a photo shoot. He'd bet his scholarship fund there wasn't a cavity in the whole lot of bright-eyed, shining teeth lot.

He scanned the area searching for his friend, Jason. The message on his answering machine had said to meet in the quad at four. Glancing at his watch, he shifted the messenger bag with his new laptop higher on his shoulder. The thing was only slightly less heavy than his desktop computer. The girl at the electronics store said they weren't too delicate but he moved it closer to his side as a pair of skateboarders whooshed by on the sidewalk. If something happened to this one, there wouldn't be a replacement anytime soon. Scholarship money only went so far.

His mind whirled with all the things he'd need for the semester. The scholarship money needed to cover it all. If not for it, he'd still be at Lake Willowbee Community College. He laughed to himself. The only time being an orphan paid off, as it had been the main requirement for the money.

He spotted Jason and his waving hand and headed across

the grass to an enormous, ancient Oak tree. As he neared, he couldn't miss the gorgeous blonde wrapped around his friend. From clothes better suited to a Polo match than a college day and the jewels wrapped around her neck, she screamed money; a lot of money.

Jason slugged him in the arm once he joined them. "Misty, this is my buddy, Chase Thanos. Dude, this is Misty Van Ellsberry."

She shook his hand with a smile that brightened her deep-blue eyes. "Jason has told me so much about you. I feel as if I already know you. Is it true that you can carve anything?"

His face heated. Helping Uncle Dimitri build furniture was one thing. It was useful and productive. His carving was something else altogether. His uncle never said it was frivolous but plenty of the old man's friends around town had.

"Did you finish it?" Jason asked.

He nodded, reaching into the front pocket of his messenger bag. He pulled out a box and handed it to his friend.

"Thanks."

"No problem," he mumbled as Jason handed the box to his girlfriend.

Her eyes twinkled as she untied the ribbon and opened the box. He stared at her gleaming necklace and wondered if he would survive her laughter at the stupid gift.

Her mouth gaped open and she stared at him.

"It's okay if you don't like it," he stammered. "It's just a little something Jason wanted me to make."

Misty frowned. "Don't ever do that. You have a gift." She pulled the necklace out of the box and cradled it in her palms, letting the box fall to the ground. There in her soft hands sat a month's worth of working after the day was done at Thanos Handmade Furniture.

His face heated more as she'd ordered Jason to take off her other necklace and throw it into her purse. Jason did the clasp on the necklace he'd made and stepped back.

"How does it look?"

He couldn't find the words. This was the first time he'd made something for someone to wear. His other projects had been knickknacks and useful trinkets.

The carved wood glowed against Misty's tanned skin. The polished grain contrasted with her light-blonde hair. The grapes shone with ten layers of lacquer and the grape leaves shimmered a deep, emerald green.

Her fingers caressed the smooth wood. "My parents are going to love this. I can't believe it was a piece of driftwood."

He nodded. "Just a piece of driftwood from Lake Willowbee."

She shook her finger at him. "There you go again. Not just a piece of wood. You took a piece of wood and make a piece of art. If you ever decide you are an artist instead of a business major, just let me know. We'll have a big showing at Ellsberry Vineyards and we can all say, ah, I knew him when," she said with a laugh between her and Jason.

He gulped past the knot in his throat. Ellsberry Vineyards was world-renowned. Their champagne was the best outside of France. Their family was on the front of magazines with the rest of the rich and famous, jetting off to Europe for a quick shopping spree.

Maybe he could give back the scholarship money. What was a Lake Willowbee kid doing here?

His thoughts were torn away with a shout of 'I've got it' and the thunder of running feet. Chase turned and found himself in the path of a wide receiver from a football game played nearby.

All he had time to do was open his arms and catch the falling girl as she leapt for the ball. They crashed to the ground with a curse (her), a groan (him), and a crackle of breaking electronics (the new laptop).

He opened his mouth to tell her off when he got the first good look at her. Her long, mahogany hair cascaded around them, carrying the scent of strawberries. Her deep-brown eyes sparkled as she smiled at him and his heart exploded in his chest. He would love the scent of strawberries until the day he died.

Her smile died as she wiggled to get off him to the tune of grinding shattered glass and plastic.

"Really, Darcy. Your mother is going to have a conniption fit if she hears about you playing football in the quad."

Misty's voice broke the connection between them.

The girl smiled. "Why do you think I do it?" She got up and put her hand out to him to pull him off the ground.

His rough palm slid along the smoothest hand he'd ever felt. He wanted to hold it forever, until the crunching noise from his messenger bag brought him back to Earth. He didn't need to look inside to know the piece of equipment was toast. Chase swallowed deeply. It would take months to save up for a new laptop. It would be paper and pen until at least Christmas, if not longer.

"I'll take care of it," the girl said, gazing at him. "It's my fault it's broken. Just let me know the model and I'll have one for you by tomorrow."

"I don't take handouts," he gritted out.

"It's not a handout. I broke it, I'll replace it," she spat back, anger making her brown eyes deepen and sparkle.

Misty's voice broke in again. "Darcy, this is Chase Thanos. Chase, this is Darcy Bennett."

His heated anger broke like a face full of ice-cold water.

"Like Bennett College?"

"Yes," Darcy said with a frown on her beautiful face. "My mother is president of the college and our family has been in charge going back five generations, blah, blah, blah."

The blood left his head, leaving his dazed and dizzy. "Okay, that just makes it doubly wrong for me to take anything from you. I'm already here on scholarship, I'm not upsetting your family."

Misty spoke as Darcy continued to stare at him as if she could wear him down into compliancy with a glare.

"I have an answer for this problem."

They both stared at her.

"You're a business major and Darcy is a failing business major. You can tutor her and get paid with a new laptop. Then it won't be a handout and Darcy won't flunk out of her own family's college."

Darcy's smile brightened her whole face and set his heart to a pace sure to give him a heart attack if it kept going. She put her hand out and he grasped it in his own.

"Deal," they intoned together.

Do I remember? I remember a feeling of shame. How could I fail at my own family's college? How could I fail at everything I tried to do? How could you see me shining so brightly when all I saw was just another mistake to cover up with money and connections? Why can't I see the Darcy you see?

Why can't I see? Why is it so dark here? Why does no one know I'm here?

FIVE

"Stupid tests," he muttered, punching his phone off and throwing it on the guest room's dresser with a clatter of plastic hitting coins.

He bent over to pick them up, finding a silver dollar among the smaller change. His thumb rubbed over the smooth surface. Years of using the silver coin as a worry stone, first by his father and then by him, had obliterated the image on it. Nothing remained except for a few letters and the year--his birth year. The then-bright shining dollar had been a gift from Uncle Dimitri to his brother, Chase's father, on the birth of his first child.

He gathered the rest of the fallen change and slammed it into his pocket with a curse. No little Thanos would ever get the handed-down memento. His family tree would end with him and his soon-to-be ex-wife.

He fell onto the bed and hung his head down between his knees. "When did it all fall apart?" he whispered. If he could just pinpoint the moment that got them here, he could fix it. As he fixed broken chairs and tables. As he fixed family heirloom knickknacks with more sentimental value than monetary. As he fixed everything he held in his hands except for his damned marriage.

Sighing, he pulled himself together. He couldn't help Darcy if he couldn't help himself. He glanced at his watch. Four hours before he could go back to the hospital. What to do with himself? As if in answer to his unspoken question, a knock came at the door.

"Can I come in?" Mrs. Macgregor's voice sounded through the wood.

"Of course," he replied, going to the door and pulling it open. "Did you need something?" he asked the older woman.

She came into his room, her arms full of clean sheets, the scent of linen, fresh air, and sunshine following her. "Tis bed turnout day."

He took the pile from her. "I have free time this morning. I can do the bed myself."

"No visit with the wife this morning?" A frown marred her round, soft face.

"They are running tests. They spotted some additional brain activity yesterday."

She smiled. "Isn't that what you wanted? This is a good thing, no?"

He shrugged. "I've been down this road before. Get my hopes up and it turns out to be a flaw in the wires or the machines are reading wrong."

"If you could do me a favor, it would at least get your mind off the hospital for a while."

"Anything," he replied, hoping against hope that it would divert his mind for a short time.

Her smile broadened. "Nick could use some help to get a tree for the inn. If you go and help he can get a nice, brawny one for the sitting room."

The last thing he wanted to do was get in the holiday spirit by getting a tree, but he would do it for this kind lady who had been there when he needed support the most. She'd been a calm voice in the turbulent sea of Darcy's hospital stay.

"Of course. I can do that. Is he ready to leave now?"

"He tis. Nick is outside getting the ropes and stuff."

Chase set the tower of sheets on the bed and grabbed his jacket. "We'd better get to it, then."

The heavy metal sounds blaring from the van's speakers set his fillings to humming. He'd asked if Nick could turn on something else. Ten seconds of holiday music had him begging for a return to the screech of what he could only assume was music to the young man's ears.

A short drive out of town had them to rolling hills and acres upon acres of Christmas trees. He spotted the familiar shape of Douglas fir and the fullness of pines. They pulled into the gravel lot with the blessed silence of the radio and the crunch of rock under the tires.

Opening the door, he inhaled deeply the scents of pine trees and fresh air. He exhaled deeply. No plume of air showed it wasn't cold enough yet in the central valley of California for frigid temperatures. His heart filled with a longing he hadn't known he had for the mountains and the lake and his small hometown. The vista here stretched for miles of unbroken rolling hills and spots of trees here and there. Only the vast green tree farm came close to feeling like home in the Sierras.

Nick got out of the van and shut his door with a slight slam. Chase followed suit and let the young man set the direction of their Christmas tree getting. He walked beside him as they passed the trees already cut and mounted on nailed boards. They passed the flocking tent and Nick shuddered at the thought of desecrating the noble trees.

"Grandma would boil me in oil if I came back with one of those 'not how nature intended' trees, as she calls them. I think she believes they are one step down from the silver aluminum ones she told me about when she was a little girl."

Chase laughed. "My mom and dad had a picture of one of those, with the color wheel turning underneath."

Nick laughed. "Do they get a real tree now?"

His laughter died. "They died a long time ago. When I was a little kid. I grew up with an uncle. He's all I have now."

Nick put his hand on Chase's shoulder. "You have Darcy."

He nodded his head but in his heart he wondered. *Did he have Darcy?*

Six

Chase grinned as his fingertips caught and clung to the covers like a suction cup. He'd cleaned his hands several times, but the sap from the tree stubbornly adhered to a couple of his fingers. The time away from the hospital had been fun and refreshing with Nick and the large pine tree now gracing the inn's sitting room. Mrs. Macgregor gushed with excitement over the large and full tree now taking up a large portion of the room. When he'd left, Nick was touching up the white paint on the front door and the molding going into the sitting room. The young man had gotten a laughing fit as they tangled among the large branches and hit every flat surface from the front porch to the room. He'd scrambled down the front steps with Mrs. Macgregor's scolding tone ringing in his ears.

The sliding glass door slid open and Darcy's doctor walked in. The smile on the man's face set his heart to racing. Steeling himself for disappointment, he couldn't help the tingling of hope taking his breath away.

"The tests went very well today. We are seeing increased brain activity. Not quite enough to pinpoint when she could wake up, but very good signs all around."

He let his held breath out. "Why doesn't she just wake up?"

The doctor shook his head. "Medical science doesn't know everything, Mr. Thanos. We've come a long way since Darcy was brought in here after her accident. I believe she is making excellent progress. Now we just wait for her to want to wake up."

Swallowing the lump in his throat, Chase spoke his thoughts aloud to the doctor. "How long can she stay like this? What if she never wakes up?"

"Mr. Thanos, we are nowhere near that concern. With the increased brain function, I have high hopes for more progress in the next few days."

"Thank you, Doctor Jameson."

He nodded and left, the sliding door opening and closing behind him.

Chase sat alone with his thoughts. The hunt for the perfect Christmas tree this morning led him down the path of his Christmases with Darcy. Each one a photograph in his memories. From the first one as her college tutor to last year when he'd been at their home alone and Darcy had been with her parents in Europe.

Each holiday an ornament on their tree. A simple frame he'd carved with their photo inside. The one Darcy made that he never could figure out what she had been trying to make. An expensive bauble her parents bought them in Paris for their fifth anniversary trip. A trip that included the in-laws.

The missing ornaments. The baby's first Christmas bought with high hopes and put away with tears when the hopes died. His mother's antique glass ornaments broken when the tree fell. Bennett family ornaments Darcy threw away in a fit of anger at her parents' attitude at Chase.

Was every Christmas tree a chronicle of a family's highs and lows?

His thoughts ripped to the present at a moan from Darcy. He sat up, his pulse pounding in his chest, his breath coming in heavy pants. He fumbled with the call button and punched it several times before a voice replied.

"Darcy is making sounds," he yelled into the speaker in the bed.

Within seconds, a nurse appeared. She took his wife's pulse while she laid there silent. Just when he thought the nurse would leave, another moan issued from her. "I'll get the doctor," she replied, a sparkle in her eyes and a lift in her steps as she left the room.

Doctor Jameson returned, a smile on his lips. "Let's see what we have here."

He moved to the foot of the bed. "We'll check if this is voluntary or involuntary."

The doctor pulled a metal tool from his pocket. He moved the covers from her feet. Running the tool along her foot,

Chase couldn't tell if the movement and moans were a good thing or bad thing from the doctor's facial expressions.

Placing the tool back in his pocket, he pulled the covers back down and patted Darcy's feet. "This is a very good sign," he commented as he moved to the head of the bed and shone a light into her eyes.

"We'll run a CAT scan in the morning, but I have high hopes Darcy is not as deeply in her coma as before."

Chase stood, tears blurring his vision, and shook the doctor's hand. "Thank you," he whispered.

"I'll check back later."

He barely listened as the man left, the slider opening and closing. His gaze locked on Darcy. A faint blush painted her pale cheeks. In his mind, she appeared to be sleeping instead of the coma that had continued for weeks now.

If it had been summer she would have had her golden tan that always seemed to linger long into fall and the beginning of winter. The girl playing football who had dropped into his lap hadn't changed much over the years. She still tried every sport and lived outdoors, far more comfortably than inside, stuck in a house.

Seven

Bennett College Library

Chase stared at his watch for the twentieth time in as many minutes. Their third tutoring session and Darcy Bennett was late again. He started gathering up his books at the library table as the door slammed open and hot air swirled into the air-conditioned room as the cold air was sucked out. He didn't need to look up to see Darcy had finally decided to grace him with her presence. He'd thought the first time she just had forgotten the time. By today, the third time, he realized Darcy had no concept of timeliness.

"I'm so sorry," she huffed out, throwing herself into the chair across the table with a creak of leather and rollers on carpet. "Basketball practice ran over."

She smelled of perspiration with a rose scent lingering underneath. Her skin glistened and her cheeks were painted with a bright-red flush of exercise. Her long hair was swept into a ponytail, with curls falling on her shoulders. Her smile didn't reach her eyes where worry pushed her forehead into rows of furrows.

The worry in her eyes was the only thing stopping Chase from slamming his books into his bag and leaving Darcy Bennett to pass or fail on her own. Their past two study sessions showed the woman had no head for business. She wasn't stupid, but anything business related seemed to put her to sleep.

"Why do you even bother?" he asked, opening a book and getting the pad of paper and pencils lined up above it.

She shrugged her shoulders, the long hair sweeping across her breasts. "Mom, dad, big business. Like I have a choice."

He swallowed deeply as the strands of hair caressed the

breasts straining against her thin T-shirt. "Everyone has a choice. With your family's money, you could be anything you wanted. Why business if it isn't what you want?"

She sighed and picked up one of his pencils. Her long fingers twirled it as she stared into space. "I'm an only child. From a long line of only children. The Bennett Foundation is my responsibility once my parents pass on. I can't let more than a hundred years of history just fall apart under my care. I won't know if I'm being ripped off if I don't know the business of business. Even if it is as boring as watching paint dry."

He took a deep breath and stared into her eyes. "Then you have to commit to this. No one can do it for you, unless you are willing to be a token figurehead and let people rip you off left and right."

Darcy slammed the pencil down on the table and stared right back at him. "I'm no figurehead. I will run the Bennett Foundation."

Chase stuck his hand out. She smiled and shook his hand. Her eyes glared with determination. He prayed it would be enough to see her through endless business classes and finals.

Hours passed as Darcy alternated from glee as understanding cost accounting to despair with her head on her folded arms at contract law. He closed the law book and concentrated on drilling her on the basics to help her pass their upcoming test. His stomach grumbled as the light dimmed in the library and the lights came on to shine across the polished tables.

Her gaze shot to his with panic in her eyes. "We can't quit yet. I have to pass the next test in Professor White's class. He's threatened to drop me from the class if I don't get at least eighty percent on the next two tests."

The tables around them cleared as the others filtered out of the room. Friday night on campus was not spent in the library. Ms. Springer, the librarian came up to them and handed her keycard to Chase. "You'll lock up, Mr. Thanos, as usual? Just leave my keycard in my mailbox in the office."

Darcy stared as the older woman grabbed her purse and turned off the outlying lights in the room until their table stood as an island of light in the dim room. "What did she mean, as usual?"

Chase coughed and stared at his book. His face heated in a flush. "I'm here most nights studying. Ms. Springer decided it was easier to let me lock up instead of being stuck here when she could be home with Mr. Fluffy."

She laughed. "Mr. Fluffy?"

"Yep, Big white cat. She has pictures in her wallet and everything."

Darcy's phone started pinging with messages, reminding him the young woman was not a lonely, older, cat lady but a sexy, popular student. She pushed the off button and the sound died.

"Don't you need to see who that is?"

"Doesn't matter," she replied, flipping pages to the next chapter.

Smiling, a smug feeling filled him at the thought of her spending time with him instead of football players and fraternity presidents. Until he was brought back to Earth with her questions about cost accounting and realized she only wanted him for his brains. It didn't matter, he told himself. He was in this to get a new laptop, not a new girlfriend.

Time passed in a rush as he taught and she listened, asking questions to anything she didn't understand. As they moved through the lessons her questions came less and less and her excitement for discussing the work grew. By the time they reached the end of the lesson, Darcy had him questioning everything he knew about accounting as her ideas outpaced his own at how to run a business. Why not? The Bennett Foundation had to be lightyears away from Thanos Furniture.

"I think you're ready for a practice test," he announced, tearing off a page from his notebook.

The pencil snapped in her hand, the jagged edge poking her palm. The pieces fell to the table at her cry of pain. He came around the table and grabbed her hand. A line slashed across her hand, filling up with bright, red blood.

She yanked her hand back and reached into her bag, pulling out a dingy shirt. He pulled it away from her. "We have to at least clean it first."

He walked over to the librarian's counter and moved to the other side. Squatting down, he came up with a white case with a red cross on the lid

Darcy laughed. "It's just a scratch. I'm not bleeding to death."

"Humor me," he insisted. "It's a lead pencil. We'll clean it up and put a bandage. You can sit still long enough for that, can't you?"

She huffed and slammed into the seat. "Fine, Doctor Thanos. Fix me." Her voice turned low and sultry.

Darcy placed her hand, palm up, on the table, leaning in with her breasts resting on the table inches from her hand.

Chase swallowed and then swallowed again. He stared as her dark eyes glittered with mischief. She knew exactly what she was doing. He placed the first-aid kit on the table and squatted in front of her. He pulled a brown bottle out and opened it.

"This is going to hurt."

Other than a small hiss she sat perfectly still. "It hurt a lot more when the doctor fixed my dislocated shoulder after I skied into a tree in Vail. It was almost worth it to see the look on Jillian's face when it snapped back into place."

"Who's Jillian?" he asked, winding gauze around her hand and tying it off on the back of her hand.

"Jillian Michele. She always goes to Vail with us."

He gulped air and starting coughing at her casual use of the name of the last president's daughter. As if he needed a reminder that Darcy moved in a whole other world than he did. His job was to tutor her. Nothing more.

Moving the first-aid kit to the side, he handed her another pencil. Her fingers shook as she took it into her own hand.

"You aren't afraid of a test, are you?"

The color drained from her face. He silently chastised himself. Lots of people hated tests. Some even feared them. If Darcy's face was any indication, some people were terrified.

"I did fine in high school," she stammered out. "College is just so much harder than I thought it would be." A shaky laugh escaped her. "I thought I would breeze through. I mean, come on, my family owns the college.

"I did great until the first test. I froze. I couldn't even remember the little I'd studied that week. It's only getting worse. If I fail one more test I'm out of here. My parents are going to be so embarrassed."

He put his hand over hers. "We'll do this. We'll practice until you get like me and like to take tests."

She stared at him as if to say he'd lost his mind. He shrugged. He was used to that look anytime he mentioned his love of tests. "It's as if the studying is the hard part. The test is the proof that the studying worked. I wish we didn't have homework, either you do it or not. But the test. The test is the proof you get it and you get to show that you get it."

Nodding her head, Darcy pulled the paper toward her. "I want that."

Soon the floor around their table was littered with crumpled balls of paper but Darcy handed him the latest test with a smile on her face. His heart raced like a horse bursting from the gate. He'd do anything to have that smile directed at him instead of at the thought of doing well on a test. He took his pen and ticked off the correct answers against the key in the back of the book. He returned her smile.

"You only missed one."

Her smile fell. "What do you mean, I missed one?"

He laughed. "You transposed two numbers on the last one and didn't move the decimal point enough spaces. I'm pretty sure it doesn't cost over a million dollars to make one teddy bear."

"It seemed like a lot but I've seen them cost hundreds of thousands, so I thought, why not?"

He sat there dumbfounded at the thought of a priceless teddy bear. The one percent truly lived in a whole other world. Writing a minus one at the top of the page, he circled it and handed it to Darcy.

"I can do this," she whispered, kissing the paper.

"You can," he managed before she ran around the table and grabbed him. Yanking him to his feet, she smiled up at him and planted her soft, warm lips on his.

Her kiss deepened. Chase tried to pull back, but her arms wrapped around his neck and pulled him in close. Her soft fingers threaded through his hair sending shivers down his spine. Her tongue slid along his closed lips and he groaned.

She took it as permission and her tongue slid along his. She tasted of oranges and cinnamon. Moving closer, he felt every inch of her firm, athletic body. Her breasts pressed into his chest. His breath caught and his heart raced. He'd wanted to do this since the moment she'd fallen into his lap.

Was she smiling? It felt as if she was smiling. She struggled to move her mouth. That kiss had been so gentle, so sweet, so perfect. Why couldn't time stand still? Why couldn't that feeling go on forever? Why did sadness and disappointment have to butt in on a perfect life? She sighed. Sinking deeper, she embraced the dark, the warm, the nothingness. No sadness, no disappointment in the nothingness. Nothing in the nothingness.

EIGHT

Chase stepped through the large open door and inhaled the strong, sharp scents of sawdust and wood stain. He sighed as his shoulders slumped in relief. The familiar sights and sounds and scents of Thanos Fine Furniture grounded him in a world he understood. Lake Willowbee and the family business was lightyears away from the confusion and angst of the hospital.

"You're back," Uncle Dimitri called from the loft office, his deep voice carrying over the buzzing of saws and dropping of boards.

"For a check-in," he said, once he reached the stairs.

Uncle Dimitri waved him up and Chase followed him into the office. He shut the door behind him, shutting out the clatter as well. His uncle took a seat behind the desk and he fell into the one in front.

"How is Darcy?"

He sighed and ran a hand through his hair. "Better. Worse. I don't know. Some days it seems like she will wake up and other days it seems like it will never happen."

His uncle opened a drawer and Chase heard the clink of glasses. The man put the glasses and a bottle of Ouzo on the desktop. Chase smiled and Uncle Dimitri poured a dollop into each glass, handing one to Chase. He took a large gulp and heat traveled down his throat to his stomach, where it warmed him inside and out.

Uncle Dimitri sat back in his chair with a creak of leather. He set the cut-crystal glass on a stomach that had expanded year by year until he looked ready to play Santa in a Christmas pageant without added stuffing. "It's the holiday season. The season of miracles."

He huffed and threw the rest of the drink back in one large gulp. "So if I get a miracle and she wakes up I could be divorced by New Year's." Chase slammed the glass down on the edge of the desk. "Oh my God, I didn't mean that."

"Of course you didn't, son," Dimitri whispered. He drank the rest of his drink, put the glass on the desktop quieter than Chase had, and leaned forward. "This has been a tough row for you to hoe. Your mom and dad would be so proud of you. I'm proud of you. You could have left Darcy to her parents' care. She was divorcing you, you know?"

He jumped out of his seat. "I love Darcy. I'm going to be there for her. Marriage isn't something you just up and leave." His voice rose until he caught the twinkle in his uncle's deep-blue eyes.

Sitting back down, he shook his head. "You played me, old man. You know I'll never leave Darcy. Certainly, not to her parents. Those two were responsible for most of our arguments."

"How's business?" He switched the subject to something easier to deal with than Darcy's parents. They hadn't liked him since day one and nothing he did or achieved in the ensuing years would change their minds. He'd finally just given up trying.

His uncle sat up straight and grinned. "We have more business than we know what to do with. I'm only giving the crew a couple of days for the holidays. We'll have to make it up to them in the spring, give them a spring break or something."

Chase relaxed back in his chair. The business on an even keel was one less thing to worry about. He didn't think he could handle one more thing on his shoulders. "Did you get the special orders I completed while at the Inn?" Thanos Fine Furniture had been his dad's and his uncle's dream, but Chase Designs was his baby.

Uncle Dimitri whistled. "Yep, shipped them off a couple of days ago. The buyers will get them before Christmas. Always surprises me to put $25,000 insurance on an itty-bitty box."

He grinned. "Not bad for a hobby everyone said would amount to nothing."

"I always believed in your talent, Chase."

"I know you did, Uncle Dimitri. I hope you know what it means to me to have your backing all these years. I could never have started the business without your help."

He stared as a flush swept across his uncle's cheeks. "Now, you know I didn't do anything but give you the tools and the space to do your work. That little girl from college was the one who got the ball rolling."

Chase thought back to Misty and that first carved necklace. She'd shown it to all her glitzy friends and suddenly his work was in demand from the rich and famous the world over. The shop had gone from a nice business for the area to being known in corners of the world he'd never dared dream about. His work now graced the necks of people from A-list actresses to a former first lady. One was on loan to the MOMA in New York City. The spillover for Thanos Fine Furniture built the business from Dimitri, Chase, and two apprentices to a staff of hundreds that employed a good portion of Lake Willowbee.

Had he let the fame go to his head? Had all the time spent building the business been time he should have spent with Darcy? He was ripped out of his thoughts by the ringing of his phone. He pulled it out of his pocket and stared at the screen. The split-second of relief that it wasn't the hospital was replaced with dread at his lawyer's name on the screen.

"Hello," he replied and listened with growing anger as his lawyer spewed a bunch of legal mumbo-jumbo that amounted to one thing--he was getting screwed by the Bennett's again.

He slammed the phone shut and crammed it back into his pocket. His uncle sat up and stared at him with a question in his eyes.

"That was Whittaker. Margaret and Steven have gotten their wish. A judge ruled they are in charge of Darcy."

"Can they do that? Your lawyer got the papers to make you responsible for your wife."

"Mr. and Mrs. Bennett say they have divorce papers Darcy filed. As her ex-husband, I have no rights, but her parents, out of the kindness of their hearts, as if, say I can come tonight and say good-bye."

"You have to fight them, Chase," his uncle urged, leaning forward in his seat. "If she had filed the papers they would have been found weeks ago."

He fell back into the chair. "Uncle Dimitri, I'm so tired of fighting."

"Do you still love her?"

"I will love Darcy 'til the day I die."

"Then go fight for her, just like you did before. You didn't give up then, don't give up now."

NINE

The drive back to San Francis and the hospital was too long and boring not to let his mind wander to what might have been. The latest legal maneuver by the Bennett's was just the most recent battle in his ongoing war with Darcy's parents. From the moment he had met them, they had been crystal clear he wasn't good enough for their little girl. Not enough money. Not enough prestige. Even when the money and the prestige came, it wasn't enough. Never enough to make them believe he could take care of Darcy. Then the accident happened.

From the day of her car wreck, they'd placed the blame on him even though they'd been separated for months and he wasn't responsible for the rain or the drunken driver. It wasn't as if they could put anymore shame on him than he put on himself first.

If they hadn't been apart.

If she hadn't been driving in the pouring rain.

If Mr. Mattson hadn't decided he could drive after seven shots of Bourbon at the local bar.

You could 'what if' until the end of time and still be left with a wife in a coma in a hospital bed. Ex-wife, if what his lawyer said was true.

The road left the mountains and swept down into the foothills, lush and green this time of year. Fog hung in the meadows, but the freeway remained clear and light of traffic. The holiday rush was just beginning to build up. Another few days and the families would be clogging the road on their way to the ski slopes of Lake Tahoe and nearby.

Once he returned to San Francis, Main Street was cluttered with holiday shoppers. Twinkling lights decorated each skeletal tree lining the middle of the street. Banners proclaiming Happy Holidays swung in bright red and green. The bell-ringing Santa had a crowd of little kids putting their dollar bills in the red bucket to get a hug and lollipop from the jolly old elf.

Feeling like Ebenezer Scrooge he pulled into a parking space and slammed out of his car. Even the lawyer's office was decorated for the season. He rolled his eyes and stepped into the office. The petite young woman at the desk smiled with blindingly white teeth and red pom-poms in her long, blonde hair.

"Hello, Mr. Thanos. My dad is expecting you back in his office."

He tried to smile back at the bubbly young lady but his heart wasn't in it. Chase trudged back to Whittaker's office, knocked on the door, and went in at Larry's yell of 'come in.'

"You look like crap, Chase."

Falling into the chair, he sighed and stared at his lawyer. "I feel like crap. How did this happen? You said they'd asked all their lawyers if Darcy had filed. Now, they miraculously have papers. I know I sure as hell didn't sign any papers. I don't buy it."

Larry held his hand up to stop his tirade in midstream. "I didn't either. But until I can find proof otherwise, we must go along with the judge's order. It's your word against theirs. You don't want to be fighting over your wife's hospital bed, do you?"

He shook his head, sinking back into his chair. "Of course not."

"Then you have to play along while I get someone on it. My daughter, Bethany is going over to the courthouse shortly. She may look all sugar and spice but the girl is a barracuda. She has friends at the courthouse. She'll find out if the papers are legit and aboveboard."

"You want me to go over to the hospital and say good-bye? I don't know if I can do that. Face Darcy's parents and act like this is all fine and dandy? You're asking a lot."

"Chase, you have to look at the big picture. You have to be the stable, reliable, dependable one. Especially if they did something hinky with the paperwork. You want the judge on your side, not just as mad at you as the Bennett's are. He could give guardianship to the hospital, and then none of you would have a say in Darcy's care."

His mouth dropped open. "He can do that?"

Larry nodded. "Yes, he can. So, go make nice while I work on this."

Somehow, he'd shook his lawyer's hand and made his way to his car. He shuddered to think how he'd driven to the lawyer's office and not remembered any of the drive there. His hands locked onto the steering wheel. He needed to pull himself together. He'd been letting the Bennett's push his buttons since day one.

His head swiveled as he stared like a tourist in a foreign land. The Bennett family home wasn't far from the college, but the estate was a world away from anything he knew. Giant wrought-iron gates with a fancy B graced the edge of the driveway. They opened as Darcy pushed the clicker and drove through. The gates silently and slowly shut behind them. The drive down the road to the house seemed longer than the trip from the college. The blacktop wound through rolling hills, vineyards, and towering pine trees alight with red, green, and white Christmas lights.

Through a break in the trees he spotted the house. No, make that castle. He expected to see a moat and resident dragon any minute now. He whistled. "Didn't realize we were going to England for the holidays."

Darcy threw back her head and laughed at his poorly done British accent. "It does look like it belongs next to Stonehenge or something, doesn't it? Actually, my grandfather had an Italian castle dismantled and transported over here and put back together. I guess that was what was done back then. I just always think of it as old and wish we had a nice, new house."

She pulled them to a stop by the front door. Darcy's shiny new Volvo looked like a used car among the Rolls, Mercedes, and lone Aston-Martin parked haphazardly in front of the house. He waited for James Bond to come strolling out of the house in his pristine tuxedo. His shoulders sagged at the thought of his usable, but ten-year-old beat-up car sitting here among the swans of society cars and was glad it sat back at the dorm and they'd taken her car.

His heart skipped a beat. What was he doing here? What made him think he belonged meeting Darcy's parents? As if she'd read his mind, she turned to him and her mouth found his. She tasted so sweet. Of honey and chocolate and cinnamon.

Her hands held his face. "Money doesn't make people any better than anyone else. What you do to make this world a better place is what makes a man. You and your uncle make beautiful furniture to brighten people's houses. The things you carve bring beauty into this world. You are a great man, Chase Thanos and don't you ever forget it."

He ran his fingers through Darcy's long, shining hair, the half-healed cuts on his fingers catching in the fine strands. He leaned forward and touched her forehead with his. He inhaled the rose scent that permeated her skin and by connection, his. His fingers slid to her petal-soft cheek. Chase could have stayed like this forever if not for the slamming of a door and chatter of multiple conversations.

Darcy looked up and out the car's windows. He stared as she planted a fake smile on her face and swept out of the vehicle to be surrounded by a group of blondes who looked enough like her to be cousins or some closely related people. He smiled as they hugged Darcy and did those stupid air kisses he thought only happened in movies about the uber-rich. She glanced over to him past a woman's shoulder and rolled her eyes.

Chase got out of the car and moved to her side. She grabbed onto his hand and pulled him close to her. "This is Chase Thanos. My friend from college."

He might have been put out by the 'friend' comment if not for the scorching looks he was getting from Darcy's family. The tone she'd used let them know he was more than a friend without using the what he'd always thought as juvenile 'boyfriend' moniker. If that didn't imply he was more than a friend, her wrapping her arms around him and pulling him in close certainly worked. The tallest of the blondes pulled away from the group and held her hand out to him. "I'm

Veronica. Darcy's cousin on her mother's side. You must be something else in bed. Darcy's never brought anyone home before." Her gaze swept his entire body.

He started coughing as he didn't know whether to laugh or stammer a denial. Or something in between. A dreaded blush heated his face as he glanced at Darcy and noted her bright-red cheeks. One of the men pulled Veronica back to his side.

"Really, Roni. Do you ever think before you talk?"

She smiled and wrapped herself around the man like a well-fed cat. "It's easier to ask for forgiveness than it is to ask for permission."

The man yanked her toward the door just opening. "Roni, you have never asked for forgiveness in your life."

The woman's husky laugh preceded them through the doorway.

They seemed unreal, like something from a movie or another planet. He couldn't figure out where Darcy fit into this picture. The girl with the torn jeans falling into his lap with a football was a distant memory he tried to recall.

She handed her car keys to a man in a suit holding the door open. "Welcome home, Miss Darcy."

"Edgar, our bags are in the trunk. Can you put them in my room, please?"

"Darcy Elizabeth Bennett. That man is not sleeping in your room." The words came in a loud whisper from a woman who didn't look old enough to be Darcy's mother admonishing her.

"I don't think there will be much sleeping, Aunt Margaret," Roni said in the sudden silence of the foyer.

Chase groaned, hoping the pristine marble floor would open up and swallow him. Death was preferable to the looks he was getting from Darcy's mother and an older gentleman who he could only assume was her father. Hell, even Edgar, who must be the butler, was looking down his pointy noise at him. Meanwhile, Veronica and the other younger people were smirking at him.

"Really, Mother. It's almost the twenty-first century," Darcy complained.

He fidgeted as his face flushed hot. Darcy's mother was

shooting him looks to kill while Darcy crossed her arms on her chest and stood her ground. The older woman was not backing down. Chase moved to Darcy's side.

"I can find a room in town. I saw several hotels on Main Street."

A heavy sigh escaped Margaret Bennett. "Mr. Thanos, there isn't a room to be had in town. It's Christmas. I do appreciate the effort though. If you don't mind, Edgar will put your bags in a guest bedroom in the North wing."

He released a big breath he hadn't known he was holding. From the looks of the bed and breakfasts on Main Street he couldn't afford a shed at those establishments, but to help Darcy he would have used his emergency credit card.

"Well, now that that is settled, let's all have a drink to bring in the holidays," the older gentleman announced, leading the way through an arched entry way into a room that defined elegance, with overwhelming dark wood and lush fabrics. The cousins headed right to the bar and helped themselves. He reached out and took Darcy's arm.

"You didn't say we would share a room," he whispered.

"I wanted to surprise you," Darcy said, a blush painting her porcelain cheeks a soft pink.

He took both of her hands. "There's no rush, sweetheart. When we have our first time it won't be under your parents' noses just to spite them."

She stood on tiptoe and kissed him. Her soft lips slid along his and took his breath away.

"We'll just see about that," she whispered back over her shoulder as she strode across the room to join her cousins at the bar.

TEN

Chase stared across the carpeted expanse of the guest room. Guest room? What a joke. Two of the single room would have been more square footage than the house he shared with Uncle Dimitri. The bed would have held six people. All at once. His duffel bag sat folded on a shelf in the closet where his small amount of clothing didn't even fill half of the space.

He buttoned his dress shirt and tucked it into his pants. The newness of the fabric rubbed against his neck. He winced at the thought of the money spent on clothing he wouldn't wear after this weekend. He couldn't imagine where he would need to wear a suit and the pricey shirts once they were back at the college.

Dressing for dinner, as Darcy had explained it, seemed like a waste of time and clothing. Uncle Dimitri would laugh his head off when he regaled him with the story when he went home for spring break in a couple of months. He smiled at the thought and stared at himself in the mirror on the inside of the closet door. Admitting he did look pretty spiffy, he buttoned his cuffs and shut the closet door.

A knock sounded at the door that he opened to find Edgar standing there. "Dinner will be served in twenty minutes, Mr. Thanos. The family is in the red dining room."

His mouth must have gaped open. Edgar smiled. "The red dining room is adjacent to the study where you were earlier."

"Thanks, Edgar."

Chase made his way down the stairs as the butler continued to knock on doors. He spotted Darcy on a staircase on the other side of the house. She looked over to him and smiled as she skipped down the stairs. They met in the foyer.

"I take it your room is in the South wing?" he asked as she slipped her hand into hers.

"Third room on the right, in case you should go walking in the middle of the night." She winked at him and licked her lips.

He shook his head, but a smile still crept across his face. "Not going to happen, Darcy. Your mother looked like she would be patrolling the hallways with a gun and guard dogs."

"Coward," Darcy whispered up to him, a smile on her face.

"No, a wise man," Roni said as she slid up to them in a cloud of overpowering perfume and wrapped herself around him. "Aunt Margaret is she-bear over her one and only bear cub. I'm surprised she doesn't still keep you in bubble wrap, Darcy dear."

Darcy frowned at her cousin, furrows deepening across her brow. Her hand tightened in Chase's. "You must be losing your mean streak in your old age, Roni," she muttered back, an ugly tone in her voice he had never heard from her. "That's the nicest thing you've ever said to me."

He untangled himself from Roni and wrapped an arm around Darcy's shoulder. Her cousin shrugged her shoulders and smiled at him. "This one is a keeper, cousin. Don't blow it."

The woman walked across the foyer, her heels clicking on the marble. Roni pulled open a door and slipped inside. The door shut with a gentle swoosh and he was alone with Darcy, although the muted sounds of conversation filtered through the wooden doors.

"We don't want to hold up dinner," he said, moving to cross the marble expanse. She clenched his hand and pulled him back.

She rubbed her forehead. "I'm so sorry about that. It's this house. It sucks me in and makes me act just like them."

He laughed and wrapped his arms around her. "Where's my football girl? That's the real Darcy." His gaze swept over her from her upswept hair held with jewels he thought might be real diamonds, to her silk dress that must cost thousands, to the spike heels he'd never seen her in that put her almost eye to eye with him.

"You look very beautiful tonight," he whispered, placing a kiss on her cheek. Darcy was beautiful in whatever she wore. Tattered jeans or a fancy dress. He loved her in whatever she had on. His breath caught.

"What?" she asked, a worried look on her face. "You're

sorry you came and met them all, aren't you? You're seeing the real me and you don't like it."

He took both of her hands and pulled her in close. "I love you."

The color left her face. "What did you say?"

"I love you, Darcy Bennett. I love you in your jeans. I love you when you're studying. I love you all dressed up, pretty as a Christmas ornament."

A smile broke across her face, happiness shining in her eyes. "I love you, Chase."

He leaned over and swept his lips across her mouth. She opened for him and their tongues tangled amid groans from them both. She tasted of honey and cinnamon. Pulling her in closer, their bodies pressed together. The blood thrummed in his veins, pounding in his ears. His heart raced in time with hers, as she pulled them closer.

A cough broke them apart as Roni leaned through the doorway and stared at them. "Aunt Margaret wants to start dinner," she whispered. "You better get in here now before she gets one of her migraines and no one will get dinner."

Her cousin slid back into the dining room as Chase pulled himself away from Darcy. "The others are waiting."

"Let them wait," she whispered as she wrapped her arms around him.

He could have stayed that way all night, but Brock, her cousin slapped him on the back as he walked by to the dining room. "I wouldn't keep Aunt Margaret waiting. You know how she gets."

Darcy sighed and stepped back. "Fine, dinner it is."

He kissed her pouting lips and smiled at her. "It's just dinner."

She sighed as he opened the door. "No it isn't. It's the inquisition. The only thing missing is the rack and the iron maiden."

China and crystal glistened on a table big enough for twenty. Margaret Bennett sat at one end and Mr. Bennett sat at the other. Folded cards sat above each plate. Chase found his seat beside Roni and another female he hadn't met yet. Darcy walked over to the other side to take a seat across from him, between Brock and another young man.

A low voice sounded on his right. "Hi, I'm Darcy's cousin,

184

Naomi. You must be Chase."

He turned to her as Darcy took her seat across the table. "Yes."

The young girl, and she was a girl, had him blushing as her gaze swept up and down his body and she licked her lips. Roni leaned forward.

"Naomi, behave yourself. Aunt Margaret will send you to bed without dinner."

"Oh, fine," she whined and turned to stare at her plate.

A bell tinkled from the head of the table. A swinging door opened behind Margaret and an army of people brought the food. He knew his mouth gaped open but he couldn't help himself. He'd thought only royalty lived this way. Like a synchronized dance, the plates of food sat in front of them and the group of servants passed silently through the door again. As if it were a restaurant instead of a home.

He glanced across the table where Darcy smiled and winked at him. His football girl seemed a million miles and a million dollars away. He sat up straighter as Margaret raised her wineglass. "To family." She glanced at Chase and pasted such a fake smile on her face he thought her cheeks would crack. "And friends."

Course followed course and glasses of wine mysteriously appeared beside his plate. He'd never been a drinker, especially since he wasn't twenty-one yet and Uncle Dimitri wouldn't have allowed it because a teen, drunken driver took his parents' lives. He took a sip or two from each glass to be polite and still felt a buzz in his head by dessert.

Margaret put her hands together under her chin as the last of the plates were cleared and everyone sat back and sipped coffee. Darcy groaned across the table and Roni laughed quietly at his side. He suddenly remembered Darcy's comment about an inquisition. He'd thought he might escape it with all the small talk at the table during the meal, but her mother looked ready to cross-examine him in a court of law.

"So, Mr. Thanos. What do your people do?"

His people? It took a moment to filter through the slight wine haze. "There's just Uncle Dimitri and me. My parents died when I was a kid. It's been just me and the uncle ever since."

"And what does this uncle do?"

"He builds furniture. He owns Thanos Fine Furniture in Lake Willowbee." He sat up straighter. They might not have the Bennett's money, but he was proud of his uncle and the things they built with their hands.

"What kind of name is Thanos?"

"Mother," Darcy groaned across the table and her face was red as he glanced at her quickly. He turned back to Margaret.

"Thanos is Greek. My grandparents came here from Greece during World War II to escape the Nazis. The family have been woodworkers as far back as we know."

"Mother, that's enough." Darcy threw down her napkin. "I brought Chase home for the holidays since he would be alone for Christmas. His uncle is on a wood-buying business trip and I didn't want him to be alone. No one should be alone at Christmas."

"Wow," Roni whispered. "The girl found her backbone."

Margaret grabbed her forehead and her face went white. "My head. I think I have a migraine coming."

He looked to the others, but they all heaved a sigh or looked away from Mrs. Bennett. Naomi muttered under her breath and he missed most of what she said after, "Oh, brother."

Darcy's face turned pale and she rushed to her mother's side. "I'm so sorry, Mom. Let me help you to your room."

Margaret pushed back her chair and leaned on Darcy as they made their way to the door. The woman turned slightly. "Carry on. I'll be fine."

The two left and a hush fell over the room until Darcy's father pushed back his chair. "I'll leave you youngsters to it. The pool is heated and you should all go have fun. Margaret will be herself by morning."

As soon as he left the room, Roni threw down her napkin and laughed. "Aunt Margaret will be fine sooner than that. Probably as soon as she gets done having Darcy fetch and carry as much as possible."

"She's faking?" His voice cracked.

"Probably," Roni admitted. "At least the doctors never find anything wrong with her. She complains of a headache and poor Darcy comes running. It's like a test."

"A test of what?" he asked.

"A test of how much Darcy loves her mother," Roni answered.

Roni, Brock, and Naomi pushed their chairs back. "Let's go swimming," Brock announced.

He thought back to the chill outside. "Isn't it a little cold to go swimming?"

"It's inside," Naomi said.

"I didn't bring a suit," he answered.

"Don't worry about it," Roni told him. "We keep extras in the pool room. I'm sure we'll find something in your size."

"Shouldn't we check on Darcy and her mother?"

Roni grabbed his arm and pulled him out of the room. "They'll be fine. Once Darcy plays the dutiful daughter she'll meet us at the pool."

He shook his head and let the woman drag him to the pool. Just as they'd said he found a suit and had barely put a towel on a lounge chair when Darcy showed up.

His heart raced when she took off her robe and he spotted the deep-green swimsuit plastered to every curve. He hadn't known she had that shape hiding under her sweatshirts and jeans. The dress earlier had highlighted her but nothing like the skintight swimsuit. He found himself regretting his quick assertion they would not make love under her parents' roof.

A horn honked and brought him speedily back to the present as a car wanted his parking space. He groaned. He should have foreseen what Margaret Bennett would do to Darcy and his marriage. That Christmas had been the beginning of her manipulation of their entire relationship. He huffed and turned the key on the car. Hindsight was always 20/20.

ELEVEN

"What in the hell is going on?" His voice started as a yell and ended on a loud whisper as he realized he was in the hospital and everyone was staring at him. Chase glared at Margaret and Steven over Darcy's hospital bed. The hiss of the ventilator set his blood to thrumming in his veins. A pulse throbbed in his temple. He was going to throw up.

Margaret moved closer to the bed and placed a hand on Darcy's. She stared at him dry-eyed. "We did what is best for Darcy. Her breathing was labored and the doctor recommended the ventilator."

He choked over the lump in his throat. Darcy's body seemed to have shrunk in the bed, surrounded by wires and machines. "She never wanted to be kept alive with machines. You knew that."

The woman glared back at him. "I know no such thing. I will do whatever it takes to keep my daughter alive."

His hands fisted at his sides. "This isn't alive," he whispered. His gaze traveled over Darcy's face, the tube breathing for her as her chest rose and fell in a regular, mechanical rhythm. *It isn't.*

Steven grabbed Margaret's shoulders and pulled her away from the bed. He looked up at Chase. "We'll leave you to say your good-bye. I don't expect to see you here again. Darcy is our responsibility. Just as she always has been."

He nodded through his anger as they walked past and left the room. His chest caved as his pent-in breath left him. Collapsing into the chair, he reached for his wife's hand. He didn't care what the papers said or whether they were forged. Darcy was his until death parted them. She'd rushed into his heart and she wouldn't leave it until he left this Earth.

Tears streamed down his face, blurring his vision of her hooked up to machines. A part of him wanted to rip the offensive plastic out of her mouth. To unplug the machines and let happen what would happen. His spine stiffened and his fingers locked onto the blankets. It took everything he had to be still and let calmness fill him.

He leaned over and brushed the hair back from Darcy's face. The strands caught the light from the window and shimmered in his fingertips. His fingers grazed her cheek and traveled along her jaw. He knew every inch of this woman, from their first time to the last.

"Darcy, do you remember our first time? Do you remember the magic? Do you remember the love?"

The silence echoed in the large guest room. His limbs grew heavy. Hours of swimming had worn out his body, but not his mind. In his mind's eye, he saw Darcy in the skintight bathing suit, her long arms cleaving through the warm water, her body moving in perfect motion. The others splashed at the shallow end of the pool as he and Darcy tread water and circled each other at the deep end. She moved closer and closer to him until her limbs wrapped around him, pulling them in close. Her lips found his, tasting sweet and slightly tangy of the pool water.

"I can't believe we are swimming in December. In Lake Willowbee the lake is probably half-frozen."

"I want to see your lake sometime," Darcy whispered as she nibbled on his ear. "I've always wanted to skinny dip in a mountain lake."

His legs stopped moving and they sank slightly before he remembered himself and kicked his legs to hold them steady in the water. "You are being bad." He smiled at her.

"Not as bad as I want to be," she replied.

He glanced quickly to the other end of the pool to find it empty. "Where did everyone go?"

"To bed, I imagine." She looked at the poolside clock. "It's almost midnight."

"It's almost Christmas Eve," he said.

They moved to the side of the pool and she lifted herself up to sit on the side. "What are your Christmas traditions, Chase?"

He hauled himself out of the pool and sat beside her. The warmth of the room surrounded them. "When my parents were alive we would get one present on Christmas Eve and the rest on Christmas morning. I never could figure out how I always got pajamas. I had to grow up to realize my mom knew which package it was and handed it to me."

"I like that," Darcy said, a wicked look in her eyes. "One present for Christmas Eve. I know what I want for Christmas Eve." Her gaze traveled over his wet body, heating his blood to boiling. She reached out and trailed her fingers down his chest to the waist of his swimsuit.

He caught her fingers before they could go any further. "Don't start something we can't finish."

Her head swiveled around. "We could finish. Everyone is gone and in bed."

Taking her hands in his, he stared into her eyes. "We are not making love on cement beside the pool for Edgar to find."

"Fine, spoilsport," she said, a sexy pout on her lips.

Darcy jumped up and grabbed a couple of towels. Chase ran it over his wet hair and wrapped it around his waist. Darcy did the same. He moved to gather his clothes in the changing room but she stopped him with a hand on his arm. "Leave them. The staff will get them, clean them, and get them to our rooms."

He shook his head, marveling at her lifestyle. What must it be like to live this way your entire life? You would think Darcy would be a spoiled brat, but she was a sweet person. Like taking care of her sick mother in the middle of everything.

Chase walked with Darcy across the cold marble foyer and up the stairs to her room. She tried to pull him in, but he managed to kiss her good night and leave. It was the hardest thing he'd done in his life. Every urge demanded he discover all of this warm, wonderful woman.

So now he laid in his big, cold bed and wondered what he'd been thinking. "You were thinking this was what you wanted, remember?" he muttered to himself, listening as his voice echoed in the enormous room. The rattle of his doorknob cut through the berating of himself.

She stood there, silhouetted in the open doorway. The light from the hallway etched her body into his mind with searing heat. His memories of seeing her like that would remain with him forever. He sat up and threw off the covers as she closed the door and returned the room to moon-lit murkiness. What his eyes couldn't see, his other senses more than made up for. The scent of wildflowers wafted across the room, bringing corny images of running across a meadow toward her as if they were in a sappy commercial. The whisper of silk against her skin hit his ears as she walked across the room toward him.

"Chase," she whispered in a sexy tone. "I'm not leaving this room until I've given you your Christmas present."

As she finished the wild promise, her arms reached out and her soft hands touched him. Her fragrance surrounded him as he took her in his arms and his lips claimed hers. Like magic, her silky nightgown lay in a pool at her feet. The clouds about the Moon parted and a glow filled the room, gilding her body in molten silver. His breath caught and his heart raced. Darcy was here, where she belonged--with him. Forever.

They fell to the bed and claimed each other as lovers.

Chase shook his head and the hospital room came into view through his blurred vision. He wiped hot tears from his face. "Do you remember, Darcy?" His harsh whisper broke in the silent room.

Chase, are you there? I remember. I do. Why can't I tell you that? I can't move. I can't see. She sank deeper into the warm darkness. *Sometimes love just isn't enough,* she whispered in her thoughts. *Sometimes, it just isn't enough.*

Twelve

The pine board crashed through the window with a satisfying thunder and the tinkle of falling glass. Chase followed it with another and another until the opening stood bare. As bare as his soul. He'd begged the Bennett's to take Darcy off life support. He'd promised them anything. Just let her go. They'd laughed at him and called security. He wasn't good enough to take care of his own wife. He never had been, as far as they were concerned. No matter the big house, the elaborate vacations, the fine jewels and artwork. It was never enough. He was still the wood-carver from Lake Willowbee and she was the Bennett princess.

He dropped into a chair with a sob. His face fell into his hands. What hurt the most, was they were right. If he'd taken better care of her, she wouldn't be in the hospital in a coma. She would have been safe and sound in their home. Far away from a drunken driver with three DUIs to his name and still wreaking havoc on the roads.

Footsteps tramped across the concrete floor with the crunch of glass as the person made their way to Chase's side.

"Are you done with your childish behavior?"

He winced as Uncle Dimitri slapped him upside the head. No matter how old you got, that slap brought you right back to being an angry young boy of twelve. Chase sat up and looked around at the damage he'd caused. The factory was empty except for him and his uncle. He vaguely recalled the workers fleeing when the wood started flying. That should have stopped him right there, but it hadn't.

"Uncle Dimitri, I'm so sorry," he whispered with a voice hoarse from screaming. "I'll get this cleaned up and someone out to fix the window."

Dimitri wrapped an arm around his shoulders and hauled him out of the chair. "We'll clean this up and put plywood on the window. We're not getting anyone out here this close to Christmas."

The older man sighed. "I've failed you, Chase."

His mouth dropped open as he picked up broken boards and threw them into the trash pile. "How can you say that?"

"You should have been able to come to me, to let me help you."

Chase couldn't help it, he smiled. "You do know I'll be forty on my next birthday, right? A little old to still need you to fix things for me."

Dimitri sighed and rubbed his eyes. "I still see that little boy. Angry with God for taking his parents. Angry at living with an uncle he hardly knew. Chase, you will always be that little boy to me." He put his hand over his heart. "In here."

He shook his head. Dimitri took that angry young man and raised him as well as his parents could have done. He'd been strict when he'd needed to and loving all the rest of the time. If Chase believed, he would think his parents looked down on them both and smiled at how well they'd done.

His ringing cell phone broke into his thoughts. San Francis Hospital appeared across the screen. He took the call with his heart dying in his chest. They had to be calling to let him know Darcy was gone. He searched his mind and his heart and his soul. Wouldn't he know if she were gone? Wouldn't he be hollowed and half-alive if his love was gone?

"Hello, Mr. Thanos? This is nurse Ann from the hospital."

"Yes," he whispered.

"Your wife is fading. Mrs. Bennett collapsed and they left. Please get here as quickly as you can if you want to be with her at the end."

"I've said my good-byes."

"Mr. Thanos, I've been doing this a long time. You will never forgive yourself if you let your wife leave this life without you holding her hand to let her go."

He took a deep breath. "I'll be there as quickly as possible."

"Thank you," the nurse said and hung up.

"That was the hospital," he told his uncle. Tears filled his eyes. "Darcy is...is dying. I have to be with her."

Uncle Dimitri hugged him and then stepped back. "Of course you have to be with her. Your place is at her side. You bring her back. You tell that woman it isn't time to go yet.

You two have too much to do yet—together."

The last words were garbled as Dimitri grabbed his chest and fell to the floor. Chase slammed to his knees beside the older man. His uncle's face had lost all color. His blue eyes stood out from his ashen skin tone and a whisper came from his blue lips. He cradled him in his arms as he pushed the buttons for 911. He didn't know what he said, but in minutes the sound of an ambulance's siren and the flashing red lights filled the factory room. The door swung open and crashed against the wall. Chase was pushed aside as the paramedics worked on his uncle. He stood there at a loss until they got him on a gurney and headed for the door.

"Are you coming with us?"

"Of course," he stammered, rushing to hold his uncle's hand as they got the gurney to the ambulance.

Mumbling came as Dimitri tried to remove the oxygen mask.

"Darcy," he whispered, his lips barely moving.

Oh my God. How could he have forgotten so easily. He couldn't be in two places at once.

He breathed deeply and felt his heart shatter into a million pieces.

He watched as they put Dimitri into the ambulance and shut the doors.

He got into his car and followed the ambulance to the Lake Willowbee hospital.

The pacing wasn't helping. Chase's mind still raced. His heart pounded in his chest. Uncle Dimitri had been yelling at him until the doctors booted him from the curtained cubicle. The swing of the ER door had him whipping around and staring at the doctor. Trying to read the man's face was impossible.

"Mr. Thanos?"

"Yes."

"Your uncle is resting comfortably right now. We'll run

some tests, but all signs point to a weak heart. From the answers to my questions, he's known about the problem for a while."

"Can I see him?"

The doctor stared over his shoulder. "He's refusing to see you. I believe his words were, 'he better not still be out there, he has places to be'."

"My wife is at the hospital in San Francis. She's dying and I was going to be with her before all of this happened with my uncle," he explained.

"He'll be fine here with us. All he needs is some rest and monitoring," the doctor said. "The nurses have your cellphone info. Go. Be with your wife."

He stood a few seconds as the man went back through the swinging door. Taking a deep breath, he squared his shoulders. He'd listened to Uncle Dimitri for most of his life. He wasn't going to stop now.

Getting into the car and watching the hospital recede in his rear-view mirror was the hardest thing he'd ever done.

THIRTEEN

Chase let himself into Darcy's room. Nurse Ann had promised to stand guard outside. His eyes filled with hot tears that rolled down his cheeks. Her body seemed to have shrunk in the short time he had been away. He took her hand, the skin dry and wrinkled. He ran his fingers across her knuckles, the bones sitting just below a thin layer of skin.

"Darcy, how did we get here?" His voice cracked and broke as he leaned his forehead to their joined hands. "We had such dreams and hopes. From the moment I made you mine, we have been together. Through good times and bad times. The ups and downs. Always."

He laughed through his tears. "Do you remember our wedding?"

Like it was yesterday, he could still picture how Darcy looked on their wedding day. When their wedding day finally arrived after a multitude of false starts.

"Darcy, honey, the guests are waiting," he called to her through the half-open door. "The minister wants to start."

"I can't do this. Not without my mom," she cried, her voice barely reaching him.

"We discussed this." He tried to be patient, but his patience had worn thin after the tenth attempt to plan and have a wedding. Along with three trips to the ER and canceled photographers, caterers, and florists.

"She should be here."

"Yes, she should be. But she made her choice. Your father is here. Your cousins are here. My uncle is here."

"I'm here," he said, his voice firm and full of the love he felt for this woman.

"But what if she really is ill this time? What if she has a tumor or something?"

He didn't know whether to laugh or cry. It had taken several false alarms, but he'd soon seen what Darcy's cousins had been talking about that Christmas. Margaret Bennett used her illness to control her only child.

"Darcy, if she were really sick do you think your father would be here? He's waiting to walk you down the aisle."

"But she called me. She's having blurred vision."

"She still managed to call you, didn't see?" he muttered to himself. "She saw the phone clearly enough."

"Darcy Elizabeth Bennett," Stephen Bennett roared over his shoulder. "This young man has waited long enough. This wedding should have taken place months ago."

The man shot him a quick wink and a smile before he went into the room and shut the door. He heard muffled voices through the wood. His deep and hers high and crying. His pacing was cut short as her father came out of the room with a thumbs-up. "We're good to go."

Stephen walked to the end of the hall and waited. Chase leaned against the door. "Darcy, I love you."

"I love you too, Chase. I'm ready."

"I'll be waiting for you in the chapel. I'll be the nervous guy in a tuxedo."

Her soft laughter filled him as he walked past Stephen and made his way to the small chapel nestled in the forest outside Lake Tahoe. The windows framed towering pines and a gorgeous view of the mountains. It wasn't the enormous cathedral in San Francis that Darcy and her mother had wanted, but after the third cancellation Father Victor told them no more. It wasn't filled with hundreds of guests, but after a comical issuance of invitations and regrets, their friends had had enough. So, the small room of folding chairs held his uncle at the front of the room as his best man. Darcy's cousin, Roni would walk in before her and the other cousins filled the front row of chairs.

As he stood beside his uncle, the music started and the doors opened. For the rest of his life he would never be able to remember what color dress Roni wore without looking at the videotape, but when the woman stepped to the side of the podium he saw Darcy and he would remember how she looked until the end of time.

Her white gown dripped with lace at her neck and wrists. She was an angel in white. Her face glowed with happiness and her smile stabbed him in the heart as he fought to catch his breath. The material of her dress clung to her curves and swirled at her ankles as she walked toward him. Stephen stopped and the minister started to speak. The words went in one ear and out the other as he gazed at Darcy who looked back at him with happiness and love shining in her deep brown eyes.

Her father took her hand and placed it in his. His hand tingled where they touched. Darcy bowed her head for a prayer and the scent of strawberries and cinnamon wafted over him with the swirl of her hair. The curls fell forward and tickled his hands. He took a deep breath as the idea of a lifetime with this woman finally felt in his reach. Uncle Dimitri nudged him and handed him the rings, which he passed to the minister.

"Darcy, you make me complete. I will be by your side through good times and bad, through sickness and health, until death do we part." He took the ring from the minister and placed it on her finger.

"Chase, you make me complete. I will be by your side through good times and bad, through sickness and health, until death do we part." She took the ring from the minister and placed it on his finger.

His mind begged the minister to stop rambling and pronounce them husband and wife already so no one could take her away from him.

In what seemed eternity, the man finally got to that part. When he said if anyone objected, he half-expected Margaret to show up at the back of the chapel in her nightgown, having risen from what she'd proclaimed was her deathbed. When not a whisper was heard, he took a deep breath.

"By the power invested in me by the state of Nevada, I now pronounce you husband and wife. You may kiss the bride."

Darcy's smile brightened the room as he leaned in and

took her lips with his. He could have kissed her forever if her cousins hadn't cheered and whistled and she pulled back with a laugh and a bright-red blush on her cheeks. His uncle thumped him on the back as the cousins swarmed Darcy and kissed and hugged her.

The ringing of Stephen's cell phone cut through the celebration. Everyone stood still as he took the call, mumbling as he turned away. He shut the phone and turned back to the group, his face ashen.

"What is it, Daddy?" Darcy's voice rose.

"They've taken your mother to the hospital. I have to go. I'm so sorry, Darcy." His gaze locked on them all. "Go to the hotel and celebrate. I'll let you know what is going on as soon as I can."

Chase shook his head. "Of course not. We'll get changed and meet you there."

Darcy gazed at him as if he'd just won a contest he didn't know he'd entered. His chest puffed out. He would do whatever it took to see that look of love and belief for the rest of his life.

An alarm on the machines yanked him back from memories he could revel in forever. From the happiest day of his life to a foreshadow of how the rest of his married life would commence. If he had known then that Margaret and her hypochondriac ways would destroy each important event in their lives, would he have changed anything? He squeezed Darcy's hand and tears fell. He wouldn't change a thing. Unless it meant he'd have more than twenty years with his wife.

FOURTEEN

Chase walked from the nurse's station to the door to Darcy's room and back again. The room was a sea of white jackets and machines and alarms. He glanced at his watch. Midnight. It was Christmas Eve. Looking up, he spotted Mrs. Macgregor walking toward him.

"Nurse Ann said you were here." She patted the bag hanging on her arm. "I've brought you some food."

"I can't eat right now," he said, pointing to the busyness of the room.

She grabbed his arm. "You will eat. Darcy is going to need you. This could go either way. You have to be strong."

"What?" His mind whirled with the woman's words.

"Never you mind," she whispered and patted his arm. "It will all go how it is meant to be."

Maybe he was too tired, but Mrs. Macgregor's words tumbled in his brain. Hell, maybe she had a direct line to God. He would take all the help he could get. He placed his hand on hers. "I'll eat, but we have to make it quick."

He let the woman pull him to the Family Room down the hall. She pulled things out of the bag and had him set up with soup and a sandwich in no time. She reached in the bag and came up with yarn and knitting needles. As he ate, she plied the needles with the click of metal and a growing square of red and green knitted yarn.

By the time he took the last bite of sandwich and wiped his mouth and hands on a napkin, Mrs. Macgregor handed him a blanket just the right size to bundle a baby. His eyes burned with unshed tears. His voice choked up as he whispered around the lump in his throat. "We don't have any children. We can't have any children."

She folded the blanket and put it beside the empty bowl and plate. "Some people make children, willy-nilly, with a snap of their fingers and some people are gifted with them when they find the one who is meant to be with them."

"Thank you for the kind thoughts, Mrs. Macgregor, but Darcy is going to die and I won't have anything left to her to remember her by."

"Tsk, Mr. Thanos. You will always have a piece of Darcy. In your heart, with your love for her and in your mind, with your memories of her. Those we love are never truly lost. Just out of our sight for a while until we are together again. My Neville is just over the hill. As I get older, he is clearer and clearer to me. I know we'll be together soon."

"Did you and Mr. Macgregor get along all the time?"

"Oh, goodness no." Her eyes twinkled as she gazed at him. "We had some awful arguments. But by the time we made up we had totally forgotten what we'd been fighting about."

Chase stared back at her, fighting tears and a burning in his throat. "I will never forget what Darcy and I fought about during that last argument. It drove her away and landed her here. It's my fault she's in the hospital, in a coma, dying. All my fault."

"You are not a child, Darcy," he said, gritting his teeth until his jaw cracked. "You are almost forty years old. Don't you think it is about time to stop running to your mother every time she calls?"

Tears shone in his wife's eyes as she put her phone in her purse but he refused to let it sway him yet again. This was too important. They'd been at Margaret Bennett's beck and call for twenty years now. Even on their wedding night her mother had managed to be an invisible ghost in their bed. When they'd finally found their beds. He'd had enough.

"What if she really is dying?" Her lip trembled and he turned away.

What if she were? At least she would leave them alone. He refused to take the thought back. They'd had this argument a thousand times and in the thousand times nothing had ever been wrong with the woman.

"Darcy, your mother is going to outlive us all." He grabbed her hands.

She yanked them away. "The doctor found a dark spot. What if it's a tumor? She said her vision is blurred and the sunshine is killing her."

"It's one weekend. We've planned this for months. The limo will be picking us up in less than thirty minutes. We'll be back home by Monday."

She crossed her arms on her chest and stared at him. "She's my family too. It's not as if we have a house full of kids. I have my parents and you."

His shoulders slumped and he lowered his head to stare at the hardwood floor. He couldn't win an argument once Darcy mentioned children. The lack of them sat solely with him. A fact Margaret brought up every Christmas at the Bennett mansion while the cousins and their screaming hordes rampaged through the house. Stephen just stared at him and sighed, shaking his head at the lack of grandchildren.

He ran his fingers through his hair and yanked on the strands. "I refuse to have this argument again. Not today. The MOMA is honoring my work and I will be there for the showing of Misty's necklace." Who would have thought the simple necklace he'd carved for his friend's girlfriend would be placed in a museum as an example of American Folk Art?

His blood pressure rose at the thought of all the events they'd missed over the years due to Darcy's mother's hypochondria. He had to put his foot down this time or it would never end. They'd be old and gray and still rushing to her bedside.

"Enough is enough, honey. She wasn't dying on our wedding day. She wasn't dying on our anniversary when we came home early from camping. She certainly wasn't dying when we had to include them in our anniversary trip to Paris because she might die while we were gone. Did I complain about the extra money? No. Because she is your mother and we are family. But enough is enough. You just saw her last week and she was fine. She'll be fine until we get back."

A horn beeped out on the drive and he snatched up his

briefcase. "Come on, we can't miss our flight."

"I'm not going," she whispered.

"What?" He tossed the briefcase on the chair. "I'm not missing this."

"Don't miss it, Chase. Go by yourself."

Tears rolled down her face. "Don't make me choose. I can't do it anymore."

He wanted to fold her in his arms but his nails dug into his palms as he held them against his sides. His jaw tightened as she gathered her purse and coat and headed to the door. She stopped, her hand on the doorknob.

"I love you, Chase. Good-bye."

His heart skipped a beat as she opened the door and walked through. He rushed to the doorway.

"Don't do this, Darcy. There's no coming back from this."

She turned at her car's door. "I know."

He stood there as she drove down the driveway and disappeared over the hill. How could his heartbeat be pounding so hard in his head when he was sure it had just been ripped out of his chest? Somehow he pulled himself together and got his stuff and into the limo. He sat in the back, leaned his head on the soft leather, and closed his eyes.

Was he wrong? Should he go after her?

"Hell, no," he murmured to himself. "I should have done this years ago."

"Then what happened, dear?" Mrs. Macgregor's voice broke into his memories.

"I went to New York. Spent the weekend with Misty and Jason and celebrated my great accomplishment," he spat out in disgust with himself.

She patted his hand. "It's not so great when you don't have the one you love to celebrate with, is it?"

"Then the hospital called and said Darcy was in a car accident," he said, his gaze locked on the chipped Formica table, his vision blurred with tears.

"Oh, no," Mrs. Macgregor gasped out. "So you had to rush back from New York?"

He looked up at her and shook his head. "No, I was back

for a month when they called."

The older woman grasped his hands in her soft clasp. "Mr. Thanos. Chase, you didn't do anything to cause her accident. She didn't speed away in anger and not pay attention to the road. It was an accident. It's why they call them accidents. They happen accidentally."

His voice broke on a sob. "It's my fault. If she had been home where she should have been it wouldn't have happened."

"Bullshit."

His mouth dropped open and he gazed at her in wonder. Did that curse word just come out of this sweet, old lady?

"It could have happened anywhere at any time. People get in car accidents on the way to the store, to soccer practice with the kids, on a trip to an amusement park. Every day and every place."

She smiled at him. "Forgive yourself, Chase. Darcy needs your support, not your self-pity." Mrs. Macgregor tilted her head as if listening to a sound he couldn't hear. "Now more than ever."

He stared at her, his brow furrowed, deep in thought as footsteps ran down the hospital corridor and a man slid to a stop in the doorway. Looking up at the sound he spotted Larry Whittaker, his lawyer. The man's face was flush and dripping with sweat. He leaned over and grabbed his knees as he inhaled and exhaled loudly in the silent room.

"I've been looking everywhere for you," he finally gasped out. Papers crinkled in his fist as he held them out to Chase. "The divorce papers are fake. They were forged."

"Does that mean...?" He didn't dare hope.

Larry nodded. "You aren't divorced. You are in control of Darcy's care and final wishes."

He let the tears fall as Mrs. Macgregor squeezed his hands. "Go to her, Chase. Do what is right for Darcy. Do what is right for both of you."

FIFTEEN

"I guess you'll have us thrown out of the hospital and arrested now?"

Chase looked up at Stephen Bennett's whisper that barely sounded louder than the hiss of the ventilator. When he'd rushed into the room just after midnight he'd dreamed of demanding they take Darcy off the machine, but with the midday sun shining into the room, his demands were as empty as his hopes of letting his wife go in peace.

"Where's Margaret?" His voice broke. He was done being angry. All that was left was Darcy.

"They sedated her. She's upstairs," Stephen told him.

Chase pointed to the seat across the bed. "Sit with Darcy."

The man's eyebrow lifted in surprise, but he pulled out the chair and fell into it.

They both jumped in their seats at the sound of singing down the hall. Christmas carols in childish voices rang out softly.

"What day is it?" Stephen's voice broke as tears fell down his wrinkled cheeks.

Chase noticed for the first time in a long time that Darcy's father had aged far more than simple years in the last few months. He didn't know what it felt like to sit by your child's bed and wait for them to die. Hot tears burned his eyes and a lump formed in his throat. They should have been there for each other through this, not fighting a war over Darcy's bed.

"Christmas Eve," he whispered to Stephen. "Darcy's favorite day."

The man laughed softly as he groped for his daughter's hand. "Even when she was a little girl, she loved Christmas Eve more than Christmas Day. She said Christmas Day comes and we open presents and it's over, but Christmas Eve is the world waiting for a miracle to happen."

"I'm done waiting for miracles." Chase's voice came out rough and harsh.

Stephen's gaze swept to Darcy's face hidden under the tubes of the ventilator. "I thought you would remove that as soon as you could."

He sighed. "Believe me. I wanted to. But they did another scan and her brain waves have increased. Whatever in the hell that means."

The older man sat up in his chair, his fingers trembling on the bed.

Chase shook his head. "Don't get your hopes up. It's probably nothing."

It's not nothing. I'm here. Can't you hear me? I'm here.

Darcy's fingers twitched in his grasp. His heart pounded in his chest as he peered into her face. Nothing. Just like all the times before. Nothing.

The sunlight traveled across the window as the men sat there, each with their own thoughts, their own memories of the woman lying still in the bed. The glass door slid open and the doctor came in.

"Sorry to interrupt. But I'd like to run some tests. The readings coming in are most unusual."

Chase pushed himself out of the chair and came over to Stephen's side. He placed his hand on his shoulder. "Let's get a cup of coffee."

The man groaned as he stood. His face gray and tired-looking. With a shock, Chase remembered the man had turned eighty years old this year. A big party had been planned with hundreds of guests. Margaret Bennett had gotten one of her migraines and the party had been canceled. He shook his head. In his self-pity, he'd forgotten the woman inconvenienced more than just his life. Stephen had been married to her for more than fifty years.

Once they got to the waiting room, Chase poured two coffees and gave one to Stephen. "Are you going to sit?"

"I think I'll move for a while. Get some circulation in the old legs, if you don't mind?"

"No problem, Mr. Bennett. I need to call the Lake Willowbee hospital and check on Uncle Dimitri."

Stephen stopped in his pacing and placed a hand on Chase's

shoulder. "I didn't know about your uncle."

"It just happened. He'll be fine. Just needs some rest and meds to help his heart."

"Still, I'm sorry."

"No problem, Mr. Bennett."

The man winced. "You used to call me Stephen."

"You used to call me son." He wanted to pull the words back as soon as they left his mouth. Stephen's face paled sheet-white and his mouth trembled.

"I guess I deserve that. We deserve that. Margaret and I have not been as nice to you as we should have been. Now there's no time left to make it up to you. You and Darcy both."

He wrapped his arms around Stephen and held his shaking body next to him. As the shaking stopped, the man moved back and wiped his wet face. "I'll let you make that call before we go back to the room."

Chase nodded, moving across the room and calling the hospital. They put him through to Dimitri's room. His uncle's voice boomed through the phone.

"You're with Darcy, right?"

"Yes. We're getting some coffee while they run some tests."

"Who's this we?"

He smiled as Stephen dumped the awful drink into the waste basket. "Me and Darcy's father."

Chase finished the call quickly as his uncle's voice grew softer and tired-sounding and he spotted the doctor coming down the hall. He ended the call and slid the phone into his pocket as Dr. Jameson walked into the waiting room.

"I've taken Darcy off the ventilator. She's breathing on her own and frankly she seemed to be struggling with it. The next few hours we'll keep watch and see how she does. The brain scans have me puzzled." He scratched his chin. "I'm seeing increased activity but she isn't coming out of her coma. It's as if she doesn't want to wake up. Very puzzling."

The doctor left and the men stared at each other. Chase held his breath. It hurt to hope. It hurt to believe. They'd been down this road for weeks. She'd seem better and then slip deeper, but if ever there was a night for miracles, this would be it, right?

Hours passed in comfortable silence as he held one hand and Stephen held the other. The only sound in the room was Darcy's breath as she inhaled and exhaled. Her chest rising and falling was the only movement in the bed. Her fingers lay lifeless in his hand. Her eyes didn't move. Only the rising and falling of her chest reassured him that his wife still lived.

He glanced up to see Stephen asleep in his chair, his chin resting on his chest, a soft wheezing coming from his mouth. Chase scooted his chair closer to the bed. His fingers swept a loose strand of hair from her cheek. She lay there like a princess in a fairy tale, even though he knew in his heart that real life didn't always have a happily ever after like a child's story.

"It's midnight, Darcy. Christmas Day." His voice trembled. "Do you remember that first Christmas? And the next? And the next? So many Christmases together. You made each one special. You gave me a family, Darcy. When I thought I didn't have one, except for Uncle Dimitri. Just you and me. We're a family. Just you and me. I don't need anyone but you."

His voice trailed off. "I love you, Darcy. Until the day we die--and beyond. Always."

You let me go. Why did you let me go? Find me, Chase. Bring me back. Please.

Darcy moaned. Stephen sat up with a start. "What's going on?"

"I don't know," Chase cried out.

Her eyes moved behind her eyelids and her moans grew.

Why didn't she wake up? Every comment he'd heard since her accident slammed into his head. He had to make her want to wake up.

He squeezed her hand and leaned over her. "Darcy, wake up for me. I need you. Your parents need you. Darcy, wake up for Christmas."

"Chase," she whispered on an exhale and then her chest fell.

His heart stopped. "No," he screamed. "Come back. You can leave me. Divorce me. It doesn't matter. You can't leave. You can't die. Come back."

She gasped a large gulp of air and opened her eyes. They stared at him, dazed and unfocused. "Chase," she whispered and started coughing.

The machines went off with loud beeps and a group of doctors and nurses rushed into the room. Doctor Jameson stopped and stared at Darcy. He smiled. "Look who woke up for Christmas."

Chase laughed until he cried. Tears burned his eyes as he let them fall down his face.

The doctor moved the others out of the room, and strode to the bed to check Darcy. He finished quickly and looked to Stephen and Chase. "I'll be back in a few minutes, we'll need to run some more tests, but I think we're okay. Merry Christmas."

Stephen sat hunched in his chair, his shoulders shaking. Chase knew how he felt. He grabbed Darcy's hand and held it to his heart.

"You came back," he whispered, staring into her eyes.

"Because you told me to," she whispered in a cracked voice he thought he'd never hear again this side of Heaven. "Because you made me want to."

A misunderstanding
and forgiveness

CHRISTMAS
at the *Granger Inn*

CAROL DEVANEY

CHRISTMAS AT THE GRANGER INN
BY CAROL DEVANEY

Ten years after Cole and Sydney broke up, the ache in their hearts remains. Now, a Christmas reunion, complete with a mischievous ghost, offers the possibility that Sydney and Cole can rekindle the love they once shared. Will they risk facing what tore them apart to find a new place they can call home?

ONE

"I. Don't. Want...Don't. Plan. To. Go." Sydney Hall gave Kara a stern glance and pressed her lips together. "End of discussion."

"Come on." Kara snagged another piece of chocolate mint from the candy dish on the counter, then popped it into her mouth. She slid her gaze sideways toward Sydney. "You know he'll be there. Right?"

"No...I don't know he'll be there. Most likely he will be, though. It's been too long...there's too much distance, and too much time, passed between us. Besides, the most important thing is, Cole is married. Married for many years. Or had you forgotten? I won't go chasing after a married man. You of all people should know that."

How Sydney sometimes wished Cole wasn't married. He'd crossed her mind from time to time since Will's passing. But then, memories of the blessed marriage she and Will had shared bubbled to the surface. She was wrapped up in getting through each day without Will, and pushed any thought of Cole Meyers aside.

"Yes, and I respect your morals. But what will it hurt to go to the reunion? Haven't you ever wanted to meet his wife? See what she's like?" Kara urged.

Quiet, Sydney reflected back to the one time she'd actually seen Cole's wife, other than a photo of their wedding announcement in the Virginia Perks newspaper. When she'd turned to leave the spa, she had faced a lovely, slender, brunette. It was no wonder the woman's petite beauty had captured Cole's interest so long ago. Sydney had been happy with Will, and also glad that Cole had found someone.

Still, there was truth in that you never forget your first love. Sydney was no different.

Later, she had been happy to hear they'd moved fifteen miles from Raddwell Corner, so they wouldn't be glaring fixtures in town. That also meant Cole wouldn't be around to run into, which was a good thing for her heart.

Time for the two of them had ended long ago. The hopes she'd placed for Cole and herself for the future, as a young girl, had evaporated like a wisp of smoke. Cole hadn't trusted her since he'd seen her hug and kiss Ron Bacon on the cheek, at a Friday night football game years ago. That hug, and kiss, had been innocent enough. Ron's mother had passed away and, out of consideration for her friend's loss, Sydney simply wanted to show her support. But Cole hadn't viewed it that way. Granted they'd both been young, still she'd never given him reason to mistrust her. But he had, and she'd been devastated.

Sydney had fallen head over heels in love with Cole, but after six short months, she'd had to deal with the loss of young love. She mourned what might have been, but to be with someone who had no faith in her...would only make her miserable. After she'd grieved for their relationship, then came to grips with it, she dusted herself off, and had gotten on with her life.

She was no fool. She hadn't looked back.

Yet looking back now, she had by no means completely forgotten her first love. She had thought the love she and Cole shared was mutual, one that would last forever. His love had vanished because of his anger and misinterpretation of the sympathy she had shown for a grieving friend.

Often she had wondered if Cole harbored any regrets that he had made such a hasty decision, and it had been hasty. He hadn't given her the chance to explain when he walked up on her with her lips on Ron's cheek. All the explanations in the world wouldn't change the truth of what had happened, even now.

It was too late for them to be together again, particularly, since he was married. It was just as well. He probably still believed his assessment of that night years ago was truth.

Sydney watched snow pile against a window pane as moisture gathered around the window inside. Mrs. Granger and her team would be busy decorating and baking for the reunion at the Inn. Sydney hadn't been to a reunion since she and Will had married. Something had always stood in the way.

She hadn't missed attending the reunions, because she'd had Will. He was enough.

Sydney smiled at Kara. "I'm sure she's a lovely person. Cole Meyers wouldn't be involved with someone less than remarkable or perfect," she said. "You know how much he valued perfection."

"As most of us do with age, he's probably softened over the years." Kara slid her feet back inside her boots and draped her coat over an arm. "Look, as you know, the reunion is a week from Christmas Eve. Won't you consider making a reservation? It's kind of late, but they may still have an available room. Anyway, it's worth a try if you'll reconsider."

Sydney glanced at the calendar on her desk, across from the sofa. "Yes. It's a sure bet they're full. Everyone usually attends and enjoys seeing old acquaintances at the reunion. It is sad, though, to learn of the ones who've already passed away. They're still so young."

Most of her friends in Raddwell were content to allow Sydney time to grieve her husband's passing in private. Kara did too, most of the time, but she always had Sydney's well-being at heart. Kara wasn't shy. She said what was on her mind, whether Sydney liked it or not.

Kara placed a hand over Sydney's warm hand. She spoke candidly, yet delicately. "You need to get out more. Be around people. I know you're still grieving over the loss of your beloved Will." She laid her other hand on Sydney's shoulder. "Sweetie, you're still too young to live like a recluse. I love you and it breaks my heart to see you this way. You're too sad...Too alone."

At twenty-seven Sydney was already a widow. Her husband, Will, of five years, had met with a horrific end at an on-the-job accident last year. When the crane operator had misjudged the boom angle, the crane had tipped over. Unfortunately, Will had been standing directly in the path of the crane, and hadn't had a chance. The doctor had confirmed he'd died instantly. Sydney prayed that was true.

She couldn't bear the thought of Will suffering.

The books she'd read on grief helped some, but mostly had little within the pages to ease her heartache. Her heart pounded every time Will's memory stirred her thoughts. He hadn't deserved to die so young and have his life snuffed out. The accident was horrible, and she couldn't get it out of her head.

Yes, her life had been heartbreakingly lonely since his death, but Sydney was doing okay now, well as okay as anyone could be after such a sudden and tragic loss. She had no intention of forgetting him. Not ever.

She also had no intention of letting Cole back into her life. Cole and the love they'd once shared was part of her past, and that's where she planned to keep him.

Although as much as she tried, and as much as she'd loved Will, there was still a part of her memory that caused an ache in her heart for what might have been.

"Hello…Sydney. Are you still with me?" Kara waved a hand in front of Sydney's face. "You've gone off into never-never land."

Sydney sighed. "Of course I'm still here. I'm just thinking about the past."

"That will never do, my friend. Leave the past where it belongs, in the past. You know I'm leaving next week to spend Christmas with my folks. You'll be alone for the holidays. I hate to think of you rambling around this big old house by yourself, especially for Christmas."

"It's not so big. I close off the extra bedrooms, then it feels warm and cozy. I'll be okay. Besides, you're such a worry wart."

Kara smiled at Sydney. "Won't you please reconsider going to the reunion and making an old friend happy?"

Sydney looked into Kara's eyes. "You're a delightful supporter, Kara." She hugged Kara, then stepped back and shuffled through the mail on the counter.

Kara walked back to the coat closet and grabbed Sydney's coat. "Let's go get you a Christmas tree. I'll stop by the house and pick-up a quiche I made this morning," Kara said. "We'll make a day of it. How does spinach, mushroom and bacon quiche sound?"

"You know it's my favorite. I'll take you up on the quiche,

but if I go to the reunion, I won't need a tree, now will I?"

Kara squealed and handed Sydney her shoes. "You mean it? You've considered going?"

"I'll think about it." Sydney slid the mail across the counter and made a face at Kara. "I'll seriously think about it. Okay?"

TWO

The sunset cast a glorious reddish-orange hue across a blanket of light snow, filtering through the trees and illuminating the view of The Granger Inn at the end of Main Street. The Inn was previously an old Victorian home the Grangers had sunk their life savings into and had refurbished a few years back.

Sydney rolled her car window down and breathed in frosty, clean air to clear her head. Despite her reservations about attending the reunion, she was here now, and for better or worse, she had no intention of turning back. Tonight was Christmas Eve, and she intended to mingle and enjoy the reunion.

Magnolias and azaleas lined the lengthy driveway, and they glowed with hundreds of tiny twinkling lights. Small, tasteful flowerbeds overflowed with multicolored seasonal plants and welcomed the guests for this weekend's holiday reunion.

Along the weathered porch, Christmas lights and decorations were strung that lit up the entire area, including the light snowfall on the ground. Several rocking chairs were arranged between tables prepared with checkers and chess games. Huge pots of vibrant red poinsettia decorated the porch and steps.

Inside the Inn, Christmas lights and decorations flooded and brightened the beautiful old home, lending warmth and a welcoming appearance. The scent of cinnamon hung heavy in the air, and that filled her spirits with delightful reminiscences of home with her mother and father. How she missed them. Christmas hadn't been the same since their deaths. Sydney swallowed back the sorrow and embraced the special times they'd shared inside her heart.

Sydney unpacked what little she'd brought with her, then

stretched out on the bed. She closed her eyes but couldn't manage to relax. She had time on her hands before Friday night's dinner, so she thought some exercise would benefit her body and mind. She followed a path down a short, slanted hill toward the lake, settled on a wooden bench, pulled her scarf snug around her neck, then slid off the lid from a cup of hot chocolate. Her breath floated in the cold winter air, then disappeared as a light gust of wind surrounded her. While she observed a squirrel scamper over the light dusting of snow that had fallen in the late afternoon, she smiled to herself and expected that he was still stockpiling enough food for the winter.

The sound of shoes crunched lightly over the snow, and prompted her to glance up to see who she'd be required to deal with. She'd wandered down the path for privacy and wasn't in the mood yet to engage with another attendee in empty conversation. In spite of her desire for time alone when she could manage it, it didn't look as though now was going to be one of those times.

As she turned around, her heart hammered at the sight of the man who stood before her. She inwardly groaned and experienced a flash of regret for attending the reunion this weekend. Tension gathered around her shoulders and neck. She had thought she was prepared, but suddenly realized she simply wasn't ready to greet the man who'd broken her heart. That knowledge cemented her to the cold bench, and a bitter breeze crawled under her coat collar.

She grabbed at her collar and pressed it to her skin. *Of all the luck.* Still, she'd known seeing him at the reunion was bound to happen. *Time to face the music.*

"Hi, Sydney. I thought I recognized you walking down here."

Even though he was only twenty-eight by now, streaks of gray had blended through his beard, around his temples and in his curly, black hair. She was reminded of that description "salt and pepper." The gray added a distinguished—"in his prime"—appearance. Despite a momentary struggle to hold back those old familiar feelings toward Cole, her heart fluttered. When she dared to look into his eyes, her breath caught.

This...not now...not now. *Please, God. Don't let me be caught in his clutches again.*

She wondered if he'd grown better looking than he'd been in high school. And he had.

Get a grip, Sydney. You've gotten over Cole. Right? She sighed at the realization. *Consciously or not, it would seem I'm not over you as much as I thought.*

She pasted on a smile while the notion of wishing the ground would open up and swallow her, flashed through her head. *Fat chance of that happening.*

Just when she'd made progress in dealing with Will's death and had slowly moved on, this new trouble showed up. Cole. Now she was certain she shouldn't have agreed to come to the Inn. Nothing like faking a smile, but she could do it. She did do it.

"Cole Meyers. What a surprise, but good to see you. How long has it been?"

Cole grinned that famous smile at her and when he did, smile lines crinkled around his eyes. "Maybe nine, ten years I think? I was eighteen, so it would've been 2006. Too long."

"It has been a long time."

He shuffled from one foot to the other. "Mind if I sit?"

"Not at all."

Liar. This...I do not need.

Sydney fleetingly wondered if he'd ever had second doubts about how innocent that hug and kiss on Ron's cheek was, and that he'd thrown away the future they might have had for no reason. "Not at all," she repeated and patted the bench. "How are you?"

"Good. You look well and haven't changed a bit. You're still as lovely as I remembered."

He's married and coming on to me? What's up with that?

"Thanks, Cole. I'm good." Her lips tightened at his intent, or what she perceived was his intent. "I've never been better."

Do I need to remind him he has a wife? Evidently so.

"I hope your wife enjoys the reunion. It's a bit hard sometimes for the spouses to have a pleasant time at these gatherings. You know, not much in common, not knowing anyone."

"Well..." Cole dragged in a deep breath and gazed at her. "I guess you haven't heard."

On alert, Sydney waited with bated breath for Cole to explain his comment. "I don't suppose I have. I have no inkling what you're talking about. Why don't you give me a hint?"

THREE

"As you probably heard, I married a few years back. My wife, Maria, started having health issues three years ago," Cole stated, then drew in a deep breath. "Things didn't go well."

"I hadn't heard. I'm so sorry. I hope she's better now."

"Sydney." Cole held up a hand and grimaced. "Let me finish, please. Maria passed away two and a half years ago, after her first diagnosis of breast cancer. Her health deteriorated from bad to worse in a matter of six months. After all the treatments she endured, her tests were looking a little more positive, but it didn't take long for them to find out the cancer had spread viciously. There was nothing...no other meds, the doctors and her team could use to prolong her life any longer. Once she learned the treatments might only lengthen her life from two to, at the most, four months, she opted not to suffer through chemotherapy again. She was already extremely weak and refused to put herself through more traumatic treatment since the outcome wasn't going to be positive. She lived only a month and a half after she discontinued treatment."

After a sobering moment, Sydney responded to his tragic news. "I can't begin to tell you how sorry I am."

Cole opened his mouth, but no words came out. He leaned back on the bench and simply shook his head.

"How horrible for both of you," she said, then glanced at him. "Are there children?"

"No. I'm not sure if that's a blessing or not. We wanted children pregnancies to full term. She miscarried around three months each time. The doctors told her she shouldn't try again, so we gave up on having children, a family."

Sydney bit her lip. She knew firsthand how hard losing a spouse was "Cole, I'm sorry. I know how tough this has been for you." She gently touched his hand and gave a little smile. "I know you miss her terribly. Death isn't easy to deal with."

"No it isn't...but I'm doing the best I can. Each day is a little bit better."

"I'm glad for you. I know it's hard without her."

"Yes it is."

She thought about that winter he'd walked out on her, which to her as a young girl was devastating, and how she'd had to live without him because of a misunderstanding. *What is wrong with me? His leaving was in the past and I've gotten over him. Haven't I?*

She shook off the memory and changed the subject. "So, tell me, Cole. What have you been up to these last few years?"

"After we moved from Raddwell, Maria and I bought a horse farm. She loved horses and I'd always wanted a farm. So it made sense to do something we both loved."

"So, you're a cowboy?"

Cole laughed and looked down at his denim jacket. "Not really. What we have, rather what I now have, is more a breeding farm."

"My grandfather used to raise horses. He's the one who taught me to ride, though I didn't learn as well as he'd have liked. I miss riding especially with him."

Cole had a wistful expression, but he quickly erased it as he brushed snow from his pant leg. "I miss riding with Maria, too."

Sydney hesitated, then offered to help. She might live to regret her decision, but Cole was a friend who'd let her down, but a friend all the same. "If there's anything I can do...you can call me at the shop. I took over the flower shop after Mom passed away."

"Thanks." He raised his head and looked at her, as though encouraged she still viewed him as more than someone who'd mistrusted her. "I think I remember the shop. Is it still on Main?"

"Yes. We're still in the same old shop. My friend Kara works with me. She'll always know how to reach me. So don't hesitate if you want to talk or whatever."

Cole held a sheepish look on his face. "That's kind of you, considering the way I handled our breakup."

After all this time, what she'd never expected to hear was an apology. But she felt he was about to offer one. "Cole...It wasn't a mutual breakup, you chose to end our ties with each other." She smiled sadly. "A breakup two days before Christmas is a young girl's nightmare. But...what's done is done."

"No, Sydney. I was wrong. Completely wrong. It's a little late for admission of guilt, but please accept my apology. My apology's a bit lame, but the only excuse I have is that when you're young, you don't think straight. I should have understood that you were simply being a friend to Ron. I was crazy in love with you, Sydney. Jealousy made my decision and for that, I'm sorry." A far-away look closed over his expression. "That decision changed the course of both our lives."

"Yes it did, but let's leave our mistakes in the past." After so many years, Sydney now held no resentment toward the young boy who'd made an unfortunate decision. She'd long given up on a relationship with Cole. "I forgave you a long time ago, Cole. You broke my heart, but a lot of time has passed since. We've both carried on with our lives and now, it would seem, we're back where we started...except we're not together. We're a little wiser, a little sadder, and we have both learned to live with loss."

They sat quietly for a minute, each reflecting on their own thoughts.

"My husband, Will, passed away last year."

"I heard about your husband's accident. I'm sorry. I understand what you've been, and are still going, through."

So he's been keeping tabs on me?

"I loved him. If you and I hadn't broken up I'd never have found him. Neither would you have found Maria. There are things we have to be thankful for. Sad, but we don't have a reasonable explanation as to why things happen the way they do."

Sydney spoke for a short time of her husband but withheld personal details. Cole had no reason to know them and she certainly had no desire to share.

Cole glanced at his watch, then stood and held out his hand. "It's dinner time. Shall we?"

Sydney paused. *What have I gotten myself into?* She got up from the bench and stood beside Cole, but she didn't take his hand. Surely, hand-holding was too personal It was too soon, maybe not even possible, to strike up any kind of relationship with him. He hadn't asked or suggested any such advance, though she was still good at reading between the lines. After all, he'd probably seen her name on the check-in sheet and sought her out this afternoon. She knew in her heart, and she felt it in her bones, that he wanted more than she was capable of giving, or even comprehending.

So, why did I come to the reunion? I knew Cole would most likely be here. Did I secretly want to run into him? Do I want more? Do I want the same as what Cole's actions imply?

Not going to happen. Her stomach did a flip-flop. Unsure if the uneasy feeling was from strain or hunger, Sydney gazed up the lighted path that led to the Inn.

"Sure. All of a sudden I'm starving."

Four

The decision to dine with Cole probably wasn't the ideal move, though now wasn't the time to be rude. It was Christmas Holidays after all. Dinner would give them a chance to catch up on what had been happening in their lives over the past few years.

Both their partners were gone now, and Cole had no reason to remain as determined or as aggressive at ending a fresh relationship, if there was to be one, as he had years ago. In fact, he gave the impression, that mending their friendship would be the right thing to do. However, there wasn't a true relationship now, and there might not ever be again. Broken trust was a hard thing to forget. Forgive, yes...but forget, no.

At least now, or so he had said, Cole realized his error at ending what might have been their future together. Since she had forgiven him, this Christmas might be a little more bearable for the both of them, now that they were face to face. They could lay aside old hurts and maybe even become friends again. *Nothing more.*

She hoped Cole was trustworthy now...he'd had plenty of time to work on that trait. She'd changed too.

Sydney found the tension from earlier on, even after seeing Cole again, had begun to subside. She concentrated on the carols that played softly in the background and filled the house with Christmas warmth. It was time to start enjoying the holiday and seeing old friends at the reunion.

By the time they reached the Inn, snow had begun a soft downward spiral, and in the moonlight, the snowflakes resembled dancing stars falling onto what appeared to be a magnificent carved fountain in the distance. Sydney couldn't remember ever seeing a fountain this large with workmanship this fine.

Sydney paused, but didn't resist when Cole placed his

hand on her lower back, as they made their way down the corridor that led to the dining room. They were seated by a window for a perfect view of the gentle fall of snow layering the immaculate grounds. The room filled with conversation and laughter as old friends met and greeted each other.

Across the table from her, Sydney assessed Cole as a matured man with a saddened demeanor. That was understandable. The woman he'd loved was now gone. That she had to remember and take into consideration. Her heart went out to him. Death was all-consuming, and she wondered how he was really faring. How he really felt. As many widowers have a tendency to do, he undoubtedly kept his deepest frame of mind locked inside.

The waiter removed their dinner plates and exchanged them with dessert—cheesecake with strawberries and a steaming mug of coffee.

Sydney tasted the cheesecake, then savored another bite. "Delectable. Undeniably, delectable," she said, then lifted her gaze upward. If there was one dessert on earth that made her roll her eyes, it was cheesecake.

He cut into his half-eaten dessert. "I agree. I've never had better cheesecake." Cole pointed to her plate. "I see you still fancy dessert," he said, and then grinned.

She trailed a single strawberry through the sauce and stared at him. "Funny you should remember that about me. It's such a minor thing."

Cole's eyes twinkled when he looked over at her. "How could I not remember? All you ever ordered, besides a hamburger and fries, was dessert, every single time. Dessert was never a minor matter for you." Somber and thoughtful, he reached to touch her hand, then pulled back. "Besides, there isn't anything I don't remember about you."

Sydney wondered if he really did, or was simply making conversation. She'd not forgotten much about him either, but she wouldn't admit it to him. She'd always admired how he'd protected her, how he'd encouraged her in whatever she attempted. She shook off the images that popped into her head. *Now isn't the time to get sentimental. He's been way too jealous on the past.*

"So, have you kept up with me for some strange reason?"

Cole grinned. "How do you know I've kept up with you?"

She looked up from the cheesecake's empty plate. "Well, one detail is you mentioned that you knew my husband had passed away."

"Mack Preston still lives here in town and we stay in touch. He's the one who told me about you losing your husband," Cole said, then frowned. "It isn't as though I've stalked you."

"I wouldn't appreciate being stalked," Sydney replied, and pushed back her plate. "I remember Mack. Always the jokester, if I remember correctly."

"That he was and still is."

"Mack ordered flowers from my shop for his wife a few weeks ago. They celebrated their third child. The second boy for them, I believe."

"Mack's a good man and proud of his family," Cole stated.

Sydney leaned back in her chair and gazed around the room. Her glance fell on the couple at the next table. Bent forward, the two were immersed in an intense conversation. Sydney leaned closer when she overheard them talking about a steady stream of hauntings at the Inn.

Surprised, Sydney caught Cole's eye. "I've lived here all my life and never, ever heard the story of a haunting here. What about you? Know anything about this place being haunted?" she whispered.

"Can't say I have. I've not heard, but most of the people here, even if they believed it, would avoid a discussion of ghosts." He chuckled. "They wouldn't want anyone believing they had gone off the deep end, you know?"

Sydney thought about what he'd said and laughed, but then quickly disagreed. "I'll bet there are older members in town that will talk about it. There are those who would like nothing better than to repeat tales, especially ghost tales. You know that. It's such an interesting topic for them to share with anyone who'd listen."

Cole's eyes flickered while he moved his eyebrows up and down. "If you're that interested, perhaps we can find someone to interrogate."

"So now you're making fun of me?"

"Oh, no. Not at all. I'm teasing you."

"Okay, I forgot how much you used to like to tease me." She made a face at him, then smiled.

Cole smiled back and gazed into her eyes, lying his fork on the side of his plate. "You should do that more often."

"What?"

"Smile," he commented, then started to place his hand over hers again, but drew back. "I've missed you and your infectious smile. You're more beautiful than ever when you smile."

Sydney's memory evoked shared smiles and kisses that came rushing back, as her heart gave a short flutter. "Thank you."

She had missed him too, but conceded he'd destroyed those dreams long ago on a cold Friday night at the football game. Two days before Christmas was no time to breakup. There was no reason to bring up the past again, best to let the past remain in the past. She'd moved on and left Cole behind. *Haven't I? Besides, Will was the perfect husband. I have to bear that in mind.*

Still...here Cole was stirring up old memories. If their meeting again turned out badly, it would be her own fault. She could have stayed home this weekend instead of attending the reunion.

"What do you say we go and mingle with the others?"

Sydney thought about the couple's conversation tonight. What if the Inn really was haunted? "No. It's still early. Let's walk to the library down the hallway. Maybe there's a book on the Inn's history. All we have to do is find it. Are you game?"

"Uh, oh. I see that gleam in your eyes. Sure you want to do this?"

"Come on. Has your adventurous edge gone astray?"

Cole laid his napkin on the table and pushed back his chair. "It's a long shot, but well...I suppose a little research won't hurt."

"I'm curious. You must remember that about me," Sydney said, then giggled. She couldn't remember the last time she'd been this excited. Who would have thought a ghost story would be what made her pulse increase?

"Okay. Let's head to the library. If all else fails, we can grab a good book to lull us to sleep tonight."

Sydney laughed again. "If a book is really good, it would keep us up until the wee hours of the morning, not put us to sleep."

FIVE

The library's door creaked open as Cole drew it wide and threw an arm toward the door opening. "After you."

Sydney walked into the library ahead of Cole, anxious to get started searching the shelves of books.

The first thing they saw was an enormous Christmas tree, with what seemed like a million fireflies, the angel tree topper almost touching the ceiling. Sydney gazed at the massive library filled with shelves and shelves of books. It was a reader's dream. In addition to the aroma of cinnamon throughout the building, she now breathed deeply that familiar leathery, scent of vintage books. Reflections of the tree lights twinkled across the covers and titles, almost bringing them to life. She could barely wait to dig into the rows of books lined up tightly beside one another.

"Oh, my." She recalled the couple's conversation at dinner, darted her eyes around the room in anticipation, then lowered her voice. "What if...what if a ghost is in here protecting the book, the mystery surrounding this place?"

"Nah. Won't happen." Cole's laughter echoed through the room. "Your imagination is working overtime."

"You don't know any such thing," Sydney giggled and wriggled her fingers. "Maybe we're about to stumble onto a sensational discovery."

"We hope not to waste our time, but I doubt it," Cole said. "The prospect of finding a book on the Inn's family background is slight."

Sydney flipped back her hair and ignored his comment. "Nevertheless, let's get started. There are tons of books to go through."

After a couple of hours, Cole ran a hand through his hair, then shoved a book back in place, leaving it out just enough to mark his stopping point. "We're getting nowhere. We may as well give up. If a diary or a book on the Inn's history exists, it's most likely not here."

"Please. Let's explore a little longer. Okay?"

"Fine, but I'm feeling a little uncomfortable."

"I'm the one who's supposed to get an uncomfortable feeling." Sydney smiled, turned a book over in her hands, then slid it lengthwise back in place. "I wish we could find something. Anything."

Cole leaned against the bookshelves, then whispered loudly. "You may get your wish." He drew in a deep breath, then dropped his voice another octave. "Lord! I think...I think I see a female ghost," he threw his arm toward the ceiling. "In the corner—look."

Irritated that Cole would pull her leg at a time like this, she refused to believe him. "Stop it. Just stop it, now. This is no joking matter. Frankly, I think you're trying to get me out of here. If that's what you want, simply say so."

"You're absolutely right, I do want you out of here. Especially now."

Sydney pointed to the stretch of shelves they hadn't searched through. "These still need going through. Come on, help me out."

"No really. I do see something. I swear. It's a shadow of a lady wearing a flowing lavender gown. Oh, wow!" he whispered. "You aren't going to believe this. Now there's a haze surrounding her. You must look, Sydney. Look. Now!" At her continued refusal to consider he was being serious, he caught her by the arm and urged her to turn around.

Sydney wasn't about to be taken in, but to appease him, she followed where his gaze ended. *Is it the lighting or is there really something there?* A flimsy section of lavender and a light haze swam before her eyes, then disappeared. She did a double take. The haze had faded as quickly as the mid-morning sun breathes upon a mist and makes it vanish. She passed it off to her overactive imagination until an icy trickle of fear shot down her spine.

Still...She thought maybe, just maybe only Cole was allowed to see its entirety. "Do...do you still see it?" she asked.

Cole shut his eyes, then opened them wide and shook his head. "No. Not now. It's…she's gone. Let's get out of here. I'm not into indulging a ghost."

Sydney pushed aside the fear that had pressed at her a second ago. "No. I'm not leaving. We're still doing a search for a diary or a book on the Inn's history. She's not going to hurt us."

Cole repeated Sydney's words. "She's not going to hurt us? And how do you know that?"

"If she intended harm, we'd already be toast," Sydney said, and laughed. "Besides, I don't sense any bad vibes from her. I'm staying. If you'd like to leave, please do."

Cole shook his head. "I'll stay here with you. I'd rather find something else to do, but I'm fine. If you get scared or change your mind, all you have to do is say so. I'll be more than happy to leave."

"That won't happen." She pointed to the corner where the alleged ghost had floated. "You take that end of the book shelves and I'll take the other side. We'll meet in the middle."

Sydney had forgotten how many generations the house had passed through, then she remembered Mrs. Wyatt had passed away after owning the Inn for only three years. Maybe one other owner before her?

"Cole. Wasn't the Victorian home owned by the Roddwell family before Mrs. Wyatt, then the Grangers, bought it?"

Cole stared into the distance for a moment. "I believe you're right. I'd almost forgotten. The home was in the Roddwell family for years, but exchanged hands once, maybe twice, before the Grangers." He hesitated. "I think the Roddwell's niece, who inherited the place sold it to a family out of New York, but they put the place up for sale a few months later. They moved out before the place was sold. That's when Mrs. Wyatt took over before the Grangers. Why?"

"Maybe there are items from the house that didn't get passed down," Sydney suggested.

"Yeah. That's a possibility."

Two hours later they were about three quarters of the way through. They had stopped for a quick cup of tea, when they heard a commotion in the hallway.

A young man, maybe in his late twenties, caught Cole by the arm. "Hey, man. Follow us. The party is underway."

"Really? Is it that time?" Cole asked, and pulled his arm from the man's grasp.

"Sorry, man. Did you forget?" the man asked.

"We were occupied in the library," Sydney stated.

The young man raised his eyebrows at Sydney, then winked. "I'll bet you were," he said, with a knowing look spreading across his face.

"Look, friend. I don't appreciate you talking to the lady in that manner." Cole dropped a hand on Sydney's shoulder and pulled her close. "I'll ask you once. Please apologize to the lady."

The young man bristled and gave the impression that he would decline until he caught the frosty stare from Cole. "Okay, Okay. I apologize, lady. Geez. I didn't mean anything by it."

"Sure you did. But thank you...I accept," Sydney said, then fixed a look on him that said, don't do it again.

The young man stared her down, then sauntered down the hall toward the sound of laughter, music and the party.

"Enjoy your party," Cole said, then swung around to guide Sydney down the hall and into the common area for tea.

"You aren't going to the party?" Sydney asked.

"If you'd like to go, I'm game. But...your little buddy will be there."

"It'll be okay. I think you took care of him." Sydney had caught the look on the young man's face and laughed. "I don't believe he'll bother us again."

"What's so dang funny?"

"You haven't changed a bit...always up for being the hero."

"Always for you." He grinned and took her hand, and this time she didn't resist. Resting her hand in his felt good. It felt right. Hand-holding was as far as this night would go though. Period.

Even though she knew somewhere down the line she'd yearn for love and companionship again in the future, there was no time in her life for men right now. Her heart wasn't quite ready to forget her deceased husband, Will. Yet.

Even with Cole. Maybe...especially with Cole and their history. Still, she understood Cole so well, at least she used to, and wondered what was really on his mind.

As if I don't know. Pangs of guilt knotted inside her throat. *Do I really want to know?*

Six

From the speakers, Brenda Lee's strong voice belted out Rocking Around the Christmas Tree when they arrived at the party. Cole suggested they dance, but Sydney begged off. "Find me a water and let's chat."

Being that close to Cole might be dangerous.

Cole came back with a water for Sydney and a soft drink for himself. "Tell me what you've been doing these past few years. I want to know everything."

"You really don't want to know everything," she replied. "Mostly I stay busy. When the flower shop isn't taking up most of my time, I take a few classes at the local college. When time allows, I volunteer at the school and hospital. Then there's the visits at the spa three nights a week and tutoring the boy next door in math twice a week. Other than that, I'm a homebody. Cooking is fun and I love to bake. You know, cookies and cakes for the school sales."

"It sounds like you have a full plate. I'm impressed."

"I haven't traveled as much as I'd like, but hopefully the future will change that."

"Me too." Cole reached for his soda can and when he did, their little buddy from earlier in the evening, plopped down beside him.

Bloodshot, glazed-over eyes, met Cole's frosty stare.

"Mind if I dance with the little lady?" the young man asked.

Cole took in the man's drunken state and darted his eyes toward Sydney. "The decision isn't mine. I believe you'll need to ask the little lady yourself."

The young man scrutinized Cole, then turned toward Sydney. "Well, what do you say? How about that dance, little lady?"

You do have your nerve, young man. "Maybe another time, but thanks," Sydney responded, then turned away and back toward Cole.

"What's the matter? Aren't I good enough for you?"

"Young man." Cole stood and kicked back his chair. "The lady gave you her answer. Take it for what it's worth and leave well enough alone."

"Who do you think you are? What do you intend to do if I don't?" the young man spat out.

"Look." Cole exhaled and shook his head. "We aren't here looking for trouble. Let it go and get back to your party."

The young man squinted. "What if I don't?"

Cole's steely eyes bore into the young man's ugly glare. "Take my word for it. You'll deal with me. I suggest you think this over and forget you ever met us." Cole took Sydney by the hand and moved toward the door.

"Hey," the young man called after them. "We aren't done here. You can't leave."

Sydney had had enough of the young man's insolence. "Consider your position, and don't misunderstand what I'm about to say to you. Pay attention. We. Are. Done. And yes, we are leaving. I suggest you find another interest."

About that time the owner's husband came to referee. "Come with me, young man. You need to sleep it off. You'll feel better in the morning. Tomorrow's going to be filled with entertainment and we'd like it to be a pleasant experience for everyone involved. Including you."

The owner's husband turned toward Cole and Sydney. "I do apologize. This young man works for us and has had way too much to drink." He gave the young man a stern glance. "Apologize to the folks if you want to keep your job."

The young man sulked, but took the older man at his word. "Fine. I'm sorry. It won't happen again."

Sydney nodded and sighed an inward moan. The day had started off fairly well but had grown progressively worse. She wasn't going to let the incident dampen the mood of her first Christmas holiday with Cole in ten years. Surprised, she realized they were fast becoming friends once again.

The Christmas season was supposed to be all about love.

Not necessarily love between Cole and herself, but love all the same.

SEVEN

Two groups of singers sang Christmas carols, while the remaining guests gathered around the fire pit drinking hot chocolate or coffee. The tree lighting ceremony would begin soon. Cole had brought a blanket for her, and she'd decided to share it with him.

Sparkling snowflakes curled down and around Sydney's head. She caught a couple on her tongue and giggled. It'd been forever since she'd done that. Memories of making snow angels with her mom and dad added a measure of sorrow that enveloped her.

"Care to share your thoughts?" Cole asked.

Sydney cast a glance at him and sighed. "I'm thinking of my parents and how much I miss them. Christmas was everything it should be with the two of them. We never lacked any of the special magic or splendor for the season. They did it all."

"My parents did too. I remember many good times with your parents, also. This is a sad season for the both of us...for more than one reason. Both of us have lost our parents and our spouses."

Sydney had the urge to put her arm around his waist, in comfort, and lay her head on his chest, but thought better of it. *Not a smart move.*

The holidays hit her hard, especially Christmas. That old heavy suffering weighed her down. "Yes, it's sad. I miss my husband, Will, and my parents."

Solemn, Cole admitted, "I miss Maria too."

"Christmas isn't the same anymore. It never will be, but we have to go on. Make the most of it. Where do you normally spend the holidays?" Sydney asked.

"Home. I tend to avoid gatherings. I'm simply not into Christmas these days."

"Since your wife passed away you mean?"

"Yes. And…since I don't have children, I didn't see the point."

"This year we'll celebrate together. Between the two of us, we should be able to find some semblance of normalcy. You know your Maria would want you to be happy, not sad. I also know Will would want that, too. Though I admit, I've not been a hundred percent successful at living a normal life since his death and haven't given much thought to getting on with life until the last few weeks. Nor have you since you lost Maria. Life just isn't normal now. Not with the losses we've faced."

"I suppose she wouldn't want me to be so unhappy. She was a good woman, in every way." He cut a peek toward Sydney. "I hope you aren't offended by my talking about Maria."

"Not at all. I understand. I've talked about Will also. It helps me to talk about the loved ones I've lost," Sydney replied. "Not everyone wants to talk of their loss. For others it does help. You know what's also sad? None of my friends bring up Will's death. They avoid it at all costs. Even if I talk about him, they change the subject. They're afraid they'll upset me, I guess."

"I get that too," Cole said. "It's like we have a disease or something…and that's depressing in itself."

"On a lighter note," Sydney said, inwardly smiled and touched Cole's arm. "I think the kids enjoyed their party this afternoon, and unwrapping gifts from their families. It was thoughtful of Mrs. Granger to allow time for the children, and the parents. This reunion wouldn't be a success if they'd had to miss out on their special Christmas occasion. I understand she also wrapped gifts for each child and left them under the tree."

"Did she, now?" Cole laid a gloved hand on Sydney's and nodded. "That's very commendable. She's a nice lady."

About that time the Grangers appeared at the temporary platform located in the middle of the garden, and officially greeted their guests who'd gathered for the festivities. The Christmas carolers returned with a few more songs and invited the group to join in. It was the time for joy, for unity.

They lit candles for the ones who'd passed away and shared a moment of silence in their loved one's memory. The moment was subdued and positive at the same time. Sydney wondered how many others were in the same circumstances she and Cole were. Quite a few, she imagined.

When the carolers finished singing, it was time to light the tree.

"Can you see good enough?" Cole asked.

"Certainly," she said, then giggled. "It looks to be about a twenty-five or thirty foot tree. If I couldn't see anything else, I'd be able to see the top."

Everyone began counting down from ten to one. At the count of one, the entire area lit up in a burst of color and dazzling effects. Cheers went up from the children and parents alike, drowning out the music that played through outdoor speakers. Hundreds and hundreds of twinkling lights sparkled in every hue imaginable. Sydney loved the blue, green and white combination that lit up their surroundings.

"Oh, this is exciting," Sydney said, and clapped her hands. "Such a beautiful huge, full tree, and even though it's snowing, maybe because of the snow, we have a fabulous night for the tree lighting."

The instant she spoke, the light wisps of snow changed to big fluffy snowflakes that began to fall gracefully from the sky. Sydney gazed up at the tree and into the stars, then released a whisper. "Oh, these huge snowflakes are one of the most beautiful sights ever!"

Cole leaned close, gazed into her light green eyes, and brushed a strand of auburn hair back inside her hat. "Not as beautiful as you," he murmured.

Uh, oh.

"Cole, what are you doing? You're moving too fast for me." She took her hands out of her pockets and hastily set out to find another hot chocolate and a cookie.

Food. Food will help me forget the way he was, the way things were between us, the way he acts like he wants things to be again.

Cole followed her, took the cup from her, then slid napkins under and around their cups. "I know what I want, Sydney."

"So now you want me...you want to pursue me?" Sydney was floored by the depths of his audacity. "Don't you think it's a bit too soon to become so familiar again?"

"Familiar? Of course not. We're both single. It isn't as though we've just met. We've known each other for years. We have a past, memories. More good than bad."

"I believe we've lost a few years. We may have known each other back then, but we've both grown and changed. Agreed?"

Cole rubbed a hand down his thick beard until the tips of his fingers met at the bottom. "Agreed, but...I've never forgotten my love for you. Never." He handed her the hot chocolate and led them to a bench at the edge of the garden.

"Cole...I..." She hesitated. "I'm not so sure I'm open to beginning again. We may not feel the same, not want the same things now. What then?"

"Then let's discuss what we want, Sydney."

EIGHT

A few steps ahead, Sydney led the way back down the path to the lake, Cole immediately behind. "Please don't take this wrong, Cole. I'm not accustomed to being pressed. No matter who's doing the pressing. We've enjoyed each other's company today and since I'll admit to having missed you, I'd like to continue to stay in touch from time to time. Still, neither of us can plan a future based on what we shared back in high school. Times have changed, and as I said, we've both changed. I honestly don't know if we could pick up where we left off. Even if I decided I wanted to, which hadn't entered my mind until you brought it up, all this is coming at me so fast it's still very confusing to me right now."

Though it pained her to admit, Sydney knew, deep down, she'd made the choice to come to the reunion in hopes of Cole possibly being here. In more ways than one, the decision had been a mistake. Or was it? She hated being confused, indecisive.

"Exactly. My feelings for you haven't changed though." Cole dusted off a section of snow from the bench, then waited for her to sit. "You may think it's because I'm lonely or needy. That's not it. I'm neither. Okay, maybe I am lonely sometimes, but that's natural after losing someone you loved. Seeing you again brought back the happy times we shared, and I simply thought we might pick up where we left off."

"We could never pick up where we left off. I suppose we could try, but it's impossible to erase ten years. Right now I can't see that happening." She sipped her cocoa and sighed. "Life throws out diverse options, then we make our decisions."

"I realize it will take time. Is it possible you could at least think about working with me? Consider to agree to begin again?"

"Maybe I'll think it through. For something I didn't see

coming, it's as though a pot started to simmer earlier this morning, and tonight the pot is boiling!" Sydney laughed.

Sydney could tell by the look on Cole's face he'd taken offense to the laugher. "I'm sorry. I wasn't making fun of you."

But then he grinned. "So you see humor in my feelings for you, do you?"

"Hey, I said I was sorry. Drink your chocolate, we have work to do."

"And what might that be?" Seemingly, Cole's expression went blank.

"Come on. You know very well what I mean. We still have the rest of the library books to search."

"Well then," he said, crumpled his cup, threw it into a waste can and lightly grabbed her by the hand. "Let's be off."

"I see the Christmas tree lights are still on. A good thing since the lamps are softly lit. Bright lights will make for a speedier search for the diary or book."

After roughly thirty minutes, Sydney slumped into a chair. She looked at her watch. "Twelve o'clock. I'm not so sure we're going to find what we're looking for. Maybe we've wasted hours searching for a piece of history that isn't here."

"This time we spent together was special. I don't call that wasted," Cole said.

"You very well know what I mean." She reached for another book, then the tree lights flickered off. "The lights are probably on a timer. We can continue tomorrow if you want to join me," she said. "I think it's too dark to make out titles."

"The decision is yours. I'm not the one researching ghosts," he said.

"But you wouldn't mind if we did, now would you?" Sydney threw a knowing glance at Cole. "Especially since we saw that apparition earlier. That has to make you suspicious or at least fascinated by the manifestation we both observed."

"I'm becoming more fascinated by the minute," he replied. "Especially since we actually saw the lady in the lavender gown. I admit seeing a ghost was spooky, but interesting."

"Yes it certainly was." Sydney slid the book back on the shelf, then turned to Cole. "You saw the entire gown on the lady, I only saw a portion, and it jangled my nerves."

"You know what really alarms me?" Cole asked.

"No. What?"

"I swear I had the shakiest feeling that it was my wife, Maria."

Sydney's pallor changed in an instant. "Come on. She's heavy on your mind this time of year. That isn't possible." She swallowed back a shudder of fear. "Is it?"

"Your guess is as good as mine." He shook his head and rubbed at his beard. "Let me try something." He clicked the lamps and they brightened the room. "There. We should have thought of checking the lamps earlier. Are you up to finishing up here tonight?"

"Sure. There aren't that many more books to go through." Sydney rose from the chair and faced Cole. "Shall we begin again?"

"Okay. You know, Mrs. Granger could shed some light on either a diary or a book on the house. I can't wait to talk to her. You have my curiosity spiked now."

Sydney winked at him. "We'll try to catch her in between responsibilities tomorrow. I understand she's pretty open about sharing information. Maybe she'll be receptive about sharing history on the house and the gossip that it's haunted. We can also try to talk to the couple from dinner last night. They could have valuable evidence...or not."

"Fine." Cole looked around the room, then ran his hands up and down his arms. "Did you feel that breeze?"

"No. I didn't feel a thing. Let's get started so we can get out of here."

Cole shivered. "The heat must have gone out. It's getting a bit chilly in here."

NINE

"Where did you leave your jacket?" Sydney asked. "Do you want to get it?"

"I don't need a jacket. I'm good. It's just that every once in a while I walk through a cool section of air. No big deal. Old houses don't have good heating systems." He glanced around. "Weird though, the way it only rushes in once in a while."

"True. These old homes have hot and cold spots, or so I've heard," Sydney said, and slid another book back on the shelf. "We shouldn't be too much longer."

"Well, I'm glad you have your coat."

They searched a little over an hour without finding anything more than when they began.

"I'm so disappointed," Sydney declared, and frowned. "I just knew we'd find something. Anything. But there isn't any history here at all on the house."

Unsmiling, Cole stared at her. "What would you do if you found an indication of ghostly hauntings anyway?"

Sydney scrunched her face. "I have no idea. I'm simply intrigued."

"Me too, but the search is over for now. At least for the night." Cole stretched, then yawned and threw an arm around Sydney's shoulder. "This has been quite a day. We may as well go to our rooms and try to get some sleep."

His touch felt warm and good, and as a result, she didn't shrug him away. Halfway to the door, she paused. "Do you think we dare to check the desk?"

"That would be criminal, Sydney. We can't possibly search a private desk, the Granger's desk. This is their home, for heaven's sake."

"Oh come on, Cole. It isn't like we're here to steal anything. We'll simply look for a book or a diary, then we leave. Simple as that."

Sydney moved toward the desk as she wrenched her head

sideways at him. "Ten steps, that's all it will take."

"Okay, but I don't approve of going through someone's desk." Cole directed a serious glare toward her.

"That's not what I had planned." They both glanced around the desktop, Sydney bit her bottom lip and muttered her thoughts aloud. "You know...if there was a book or diary, it wouldn't be in plain sight," Sydney offered.

"Oh, no. Don't even think of it. We're not going through the desk drawers. Come with me, we are leaving now. I can't, in good conscience, let you put yourself at risk of getting arrested."

Sydney's jaw clenched. "Oh, all right. Of course you're spot-on. This isn't being a good and honest guest," Sydney admitted. She slapped her hand on top of the desk, then trailed her fingers along the back edge of the desk as they moved toward the door.

On the way out Sydney straightened a couple of books, then sighed. "Maybe tomorrow will be more productive."

"If you're lucky."

"Wait! This wasn't here before. Come over here, Cole."

"Just when I thought we were out of here. What did you find now?"

"This section of the wall simply opened up. But how? I must have touched something while we were at the desk," she said, her voice filled with excitement.

"You think?"

"I want to push that door open so badly, I can hardly stand it." Sydney held her hand over her heart.

"Look, I've checked through hundreds of books today. I'm sure Mr. and Mrs. Granger didn't mind. But this...this is too much. I'm not creeping into a sealed off room in a stranger's home. You do what you want, but leave me out of this shenanigan. Please, Sydney, let it go."

"How can you say that, when we've come across a secret door? I'm not so bad. Mrs. Granger may allow us inside tomorrow," Sydney muttered, with a frown.

Cole crossed his arms and stood back a step or two. "Wait until she finds out we were at her desk...if that's what happened to open the door."

"I'm not sure how it opened, but I'm afraid to try to shut the door. I only hope she doesn't call the police. Oh, Lord. Wouldn't that be a fine mess?"

"I'm not here to tell you what to do, but I think it would be a smart move to leave. Now. This innocent search is getting out of hand."

"Okay, we will. Just one little peek." Sydney pushed on the door and it creaked open about six inches.

"Be careful." Cole's voice tightened while he held onto her arm. "What do you see? Anything?"

"Turn loose of my arm, Cole. I'm not going inside. I only wanted to see if there was anything of interest."

Cole loosened his hold on her arm, but stood close enough that she felt his breath on the back of her neck.

"It's so dark inside it's hard to see anything," Sydney whispered.

A cool breeze brushed by her face and she swiped a scattering of dust away. "Cold inside. Any second now, my eyes should adjust to the darkness. Yes! Now I can barely make out bookshelves, several of them, and some boxes. Wow!"

"I hear someone coming down the hall. Quick, pull the door to and back away."

"Dang. Not enough time to see much." Sydney let out a ragged breath, and pulled the door to.

"Hey. What are you doing in there?"

They'd been caught. Now what?

TEN

Cole quickly yanked a book from the closest shelf and pushed open the door. There stood the drunken young man from earlier in the evening. Cole held up the book and shrugged. "Can't sleep in strange places without lulling myself to sleep with a book."

"What's it about? You know the book?" The young man asked.

Cole squinted his eyes and gazed sideways to make out the title. "The Art of Making Sweet Breads. By the way, I thought you'd gone to bed to sleep off your stupor."

"Not much substance for late night reading," the young man said, then laughed. "For your information, it takes little sleep for me."

"Anything to read helps make me sleepy." Cole commented, and pulled the book to his side. "We'll see you in the morning at breakfast."

"You got it, man," he said, and strolled back down the hall.

Before they could leave the room, a cool breeze closed the door for them.

Cole jerked his head around and glanced at Sydney. "What the..."

Floating close to the ceiling was the same lavender gown they'd seen previously.

Sydney lurched toward Cole, took his arm and swallowed hard. She tried to absorb what they were seeing. "Cole. What do you think she wants? Why are we seeing her?" she asked, her voice trembling.

"I have no idea, but this is twice so it must mean something. Maybe she's trying to tell us something. But how will she do that?"

"I'm at a loss," Sydney said, and moved against Cole, enough to feel the warmth from his body. "And...I'm beginning to feel alarmed. I wish now I'd left well enough alone."

Cole turned and wrapped an arm around her shoulders. "Aww...Come here. There's no need to be frightened. I feel no fear from the apparition. Don't ask me why, I simply don't."

"Then why am I frightened?"

"Probably because you're allowing the anxiety of something you've never seen to take over. I imagine if this thing intended harm, we'd feel it. We'd be running out of here...fast."

"But I *do* have a weird sensation," Sydney said, then shivered. "I *do* want to run out of here, but we can't get the door open! What's that all about?"

"Take my word for it. Again, if whoever this ghost is meant harm, we'd already know."

The door to the library whooshed open wide.

Both of them looked at the other, amazement clouding their faces.

"Time to go while we have the chance." Cole hugged her, then guided her to the door. "Everything is okay. Let's see if we can find a cup of tea before heading to our rooms."

Sydney shivered. "Fine by me. Some normalcy will be a good thing. I'm not so sure about sleeping tonight though."

They looked back, both at the same time. The lavender gown began to disappear, as it jetted like a streak of lightening inside the secret door. Then the door slammed shut.

It was all Sydney could do not to take off in hot pursuit of her car and head toward the safety of home.

Cole set a steaming cup of tea in front of her and inched the sugar bowl toward her. "Are you hungry? I can make you some toast."

"Uh, no. I wouldn't be able to get a bite down. I'm praying the tea will stay down and settle my stomach."

"If I remember correctly, you're stronger and braver than this. I always admired you for those traits. You're going to be okay. You have me to protect you, so you needn't concern yourself. Even from a ghost."

"You always did," Sydney said, then smiled across the

table and winked at him.

If only you'd have trusted me more. But that wasn't the way life pushed the cart. It's always been 'Don't put the cart before the horse'. Whatever that means.

ELEVEN

At breakfast the next morning, Sydney leaned over and snagged a piece of Cole's bacon. "You don't mind, do you?" she laughed as he raised an eyebrow and playfully wrapped an arm around his plate.

"No, but if you'd like more, tell me and I'll call the waiter. You don't really need to steal mine." He grinned at her. "Could I get you more coffee?"

"The more caffeine this morning, the better." She pushed her coffee cup forward. *Are you always this nice or are your actions and words for effect?*

Cole poured steaming coffee from the carafe. "Say when."

Sydney held up a hand. "For whatever reason you're acting like a gentleman, it's working," she said, and stirred cream into her coffee while she smiled. "So far."

"I couldn't be happier." He tugged on his beard. "I thought I'd always been a gentleman. Well, except for that one time at the ballgame."

"I may or may not agree with you, but I'll leave comments on that later. The verdict is under consideration."

"Please be gentle," he said, then chuckled.

"By the way, I called Mrs. Granger early this morning. I explained we'd searched through her library a while last night for a diary or a book on The Granger Inn's history. She admitted she'd heard there was a diary somewhere in the house. When they first moved here, they organized a thorough inspection of the house, but that had produced nothing in the way of a diary or anything related to its history."

"Did you ask if she'd heard rumors that the Inn was haunted?"

"Yes. Yes I did. At first she kind of hesitated, then a short, light giggle came across the phone, and she admitted she'd heard rumors. The original owners were the Raddwell's, who had the house built in the late 1800's. Being handed down to so many relatives over time could have been the reason for a loss of information. Not everyone keeps good records, no matter how people believe they did back then. Then there was Mrs. Wyatt who purchased the house from the Raddwells. Who knows what she could've found in the house?" Sydney shrugged and took the last sip of coffee. "Who knows what she may have hidden away, or worse, destroyed."

"Let's hope none of the house's history has been done away with. That would be a shame. Did Mrs. Granger give you a time she could meet with us?"

Sydney nodded. "She's expecting us in her office after breakfast."

"Before we begin, there's some information you should be aware of." Sydney took a deep breath and glanced at Cole for support.

"Go ahead, Sydney. What we did...well, she has a right to know."

Mrs. Granger looked from one to the other, her gaze and expectation suspicious.

"Okay. We overheard a conversation at dinner last night about the Inn possibly being haunted. The rumor, if it is a rumor, intrigued me. I talked Cole into going into the library to search for a book or diary on the house. I didn't think you'd mind us looking around. If so, I take full blame for everything."

Mrs. Granger held up a hand to interrupt. "Why didn't you come to me last night? It's not a problem for you using the library, but I could have relieved your minds then."

"You were so busy with the dinner, the tree lighting and whatever else, we only intended to search for the items on library shelves." Sydney weakened and wondered how Mrs. Granger would take the news that she'd had the gall to look around her desk.

I should have given up the search, before it became so involved.

"Something happened. Something you aren't going to be happy hearing." Hesitant, Sydney continued. "Last night we..." She couldn't go on.

Cole came to stand by her side and whispered in her ear. "You can do this, Sydney. If you can't, I will."

She had a mental block and had to get past it. *If it's the last thing I ever do, I'm going to apologize to this woman for snooping in her library, around her desk. Even though I did something I'm not proud of, I've never been dishonest and won't start now.*

Sydney sent Cole a grateful look, and mouthed a thank you.

"When we couldn't find a diary or a book on history, I had the worst idea. The desk seemed to be a good spot for a book or diary." Sydney held Mrs. Granger's attention.

Her face tightened as she waited for Sydney to continue. "Go on."

"I promise we didn't open any of the desk drawers, we only scanned the top."

"I have a feeling this is only the beginning of your story." Mrs. Granger raised an eyebrow, then commented, "You needn't have bothered though, the library and desk is empty of any important items since so many use it for reading or whatever. I can't imagine why you thought something that significant would be in plain sight."

"You're correct. But...what I did next was completely unintentional. We decided what we were doing wasn't right, so we decided to leave and were on our way out. As I came around the desk, I must have hit a button or something. That's the only explanation I have for what happened next. As we were leaving, at the end of the last book shelf, I noticed a door ajar that wasn't opened before. Unable to resist, I poked my head inside the opening for a quick peek."

Mrs. Granger gasped and clenched her fingers around her water bottle.

"Are you aware of a secret door in the library?" Sydney asked.

"No. We've owned this Inn for eight years and this is the first I've heard of a secret door. I can't imagine someone not having found it before now."

"I agree. Surely someone must know about it," Sydney said, hopeful.

"Unless someone in town knows, I wouldn't think so, since

all the previous owners are long gone." Puzzled, Mrs. Granger leaned forward. "Perhaps you can remember the exact area you came in contact with the desk."

"I'll try to remember. I'm not even sure that's what caused the door to open." Sydney had no idea where, but she would show her how she'd come from around the desk. "Very well. Now I'll tell you the rest of the story."

"You mean there's more?"

"Yes, and it's fascinating," Sydney said. *I wouldn't blame her if she threw us out right now.*

"Indeed?" Mrs. Granger questioned, a slight twinge of irritation in her voice. "Tell me more."

"Earlier in the afternoon, we'd begun to search for the book, found no diary or book and decided to have a cup of tea and come back later. It was after the tree lighting, that we went back to the library for one last look. That's when I found the door."

"I wish you'd informed me right away."

Sydney shot a look at Cole, who sat and watched the two of them, Sydney on edge and Mrs. Granger skeptical.

"Well...There's more. I'm not so sure how believable this will be, but it's what happened. Both of us can testify to what I'm about to tell you," Sydney said, then took a deep breath.

"I may as well hear the entire story."

"As I said, we'd gone in late afternoon on a whim that we'd find some kind of information in the library about the house."

"You've already admitted you found nothing, so why go back?" Mrs. Granger questioned.

Sydney laughed. "You have a ton of books. We hadn't finished going through all of them."

The corners of Mrs. Granger's lips lifted in a slight smile. "Yes. There are many, many books. We're proud of our collection."

"Okay. This is where there were two incredible occurrences. The first time we were in the library, Cole felt a cool breeze. Nothing strange about that though, except this time of year no one uses their air conditioning. It's what occurred next that knocked our socks off."

TWELVE

"Do you believe in ghosts, Mrs. Granger?"

Mrs. Granger scoffed. "Of course not. There's no such thing. Do you believe in such things?"

Cole and Sydney exchanged knowing glances.

"I never did in the past, but the events from yesterday leads me to consider otherwise," Sydney said, and stole another glance at Cole. "I'm not so sure anymore."

"While we were in the library, Cole saw something that shook us both to our cores. At first I thought he was playing a joke until a few seconds later, I saw for myself."

"And what did you see, Sydney?" Mrs. Granger asked.

She had no choice but to simply tell the woman what happened. She couldn't put it off any longer.

"Okay, this is the way it played out. Cole saw a female apparition in a lavender gown floating between the floor and the ceiling, engulfed in a haze. When I turned around, the only thing I saw was the bottom of the gown, as it had started to fade away."

"You...you can't be serious." Mrs. Granger stood up, gulped and all but lost her breath. "Young lady, what kind of prank is this?"

Sydney saw that she was getting nowhere in her hope of convincing Mrs. Granger. *This entire conversation may well be a waste of time.* If she couldn't convince the woman they weren't deceiving her, she'd never find out if there were documents on the Inn's history. Worse, Mrs. Granger had every right to call the police and she very well could. "I promise you this is no prank."

"Sure sounds like one to me." Mrs. Granger said. "I think this meeting is over."

"I promise you it's not a hoax. Please hear me out. I haven't gotten to the contents of the room where the secret door led."

"Fine," Mrs. Granger said, and sighed. "Go ahead with the

rest of your story, but I can tell you now, I don't appreciate your going into a secret room in my house."

"Thank you," Sydney replied. "Neither one of us actually went inside. I only peeked inside through the darkness. When we went back to the library the second time, we saw the apparition again. Only this time, I think she caused the library door to open and close."

"I'm sorry, but I believe those kind of happenings only occur in the movies."

Sydney had to find a way to change her mind, because it did happen. She also believed it had happened before and had a strong feeling it wouldn't be the last time.

"Well, something or someone did, because it slammed shut and opened again quite fast. No one else was around, except Cole and me. Come to think of it, the ghost could be the one who also opened and closed the door to the secret room. Think about it."

"You have no proof." Mrs. Granger sat back and crossed her arms. "Do you understand how hard this tall tale is for me to swallow?"

"I can promise you this isn't a tall tale," Sydney said. "According to the lady in the dining room, the ghost is rumored to be someone who used to live here. Cole has a strange notion it's his deceased wife, though I don't think so. Whoever it is wants us to know something. Maybe there's more to the story than any of us wants to accept."

"Ghosts are nothing but rumors people use to make up to pass the time," Mrs. Granger stated. "In my opinion, it's nonsense."

Sydney let that statement pass. "If you have time now, and are still interested, I'll show you the section of the desk I touched."

In her mind, Sydney saw the door that had opened, and how she wanted so much to discover what was hidden inside the secret room.

"I don't really see the point. If you could give me the location, I can try it myself."

"I wish I could, but have no idea which spot it was."

Mrs. Granger sighed. "Very well then. I suppose it won't hurt to check out the library and this supposed secret room." She checked her watch. "I have to oversee lunch in a little while. Now is good for me if you're okay with the timing."

Sydney's heart jumped. Yes! She was going to see inside the secret room if the door opened again and if Mrs. Granger allowed her inside. "Most definitely." She glanced toward Cole. "Is now a good time for you?"

"I'm all yours," he said, grinned, then winked at her.

Sydney stood in about the same position she hoped she'd been when the door to the secret room had first opened. "When I came around the desk, I hit the desk about here, and my fingers ran the length of the desk."

"Wait," Cole said. "I'll stand by the door, then we'll know the exact spot so Mrs. Granger can use it again."

"That is probably a good idea," Mrs. Granger admitted.

"Okay. I'm in place." Sydney moved slowly and precisely around the desk, her fingers running the edges. "Anything yet, Cole?" Sydney called out.

"Nada."

She tried it again. "What about now?"

"Nope. Nada."

Mrs. Granger stood back, tapped her foot, and checked the time. "Nothing is working. Evidently something else tripped the door, if indeed it was tripped at all."

Yes, something like a ghost! Sydney thought back for a moment to when the door had opened. "What if it wasn't my hand touching something after all, but my foot?"

"That doesn't make sense. Can you imagine how many people over the years that have walked behind that desk? No amount of repeating the steps is going to trip the door. Look, I have responsibilities in the kitchen and I'm running late. Sorry folks, I'm leaving."

"I'm so disappointed. Something opened that door.

Something—anything."

Mrs. Granger headed to the door and noticed the last book was placed too close to the edge toward the end of the bookshelf. She pushed the book back even with the other books, and when she did, the door to the secret room creaked open.

"Oh, my," she whispered. "Oh, my." She pulled the book out, then leaned in close to examine the bookshelf. "Come look at this. In the corner is a tiny button. Of all things. I'd never have believed this in a million years. In all the times these books have been moved, dusted and put back, I'm wondering why and how strange it is that the door hasn't been discovered earlier."

"Maybe someone did find the door and you just don't know anything about it. That's the book I left out to mark my spot! I must have let the edge of the book come in contact with the button when I slid it in place." Sydney clapped her hands in excitement. "Wow. You did it. It wasn't my snooping after all. Whew. I feel so much better."

Excited, Mrs. Granger stared at her. "Your snooping, as you call it, is how this discovery came about. If you, hadn't left this book to mark your place, we'd never have found the secret room."

"So you aren't annoyed with me for snooping?" Sydney asked.

Mrs. Granger laughed. "Annoyed? I suppose I should be, but no. Not now, since we're standing in front of proof on your outlandish story. Please wait for me before going in. I'll let the crew know they're on their own for lunch."

Even though Sydney was itching to get inside the secret room, she respected the woman's request. "Yes, ma'am. We'll be right here...waiting."

Thirteen

Mrs. Granger passed Sydney a large, heavy flashlight and one to Cole. She allowed him to enter first since he was the tallest, and because he'd offered to swipe at the spider webs and knock back dust with the wet cloths she'd brought from the laundry room.

A strong musty scent seeped from the open door and into the library, which caused all three of them to break into spasms of sneezes. Mrs. Granger reached inside a pocket of her jacket.

"Put these masks on. Thank goodness I had the foresight to grab a few. I don't want any of us to get sick from the dust. Lord only knows how long since it's been cleaned. Years, from the look of the room. We certainly haven't cleaned it. I didn't even know it existed."

Once inside they uncovered antique furniture stacked floor to ceiling that covered most of one side of the room. Boxes of silver, china, crystal, linens and vases filled another side of the dust-covered sanctuary.

All three stumbled out of the room for some fresh air. "That's a hundred years' worth of dust if it's a day," Sydney managed to say through a coughing spell.

"There's quite a treasure in that room. I wonder how long it's been since anyone stepped foot in there?"

"It's hard to tell, Mrs. Granger," Cole remarked, and looked around the floor. "There aren't any footsteps through the thick dust, so it's been a long, long time since anyone has ventured in."

Sydney flipped her flashlight on, then went back inside and resumed her search of the room. "I see a table in the corner, and it looks as though there may be something on top. Let's check it out." Sydney handed her flashlight to Mrs. Granger. "Would you help me move the boxes on top of the table, Cole?"

On the table, several small, rusty metal boxes were stacked on top of one another. Beside those was a long, flat, metal lockbox. Cole brushed aside the dust that revealed the rusty treasure.

"Check three of the boxes, Sydney and I'll check the other four," Mrs. Granger said. "Cole, would you mind getting the letter opener from the desk? I really hate to damage the boxes, but if there are keys, I have no idea where to look. The locks shouldn't be too hard to pop open, they look pretty rusty."

Cole wrestled with the lock and finally broke into the largest box. "Bingo! There are four diaries in this box."

Sydney reached for Cole's hand, squeezed, and smiled up at him.

They continued opening the boxes, each one filled with letters or a stack of ribbon tied stationery. A few steel nibbed writing pens and a dried bottle of ink filled another box.

Cole had reached down to pick up one of the diaries, when all three of them suddenly stopped and rubbed at their arms. A swift cool breeze blew through the room, bringing with it the intoxicating scent of Gardenias.

"Oh, my," whispered Mrs. Granger. She chafed her hands up and down her arms again. "It's getting very cold... Oh my word! Look. Quick."

Cole and Sydney both fixed their eyes in the direction of her stare with intense curiosity. Each of them drew in a quick breath at the lavender gown and the haze around it, floating in the Gardenia scented air.

"Don't be frightened, Mrs. Granger. It's her. She's back, but she won't harm you or us." Cole said in a low calming voice.

"Her? Her? Who is the *her* you're talking about?" Mrs. Granger's flashlight shook uncontrollably.

Gradually, the ghost's long black hair and face had begun to surface, while she hovered over the lockbox Cole had broken into. She moved and pointed a long slender finger to each box, then disappeared without warning through a back wall as quickly as she'd appeared in the room.

Cole pulled his denim jacket collar around his neck and shivered. "I don't know if she's unhappy or telling us to take the diaries. Isn't this one for the books? She's definitely trying to tell us something. Obviously we need to figure out what."

When Sydney placed a hand on Mrs. Granger's shoulder, she leapt toward Cole.

"I'm sorry. Are you all right, Mrs. Granger? You haven't said a word."

"I...I think I'm fine, but terribly shaken. Never would I have believed what we experienced had I not seen it for myself." She pulled in a ragged breath and rested a hand over her heart. "Wow. You two weren't playing a prank after all."

"We wouldn't do that to you," Sydney offered.

When she'd gathered her wits about her, Mrs. Granger asked. "Can I trust you two to be discreet?"

"Yes, of course," Sydney said. "May I ask why?"

"There isn't any reason to upset the other guests and ruin their weekend. As Cole said, the lady ghost isn't going to hurt anyone. We hope," she replied. "I'd like you to take these letters and diaries to your room and hide them in a safe place. After lunch we'll get together, read through them. Then I'll discuss with my husband how to handle the items and what they mean for the Inn and the town. That is what you'd like to do, isn't it?"

Sydney shook her head. "There isn't anything I'd like better. Thank you for allowing us to read them. They should prove to be informative as to why the ghost is here. Maybe."

"Very well. I'll see you at lunch, then we'll go to your room, Sydney, if you don't mind. I'd rather we do this in private."

"Would you mind if Cole meets with us?"

"Oh, of course not. He's more than welcome to join us. I only meant others from the reunion."

Cole stepped up. "Thank you, Mrs. Granger."

"Certainly, Cole. Perhaps we'll be lucky enough to tack on a bit of history to this old place. Surely something in the letters or diaries will shed some light on this incredible phenomenon the three of us witnessed."

Mrs. Granger shook her head in disbelief, and stepped from the secret room.

FOURTEEN

Cole led Sydney down the hall and into the common room. Steam rose from the cups filled with strong coffee, to which he added warmed cream. He set a cup in front of her and seated himself across the table from her. "I'm at a loss as to what happened in the secret room," he said. "We may as well forget it until Mrs. Granger returns and we are able to find out more about the house. I have a feeling the diaries will spill the beans."

"I think so too. My heart is beating so fast, I can't tell you how excited I am right now. The key must lie in the diaries and letters, especially since the ghost hovered over the boxes. I, for one, can barely wait to read them. Can you imagine what's inside those diaries?" Sydney chuckled, then drained her coffee cup.

"I hope it's more than light conversation between the correspondents." Cole leaned back and stretched. "I think I'll lie down for a while before lunch. I didn't sleep well last night. I kept seeing a floating dress, while its image danced around inside my head most of the night." He laughed and ran a hand down his beard. "I'd prefer if it were you doing the dancing."

"I haven't danced in quite some time," Sydney said, then grinned. "I'm not really hungry either. A nap sure sounds good. We should be rested when we dive into this afternoon's treasures," Sydney said, then yawned.

"Agreed. The afternoon could prove to be a long one, but one I'm looking forward to."

Sydney gave Cole a long look. "By the way, you're terribly handsome with the beard. How long have you worn it?"

His eyebrows arched upward, making his eyes open wide. "Three and a half, maybe four years. I really can't remember. I had a motorcycle accident and got a scar on my chin because of my love of speed. Yes, I still love speed, but I have slowed down since the accident."

"When did it happen, about the time your wife became ill?"

"Umm...a month or so before. Maria liked the beard too," he admitted, then looked in her direction. "So you think I'm still handsome?"

Sydney laughed. "As a matter of fact, I do. I have always thought you were handsome. Don't let this go to your head, but you're more handsome now than when you were younger."

"Why, thank you ma'am." Cole smiled and bowed from the waist. "You're the loveliest and sweetest lady I know."

"Your charms aren't lost on me, Cole." Sydney sent him a regretful stare. "They never were."

"Thank goodness. I thought I was wasting my time," he said, and laughed. "I do have my moments."

"That you do." *I shouldn't be boosting his ego. Dang! He'll probably get the wrong idea.*

"I'll be sure to keep you charmed, lovely one." Cole winked, ran a finger down her hand, then stopped at her rings.

"It's only been a year since Will passed away." She glanced down at her wedding rings and twirled them around her finger. "That was the longest year of my life. So you see, there are complications. Complications of the heart aren't easily resolved."

"No. No, they aren't." Cole stared out the window, his expression lost in the past. "I wonder why I think Maria would show up when you and I are together and why would I feel her so near when we see the apparition?"

"I have no idea. Neither am I sure it's Maria and not a descendant of the Raddwell family." Sydney stared at the tan line surrounding Cole's ring finger. "No offense to you or Maria." She pointed to the tan line where he'd worn his wedding band. "Do you think the reason you think and felt the ghost may have been Maria, and that you want to see her so badly?"

"It's a possibility. We've talked a lot about her this weekend, maybe she's been pushed to the front of my memory bank." He sighed. "I don't know. I'm not sure of much of anything anymore."

"You're only now beginning to find some peace with her

loss and ease in your grief, and it's been two and a half years. Will has only been gone a year. I'm still not ready to venture into another relationship. It's too soon. I can't get past the loss and his memory."

"What did you tell me?" Cole asked gently. "You need to get on with life. Isn't that right? Will would want you to be happy, too. Give yourself some time. Love his memory, keep it close, and try to find some happiness." He stared into her eyes and smiled. "You're too young to be alone and unhappy."

"You aren't supposed to remember everything I say," Sydney said, then frowned.

"Aw, Sydney. I'm not trying to push you. I know how you hate pressure." Cole leaned over and placed a finger under her chin and a thumb on top. "Promise you'll keep an open mind though, where we're concerned. Don't forget what we once had was more special than most people ever find. With a little luck, you may find that love is still there. I haven't forgotten my love for you...I never will."

"True love isn't easily forgotten, Cole." She sighed. "You know how I loved you. We simply didn't have a chance to see if it would last. You made sure of that. Now. I'm not sure of anything either."

"Sydney, I've forgiven myself and finally have the chance to ask for your forgiveness. Can you please try to put that awful night in the past where it belongs?"

"I have forgiven you. I forgave you years ago so I could get on with my life. It's just that there are times I have those old feelings that creep back in, especially over this weekend. Seeing you again brings back too many memories...feelings too strong to deal with right now. You understand, don't you?"

Cole stacked their cups in the sink, then stood beside her. "Sure I do. I'm not unfeeling. Never doubt for one minute, that the love we had for each other isn't still suspended in the background. It's there waiting. Waiting for us to make up our minds. Love is patient, sweetheart."

Sweetheart. I'm not so sure he should be so personal. Sydney looked directly at him and bit her lower lip. "I've made up my mind about one thing, I'm going to take that nap we talked about before we get into a deeper conversation I'm not ready for. How about you?"

"Sure. I'll set my phone's alarm for an hour so we won't oversleep. I'll knock on your door and wake you, if you like." He grinned at her. "Remember love is waiting for you to make up your mind. My mind is made up. I know what I want."

FIFTEEN

"Clearly that explains why over the years, some guests have mentioned they've heard crying in the night. Plus others have said they've heard gentle footsteps in the hallway. I never imagined there was anything to the tales people repeated to me ever so often, because I've never heard any sound or seen anything in the entire eight years we've been here."

"Surely you've heard something. Maybe you thought it was the wind, or the house creaking," Sydney urged.

Mrs. Granger got up from a chair and paced around the room. "I have heard those things, but paid no attention. I passed them off as people making more of the situation than it was. People hear rumors and blow them out of proportion, you know."

"So let me get this straight. Lylia Raddwell's husband was returning from England when his ship went down, but they never found the bodies of the men who were on board. And this incident took place in the late-eighteen hundreds," Sydney said. "Is that about right?"

"Right," Cole and Mrs. Granger said together.

"Lylia refused to believe her husband was really gone and on her darkest day, had a breakdown. One stormy night, here at her home, she fell down the stairs and broke her neck, dying instantly. Since she hadn't had closure, her spirit remains here on earth. Or back and forth, wherever she goes. I simply don't understand this phenomenon." Sydney shook her head and stared at Cole.

"Do you have anything else you'd like to add?" Mrs. Granger asked Cole.

"Don't forget...Lylia must remain in this house because she's still waiting for her husband to come back to her, Mrs. Granger," Cole reminded her.

Mrs. Granger sent them a crooked smile. "Since Lylia hasn't hurt anyone so far, I don't imagine she'll start now.

Sydney rubbed her neck and feigned a smile. "I'm sure she's harmless. At least she seems to be each time we've seen her."

Mrs. Granger stacked up the diaries, tied a ribbon around the letters, and boxed them. "By the way, getting back to real life, don't forget the Christmas party after dinner tonight." She turned to leave. "Semi-formal."

Cole eyed Sydney. "We'll be there. Is that okay with you, Sydney? Shall I drop by for you?"

"I'd like that, Cole," Sydney said, then turned to Mrs. Granger. "And thank you. I wouldn't miss getting together for anything. A Christmas party sounds like fun."

"This will be our little secret, okay?" Mrs. Granger whispered, as she gripped the doorknob. "You know, about what we saw. The ghost?"

"Of course. Our secret." Sydney made the motion of zipping her lips. "No one would believe us anyway."

"Bundle up. The temperature has dropped. There's a fountain on the other side of the garden I want to show you. We won't stay long." Cole positioned himself behind her, helped guide her coat on, then wrapped an arm around her shoulders.

I'm more distracted than annoyed and not sure when I've encouraged Cole too much.

She realized in several little ways, she'd indeed encouraged him. Whenever, or whatever it was, hadn't been a smart move on her part. Had he had gotten the wrong idea from her? Had she nurtured his attention in some way more than she should have? Best to put a stop to it right away.

But is that what I really want?

Sydney gazed upward at the sky, which was turning a chilling gray. She shrugged from his embrace, then stepped aside. "Taking liberties, are you, Cole?"

"Hey...and here I thought we were doing so well." Cole patted her on the back and let his arm slide down to his side. "Sorry. I don't mean to give you the wrong impression, Sydney. A shoulder hug seemed natural at the time. Like old times."

"The last time I looked, we weren't a couple, so natural doesn't work. We're becoming familiar, more comfortable, with each other again, which is okay, but I'd like to keep a safe distance between us."

"Okay. We'll take this one day at a time and see where it goes. Does that sound okay with you?"

"A reasonable statement and question, Cole. I'm glad you've learned to control your feelings...somewhat." *So why haven't I learned to control mine? I love Will. Yet, I've found I still care about Cole. What's wrong with me? How can I care about two men at the same time?*

"You have no idea how long it's taken me to arrive at this stage in my life." He cleared his throat. "Ready to go see the fountain?"

Sydney started to comment on his statement, but let it go. "I am. I didn't realize there was a fountain here until earlier today. I saw it as I drove around the back while looking for a parking spot. I guess I didn't remember or scan the brochure good enough. A fountain makes sense though, since this is an old Victorian."

"Watch your step. Actually the fountain is around the back in the middle of the Rose garden." Cole guided her around to the back of the house, Sydney's elbow in his hand. "I ran across it yesterday when I walked the grounds before you got here."

"Do they have the fountain running in December; in this weather?"

"The water wasn't on yesterday. Too cold. Most likely won't be on today either in case of a freeze. Of course the roses aren't in bloom either, but we can use our imagination," Cole said. "What I want you to see is how fabulous this fountain is."

The fountain rose approximately fifteen feet in the air. Three elaborate tiers tapered to the top to showcase the figure of a woman, fully clothed in what appeared to be a filmy nightgown.

"Wow! That's some fountain," Sydney exclaimed, as she wound her way around the entire fountain. "The sculptor did a remarkable work of art."

"If you remember, in one of the diaries, Lylia mentioned a sculpture that was commissioned from a sculptor out of New York. She wrote of her excitement when the sculpture arrived a few months after the house was completed."

Fascinated, Sydney concentrated on the sculpture's flowing gown. "This is such an intricate piece. You can all but see through the gown. Amazing work.

"I wonder how much time this piece took to sculpt?"

"Plenty, I would suspect." Sydney shivered. "There's an eerie sensation surrounding the fountain. Do you feel it? And I wonder if the lady in the lavender gown posed for the sculpture?" She shook her head. "No. No, she couldn't have, because she was here. Maybe they used a photograph of her."

"Yes. I can see where using her photograph was a possibility. Honestly, I encountered the same sensation yesterday, too." Cole looked away and raised his eyebrows. "I didn't say anything, because I wanted to see if you had the same gut feeling I had. Sometimes what we see, or think we see, are things that we have previously experienced out of speculation, or out of expectation."

A brisk breeze surged around both Cole and Sydney. Sydney inhaled a light hint of Gardenia, the same scent that she'd smelled in the secret room.

"We're not alone, Cole," she whispered. "We have company."

Sixteen

"There's definitely something going on here." Sydney glanced around, sensing the same ill-at-ease feeling she'd experienced earlier in the secret room. "We shouldn't treat this sensation lightly, Cole. I'm not so sure I'm comfortable with it, either. Not as much as I was in the library. Something simply isn't natural here."

"Let's go." Cole stretched his hand out to Sydney. "I think we're finished here. We can go back inside if you prefer. I don't want you to be uncomfortable."

Sydney reached out and closed her own around Cole's hand. "I'd rather go back inside. I suspect we've been followed."

A strange feminine voice was vague, but softly spoken. *"My love is gone, don't leave yours alone."*

"What in the world was that?" Cole asked, while he looked around and in the direction of the voice.

As Sydney gasped, her eyes opened wide. "What? You mean *who* was that, don't you? Unmistakably, we're being addressed...and what was that riddle about? What does she mean by *your* love? Is she talking about me? She knows nothing about us."

"I'm sure I don't know," he said, and smiled. "Unless she can read my mind and see inside my heart."

"This definitely is no time for romance." Sydney stared at the lady in lavender a moment, then back at Cole. "I am not your love."

"We'll see, my love." He chuckled. "We'll see."

"Stop calling me that," Sydney threw at him.

The lavender gown circled slowly twice around the fountain, then came to rest on the sculpture's arm. The shape of a body slowly swelled inside the gown, its flowing black hair covering the face, the gown continuing to billow out in a delicate breeze.

Sydney stared, a look of panic on her face. "Oh. My. God.

Cole...Cole...do you see what I see?"

"Do you mean the lady in the lavender gown sitting on the sculpture? Yes. Yes I'm afraid so."

"She's in full form now," she whispered. "How does she do that? Why is she following us? We have nothing to do with her. We're from her future and she's lost in the past. I don't understand what's happening at all."

"Ghosts can do anything they want," Cole whispered, then gently pushed Sydney behind him. He stood protectively with his arm wrapped backward around her waist.

Then he gazed up intently at the figure. "What do you want with us? What is it you need? Why do you keep showing up? We can't help you. Please go away."

When she spoke again, it sounded as though she were speaking under water. "*Do not be alarmed. I'm not here to bring you harm.*" The figure raised an arm and pointed toward a lighted window where the young man who worked at the Inn stood in the shadows observing them.

Cole viewed the young man, his fingers holding back the curtains, eyes fixed on them. "What?" he asked. He looked up again at the ghost in the lavender gown. "What does he have to do with you? With us? Who is he?"

"*Bring to a close. Inquire what he knows.*"

Sydney remembered how nosey the young man had been when he caught them in the library. "That boy knows something. I feel it in my bones," she blurted out.

"You may be right." Cole pointed toward the ghost. "She should know."

Cole raised an arm and motioned for the young man to come down. "We'll find out if he knows anything."

He lowered his arm and wrapped it around Sydney. She didn't budge. Together they waited.

As did the ghost.

The young man walked close enough to them that Sydney could smell no alcohol on his breath. Evidently he hadn't been drinking. Good. They were about to pick his brain for some intense information, and needed him sober.

The young man ambled toward them calmly, and

apparently without a care in the world. "What can I do for you folks?"

"We saw you watching us. Tell me why," Cole questioned.

Guilt spread across his face as he glanced down at the ground. "I realize you saw me. I also saw the lady in lavender. I couldn't take my eyes off her."

"What do you know about her? The ghost. She is a ghost, you know."

"Hey, man. I know she's a ghost." He shrugged and shuffled his feet in the snow. "How would I know anything?"

When the lady in lavender whizzed by the young man's head, he turned as white as the snow beneath his feet. He ducked and tugged at his coat. He turned to leave. "I'm out of here."

Sydney was amazed that the ghost could hear and understand them, and wasn't surprised at the young man's fear. "Oh, I wouldn't do that if I were you. I believe she wants you to talk to us. Maybe you'd better come clean."

"Then it's time to tell my story. I hope you'll believe me."

"You mustn't be afraid of her. She's only trying to get your attention," Cole said to the young man, then turned to Sydney. "We should include Mrs. Granger in the remainder of the conversation. After all, the house and ghost belong to her."

Cole and Sydney lead the way, while the young man followed them back inside, close on their heels.

"Are you okay, Sydney? Not frightened or anything, are you?" Cole asked, as he leaned near her when he turned the door knob.

"I'm fine, thanks to you." She rested her forehead against his and smiled sweetly. "You've always made me feel safe."

He pulled open the door and whispered. "I'll see what I can do about keeping you safe, my main concern."

SEVENTEEN

Mrs. Granger met them a few minutes after Sydney called her on her cell phone and explained that they may have valuable information on the ghost. Could she meet with them in the library?

After Sydney, Cole and the young man seated themselves, Mrs. Granger pushed the door to the library closed, then locked it. "Well, young man. It seems you have some important information to share."

He rubbed his hands up and down on his jeans and let out a shaky breath. "I suppose I do. Probably more than you want to hear, but it's time the truth is told." He hung his head and muttered. "I'll be glad to get this over with and put the ghost to rest."

"So you see, Mrs. Granger, we aren't the only ones the ghost is visible to," Sydney replied. "But I'll let him tell you what he knows."

"Lylia Raddwell is your ghost. My full name is Landon Raddwell Spencer. My great-grandfather, James, was Lylia's husband's father."

"Raddwell? You're a Raddwell?" Mrs. Granger squinted at the young man. "So you lied to us. You lied about who you are and your last name? But your social security card, and your birth certificate lists you only as a Spencer. Why did you feel the need to lie? Why did you do that?"

"When you first offered me the job, remember I asked if I could get back to you? I almost turned it down. Then, after I'd had time to think about living and working in my family's old home, I couldn't resist. All my family is gone now and I wanted someplace I'd feel close to them. A place to call home."

"I'm sorry," Mrs. Granger uttered.

He looked her directly in the eyes. "My last name, Spencer, is correct. There had been bad blood between Leon Raddwell and his brother, Henry Raddwell, who was Lylia's deceased husband. Sarah, a recent widow and Leon's sister, was aware of what she deemed the truth to be, regarding Lylia's death. In a heated argument, she'd admitted to Leon what she'd witnessed the night Lylia had died. Furious, Leon ordered his sister, Sarah, to depart from the Raddwell home. He had paid Sarah a substantial sum of money and demanded she sign a statement, that she'd never reveal the truth and never contact the family again. What the Raddwell's didn't know was, Sarah was pregnant with my father. Later, after my father's birth, Sarah remarried and became a Spencer. To keep down gossip, Mr. Spencer quietly adopted my father. When I was born, they gave me my family name, as a middle name. Raddwell. I may have been legally born a Spencer, but my bloodline is Raddwell.

"Poor Sarah, and the rest of you. To be torn from family that way is appalling," Sydney said.

"I apologize for lying to you, but I'm indeed a Raddwell."

"How sad for you, Landon. Again, I'm sorry," Mrs. Granger said.

"I lived through it okay, but my father had a difficult time dealing with the Raddwell's behavior toward Sarah and her unborn child."

"You have a home here with us as long as you'd like," Mrs. Granger said.

"You can't imagine how much I appreciate your offer and kindness." He grinned. "That news is the best I've heard in a long time. Thank you so much."

"You're welcome. Be good to yourself and make us both proud," Mrs. Granger replied.

"I will. You can count on it."

Landon leaned forward on the sofa and resumed his account of the mystery. "Lylia died on Christmas Eve. She's been most active on Christmas Eve and Christmas Day, so I've heard, but I've also heard she walks the halls and sometimes cries at night...off and on."

"Have you ever seen her before tonight?" Cole asked.

"I've heard weeping in the night...and yes, I've seen her a couple of times before."

Mrs. Granger jerked her head in the young man's direction. "Really? Where?"

"Each time she was in the library huddled at the edge of the bookshelves."

Mrs. Granger, Cole and Sydney, each drew in a sudden breath.

Sydney breathed deeply. She had to know where he'd seen the ghost. "Show me the exact place you saw her."

"She was always here." The young man walked over to the area of the secret door's location. "The lights would begin to blink, then she'd show up. She always wore a lavender gown. I gotta tell you, she scared the bejeezus out of me."

"Why didn't you say something?" Mrs. Granger asked.

He simply looked at her, but didn't bat an eye. "Would you have believed me?"

"Probably not. Since you sometimes have a drinking problem, I'd have assumed you were having hallucinations from the drinking."

"Right," Landon said. "I understand."

Landon turned to Sydney. "I overheard you talking about a diary or letters that may be in the house. I have the evidence, not here of course, that will prove what I'm about to tell you."

"Please continue, Landon," Mrs. Granger urged.

"Before Sarah left, she wrote a letter, and in the diary, then gave it to my other great-aunt, which she kept hidden in her blanket chest. My great-aunt became ill, and swore a young housekeeper to secrecy. The diary and letter were to be hidden and never to be passed into the wrong hands."

"How did you come to have possession of the diary and letter?" Mrs. Granger asked.

"My grandmother, Sarah, had always been kind to everyone at the Raddwell home, no matter their status. The housekeeper, who Sarah had entrusted her diary and letter to, was getting up in years and wanted to return them to Sarah. She'd always trusted Sarah and discovered where she lived. One day she showed up on my grandmother's doorstep and left them with her. After my grandmother passed, my father and I found them hidden away in her room in an old foot locker."

Mrs. Granger regarded Landon. "I don't know how long you've had them, but why didn't you return the documents to the rightful owners of the house?"

"If truth be told, I have no satisfactory excuse except that they were the only items that tied me to the Raddwell family." Landon blew out a long breath. "I wasn't ready to relinquish that bond."

"I can understand wanting something that belonged to the family...your family. However, there is the responsibility to the history of the house," Mrs. Granger commented.

"That's true," Landon said. "Anyway, there's more. Leon, had gone mad because Lylia wouldn't marry him. Lylia had discovered her pregnancy after her husband, Henry, was lost at sea. Even though she was pregnant with Henry's child, Leon still wanted Lylia and the child as his own. He and Lylia had a dreadful argument, because she refused his advances. When the argument grew heated, Leon turned to wrench Lylia's arm, he inadvertently pushed her, or so Lylia's sister-in-law, Sarah, had written. Lylia tripped, or was pushed, then tumbled down the stairs. Her neck was broken. Leon had lied about what had happened, probably because he knew he'd be accused of her death and he wasn't going to take the blame. He'd informed everyone that she had evidently gone mad, and in her grief, had thrown herself down the stairs. He had no way of knowing his sister had observed the entire argument and the subject of their discussion."

"That's quite a story. Could we see the letter and the diary?" Sydney asked, then turned to Mrs. Granger. "If you don't mind."

"I have no qualms if you and Cole would like to read them." She looked at Landon. "You are going to turn over the documents to me, aren't you?"

"I suppose it's the right thing to do." Landon hesitated, as his face crinkled with concern. "Yes. I'll get them when we wrap up here. The papers belong at the house. History should be kept with the home."

"Thank you, Landon." Mrs. Granger said. "You're doing the honorable thing."

"Cole, you've been awfully quiet," Sydney said.

Cole nodded at Sydney. "Landon, I think the story is remarkable, but why do you think Lylia has shown herself to us?" he questioned. "Why us, when we have nothing to do with the family?"

Landon studied Cole for a moment. "Lylia must have trusted you two, or she wouldn't have made herself visible when she did. I think she wants the truth to come out about her death, so she can be at peace. Not that this is a proven fact, but I believe some ghosts can feel other people's hearts, decide whether they can rely on them, or not."

"We certainly followed her wishes, didn't we, Sydney?"

"Yes, and if I hadn't been so inquisitive, we'd never have gotten to the bottom of this mystery."

The room grew chilly and eerily quiet.

All four of them gazed at each other. They realized Lylia had invited herself into the room.

Still dressed in her lavender gown, Lylia hovered at the top of the secret room's door. *"You've done your best...I can now rest."* With those words, she disappeared through the secret room's door. Immediately warmth returned to the library.

"Wow." Landon said, and swallowed hard. "I see now that I should have given you the articles long ago."

"Don't blame yourself for her long suffering. Now may have been the time Lylia was waiting for," Cole said. "Perhaps we were simply in the right place at the right time."

"Well I, for one, am glad that this whole ghostly mystery is resolved. At least I hope so," Mrs. Granger uttered.

Mrs. Granger straightened a painting on the wall, then went to the library door and unlocked it. "Come, my friends. We have a Christmas party to attend."

EIGHTEEN

"May I have this dance?"

Sydney set her glass of punch down and smiled at Landon who had a big grin on his face. He looked so handsome in his suit with his hair slicked back. "Of course, it is Christmas. Just don't step on my toes," she said, then laughed.

"Never happen, pretty lady. I learned to dance from the best." Landon bowed from the waist and proceeded to guide her expertly around the dance floor, Sydney following his precise steps.

"You're a very good dancer, Landon. I must say, you look dashing tonight."

"Thanks. My grandmother taught my mom and my mom in turn taught me. Dance was important and required in her day and at the Raddwell household. As I understand from my mom, they all were a pretty strait-laced bunch."

Sydney couldn't be happier for Landon. Not only had he found a place to call home, but also he had declared he would stop drinking. Yes, Landon would be okay. He now had a family to rely on, someone to encourage him in times of trouble.

When the music stopped, Landon led her through the crowd and back to her table. "Thank you for the dance, Sydney. I want to thank you for being so kind to me, especially after I was so rude when we first met."

"My pleasure. I enjoyed every minute. As I said earlier, I forgive you. You've made some positive changes and I admire that it didn't take you long to choose how you want to be perceived. Keep doing what's right and you'll turn out fine. You're a fine young man now, but, you'll be a fine man one day. I'm sure of it," Sydney said, and patted him on a shoulder.

Sydney had noticed the way one of the servers had watched Landon while he'd danced with her. "Now, I know you aren't working tonight, but there's a very pretty young server at the dessert table who's kept an eye on you, especially while we were on the dance floor. Maybe you could see if you can help her, or ask her opinion on which dessert she recommends. You know, break the ice?" she smiled.

"Is that right?" Landon glanced across the room at a pretty brunette, a slow grin breaking across his features. "Okay, thanks. I know her. That's Kinsey Wade, and she's a real hard worker and a sweetheart." He turned back to Sydney and beamed. "Excuse me, I feel like a little dessert. Enjoy the rest of your evening."

As Landon walked away, Sydney felt a hand on her shoulder and warm breath at the back of her neck.

"I couldn't wait for your dance to end," Cole whispered.

"You could have cut in," she replied.

"What? And break a young man's heart? No way. He's wanted to dance with you all weekend. You're all mine for the next one," he said, and straightened his shoulders. "That is, if it's all right with you."

"Of course, Cole." She looked around and shrugged. "Unless there's another young man willing to step up and nip your good fortune in the bud."

Cole threw back his head and roared. "There isn't anyone in this room brave enough to endure my wrath."

"Is that right?" Sydney laughed. "You're pretty sure of yourself."

"Come on. I know you only have eyes for me," Cole teased.

"Well, I sure did at one time. Regrettably, you took care of that."

As Cole's smile faded, it was replaced by a look of sadness. "I thought we'd made our peace. I'm devastated that I hurt you, Sydney. Can we please call a truce? Are you going to throw away what, I hope, we've started to rebuild?"

"We have already made peace, Cole." Sydney sighed. "Some things never go away, though. You simply can't rush a relationship. Or people. It's not natural."

All of a sudden, the music and words of *Blue Christmas* filled the room, bringing with it a flood of memories, some good, some sad. Cole held out a hand, and while she thought her feet were cemented to the floor, he had pulled her onto the dance floor before she knew what was happening.

She fought against the feeling, but being back in his arms again felt good, felt familiar. Felt as though she were wrapped in a warm cocoon. She thought of stopping this nonsense and returning to her table, but gave in to the closeness and rested her head on his chest. *It's only a dance, right?* So long. So long between the time she'd last sensed the safety of his arms...and the crushing blow he'd dealt to her young heart. For her own peace of mind, she had to remind herself that she'd forgiven him and had meant it, for him and for herself. Still...

Sydney raised her head and gazed into his chocolate brown eyes. "You know you really take a lot for granted, Cole. You're rushing whatever you think we could become to each other. If there could be a future for us, I think it has to happen naturally."

"I'm sorry." Cole dipped his chin and caught her light green eyes with his own. Then, with a thumb and a light touch, he brushed a wisp of dark brown hair from her face. "I don't mean to push. It's been so long since we've been together, or danced, or since I've held you."

Sydney had to admit while she danced with Cole, the nearness had stirred old responses for him, but she was beginning to feel uncomfortable. "You're moving too fast. It was only yesterday that we saw each other after nearly ten years," she blurted out. "Don't you think it's a bit too soon to pretend those years never happened? That we can pick up where we left off?"

"The years did happen. Neither one of us can do anything about the past." Cole stopped them right in the middle of the dance floor and took her shoulders in his hands. "Ten years, ten minutes, ten seconds—my feelings for you will never change. Never."

"How can you be so sure? As we discussed earlier, both of us have changed over the years." She made a great effort to laugh, but it appeared forced, unnatural. "Who knows? You might despise me once you get to know me better."

"I doubt anything could ever change my opinion of you." He grinned. "So does that mean we're not done here? That we have a chance to discover each other again?"

She wanted to say, not on your life, buster. Instead, she shrugged out of his grip and walked off the dance floor as *You're All I Want for Christmas* began to play. She almost lost it listening to the words. The words her mom and dad had lived by all their married lives. Words that struck a chord in her heart. Words that caused her to pause and wonder if she could be brave enough to take a step toward the future. A future with a man, who no matter how hard she tried to put him out of her mind, still held a special place in her heart.

No matter how much she'd like to make a decision and put Cole's mind at ease, she wasn't ready to jump into a relationship simply because she was caught up in the moment. And she wouldn't say yes to something she wasn't sure of, just to please him. She'd not lived her life that way and wasn't about to begin now.

She turned to glance back at Cole. "You really must stop staring."

Nineteen

Cole pulled out her chair, seated her, then leaned over and whispered. "You're the most beautiful woman in the entire room. Why shouldn't I stare?"

"Maybe because it's rude. Maybe I'd prefer you didn't, because this weekend has plunged me into the past, too many memories...too soon. Maybe because you're making me uncomfortable that we're clearly so at ease with each other, even after all this time. Maybe because you're still the same old Cole?" Sydney questioned, then heaved a sigh. "I don't know."

She didn't know. Too many emotions had passed between them these past two days. Too soon. Way too soon.

"No. No, I'm not the same. Neither are you, remember?" Cole leaned back in his chair and studied Sydney. "I'm glad you still have some pleasant memories of our past. We can work through the bad times and start fresh. A fresh start...that's what we can do. If you're willing and if it feels right."

Sydney sighed and took a sip of punch. "There's still Will, not to mention Maria to consider."

What do they do with their other loves? How do they get past the grief each one still carried for their loss? Dealing with grief wasn't an easy undertaking.

"They're part of our lives. Period. Nothing will change our love for them. But...we can go forward, take each day as it comes and see how we get on with the grief and letting go."

Sydney's back stiffened. "I'll never let go of Will's memory. Don't even go there."

"Sweetheart, I'm not asking you to forget Will. I won't forget Maria either." Cole chewed on the inside of his lip. "Both of them meant too much to us to forget. Letting go means to always hold your loved one in your heart, and go on living. They both would want us to be happy."

"Yes, I believe they do or would." She and Will had

discussed this very concern for the two of them a few months before he'd passed away. Now she found it ironic that Will had insisted on talking about what would happen if one of them were left alone. She hadn't wanted to discuss death, but Will had insisted. He'd said the same as Cole had pointed out. He wanted her to be happy. *But…approaching that time and putting it into practice, would be easier said than done.*

"Certainly," Cole stated. "They loved enough to want us happy. We're both still young. We can love again."

Sydney stared at Cole as she remembered Will's expression while they had talked about loss. "When you lose a loved one, it takes time to come to grips with even the slightest possibility of replacing them. They can't ever be replaced. You find another to love, but not to replace. Not a topic to be taken lightly."

Sydney saw from Cole's expression, their conversation was getting to him too.

Cole leaned close to her and patted her hand. "Okay. Let's change the subject. How about that dessert you wanted to try?"

Sydney rubbed her tummy. "I shouldn't, but I can never turn down fresh coconut cake."

Her mom had made the best coconut cake ever. If she were helping her mom and stood still long enough, she'd be able to taste the warm coconut milk that was always drizzled over the top and left to soak inside the yummy layers. Times like this were when she missed her mom the most. The holidays…someone to pour her heart out to, someone to call in the middle of the night if problems weighed heavy on her mind.

Cole strolled behind Sydney, stopped at the dessert table and looked over the assortment of tempting calories. "I'm easy. I'll have a slice of pecan pie," he said to Kinsey.

"I remember how much you love warmed pecan pie," Sydney said, as she slid a napkin under her plate and picked up a fork.

"Would it be too much trouble to warm the pie?" he asked Kinsey.

"If course not. I'll be right back," Kinsey replied.

Cole turned and lifted an eyebrow. "It seems you

remember a lot about me. The things I like and don't like."

Sydney scoffed. "I should. We've known each other all our lives."

"Merry Christmas to both of you," Kinsey said when she came back, then handed Cole the pie. "Be careful, the plate is hot."

"I will. Thank you, Kinsey. Merry Christmas to you, too."

He held the plate under his nose and breathed in the scent of fresh warmed pecan sugary goodness. "Umm, this is delicious," he said, then dug in for another bite. "What else do you recall about me or our childhood?"

"I remember when your mother threw away a pair of ragged shorts several times. Each time, you'd dig them out of the trash and throw them in the washing machine," she laughed. "What about those cowboy boots you wore with them? Those were a hoot!"

"You see, Sydney? You haven't forgotten a thing about me," Cole said over a shoulder, as he took their plates and followed her back to the table.

She had to admit, she couldn't deny what he'd said when the memories came spinning back. She told herself it was only because they'd grown up together and he was forever at their house. Her mom had always set a place for him at the table. "Just in case," she'd say. *Ha.* There weren't too many nights he missed dinner at their table.

"Coffee?" Cole interrupted.

"Yes, please. Light cream."

"I remember," he remarked, then winked.

She and Cole had been like brother and sister until one day at the age of fifteen, everything had changed. Under a tree in her back yard, Sydney had fallen off the tire swing because she'd wanted to stand up in the tire and show off. Even though she was a bit of a Tomboy, little did she know tire swings could twist and flip you if you only used one foot. Cole had rushed to pick her up and before he'd released her, he'd kissed her. Annoyed, but surprised, she'd asked him why he'd kissed her.

Cole had shuffled his feet and looked startled at what he'd

done. "Gosh, I don't know. I had this feeling come over me and before I knew it, I'd kissed you."

Cole had been a somewhat shy young man at times, but Sydney saw a huge difference in then and now. How he'd changed.

"Well, don't do it again," she'd ordered. Even at the time, she wasn't convinced she meant what she'd said.

Over a matter of weeks, Sydney thought about their first kiss, one thing had led to another and before long, she and Cole were inseparable. They'd vowed to let no one come between them, they'd be together for a lifetime.

Once they'd finished dessert and took their plates to the counter, they found themselves standing beneath a spray of mistletoe. Without warning, Cole's arms wrapped around her in a warm embrace. He tilted her head and pointed to the mistletoe hanging above them, then grinned.

Okay, it's only mistletoe. A light kiss won't mean anything.

She didn't drop her head or move, so Cole took his cue from her.

He leaned in and kissed her gently, but he let the kiss linger a little too long. "Wow," he whispered in her ear. "I've missed you more than I realized."

"Cole, it's only a Christmas kiss. Please don't read any more into the kiss than what it meant. Friendly, nothing more."

"Fine, but I won't apologize."

"Just so you know where we stand," Sydney murmured.

That kiss and the scent of him when he bent near her, all but did her in. She'd better take care of where her own heart stood.

Sydney rubbed at her arms to warm them. She hadn't felt anything except a cool breeze, she hadn't seen anything. But...she had smelled the familiar scent of gardenia as the light chill ran up her spine. She'd had the same experience as when Lylia had first revealed herself in the library.

"Never mind that, Cole." She pulled back her shoulders and slanted her head sideways. "Do you feel anything, or notice anything strange?"

Cole hugged her tighter and breathed in the fragrance of her hair. "I only notice you...how nice you smell and how familiar you feel in my arms right now."

"Come on, Cole. Listen to me. I'm serious." Sydney pulled away and spoke in a low, tense manner. "Don't think I'm crazy, but I sense Lylia around us. She's supposed to be at rest now, since the diary and letter exposed the truth of her death."

She hadn't seen Lylia, but glanced around, if only to acknowledge she wasn't there. At least, if she was around, Sydney was unable to see her. Funny, but she would miss their ghost in lavender.

TWENTY

Cole dropped his arms from around Sydney and declared, "Lylia did call you my love. Maybe she's hovering around to make sure we follow up on her suggestion."

"Oh, please. As if that's going to happen," Sydney said. "I rely heavily on my own decisions, not on a ghost."

"Are you two enjoying the evening?" Mrs. Granger asked, cutting short their banter.

Sydney turned to greet Mrs. Granger, happy for the interruption. "You've been very hospitable and accommodating. Thank you for all your hard work to make the reunion a success."

"My pleasure. I hope you'll come again," she said, and smiled. "You're welcome here anytime. Try not to wait until next year for your next visit."

"I hope Lylia doesn't follow me home, because she was here a few minutes ago. She may still be here," Sydney said quietly, as she directed her comment at Mrs. Granger.

"I'm so sorry. She must have taken a liking to you, Sydney. I wouldn't worry about her following you home. As I understand ghosts, they normally remain in the house where they died." She handed Sydney a card. "Give me a call if you have any more problems."

Sydney slid the card in a pocket of her slacks. "Thanks, I hope I won't need to get in touch with you."

"Merry Christmas to you both. I wish you a safe trip home, if I don't see you in the morning at breakfast. Try not to miss breakfast though. We're breaking all the year-round rules and serving an enormous smorgasbord." She laughed. "My husband's favorite meal of the year. He jokes that if he died after Christmas breakfast, he'd die a happy man."

"Yum! You can count on us. We wouldn't miss breakfast for anything," Sydney responded, then waved goodbye to Mrs. Granger.

"Hey, Sydney. Are you working tomorrow?" Cole asked.

"I'm not sure. Why?"

"Most of the town will be closed for business. As you know, they normally give employees off the day after Christmas so they can spend time with family."

Now what? Sydney continued to gaze at Cole. "So what's your question?"

Cole held his arms close to his chest, palms out and gave her an inquiring look. "On impulse, I hoped we might visit my farm after breakfast. We can go horseback riding or take in a few hours of fishing, or simply relax. I'd like to show you around, let you see what I've been up to the last few years."

Sydney understood if she visited his farm tomorrow, that would undoubtedly be the first step at a new beginning if Cole had his way. One, Cole wanted a new beginning, two, she still wasn't convinced if she wanted a new beginning. Sure, she had her own doubts, but she took into consideration Will's words before he'd passed away. He'd wanted her to find someone else to love. No matter how much she recalled their discussion, when it came down to the wire, the decision was hers. Hers alone.

The past two days had given her a lot to think on concerning her future. Would she live out the rest of her life alone, or accept that she would eventually choose another husband.

"On one condition."

"What condition is that, Sydney?"

"You won't talk about us getting back together. If we find there's still something worth saving between us, then it should be mutual and voluntary, definitely for the both of us."

Cole's eyes lit up. She almost laughed. He reminded her of the young man from way back when. How was she going to be around him and not think of the good old times? To remember those times? To want those times back again? Considering how much her heart had already softened toward him, she'd best be on her toes. Better yet, she'd best guard her heart, because if she knew him as well as she thought she did, Cole always went after and got what he wanted.

He ran his hands through his hair and blew out a ragged breath. "You drive a hard bargain, woman, but it's a deal. I agree love isn't, or shouldn't be, one-sided. I promise not to push myself on you. It'll be your call."

She grinned. "So you're putting me on the spot, are you?"

"As I said. Your call. Take it any way you choose," he said and chuckled.

"Okay then. I'll follow you to your horse farm tomorrow." She smiled at him and winked. "I'll expect a steak dinner with all the trimmings, too. Oh, and if we ride, I'll have nothing to wear. I didn't exactly pack for a trip to a farm."

TWENTY-ONE

"Promise not to hate me." Cole scrunched up his face and made a growling sound. "Let me finish before you say anything, okay?"

He looked like a big old bear who'd lost his last meal.

Sydney bit her bottom lip to keep from laughing. "I'll think about it."

"Please do. You are almost the same size as Maria. There are several riding habits at the house, if you wouldn't mind wearing her clothing. Everything has been dry cleaned, so cleanliness won't present a problem."

I can't believe you asked me to wear your wife's clothes. "I'm not thrilled about wearing your deceased wife's clothing, Cole. We can stop at the mall and I'll buy something appropriate."

"Raddwell's a small town, remember? The mall will probably be closed except for a few restaurants," he reminded her.

"Of course you're right. It isn't mandatory we ride tomorrow, Cole. We'll need to stop by the grocery store though."

"Always thinking of your tummy," he said in a joking manner.

"Oh, you!" she said, and popped him on the arm. "If I remember correctly, you're worse than I am. You can put away some groceries."

"No worries. No grocery store. You should see my pantry. I'm a single man who shops for enough groceries to last weeks at a time. Except for milk, bread, eggs and a few other incidentals."

"And you're sure you have steaks, salad makings, and potatoes?"

"Yep. Made a run a couple of days ago. We'll lay the steaks out when we get to the house. There isn't much time to shop with everything there is to do on a farm."

"You could have groceries delivered, you know." Sydney thought how hard living alone on a farm must be. She hadn't been raised on a farm, but appreciated there was always something to do. She admired the men who had chosen that line of work. She realized her admiration for Cole had shot up a few notches.

The next morning breakfast was everything Mrs. Granger had promised, that and more.

"I've packed baskets of peach muffins for each of you to take home," Mrs. Granger said. "Promise me you'll visit again and I'll bake something special for you two."

Sydney hugged her. "We'd love to visit as often as we can." She glanced at Cole. "Oops. I'm sorry, Cole. I shouldn't speak for you."

He shrugged and stood so he could shake Mrs. Granger's hand. "Not a problem. I'll visit whenever you'd like. My best to your husband."

"I look forward to seeing both of you again, and I'll give my husband your message. Be safe driving back home."

Sydney waved goodbye to Mrs. Granger, then turned to Cole. "I'm all packed and ready to go, when you are."

"I'm about forty-five miles from town. We should be there before noon if we don't run into any problems." Cole loaded their cars and headed for the farm, Sydney following his lead.

Sydney lived at the edge of Raddwell, in her mom and dad's old home-place, which she found heartwarming. Plenty of memories surrounded that old house, and they were what counted. As much as she loved the country, her hectic schedule hindered traveling as much as she'd like since she'd taken over her mom's flower shop. Still, she had her friends and was as relatively content as a grieving widow could be.

Once on the road, she observed mile upon mile of fenced pastures and long gated driveways, now laden in snow, that rushed by leaving her in the wake of its beauty. The snow had fallen steadily since they'd left The Granger Inn, and had gained strength the closer they got to Cole's home.

Cole pulled onto a graveled driveway and waited for the

gate to open, then pulled forward to allow Sydney access to the farm before he closed the gate.

A rapidly thickening blanket of frosty shimmers layered the rolling hills and pastures beyond a sprawling ranch style home that sat atop a hill surrounded by stands of bare trees. Further down the hill, from the house, were the stables and barns.

Sydney drew in a quick breath. The farm, what she could see, was picturesque and inspirational. What she wouldn't give to have canvas and paints with her. Maybe Cole would allow her to bring them another time and paint parts of his farm.

Cole parked the car, then walked to hers and opened the door. "Is there any reason you may need your bags?"

"No. I'm good."

Cole saluted her and pulled his bags from the trunk. "If you change your mind..."

"I can barely wait to get inside the stables and see what breed of horses you have," Sydney said, then pulled her coat tight against her neck to block the wind.

"First things first, Sydney."

She followed Cole to the wrap-around porch. Even though the sun's warmth had broken through, she breathed in frigid air, then blew it out slow and easy. She chose a rocking chair at the end of the porch, giving her a view of pasture and mountains.

"I'd forgotten how beautiful the foothills of the Blue Ridge Mountains are. Your farm is breathtaking! No wonder you love it here."

"I've never been happier."

As she looked out at the vast land, then back at Cole's face, she knew he was home. "You were right to buy this place, Cole." She smiled up at him as she moved back and forth in the varnished rocking chair.

"This place is in your blood."

Twenty-Two

"Steaks are up. Mind looking in the cabinet and bringing me a clean platter?" Cole fanned at the smoke and turned off the grill. "Hope you still prefer your steak medium rare," he called out.

"Check on the table. I've already brought out a platter," Sydney called from the patio and shook her head. "Yes, you remembered correctly on the steak."

Cole had cleaned the table and Sydney had rinsed last of the dishes when the phone rang.

"Hi, Ted. How are you? What? Hold on. I'll be right there."

"Sydney, please wait for me to get back before you leave. I can't explain right now but there's been an accident down the road." He reached over the counter, pulled her to him and kissed her soundly on the lips. "That'll hold you until I return," he remarked, then chuckled.

She stumbled back and grasped the counter. "Cole Myers. You promised not to push me."

"I didn't push. I kissed. Not the same thing." He grinned at her. "By the way, you're a natural behind the sink, and you make a mean salad. Wish I had a camera handy."

"I should leave right this minute," she pouted.

"Please don't. I love having you in my home. It feels warm, full of life and inviting again. I'll be back soon." He pulled on his heavy coat and added a hat. "My cell phone number is on the fridge if you need me."

As much as I hate to admit it, you're making me need you. Making me want to stay. To never leave.

"I'll be fine. See you shortly."

He grabbed the keys to his truck and as he passed by her, kissed her lightly on his way out the door. "We should make this a permanent thing."

Sydney frowned and crossed her arms at her chest. "You broke your promise. Are you not trustworthy?"

"I know. I know I broke my promise to you. It was too hard to keep. Yes you can trust me." He winked and chuckled as the door closed behind him.

Over two hours later, Sydney became concerned when Cole hadn't gotten back home. She'd paced the floor and tried his cell, but got no answer. She checked her watch and peeked out the window. It was now going on ten and she wasn't keen on driving late at night, especially in the heavy snow, which continued to fall. Since there wasn't much traffic around here late at night, the roads would be covered in snow. Maybe ice, she hadn't heard. Surely he'd be home before long.

Sydney dug around the cabinets in search of coffee. She finally found it in a huge ceramic jar on the counter. When the coffee pot began to gurgle, she poured cream in a mug and warmed it in the microwave.

She kicked off her shoes and went to the living room and flipped on the lights, the television, then searched for the weather station or the news. The weather report didn't help matters any. She groaned. They were predicting more snow for the next two days, with no let-up in its torrent.

It was still the Christmas season. Sydney turned off the TV, then roamed through the radio stations until she found a station that still played non-stop Christmas carols.

She wouldn't be going anywhere. But where was Cole? How would he feel when she'd be stuck here for a few days? Knowing him, he'd be thrilled she wasn't able to leave.

What about tending to the horses? She barely knew how to ride, much less take care of his horses, but she'd make a stab at it if she had to. Certainly Cole would be home before she had to make such a decision. He employed two work hands, but they were off for the rest of the week. So much for help.

Automatic feeders! Sydney recalled Cole mentioning that he'd installed automatic feeders for the horses since he sometimes left for days at a time.

Thank God. She wouldn't have to go out in this snowstorm. If anything happened to Cole's horses he'd probably be bankrupt.

The coffee's aroma filtered through the room. She'd forgotten about putting it on, got up and poured a mug full. She'd barely raised the mug to her lips when the phone rang. Hesitant that she should answer Cole's phone, she took a sip of coffee, shrugged, then picked up the kitchen phone.

"Sydney?"

"Cole? Where are you? Is everything okay?"

"I'm fine now. I'd have called you sooner, but they wouldn't let me use the phone until they ran tests."

"Tests? Are you at the hospital? Are you all right? What's wrong? Are they going to keep you? Do I need to come down?"

"Whoa. So many questions. No. Please don't try to come down. They're going to release me in a little while. At first, they thought I had a mild concussion, but thank God I don't. Terrible headache though. The CT scan result was negative. I talked them out of keeping me since I have no concussion and you're at home."

Since you're at home, he'd said. Is he okay, or simply telling the doctors I'm here so he could come home?

"How did you know I wouldn't have driven home already?"

"Not in this weather, besides I understand you, remember? You don't drive in heavy snow."

"Yes, that's true. I want to know what happened to you, but we can talk about it when you get here. Wait. Are you able to drive?"

"Yes, I'll be there before long. Hold on, Sydney. The nurse is here to remove my IV."

"I'll talk to you later. Do what you have to."

"Hang on." He paused for a minute, while the nurse gave him instructions. "Okay. I'm back."

"Don't be frightened when you see a snowplow coming to the house later on tonight. I was lucky enough to catch Paul, the manager, in the area, plus he's a friend. He'll plow from the hospital to home and I'll follow."

"You're also lucky you live in a small town with caring folks willing to help you in time of trouble."

Sydney couldn't imagine what trouble Cole would be in, if he had lived in a metropolitan town. There was definitely something to be said for small towns and good neighbors.

"The nurse gave me my walking papers. Have to run so I won't hold up the snowplow."

"I'll be here waiting for you. Hurry home."

Much to her surprise, her heart had thawed toward Cole. *When had that happened?*

TWENTY-THREE

Following behind the snowplow had taken Cole approximately an hour before he finally, pulled into the driveway. Sydney was on her third mug of coffee when the snowplow's headlights bounced their way up the hill and stopped at the house.

Sydney had rummaged through Cole's pajama drawer earlier, and found suitable nightwear and a pair of heavy socks. She'd already made up both of the sofas in the living room, so she would be close by in case Cole called for something during the night. It was just as well, she wasn't going home, at least not tonight.

At first, it had been the snow that kept her here, now she wouldn't leave him, even if she could, when he needed her. He did need her, at least now, whether he wanted to admit it or not.

Cole wasn't her responsibility, but she had no reason to abandon him. Those old loving feelings rushed inside her head, and worse, inside her heart. She was in trouble, but she wouldn't dispute it or try to deny what she saw coming at her head-on.

She'd lost her heart to Cole. Again.

Sydney settled Cole on the sofa and brought a mug of coffee to warm him.

"Thanks for the coffee. You look adorable in my P.J.'s and floppy socks, by the way," he said, then failed at concealing a chuckle.

The pajama legs were rolled up, as were the sleeves, which she had to keep pushing back in place. "I'm sure they look funny, but you're a big guy. There wasn't much of a choice."

Sydney saw Cole open his mouth to speak, then close it immediately. She wondered if he was about to suggest her wearing Maria's clothes again.

She took a deep breath and jumped in. "Don't you dare leave me again, Cole Meyers. Do you realize how worried I was?"

"Not on your life, my love," he mumbled. Cole cocked an eye open and smiled through his pain. "Now who's being aggressive?"

Suddenly, Sydney had second thoughts of baring her soul to Cole. But then, if she didn't speak up now, she might never. "I suppose I am. Like you, I realize what I want. What's important."

"And that is?"

"You. You big lug." Sydney leaned down and kissed him gently on the lips. "I've missed you, too."

Cole pulled her down on the sofa and stared into her eyes. He slid his hand around her neck, wrapped her in his arms and rested his head against her forehead. "Now we're getting somewhere. You know how I feel about you," he whispered. "You're all I want. I love you."

She wanted to say I love you too, but the words stuck inside her mouth.

"You scared me. I thought you weren't coming back." She laid the back of her hand on his forehead. "You look so pale. I'll go get a pillow and elevate your head," she stated, then patted him on the chest. "Don't go anywhere."

"Ha. As if I could," Cole responded.

Sydney headed for the bedroom and halfway down the hall, to her left, a flutter of lavender caught her eye. Then she smelled the fragrance. Lylia's fragrance. Gardenias.

"Hello, Lylia," she whispered low so Cole wouldn't hear. "I think I'm aware of why you're here. Thank you for helping me to gather courage to admit my love for Cole."

Lylia danced around her with the sweetest scent Sydney had ever experienced. "Go on home. It's time. Go be with your love. Goodbye, Lylia. Rest in Peace."

Sydney smiled and nodded as the sweet scent of gardenia faded, and the lavender gown floated out of sight. "I don't believe we'll be seeing you again," she whispered.

When Sydney returned with the pillow, Cole was sitting up. He patted the sofa. "Come sit by me for a while."

Since they'd both been involved with Lylia, she shouldn't withhold Lylia's visit. "I wasn't going to say anything, but you deserve to hear this."

Cole appeared to be uneasy. "What is it? What's wrong?"

"Nothing's wrong," she replied and pulled the blanket back over Cole's legs. "Lylia, appeared while I was in the hall."

Cole perked up, surprised at what she'd told him. "She did? That's weird. Normally ghosts don't leave the home where they died."

"I know, but for whatever reason, she was here. I believe her job was completed and she came by to say goodbye. Her spirit is finally free."

"Wonder why she didn't appear to us both?" Cole paused, then questioned. "What do you mean, her job was completed?"

Sydney smiled. "Once she'd made herself visible to us. I believe she sensed what was hidden in our hearts. She felt we should be together, and played the role of matchmaker." She laughed. "We've been had by a ghost."

Cole chuckled and folded her in his arms, hugged her tight, then sat back and rubbed his temples. "Can't say I'm unhappy with her. Meeting Lylia was quite an experience." Cole nudged her. "She gifted us quite a Christmas."

"That she did," Sydney agreed. "Do you need anything? Is your headache coming back?"

"A slight ache, that's all. I'll be okay. I may take something in a few minutes."

Sydney thought if she could get him to talk, he might forget the headache. "Care to discuss what happened tonight?"

"Would you mind nuking my coffee first? I don't enjoy cold coffee."

"Sure." Instead, Sydney poured fresh coffee, then warmed it.

Cole took the mug from her and continued. "I'd pulled Ted out of the ditch, then we checked his car for damages. We were about to leave, when a truck came around the curve right before the bridge. The truck was going too fast and when he tried to slow down, the truck slid into the bridge. When he hit the bridge, the truck rolled on its side. Thank God he didn't roll into the river."

"But that doesn't explain how you were hurt."

"I didn't move quick enough and while standing on part of the bridge where the truck hit, I took quite a tumble when part of the bridge gave away. I barely escaped hitting the water." He sipped at the coffee and sighed. "My head hit the concrete and left this gash in my head. The truck driver is in the hospital for observation."

Sydney hugged him. "You're safe now. Nothing else matters."

"There is one thing."

"What's that?"

"Since the bridge is out, you won't be able to go home until it's repaired."

Twenty-Four

Sydney blinked hard and let out a low whistle. "So all of us on this side of the bridge are stuck for the duration?"

Cole shook his head. "I'm sorry. It appears so. Nothing to do but put up with me for a few days."

Sydney grinned and winked at him. "I think I can handle your company. Maybe we won't tire of each other," she said, while she pulled her hair back from her face.

"Never would I tire of having you around. It's a bit of bad luck, especially for you, but nothing will please me more," he answered.

"You know, Christmas is a special holiday for us to spend time together. Become familiar with each other again." Secretly, Sydney hoped this would prove to be a new beginning for the two of them. The prospect of having Cole back in her life, was a new beginning, one she was looking forward to getting underway. She backed up her thoughts. They were already ongoing.

"It'll be like old times. We'll have fun. No work, only fun," he said, and grinned.

"Not the perfect vacation from work either, but I'll make the best of it. I'll call Kara tomorrow and let her know. She can handle the shop until I get back."

Sydney glanced at Cole, only to find he'd dozed off. She covered him, then took their mugs to the sink and rinsed them. She was tired too. After she'd checked the doors, she flipped off the lights and slipped under the covers on the other sofa beside Cole. Sleep was what she wanted right now.

The scent of coffee filtered to the sofa and woke Sydney early the next morning. Cole had already gotten up and was standing on the front porch, coffee mug in hand staring out over his land. She grabbed a mug and filled it, then headed out the door to join him.

She slipped an arm around his waist from the back, then laid her head on his shoulder blade. "Good morning," she said, in a cheerful voice.

Cole pulled her around, gave her a big bear hug and kissed her. "Good morning yourself, my lovely sleepyhead."

She yawned and breathed in the cold crisp air. "What time is it, anyway?"

"Seven. I woke up at five, but I didn't want to wake you, so I stayed in bed as long as I could. By the time I eventually crawled off the sofa, it was around six. You were still sleeping pretty hard."

"I'm surprised I didn't hear you earlier. I must feel safe here, because I slept through the night," she said, as she giggled. "I was tired last night. How are you feeling this morning?"

"I'm fine, a little sore, but okay." He glanced down at her. "You're safe with me. Always will be," he stated.

"I'll change your bandage in a while." She hesitated momentarily. "Unless the nurse said to wait until tomorrow."

"Yes. Tomorrow is when she said to change it. Thanks, though. I can probably replace it."

"I'll be happy to take care of the bandage." Sydney placed a hand on the side of his face. "You have nothing to prove to me. I know you better than you think I do."

"We do have that in common," he said, and laughed.

"I could get used to seeing this amazing view every morning." Sydney sighed and took a long sip of coffee. *We have more in common than you possibly realize.*

Cole looked at her, then hesitated as though he had another comment ready to share. "Feel free to come over any time you'd like. My home is yours whenever you can make time to visit."

A visit. What I'd like would be to live here, with you, but that decision is yours to make. But then how would he know that, since he had no idea how she really felt about him. And she was too nervous to tell him exactly how she felt. Maybe one day soon she would.

"When I woke to find you on the sofa, I thought how wonderful it would be to find you here every day. Permanently." He took both their mugs and set them on a table, then turned her to face him. "I let myself imagine that it could happen one day, and how happy we would be together."

"Cole..."

"I'm not pushing you, Sydney. I'd never push you in any way. I only want you to understand how I feel and how much you mean to me."

"What do we do about Will and Maria? How do we get past loving them? Missing them?"

"I'm saddened every day at losing Maria, and I'm sure you feel the same about Will. We had our allotted time with each of them. They're still part of us, no matter what we do or where we go. They'll remain in our hearts forever." He ran a hand through his hair and pulled his coat close to his chest. "The past couple of years were the hardest I've ever spent. I don't want to go through that kind of grief again, but I do want to love again...I want that love to be you. Only you. I'll never love another woman as much as I love you, Sydney. Ever."

"Thank you, Cole. I appreciate you baring your soul and being honest with me. That took a lot of courage to admit."

Cole had grown up. Grief had the means of ripping out your heart, of touching your soul and changing you in ways you never thought possible.

He leaned down and kissed her gently, then whispered. "You may see it as courage, I see it as truth."

Cole was an incredible man, one who loved her, and the man she loved in return. She'd had reservations of putting her heart on the line, but gathered enough courage to admit she still loved him. Not the young boy she'd fallen in love with as a teen, but a full-grown man who gave freely of himself. He was kind, yet full of strength. Part of his strength came from grief. She should know, part of her strength came from the same place.

Sydney had no doubts that Cole would prove himself a

loving and attentive husband. What more could she ask for?

Then there would be a new place to call home. Home would be wherever Cole was. Her heart would be full, content.

A new home with a considerable amount of land to work. Land for the horses to roam. There would be foals, then extra responsibilities to keep them busier than they probably wanted, but farms demanded hard work and dedication. She had no qualms about being accountable.

In her heart's mind, she wondered, *if* there would be children...Or should she be so positive as to ask *when* there would be children? She could only dream. And dreaming, she was.

Now was as good a time as any to let him know how she felt too. Cole had not mentioned marriage. Of course he wouldn't without knowing how she felt about him. Too, they'd only been together for two days since she was fifteen.

"Cole...I've fought against loving you, but the pull is too strong. I can't fight both you and my heart any longer. I also want you. I love you. I love you more than I did at fifteen. I love you more than I did yesterday, because today, I'm unafraid. I'm not afraid to love you again. We can be happy together, because we both want a good, honest relationship, a love that will last."

Cole looked at her as though she had two heads. His eyes popped wide open as his jaw dropped. "Are you serious? Does this mean what I think it means? Are you willing to become my wife?"

"Well, Cole, that remains to be seen," she said, then giggled. "You haven't asked me yet."

A huge grin broke over his entire face. "Well then, woman. Never let it be said that Cole Meyers didn't go after the love of his life."

Cole got down on one knee and took both her hands in his. "Sydney Hall, would you do me the honor of being my wife? My love? My everything?"

Sydney pulled him to her and threw herself in his arms. "Yes! Yes, Cole Meyers, I'll be your wife."

Cole feigned a look of shock. "What? You aren't going to

make me wait for an answer?"

With a smile big enough for her dimples to stand out, she shook her head. "Why should I when we both know what we want? We've gotten a second chance at love, and I'm not going to waste one minute."

Cole's stuck out his chest so far, she thought the buttons would pop off his shirt. "You've made me the luckiest man in the world, Sydney."

"I'm a fortunate woman to have you return my love," she said, through the tears that ran down her face.

Cole wiped away her tears, hugged and kissed her fervently, yet lovingly. "Oh, my sweet, sweet, Sydney. I thought I'd lost you forever."

"Never happen, my love," she breathed in, through his tender bear hug. "Never again." She raised her head. "Cole," she gasped.

"Yes, honey?"

"You'll need to lighten your grip. I'm having a hard time breathing."

Cole immediately loosened his hold on her. "So sorry. Get used to being hugged, though," he said, then with one hand he tossed his hat in the air. He caught her up in his arms and swung her around and around the porch, the wintry winds and snow blowing through their hair.

Here she was planning a wedding two days after she and Cole had found each other again. How crazy was that?

They'd both decided to hold the ceremony at the farm next spring, six months away.

What better place for them to join in matrimony?

She was right. Christmas was all about love and forgiveness.

How could I ever wish for a more perfect Christmas?

Susan R. Hughes

Christmas
at *The Roses*

CHRISTMAS AT THE ROSES
BY SUSAN R. HUGHES

All Ellie wants for Christmas is to avoid it altogether. Reeling from her broken romance with Spencer, she plans to spend the holidays at the historic Roses Inn writing her novel. Spencer has a plan of his own—to rekindle both her love for him and her fondness for the holidays. To win back her stubborn heart, he might just need a little help from the inn's resident ghost.

PROLOGUE

You're spending Christmas *alone*?" Gwen braced her shoulder against the frame of Ellie's bedroom door, her arms folded, as she pinned her roommate with a skeptical look. "At some hotel?"

"Not just some hotel," Ellie replied while tossing a pair of jeans into the small suitcase lying open on her bed. "The Roses Inn. The one owned by Abby Wells."

"You mean the haunted inn?"

Ellie rolled her eyes. "Supposedly haunted, but any place over a hundred years old gets the reputation of having a ghost or two, especially in Niagara-on-the-Lake." Ellie opened the top drawer of her dresser and plucked out a few pairs of plain white socks. She wouldn't need anything fancy to wear during the six days she'd be away from home. "It's just a lovely little inn in a picturesque town. It'll be quiet, and I'll have time to work on my new novel."

"But over Christmas?" Gwen cocked her head, making her unruly copper curls spill over one shoulder. "You can't do that. It sounds just dismal."

To Ellie, it sounded perfect. What a relief it would be to forgo the forced cheer and obligatory gift-exchanging that she'd been dreading. She might even manage to avoid the garish decorations and Christmas tunes that chafed her nerves. Instead she'd enjoy a restful midwinter break, a chance to recharge and catch up on her writing—and with any luck, she just might meet her publisher's deadline.

"A week alone is just what I need," she said. "Besides, my parents and sister are spending the holidays with my grandmother in Boston."

Gwen stepped into the room, sliding her hands into the back pockets of her jeans. "You could have gone with them."

"They wanted me to, but I'm happier staying behind. I'll visit Grandma in the summer." She tucked the socks into her suitcase, next to her pink flannel nightgown, and headed to her closet to select a few tops.

"Come back Christmas Day, at least," Gwen pressed. "Have dinner with me and my parents."

Pausing with her hand on the sleeve of her favourite purple chenille turtleneck, Ellie glanced over her shoulder at Gwen. "I appreciate the offer. But I'd rather not pretend I'm into the season when really I'm happier treating it like just another day."

Gwen was quiet for a moment. "Ellie, I've known you forever. You're not the Grinch you pretend to be. I *know* what this is about."

"Can you blame me for wanting to skip the celebrations? Of anyone, you should understand. Last Christmas, you're the one who dragged me off to the Dominican Republic."

"Yes, but I was just getting over a break-up," Gwen countered.

"So am I." Ellie pulled the sweater off the hanger and spread it out on her bedspread, avoiding her roommate's probing gaze.

"Sure, but it's not the same. I wasn't moping alone in the Dominican. I had my best friend with me to take my mind off the trauma."

"I'm hardly moping—"

"And *you* didn't catch your boyfriend cheating on you, like I did," Gwen pointed out. "You were the one who broke Spencer's heart."

A tumbling sensation in Ellie's chest made her breath catch. Inhaling deeply, she managed to tamp down the tangled emotions that tended to bubble up whenever Spencer Brooks entered her mind. Her gaze skittered over the pillow laid neatly against the headboard on the right side of her bed—the side that used to be his whenever he stayed over. The last thing she'd wanted was to hurt him, but there was no denying she had done just that.

It wasn't all her fault. If he'd listened to reason, and respected her feelings instead of pushing his own agenda on her, they might still be together.

"It was his choice," she told Gwen, yanking her gaze back to the purple sweater. With her free hand, she folded the sleeves inward before rolling the garment into a cylinder shape. "He knew how I felt, and he put me in an impossible position. He forced me to make a decision."

"You sure you made the right one?"

"Of course," Ellie replied with conviction, though her throat felt uncomfortably tight. She swung around and grabbed a few more sweaters from the closet. Giving up her fight to hold back the tears welling in her eyes, she blinked rapidly to clear her vision, and silently scolded herself for letting her emotions get the better of her.

And for letting those niggling doubts back in.

And for still missing him with such an intense ache that she sometimes couldn't breathe.

She cleared her throat and added in a thinner voice, "Don't try to make me feel guilty."

"I'm not trying to hurt you," Gwen said gently, taking a couple of steps closer. "I'm worried about you. Joel's been out of your life for two years. Don't you think it's time you stopped letting him spoil your chance to be happy?"

The emotions churning inside Ellie lumped into a sour ball in her stomach. Turning toward the window, she closed her eyes briefly and steeled herself, refusing to let Joel into her mind. Gwen meant well, but she had it all wrong. Ellie almost never thought about him anymore, so how could he affect her at all?

She opened her eyes and watched the snowflakes tumbling through the grayness outside her bedroom window. The tiny twelfth-floor apartment she shared with Gwen had little to brag about, other than the impressive view it gave of downtown Toronto, with the CN Tower jutting high above the skyscrapers, now obscured by swirling snow.

"Ellie?"

Forcing a smile to her lips, she faced Gwen. "I'm perfectly fine. And I'm sure this will be the best Christmas I've had in years, now that I've resolved to ignore it." She tossed the sweaters into her suitcase without bothering to fold them, and shut the lid.

ONE

Her suitcase in her hand and her laptop case slung over her shoulder, Ellie paused below the decorative sign above the entrance of The Roses Inn. She gazed up at the rectangular two-story building, plain and sturdy in a distinctive Georgian style, with pale yellow siding and deep green shutters. Soft snow clung to the windowsills and formed downy peaks on the coach lanterns on either side of the door. The inn was really only six years old, having been restored after a fire destroyed much of the original interior, but according to Abby it looked the same as it had at the turn of the nineteenth century when it was first built.

Shivering in the early evening chill, Ellie opened the green paneled door and the holly wreath hanging there swung side to side, jangling the tiny bells affixed to its branches. In the welcoming warmth of the foyer, she stamped her boots on the doormat before stepping onto the brocade rug laid over hardwood flooring. The small space, with its homey décor of exposed beams and knotty pine wainscoting, only accommodated a dark wood counter and a single upholstered chair. A staircase to the right led to the second floor.

The man behind the desk, black haired and stocky, greeted her with an affable smile. "Welcome to The Roses, lass," he said in a broad accent that Ellie recognized as Northern English.

"Nippy out there," she remarked.

"That it is. But the fresh fall of snow is beautiful, isn't it? The way it glistens under the lights, one almost doesn't need Christmas decorations on an evening like this."

Silently adding that she could do without them altogether, Ellie acknowledged his words with just a slight dip of her chin. She set down her cases on the rug and tugged her gloves off her fingers. "I have a reservation."

"Your name, please?"

"Ellie Lynd."

A grin spread across the man's round, ruddy face. "Ah, yes. Abby's author friend."

Ellie nodded, though she wasn't sure she and Abby could be properly called friends. Colleagues, maybe. They shared the same publisher, and after meeting at a book signing, they'd run into each other at a few other authors' events. "You must be Oscar."

"I am, indeed. Glad to meet you, Ellie." He glanced at a computer monitor on the counter. "You'll be staying for five nights, leaving on the twenty-sixth?"

"Yes." Ellie rested her purse between the monitor and a bright crimson potted poinsettia.

Oscar tapped on the keyboard. "Have you stayed with us before?"

"No, but when Abby told me she owned one of the oldest inns in Ontario, in one of the prettiest towns in the province, it sounded like the ideal place to get away for a few days."

"Don't let the weather dissuade you from getting out and about. There's plenty to do here during the holidays." Oscar plucked several glossy brochures from a rack behind him and slid them across the counter. "You missed the Santa Claus parade, unfortunately, but you can still walk around town and enjoy the displays of Christmas lights, or better yet, take a horse-drawn carriage ride. There's a gingerbread house auction tomorrow that you shouldn't miss. And Christmas Eve, you can join a local church choir on a candlelight stroll through town. Oh, and of course if you like wine, some of the wineries in the area are holding festive events."

Ellie took a cursory glance at the brochures. "Thanks, but I'll be in my room writing most of the time."

His smile slipped just a little. "I'm sure you'll be comfortable in the Captain's Room." He pressed a key on the keyboard and the printer whirred behind him. "Our pub is open for lunch and dinner, and there are a few places nearby that serve breakfast."

"Sounds perfect."

Oscar pulled an invoice off the printer and handed it to

Ellie, along with a pen. "Let me help you with your suitcase," he offered, while she signed the paper.

"It's not necessary. I can—"

Before she could finish objecting, he had her small suitcase in hand and was headed up the stairs. Setting down the pen, she grabbed her purse and laptop and jogged after him.

At the first room at the top of the stairs, he slid a key into the lock and opened the door. Ellie followed him into the room, while he placed her suitcase beside the four-poster bed and left the key on the nightstand.

She stepped out of her damp boots and gazed around at the room's simple, sturdy oak furnishings and plain cream walls. The small table and chair in the corner would serve as a perfect writing desk. She turned to Oscar, whose broad frame filled most of the doorway. "The room's lovely. Abby's done a wonderful job restoring the place," she said.

"She'll be chuffed to hear it. Would you like me to ask her to ring up when she arrives?"

"Yes, please."

"I want to mention that I read your book, *The Last Prince of York*." Oscar ran his hand over the bristly dark hair at the back of his head, as though shy to admit he knew her work. "I'm not much of a fiction reader, mind you, but Abby left the book in the lounge, and since I'm from Yorkshire, it caught my eye. Once I picked it up and skimmed over the first page, I couldn't put it down."

"That's the ultimate compliment." Ellie smiled with genuine pleasure. "I'm...chuffed."

Returning her smile, he gave a deep nod. "Grand. If you have any questions, you know where to find me."

"Any hauntings lately in this room?" she asked glibly as he turned to leave.

His hand resting on the doorknob, Oscar twisted to face her, one thick black eyebrow rising. "Not recently. Since the fire, Rebecca tends to be more selective about who she chooses to visit."

"Rebecca?"

"Abby didn't tell you about Rebecca Norris?"

"She said there was supposedly a ghost here," Ellie said, curious. "She didn't go into detail."

Oscar's expression turned subdued. "Rebecca was an ancestor of Abby's husband, Jason. D'you know Jason?"

"I haven't met him."

"Well, Rebecca's family lived here during the War of 1812. Her husband, Jack, was killed in battle, and she passed away just after their baby was born, in one of the rooms here."

"Wow. How tragic. Well, it's no wonder her soul hasn't been able to rest," Ellie remarked. Though she didn't believe in ghosts, she understood how spooky stories could develop in the wake of traumatic events. "Have you seen anything unusual while working here?"

"Not for some time, as I said. Don't let it worry you. If she does show herself, she'd not harm anyone."

"Oh, I'm not worried. Thank you, Oscar."

After he left the room and closed the door, Ellie placed her laptop on the small table, and then lifted her suitcase onto the bed and opened the latches. Humming to herself, she extracted her toiletries bag and carried it into the bathroom, where she brushed her teeth and ran a comb through her hair to tame the tangled long strands.

Emerging from the bathroom a few minutes later, she stopped short when a waft of cool air touched her arms. She glanced at the window and noticed the filmy curtain billowing inward as though nudged by a breeze.

Shuddering from the cold, Ellie stared at the swaying curtain for a moment, puzzled as to why someone would leave a window open this time of year.

Come to think of it, why hadn't she noticed the chill in the room when she first walked in with Oscar?

Striding across the rug to the window, Ellie pushed back the curtain. She scanned the double-hung panes in search of a way to close them. It took a moment for her mind to register the fact that the window appeared to be firmly shut.

She pushed down on the sash, just to make sure there wasn't a small crack, but it didn't budge. She then ran her hands around the frame and along the sill, and felt no hint of a draft.

The cold air was gone, and in its place only warmth radiated from the baseboard heater.

Even with warm air flowing up her body, a chill crawled down her back. She wrapped her hands around her arms, rubbing the goose bumps that prickled her flesh.

Well that was weird.

She drew a long breath and expelled it as an uneasy laugh. Obviously her conversation with Oscar had worked its way into her imagination. Shaking her head, Ellie turned away from the window and moved to the bed to finish unpacking her suitcase.

She jumped when the phone on the table rang. Leaving her sweaters in a pile on the bedspread, she went to the phone and picked it up. "Hello?"

"Hi, Ellie. It's Abby."

"Hi, Abby," she said, her tone bright with gratitude for a moment of conversation to fill the quiet in the room. "This place is gorgeous. Are you downstairs?"

"Thanks. I'm glad you like it. I am downstairs, but I'm sorry, I don't have time to see you right now. I have to pick up my daughter from a play date in a few minutes. Would you like to get together tomorrow?"

"Yes, I'd love that."

"Do you have plans with family or friends in town?" Abby asked.

"No. I'm not here to visit anyone. I'm just here to write."

"Really?" Abby paused. "I'm amazed you can find time to get away and write so close to Christmas."

Ellie lowered herself into the Windsor chair by the table, as she offered her most concise explanation. "I'm not celebrating. I recently broke up with my boyfriend, so I'm not exactly in a festive mood."

"I'm sorry to hear that. So what's your new book about? Last time we spoke, you were struggling to come up with a new story."

"Inspiration hit when I saw a program about a castle in Somerset, England," Ellie said, thankful Abby had introduced a more comfortable subject. "One of the towers is called the

'Lady Tower' because the lord kept his wife imprisoned there for several years."

"And did she finally manage to escape, or was she released?"

"She got out when King Henry VIII had her husband charged with treason for colluding with Thomas Cromwell. Both men were beheaded," Ellie said.

"A common hazard for nobles back then, I suppose," Abby remarked.

"I started thinking about what this woman went through and what happened to her afterwards, and how she might've found happiness in a time when women had so little say in their own fate. I hope readers will find it interesting."

"It sounds to me like your story has great promise."

Elle wandered toward the window, her thoughts flickering back to the baffling moment of coldness in the room that she couldn't yet explain. "I am curious to know more about this place. You never told me the ghost is your husband's ancestor."

"Long story. I'll tell you about it tomorrow. Have a good night, Ellie," Abby said, adding with a laugh, "Just tell Rebecca you're a friend of mine, and she'll be good to you."

Two

Summer 1537, Farleigh Hungerford Castle, Somerset

On her sixteenth day in the tower, Lady Elizabeth Hungerford looked at her hands and wept. It was the first time she had thought to notice how they'd changed. She could not see the rest of herself, but her hands she studied earnestly, as she held and turned them in the light of the tower's east window. The skin, parched and cracked, drew tightly on the ragged nails, caked with grime. These were no longer her own hands; they were the hands of a woman much older than her twenty-seven years.

Lowering her face into her pitiful hands, she wept bitterly. No one heard or came to comfort her, and her sobs echoed unanswered against the stone walls of the tower. Each of the past sixteen mornings, she had opened her eyes with the fleeting hope that she might finally be awakening from this nightmare; that she might find herself home at Sleaford, still a young girl in her father's house, never having fallen into the grip of Walter Hungerford. But here she remained, the lady of the manor, locked away with nothing to do but wipe the hot tears from her cheeks and pray for God's mercy.

Ellie stared at her laptop screen for several minutes before the words she'd typed began to blur together. Slumping against the rigid spindles that formed the back of the chair, she rubbed her fingers across her eyes and heaved a deep sigh.

She'd hardly budged from the chair since breakfast, but it was past noon now and she'd written only four new pages. She wished, for the umpteenth time, that she could send her draft to Spencer for his suggestions. He'd have a ton of ideas to prod her reluctant muse back to work. But it wouldn't be fair to ask him. She hadn't even spoken to him in several weeks. He'd moved on with his life, and she was trying to do the same.

But moving on wasn't exactly getting easier. Writing a novel without Spencer's input felt strange and arduous. They'd met while she was plotting The Last Prince of York, when he was referred to her as an expert on Plantagenet and Tudor royalty. He taught history at a private school not far from the museum where she'd worked as a tour guide. He'd been nearly as excited as she was about the project, and they'd spent long hours working together on her fictionalized account of true events from King Henry VII's court. Spencer had provided historical details while she shaped the prose, bringing to life the mysterious figure Perkin Warbeck, who in 1495 claimed to be one of the princes purportedly murdered by Henry's predecessor, King Richard III.

Spencer's passion for the subject had ignited Ellie's creative fire and she hadn't been able to fill pages fast enough— although at times she'd had to fight to keep her focus, when a mere glance of his sea-blue eyes made her pulse skitter, and his easy smile triggered warm ripples in her chest. Six months after Joel had broken her heart, she hadn't felt ready to let someone else in. But she'd fallen hard for Spencer anyhow, and by the time her novel topped the bestseller lists for historical fiction, and she'd quit her day job, they were spending nearly every night together.

Now on her own, professionally and personally, Ellie found herself struggling in both spheres. At thirty-two, she knew she was lucky to be successful enough to support herself with her writing. And she'd been lucky to have Spencer, for as long as it lasted. Maybe she'd depended on him too much. If there were any ghosts in the room, they were merely visions of Spencer that refused to be banished from her mind.

After saving her document, Ellie stood and arched her back, stretching her arms. A quiet room usually helped her concentrate, but right now she wouldn't get any more done if she couldn't wrench her thoughts away from Spencer and into the head of Lady Hungerford. She glanced through the window, out at the snowy street, where an elderly couple strolled past along the sidewalk, their arms linked. A walk just might help clear her head, and anyway, her stomach had been growling for the last half hour and she needed to eat.

She grabbed her room key from the nightstand, slid on her runners and headed downstairs. With the noise and aromas of the pub below meeting her before she reached the landing, her stomach rumbled with more insistence.

In the dining area, she found a small table near a stone fireplace opposite the bar. She settled into one of the dark wood captains' chairs, appreciating how the antique rustic furniture and aged oak floors and beams reflected the inn's humble roots. A fire crackling in the fireplace warmed the room. Though she enjoyed the ambiance, Ellie had always felt awkward eating alone in restaurants. She ordered a roast beef sandwich and a chef salad, and while she waited, occupied herself studying the landscape paintings on the walls. When her meal arrived, she ate quickly and returned to her room.

She stayed only long enough to don her coat and boots before heading back downstairs. The day manager at the front desk, a sandy-haired man who was younger and leaner than Oscar, greeted her affably.

"Good afternoon. Can I help you with anything?"

"I'd like to go exploring," Ellie said, while slipping her gloves on her hands. "I haven't been to Niagara-on-the-Lake since I was a girl and I can't remember where anything is. Can you tell me which direction I should head in to get to the shops?"

"You'll want the heritage district. Queen Street is just a block down." He motioned toward the window on his right side. "It's very pretty in the summer with all the flower displays, but this time of year the street has a special charm."

"Thanks."

Flipping her hood over her head, Ellie pushed through the door and stepped out into the afternoon sunlight. The cold air nipped her face, but thankfully there was little wind and the sun glowed bright in a clear blue sky. Pulling her scarf up over her cheeks, she glanced along the road to the spot where she'd parked her car—on a corner that branched into a quiet, tree-lined residential neighbourhood—then walked the other way as she'd been directed.

When she reached the corner, she paused to scan the length of Queen Street, its wide sidewalks edged with narrow snow banks. "Charming" fittingly described the old-fashioned storefronts that brought a Victorian postcard to mind. Holiday lights were strung along the windows and doorways, around light posts, and among the bare limbs of the trees that lined the sidewalks. Ellie imagined that after nightfall, the illuminated lights would make a gorgeous display.

She strolled for several blocks, passing boutiques and gift stores, sweet shops and ice cream parlours among wine bars, coffee shops and bistros. Toward the end of the shopping district, she recognized the cenotaph clock tower that rose from the median in the centre of the street. While she walked, Ellie watched an old-fashioned horse and carriage amble along the far side of the road, transporting a foursome of sightseers bundled in warm coats. The idea of renting a carriage for a short jaunt flitted through her mind, but she supposed a carriage ride for one would be even more dismal than eating alone.

When she turned her attention back to the shops, her gaze fell on the window display beside her and she slowed her steps. Garlands and red bows trimmed the outside window frame, while inside, tiers of shelves displayed apple-cheeked elves in velvet costumes, light-up snowmen, fat glittery candles and quilted stockings. Crystal angel and snowflake ornaments strung in a row stirred in a breeze from the door when it opened. Below, a tiny steam train wobbled along an oblong track, circling a row of brightly painted nutcrackers and Santa figurines in long fur-lined coats. Tucked in the far corner, a wooden nativity scene featured tiny figures carved in intricate detail.

Ellie's breath caught for a brief moment. The sight of so much Christmas glitz tugged at her, sparking the tiniest glow of girlish excitement. Memories spun back to her mind— she'd forgotten, but she was sure she'd been to this shop when she was a child. She didn't quite recognize the place, but a sense of enchantment still resided deep in her memory, from a time when Christmas had cemented her belief in magic and miracles. And she had a dim recollection of her mother having to drag her by the arm out the door.

Tearing her gaze away from the window, she shrugged away the nostalgia pulling at her. No use letting herself get sentimental about things she couldn't enjoy. Instead she turned and ducked into the gourmet food shop next door.

Sidestepping a long line of customers at the cash register, she roamed around the perimeter of the shop and scanned the shelves packed with jams and chutneys, syrups and sauces, relishes, oils and every variety of exotic-looking condiments. On each lower shelf, sample jars sat open next to bowls of pretzels for dipping.

This was more like it. Ellie unzipped her coat and stuffed her gloves into her pockets as she perused the displays, breathing in tempting aromas. She stopped at a corner table stacked with a variety of sweet and spicy mustards. Taking a pretzel, she dipped it in a sample jar of ice wine mustard and tasted it.

With the tangy blend of flavours lingering on her tongue, she picked up a jar and studied the label, noting that the mustard was made with Niagara ice wine from Brinleigh Estate Winery—wasn't Brinleigh Estate owned by Abby's husband? She made a mental note to ask, and in the midst of considering how many jars to bring back for herself and Gwen, a familiar voice behind her made her spine stiffen in alarm.

"Fantastic stuff, isn't it? I might just buy up their entire stock. It's supposed to be amazing on barbecued chicken."

Ellie spun around, her gaze connecting with a pair of eyes that were sea-blue, flecked with gold—dazzling like sun-sparked water.

In the moment it took for her shock to wear off, she placed the jar back on the shelf and squared her shoulders, aware of the erratic rhythm of her pulse. "What are you doing here, Spencer?"

"Same as you, filling up on free samples of fancy dips." With a mischievous lift of his eyebrows, he grabbed a pretzel, dunked it in the chipotle mustard sample jar and popped it into his mouth.

"I'm not... I've had lunch," she stammered, staring at him, assessing his reaction to bumping into her that struck her as far too casual. "I mean, what are you doing in Niagara-on-the-Lake?"

"I could ask you the same thing." He returned her searching look with narrowed eyes, and his lips curled into a playful smile as he asked, "Have you been following me?"

"Of course not. I didn't know..." She clamped her mouth shut and exhaled sharply through her nose. "You're the one who doesn't seem surprised to see me here."

"Not completely. I spotted you from across the street half an hour ago. Then when I saw you in here, I figured I'd say hello." He tugged off his toque and ran his hand through the ruffled strands of his thick dark hair. "It's all right to talk to you, isn't it? We're still friends—aren't we?"

Ellie angled her head in a jerky nod. She'd been the one to use the word friends the last time they spoke, though she wasn't sure such a thing was possible. Not when her heartbeat couldn't seem to follow any sort of natural rhythm in his presence. Suddenly she felt too warm in the crowded shop, and wished desperately to either shed her heavy coat or escape to the cold air outside. "You still haven't told me why you're in town," she said in the most casual tone she could manage.

Spencer selected another pretzel and scooped up a dollop of honey mustard. "Remember my old friend Gino? He and his wife run the local Helping Hands Centre. I think I told you about it—they collect food and clothing for the disadvantaged."

"I remember," she said. "I met Gino once when he came to Toronto for the weekend."

"Well, the centre is holding a holiday party tomorrow, and he asked me to play the part of Santa Claus for the kids."

Lifting her chin, Ellie peered at him with a skeptical arch of one eyebrow. "You came all this way just to do that?"

"It's not that far from home," he said, nipping off the end of the pretzel. "Just a couple hours' drive, and it's a great cause. You're here too, three days before Christmas, for some reason you haven't shared with me yet."

"I'm writing."

A smile of genuine pleasure flitted over his lips. "A new book? That's great."

"So that's why I'm here, to have some time to myself to work on it," she said crisply, finding her gaze drawn to the appealing little crease that always formed beside his mouth when his smile slanted to one side. She jerked her eyes upward to meet his. "I booked a room at an inn. I need a few days without any distractions to make some progress on the first draft."

"So close to Christmas?"

"Makes no difference," she said with a quick lift of her shoulders. "I'm not really celebrating."

Spencer's smile tightened. "Same as last year, huh?"

"Last year I supported my friend in her time of need. You said you understood," Ellie muttered. Why was she explaining herself? He wasn't even supposed to be here. She'd left Toronto to get away from diversions, and even though his presence sparked a reflexive warm glow beneath her breastbone, she couldn't think of a worse distraction.

"I did understand," he said. "I still do." He studied her with his unwavering gaze that had always made it impossible to conceal her feelings. "If we're going to be friends, you can't keep looking at me like that."

"Like what?"

"Like I've committed an unforgivable crime. All I did was ask you to marry me. You turned me down. End of story."

Ellie shuffled sideways, making room for the shoppers reaching around her to access the mustard samples. "That's not exactly what happened," she said.

Spencer faced her, resting his hands on his hips. "Right. I had the nerve to refuse your offer to live together and settle for calling you my girlfriend for the rest of our lives, when I only wanted to call you my wife." His tone roughened a little, yet the warmth remained in his eyes, and the passion in his words quivered through her chest. "My bad, I guess."

"Well, I suppose you're right about one thing. If we're going to be friends, we have to put all that behind us." Ellie drew a settling breath, letting her gaze skitter over the black buttons on his coat, and then the drawstrings dangling from his hood. Anywhere but his eyes would do.

Without thinking, she'd used the word friends yet again—that empty promise former lovers used to ease the sting of their breakup, but almost never followed through with. She couldn't imagine being around him and resisting the urge to touch him—or, far worse, seeing him touch another woman when he decided to date someone else.

Releasing a slow sigh, he dropped his hands to his sides. "So you're staying somewhere in town?"

"The Roses, just down that way." She motioned in the general direction of the inn. "Are you staying with Gino?"

"Yeah. He and his wife Sonia have a house just outside of town, overlooking the escarpment."

"I have to get back to work," Ellie said at last, her emotions twisted in a tug-of-war between the comfort of his familiar presence and desperation to be away from him. Out of habit, she rested her hand on the sleeve of his coat, before snatching it back. "Nice seeing you, Spencer. Enjoy the party."

"Merry Christmas," he said. He caught her hand and lifted it to his lips, brushing a kiss against her knuckles. The brief contact and the warmth in his eyes made her heart flop in her chest.

THREE

Spencer watched her march toward the door, her boots thudding on the hardwood with each hurried step. She shoved the door open and the tiny bell above jingled pleasantly. When she stepped outside, a single red glove tumbled from her pocket and landed on the doormat just inside the door.

Weaving around throngs of shoppers, he made his way to the doormat and bent to pick up the glove. He glanced up and caught a glimpse of Ellie passing the window, just a flutter of honey-brown hair that bounced on the shoulders of her coat as she retreated along the sidewalk.

Spencer drew a long breath to ease the tightness in his chest, watching the woman he'd intended to spend the rest of his life with run away from him again.

Six weeks after the last time he saw her, it still made no sense.

He stroked the soft angora glove with his thumb. Her warmth lingered in its fibres. Though he could easily catch up to her and return it, instead he tucked the glove into his pocket. It was a stroke of luck, really—or maybe fate—providing the perfect excuse to see her again. Much more convenient than trying to think of another reason to show up uninvited at The Roses.

She'd looked surprised to see him, but he'd had a hard time gauging the other emotions churning within her dark eyes. For his part, he figured he'd managed to come across cool and casual, as though his pulse hadn't been thundering in his ears the whole time they talked. She might not have guessed that he was frozen to the bone from walking the streets all morning, lurking near The Roses, waiting for her to emerge.

He hadn't enjoyed feeling like a creepy stalker, or lying to her about his reason for coming to Niagara-on-the-Lake. Well, he hadn't lied completely, just bent the truth. Gino hadn't exactly asked him to play Santa Claus—but Spencer couldn't very well admit that after hearing from Gwen that Ellie had headed to The Roses for the holidays, he'd called Gino and begged him to hand over the red suit. Spencer knew full well that if he showed up in town just to throw himself at Ellie's feet, she'd run the other way.

He had no intention of begging her to take him back, and compromise wasn't on his agenda, either. Getting her back, without giving in, wasn't going to be easy.

A straightforward approach hadn't worked before. He should've known, of course, when she'd told him plainly from the beginning of their relationship that marriage wasn't for her. Later, once she opened up about Joel and their cancelled wedding, Spencer had understood her reluctance—but he'd proposed anyway, in a moment of blind optimism during a Sunday walk through Toronto's High Park. With the trees glowing orange and red in the golden afternoon sunlight, and a crisp November breeze tugging at their jackets while they strolled hand in hand, the moment had felt too perfect to let pass.

He'd never forget the look of alarm on her face when he sank to one knee and asked her to be his wife. Her tremulous voice when she replied still echoed through his memory as clearly as the day it had happened, along with the crushing sensation in his chest that had followed.

"Please don't, Spence. Things are so good between us. I don't want anything to change."

"Things have to change. We have to move forward." He *gripped her hand, holding her gaze, willing her to see the depth of his love for her in his eyes.*

"Let's live together," she blurted. A small smile chased the panic from her face as the idea settled. "It's the perfect solution. I'll move into your place."

Spencer remained on the ground, the chill of the hard earth beneath his knee seeping through his jeans. For a brief moment her enthusiasm gave him hope, but he realized just as quickly that she was offering him something less than he was willing to accept. "That isn't what I want, Ellie. I want to be married. I want forever with you."

She bit the corner of her lip, her brow furrowing. "I want forever, too. But we've talked about this, and you know how I feel about marriage. Besides, we don't need a legal document to keep us together."

"If you're so dead-set against the document, I have to wonder if you're really all that sure what you want." Releasing her hand, Spencer climbed to his feet and brushed away the fallen leaves clinging to his knee. His pulse hammering in his throat, he fought to push down the anger, hurt and humiliation roiling inside him. "I know what I don't want, and that's a live-in girlfriend who's holding back from a full commitment—using a broken engagement as an excuse."

Ellie folded her arms over her chest as her beautiful dark eyes hardened. "So you're saying it's marriage or nothing? You won't compromise?"

"Jesus, Ellie, this isn't the kind of thing you compromise on. I'm one-hundred percent committed to you. Until I met you, I didn't know it was possible to need somebody this much. Sure, it's a little scary putting your heart on the line after you've been hurt. I get that. But if you're not willing to take the chance, what does that tell me about your faith in me?"

Raw emotion flickered in her eyes, but only briefly before her expression closed over—as though a door had slammed shut, locking him out. She glanced away, holding her arms tighter around her. "Sounds like you're the one who doesn't have faith in me. I guess we're just wasting our time. Bye, Spence." She spun on her heel and marched away from him, kicking aside leaves in her path as she walked.

Spencer could've sworn his heart stopped dead in his chest. He could barely catch his breath as he lurched to a nearby picnic bench and sank onto the wood-slat seat.

He should've chased after her. Maybe he could've reasoned with her. But he'd figured she'd come around on her own. He'd dug in his heels just as deep as she had, telling himself that if she wasn't willing to make their relationship official, their future was doomed anyhow.

His friends had told him if he was so hell-bent on marriage, he should find a woman who wanted the same thing. The trouble was he didn't want anyone but Ellie.

Spencer waited until mid-afternoon to make his way to The Roses. He'd never seen the inn up-close before, but he'd read about its past, along with the many other historic buildings throughout Niagara-on-the-Lake. His background as a historian gave him a special appreciation for the pretty lakeside town that had served as the original capital of the British colony of Upper Canada. Known back then as Newark, situated across the Niagara River from the United States, the town had played a central part in the War of 1812. Following the bloody Battle of Fort George in 1813, Newark had been seized by American forces, and later burnt to the ground as the troops withdrew. Tossed from their homes in the middle of winter, the resilient residents had rebuilt their town, including the original Roses Inn. Most of the military sites and several of the old homes had been restored and stood today as heritage sites.

The town's violent history had produced scores of ghostly legends that led to Niagara-on-the-Lake's reputation as the most haunted town in Canada. Reports of paranormal activity in local homes and businesses continued to draw curious tourists for nighttime ghost walks, and a chance to sleep at one of several reputedly haunted inns, The Roses among them.

Spencer climbed the steps to the door and stepped inside to find the small foyer deserted. Muted noise drifted in from the adjacent pub. He unbuttoned his coat while he waited by the desk. After a minute or so, when no one came, he wandered toward the door to the pub.

Ellie's voice nearby made him stop and glance around.

"That's amazing," she said. "Do you think everything you experienced was really supernatural?"

"I don't know," another woman's voice replied. "The rational part of my mind tells me that just because you can't explain something, that doesn't mean there isn't an explanation. I thought the apparition I saw in the window of your room six years ago looked a lot like Rebecca's portrait, but from down in the street it really wasn't that easy to tell."

Following their voices, Spencer discovered an open doorway opposite the pub entrance.

"You have a portrait of her?" he heard Ellie ask.

"Yes. We have the original at home. I used to have a copy hanging upstairs, but it was destroyed in the fire. I made another copy to hang in the pub. It draws a lot of interest from visitors who come to town for ghost tours."

The woman stopped talking when Spencer leaned into the room, which turned out to be a cozy lounge with a fireplace on the far wall, next to a bookcase overflowing with paperbacks and magazines. He found Ellie seated on a floral-print sofa beside a brunette who looked to be in her late forties. As both women turned their gazes on him, Ellie's lips parted, her expression registering disbelief and just a hint of umbrage.

The brunette stood. "Are you checking in? I'm sorry, Jeremy just stepped out. I can help you."

"Not checking in, actually." Spencer pulled the red angora glove from his pocket. "I'm a friend of Ellie's. Just returning the glove she dropped when we ran into each other earlier."

"Abby, this is Spencer Brooks," Ellie said after a moment, her uneasy gaze darting between the two of them. "Spencer, this is Abby Wells."

Abby's eyes widened a little, as recognition of his name flashed through her expression. "Good to meet you, Spencer." She held out her hand to him.

"Abby Wells, the mystery writer?" he said, grasping her hand. "Oh, that's right, Ellie told me you own an inn. I didn't put two and two together. This place is magnificent."

Abby smiled. "Thank you. Ellie told me you teach history at Elmview Academy."

"I do," he said, with a flush of pleasure to learn that Ellie had been talking about him. "You know the school?"

"Know it? I went there for three years, when I lived in Toronto. Back when you were in diapers, I'd imagine," she said with a laugh. "The uniforms were dreadful, but Elmview has always been known for its top-notch faculty. I give credit to my English teacher, Ms. Charles, for encouraging me to pursue my writing."

"Deena Charles? She's a wonderful teacher. She just retired, but if I see her, I'll pass along your regards."

"Please do. If you'll excuse me," Abby said, "I'd better see what's keeping Jeremy." She strode around him through the doorway and disappeared.

As the click of Abby's heels receded, Spencer turned to Ellie. He stepped closer and held out the glove.

Taking it, she settled a guarded gaze on him. "If you think I dropped it on purpose—"

"I'm sure you didn't," he said, "judging by those daggers in your eyes."

She looked startled at first, before the rigid lines in her face softened. "Sorry. It's just a little...awkward running into you like this. Thank you for bringing my glove."

"I brought you this, too." Reaching into his other pocket, he extracted the jar of ice-wine mustard he'd bought before leaving the shop. "You looked like you were thinking of buying some before I distracted you."

"I was." She accepted the jar and glanced down at the label. "Thank you."

"I'm not here to bother you, Ellie," he added. "I realize you don't want distractions while you're trying to write. But it is good seeing you." Briefly he scanned the length of her body, appreciating her striking figure even in a pair of old jeans and a pale pink hooded sweatshirt. His gaze skittered over her honey-brown hair, loose around her shoulders and a little dishevelled from her walk outside. He could almost feel its silky strands between his fingers. She wasn't wearing any makeup, but he'd never thought her naturally full lips, pearly complexion and haunting dark eyes needed enhancement.

"You're not bothering me," she said mildly. "I was taking a short break, but I'm about to head back to my room."

She might have meant to dismiss him, but Spencer wasn't quite ready to leave her. When he sat next to her, her brow puckered a little but she didn't protest.

"I heard you talking to Abby about the hauntings here," he said.

Ellie twisted her body slightly to face him. "She and her husband have both had some strange experiences, but I slept like a baby last night and I didn't notice a thing." The corners of her mouth lifted slightly. "I didn't expect to, but I was almost disappointed."

Even her faint smile bolstered him, and he added, "That Victorian bed and breakfast we stayed in at Stratford last summer was supposedly haunted by a headless spirit, according to the brochure. But we didn't see anything unusual. Of course, we were too preoccupied those two nights to notice even if a whole chorus line of headless ghosts had sashayed across the room belting out show tunes."

She breathed out a short laugh, a sound he hadn't heard in weeks, and it still triggered a warm swell in his chest. Pink smudges bloomed on her cheeks, and her gaze dipped again to the jar in her lap. It thrilled him to know that memories of that weekend still made the blood rise in her, just as they stirred prickles of heat in lower areas of his body.

"You were disappointed?" she asked after a moment, tossing a quick, probing glance at him.

"Are you kidding? That was the best weekend of my... Oh, you mean about the ghost not showing up?" He shifted a little on the sofa. "It wasn't at the top of my mind." He'd been too focused on Ellie, wrapped up in her, both figuratively and literally, with plans for a marriage proposal already gelling in his brain.

"Mine either," she said quietly, and pressed her lips tight, as though trying to squelch whatever emotions those memories had dredged up. She was a pro at smothering feelings that made her uncomfortable, or at least she was good at hiding them—a frustrating habit for a guy like Spencer who had a tendency to blurt out whatever popped into his mind. But on those rare occasions when he'd managed to coax her to open herself to him, he'd found a tender, loving heart that made his efforts and patience worthwhile.

"What are your plans for Christmas dinner?" he asked.

"I found a Chinese restaurant not too far from here that's open."

"But you'll be alone."

She shrugged, absently running her finger around the lid of the mustard jar. "Doesn't bother me."

He didn't believe her, but didn't press the point.

"How about you?" she asked.

"Gino invited me for Christmas dinner at his place. He's a professional chef, so the meal should be out of this world."

She looked up, her brow creased in curiosity. "What about your family?"

Spencer drew a short breath, feeling his chest constrict a little. "Well, my mother went to Newfoundland to finally meet that guy she's been dating online. We'll see how *that* goes. Dad's with his new girlfriend, Bethany, visiting her parents in Ireland. And my sister lives four thousand kilometres away in Victoria, so..." He spread his hands in a conceding gesture. "We're all over the place. Story of my life."

Ellie was quiet for a moment. Then she stood abruptly, clutching her glove and the jar of mustard to her chest. "Spencer, I really have to get back to work. It was good seeing you."

Spencer got to his feet. "Yeah, it was. Good luck with the book. Merry Christmas, Ellie."

With an uncertain smile and a quick bob of her head, she turned and headed for the stairs.

Four

Immersed in the words on her laptop screen, Ellie hadn't noticed the shadows deepening across the room as the sun sank behind the buildings across the road. Pushing the chair back, she closed her eyes for a moment and rolled her stiffening shoulders. She then leaned forward to switch on the lamp at the edge of the table and glanced out the window at the street below, where streetlamps pierced the evening darkness, casting harsh light over the snowbanks.

While she'd sketched out a few scenes, she hadn't written much since leaving Spencer downstairs a couple of hours ago. Their conversation kept edging into her mind, yanking her thoughts away from King Henry's court and back to Spencer's sea-blue eyes.

If you think I dropped my glove on purpose—

Dumb thing to say. She wasn't the type of woman who resorted to coquettish ploys to get a man's attention, and he knew it. Besides, he was the one who kept showing up where he wasn't supposed to be. He should be back in Toronto, or elsewhere with some portion of his scattered family, trimming a tree and hanging stockings like he'd tried to cajole her to do last year, before she'd escaped to the Dominican with Gwen. She wouldn't have been good company for him, but still, she'd felt like a heel abandoning him when he hadn't been all that keen on spending the holidays with either of his parents.

We're all over the place, he'd said. *Story of my life.*

Ellie had felt the strained undercurrent to his comment. Early in their relationship, he'd opened up to her about his childhood, explaining that while he'd always felt loved, he'd never felt he belonged. His parents had flitted in and out of romantic relationships, pulling him from one cobbled-together family unit to another. Envy had flooded his face whenever she talked about her formative years, growing up in the most solid, conventional family imaginable—living in the same split-level suburban home until she was twenty, with her optometrist mom, podiatrist dad, and a younger sister, along with various dogs and cats. She'd been a high achiever in school, popular with her classmates, and her summers had been filled with long, glorious days at the family cottage in Muskoka.

In light of Spencer's upbringing, she understood why he'd idealized marriage, craving the stable family life he'd never had. But she also knew he was chasing a dream—the same dream she'd believed in wholeheartedly when she placed her faith in a future with Joel.

Joel. She slammed a door in her mind, refusing to let him occupy her thoughts. But his name brought her back to her conversation with Gwen before she'd left Toronto, and it dawned on her that she hadn't called her roommate as she'd promised. She reached for her cell phone on the table and selected Gwen's number. After four rings, Gwen's voicemail picked up.

"Hi, Gwen," Ellie said after the beep. "Just checking in. You'll never guess who I ran into this afternoon. Well, I suppose we'll talk about it later. Bye."

As she was setting the phone down on the table, a ripple of cold air danced over her shoulders. Spinning around in the chair, she pulled in a breath and held it while she scanned the room.

Nothing moved. Nothing looked out of place—her suitcase beside the bed, the bathroom door standing open, the nightstand and dresser holding only a clock radio and a TV, all cloaked in the room's deepening shadows. The open curtains hung motionless, framing the window that remained firmly shut. Releasing her breath at last, Ellie reached her hand toward the floor and detected only a slight stirring of warm air from the baseboard heater. Yet there had to be a draft coming from someplace she couldn't see. The fine hairs on her arms prickled with a lingering sense of unease.

Shaking off the feeling, she stood and switched on the overhead lamp. The bright light flooding the room soothed her apprehension, but she still sensed a drop in the temperature—maybe only due to her metabolism having slowed from sitting still so long.

She picked up her suitcase and laid it on the bed, opened the latches and lifted the lid. Rummaging through the garments she hadn't bothered to hang in the closet, she located the cardigan she'd brought just in case she needed a little extra warmth. When she pulled it out of the case, a rectangle of thick, bright white paper fluttered out with it and cartwheeled to the floor.

What the...?

She stared at the blank white card on the floor for a moment before bending to pick it up. As she flipped it over, her heart tumbled when she saw the embossed red script on the other side, surrounded by holly leaves and bells. Her gaze skittered in disbelief over the familiar text.

The honor of your presence
is requested at the marriage of
Ellie Marie Lynd
to
Joel Robert Hanson
Saturday, the twentieth of December
at half past four in the afternoon
Villa Toscana
244 Mulino Street
Toronto, Ontario

Bewildered, Ellie studied the invitation a few moments longer, turning it again in her hands as though the card itself might explain its presence in her suitcase. She didn't remember tucking it into one of the elasticised pockets when she'd packed for her aborted honeymoon two years ago—but obviously she must have. Just as she must have unintentionally left it there during her hasty unpacking.

A fresh wave of anger crashed through her, catching her off guard. She hadn't thought she had any anger toward Joel left in her. She'd long since recovered from the crushing blow he'd dealt her when he cancelled their wedding.

Hadn't she?

Well, obviously not entirely. The approach of the Christmas season still made her stomach roll with queasiness. Traditions that used to bring her joy only triggered an ache in her chest, pulling her emotions back to that frosty December evening when the man she'd planned to spend her life with told her he was no longer sure he loved her. She'd had her final gown alteration completed that afternoon, and was fine-tuning her speech for the reception when he dropped by her apartment. Self-conscious in her old tattered sweatpants, she'd asked him to wait while she changed. He'd stopped her, gripping her hand, and blurted that he couldn't marry her. She never wanted to experience that feeling again—the feeling of her whole world abruptly dropping out from under her feet.

Funny that she'd thought briefly of Joel just before she found the invitation, and now there was little point in fighting off those memories. Her three years with him had unfolded like a fairy tale, with Joel fitting every romantic fantasy she'd cultivated since she was a little girl. A successful architect who had designed a new wing at the museum. A gentleman, sexy and confident with a quick wit and a bone-melting smile. Too good to be true, Gwen had remarked blithely, whenever he'd brought Ellie a bouquet of flowers for no reason, or rubbed her aching feet after a long day leading tour groups through the museum. He'd been her strength and her solace when her father barely survived a stroke. After her dad recovered, when she and Joel had traveled through Europe together, he'd proposed among the magnolias in the gardens of the Palais Royal in Paris. He'd agreed readily when Ellie asked for a Christmas wedding.

Joel was the first man she'd given her heart to, completely and unreservedly, and she still couldn't figure out what went wrong, or how she'd missed the signs that he wasn't happy in their relationship. All she knew was that every red silk bow, glittery garland and poinsettia plant now reminded her of the unused wedding decorations she'd had to throw away. The agony of her heartbreak had become so hopelessly entangled with the season that she doubted she'd ever enjoy

Christmas as she had as a girl, with a wide-open heart—just as she'd loved Joel.

But she didn't love Joel anymore. She loved Spence.

Correction—she *had* loved Spence. Maybe she still did, a little bit. Guilt still nettled her when she thought of the despair in his face when she'd turned down his proposal. But she could never have lived with herself had she said yes just to please him, then changed her mind at the last moment, the way Joel had.

With a flick of her wrist, Ellie tossed the invitation into the trashcan beside the dresser. Best to get back to writing and immerse herself in a time and place other than her own.

As she moved to the chair, a noise from somewhere outside her room broke the quiet. She spun her head and listened to the low, rhythmic sound.

Creeek. Creeek. Creeek.

She couldn't tell where it was coming from. Curious, she stepped closer to the wall beside the dresser. The noise grew more distinct, and her cheeks heated as it dawned on her that there might be an amorous couple making use of the bed in the next room. Well, at least someone was enjoying success in their relationship, or having a good time at any rate.

Yet as she listened, Ellie didn't think it sounded quite like bedsprings. She stepped closer and pressed her ear to the wall, straining to hear. Moments later, the noise stopped, leaving only silence.

The ringtone of her cell phone made her jump and release a startled squeak. She let out a settling breath and strode back to the table to pick up the phone. It was probably Gwen returning her call.

Instead the screen displayed Spencer's name.

Good grief, what could he want now? He knew she didn't want distractions. Ellie hesitated, considering letting the call go to voicemail. Exasperation and resentment pulsed through her, coupled with an unbidden glimmer of pleasure at the thought of hearing his voice again.

Stay strong, Ellie. Don't answer. You made it clear enough you want to be left alone to write.

But had she? She'd certainly implied it, but to be fair, maybe she needed to ask him explicitly not to interrupt her.

Finally she swiped the screen and lifted the phone to her ear. "Hello, Spence."

"Ellie, I know you're busy writing," he said, rushing his words to forestall any protest, "but I have a proposal for you."

"A proposal?"

"Don't panic," he said with a soft chuckle. "It's not the marriage kind."

Ellie sat on the edge of the bed, curious despite herself. "What is it?"

"I'll tell you over dinner."

"I don't think—"

"Before you turn me down," he said quickly, "consider that you've got to eat anyway, and a purely platonic meal with your delightfully charismatic ex *has* to beat eating alone."

Ellie couldn't help the small smile that curled her lips. "Where?"

"I'm in the pub downstairs."

"Presumptuous," she muttered, slightly annoyed, yet still intrigued.

She glanced at her laptop screen, dark now, since the computer had gone into sleep mode. Her heart sank when she thought of staying in her room, trying to coax more prose from her overtaxed brain. Her spirits lifted a notch at the thought of sharing a meal with Spence. Maybe she could bounce a few ideas off him. Treat this as the first tentative step toward the friendship both of them had claimed they wanted.

"I know," he said. "But I can't pass up a good prime rib, and Gino tells me The Roses serves the best roast beef in town. Listen, you don't have to join me, but I'm here now, so if you'd like to eat with me, you're more than welcome. I'll save you a chair."

Ellie paused, her teeth embedded in her lower lip. She squeezed her eyes shut and replied, "Okay, I'll come down in a minute."

After ending the call, she hesitated only a moment longer. Throwing off her cardigan and sweatshirt, she changed into her purple chenille sweater, then headed into the bathroom to run a brush through her hair. Examining herself in the mirror, she decided her lips needed a bit of colour and smoothed on the subtle pink lipstick she kept in her toiletries bag.

When she dropped the lipstick tube back into the bag, she noticed the little bottle of gardenia perfume Spencer had given her for her birthday. She loved the scent, but she didn't remember packing it. A soft, sardonic chuckle escaped her. Either she was losing her marbles, or the stress she'd been under had distracted her more than she'd realized. How many more little surprises would she find in her bags?

On impulse, she pulled out the bottle and sprayed a little on her neck.

Shouldering her purse, Ellie strode into the hallway and locked the door behind her. She turned to head down the stairs, but stopped when she caught sight of a rocking chair sitting in the corner below the window.

She hadn't noticed the chair before. She ran her gaze over its sturdy ladder back and gently curved armrests. It was a basic, practical piece that looked to be a well-preserved antique. A slim embroidered cushion sat propped against one of the armrests.

The rhythmic sound she'd heard just before Spencer called leapt back into her thoughts. So that explained it— some other guest must have been sitting in the chair, rocking it so that it creaked, and they'd gone away.

With a smile and a shake of her head, she turned and bounded down the stairs.

FIVE

Ellie stopped by the bar and craned her neck to scan the pub. A waitress squeezed by, carrying trays of food and drink. The place was packed, with every table and barstool occupied. The clinking of dishes melded with conversation and laughter into an indecipherable din.

At last Ellie spotted Spencer at a table for two by the window. A tall glass of beer sat on each of the placemats.

With her feet rooted to the wood-plank floor, she let her gaze roam over his jeans and casual blue pullover, and then linger on his face. She studied his masculine profile—the straight slope of his nose and the strong curve of his jaw that were so familiar and comfortable to her eyes, yet still tugged at her feminine sensibilities. Her chest fluttered with a tumble of emotions. Though they'd talked on the phone a few times, before today she hadn't seen him since the day he proposed in High Park, and she'd walked away from him, her heart crumbling with every step.

Ellie forced her feet forward. Threading her way through a group of patrons gathered near the bar, she approached Spencer. When their gazes connected, he straightened and smiled.

She pulled out the chair opposite him and sat, then lifted her chin toward the two glasses of beer. "You were confident I'd show up."

He spread his hands and grinned. "If you didn't, I'd have an extra beer to drown my sorrows."

Her laugh emerged as a brittle sound. She picked up her beer and gulped a mouthful, letting the cold ale soothe her dry throat. "So what's the proposal you mentioned?"

"I'll get to that. Why don't we order first?" Spencer bent his head to scan the menu that lay open on his placemat. "What's good here?"

Ellie opened her menu, though she already knew what she

wanted. "Everything looks great. I had the roast beef sandwich for lunch, and tonight I'm trying the chicken pot pie."

"I was thinking prime rib, but chicken pot pie actually sounds amazing." He shut his menu and leaned back in his chair. The mellow smile lingering on his lips pushed that appealing little crease into his cheek. "Did you get a lot of writing done today?"

"Some," Ellie said, Spencer's relaxed posture and expression putting her at ease. She stopped short of admitting she'd been struggling to piece her story together. "It's coming along."

"So tell me about it," he said. "When's it set?"

Ellie took another long swallow of beer before answering. "During Henry VIII's reign. It's about Lady Elizabeth Hungerford of Somerset, whose cruel husband locked her in his castle tower." Telling him about it at last sent a warm flush of pleasure through her.

"Sounds like a fairy tale."

"It sort of does, but it's a true story, with no dashing prince coming to her rescue. Of course, not many details are known about her life, so I have to embellish. For instance, I'm trying to work out how she meets Lord Walter Hungerford. I've placed her at Henry's court, in Greenwich Palace, as one of Princess Mary's ladies-in-waiting. But I haven't quite decided how she meets Lord Walter. Presumably the marriage was arranged, but still, I want a dramatic moment when destiny brings them together—though she has no way of knowing the fate that awaits her."

"What year?" Spencer asked.

"Sometime before 1532, the year they married." Expectation sparked in her as she watched his brows gather—she knew this look, the one that signaled he'd begun rifling through the stockpile of historical knowledge crammed into his brain.

"An interesting period to write about," he remarked. "You've got King Henry coming under the spell of Anne Boleyn, and then initiating the Church of England's separation from Rome so he can divorce Queen Catherine and marry Anne. Plenty of palace intrigue to work with."

"I know. I've been researching the era."

A young waitress arrived at the table, interrupting their conversation. After filling their water glasses, she took their orders and flounced away.

Spencer snapped his fingers and leaned toward Ellie. "I might have something for you. I think it was in 1527 that a delegation of French dignitaries came to England to negotiate a treaty, and Henry threw a famously elaborate reception at Greenwich Palace for them. There were lavish banquets, jousting matches and performances with dancing, music, drama—"

Ellie nodded. "Yes, the entertainments were called masques."

"Right." Spencer's blue eyes gleamed. "They hired professional musicians and actors, but the courtiers themselves were usually involved in the dancing. At the end of the performance, the players would remove their masks to reveal their identities. How about you have Lady Elizabeth participating?" His brows arched dramatically. "The moment she removes her mask, she catches the eye of Lord Hungerford, and he's enthralled by her beauty and innocence. Their gazes lock. He's a handsome enough fellow, but there's something predatory about the look he gives her that sends a cautionary chill down her spine."

"It's perfect. Thank you, Spencer. I owe you one." Ellie grinned, her pulse surging with yearning to collaborate with him again. She reached for her purse, meaning to type a few notes into her phone, then realized she'd left her phone in her room. "Do you have a pen so I can jot this down?"

"Don't worry about that now. Just give me a call whenever you need details."

"Okay. Thanks." Ellie tapped his hand in an appreciative gesture, only for a moment, but as she slid her hand back to her lap, her gaze remained locked on his fingers. She couldn't help the flood of tactile memories that swept in. She could still feel his fingertips tracing an electrifying path on her skin—over her face and lips, in her hair, along her thighs, and in every secret place on her body.

"So what happened to Lady Elizabeth?" Spencer asked. "No daring rescue?"

Jerking her focus back to his face, she cleared her throat.

"The village women smuggled food to her, and eventually she was released when her husband was arrested for unrelated crimes. After that, she married Lord Robert Throckmorton whom, for the purposes of a happy ending, I'm going to portray as her true love and soulmate."

Spencer smiled. "A happy ending. Sounds perfect, Ellie. I can't wait to read it."

"Well, I—" She snapped her mouth shut for a moment and began again. "I suppose it's a normal part of the writing process to feel overwhelmed by the work ahead, and wonder whether you'll actually be able to pull it off."

His gaze held hers, direct and intent. "Sure it's normal. But I've seen you in action. You've got that magic combination of talent, willpower and passion. So I haven't got an ounce of doubt that you'll come up with something brilliant."

Ellie exhaled, gripping her napkin in her lap. A few words of encouragement from Spencer had her heart soaring. "I think it's time you end my suspense and tell me about this proposal you mentioned," she said mildly, one corner of her mouth curling upward. "I'm beginning to think it was just a fabricated excuse to lure me down here to talk about my book."

"I won't deny it made a good excuse, but my proposal is perfectly real. And since we've established that you owe me a favour..."

"Here we go."

He folded his hands on the table. "Just after you and I parted company earlier, Gino texted me and told me a couple of the volunteers he had lined up for the Helping Hands party dropped out. He asked if I knew anyone who might be willing to step in."

Ellie regarded him with a skeptical tilt of her head. "And you thought of me?"

He offered one of his soft, enticing smiles that used to make her heart trip over itself—and still did. "I realize you're determined to skip Christmas, but wouldn't you like to get out of your room for a couple of hours and help a worthy cause?"

She smirked. "It's kinda hard to avoid Christmas when you're surrounded by tinsel and carollers and your escort is dressed as Santa Claus."

"It's for the kids, Ellie," Spencer countered, his expression sobering. "A chance to give them a few presents when they might not get any otherwise. Remember what Christmas morning meant to you as a kid? The anticipation, the gifts piled under the tree. The magic. Now imagine if Santa didn't come to your house. All your friends get showered in presents, but not you. Imagine, as a child, dreading Christmas morning the way you do now."

Ellie heaved a long sigh. He knew just which of her buttons to push to break her resistance. "What would I have to do?" she muttered.

"Well, if wrapping gifts or hanging decorations is too festive for you, there are plenty of other jobs. How are you with face painting?"

"Any other options?"

"You could help serve at the ice cream bar."

"I'll think about it, all right?" Ellie said.

Spencer bobbed his head, his shoulders straightening in triumph. "Good enough. And just in case you're worried, I promise not to try talking you into marrying me," he added, drawing an X with his finger across his chest.

Six

After they finished their meals, the waitress brought separate cheques, as Ellie had requested, each on a small plastic tray, along with a frosted glass ball ornament imprinted with The Roses' logo.

"A little gift for you," the waitress said, flashing a pair of deep-set dimples. "You can pay at the bar. Merry Christmas."

"Merry Christmas," Spencer echoed, returning her smile.

Ellie, on the other hand, eyed her ornament with a sour twist of her lips, then picked it up by its red ribbon and passed it across the table to Spencer. "You can have mine."

Reluctantly, he accepted it and placed it next to his identical ornament. "So you're really determined to hold onto this grudge against Christmas?"

"You don't understand."

"I think I do."

She tilted her head, considering him with a slight frown wedged between her brows. "You said that yesterday. But if you really did understand, you wouldn't have given me an ultimatum to get engaged, when you knew I wasn't ready," she said in a rush, then pressed her lips tight as though regretting the outburst.

Leaning forward, Spencer propped his elbows on the table. He liked the way she filled out the purple sweater she'd worn frequently last winter, and he remembered the softness of the yarn when he'd stroked his hands down her back. With her hair waving over her shoulders and a hint of lipstick colouring her lips, she looked as though she'd spruced herself up for him before coming down from her room. But it was the scent of her gardenia perfume, a gift he'd given her, that sparked hope in him—even in the middle of a tense discussion.

"You never told me you weren't ready," he said evenly. "You said in no uncertain terms that marriage wasn't for you and you weren't likely to ever consider it."

"That's right. You knew that from the start." Ellie tapped her index finger on her placemat, then sat back and folded her arms, her expression rigid. "And can you blame me?"

Spencer blew out a ragged sigh of frustration. He should have kept his mouth shut. The meal had gone so nicely, the conversation flowing as it used to, and he'd sensed her growing comfort with him. Even so, he couldn't quite hold back from speaking his mind.

"Okay, I admit it. I really *don't* understand. Joel canceling your wedding the day before the ceremony was cruel and awful, and I get that the timing at Christmas has put you off the season altogether. But I don't get why all that anguish didn't just evaporate when you met me. When *we* fell in love."

She stared at him, her dark eyes stern. Then she looked away, as she'd taken to doing whenever he made a point that she couldn't counter. "I can't explain it."

"Ellie, we should have both thanked our lucky stars that Joel did what he did." Spencer softened his tone. "His boneheaded mistake was the best thing that ever happened to me. If you didn't feel the same—"

"Of *course* I did. I didn't want to lose you, Spence." When her gaze snapped back to his face, the flash of raw pain he saw in her eyes tore at his heart. She shook her head and closed her eyes briefly. "I just didn't want to get married. Why does a piece of paper matter that much to you?"

"Because it does." Spencer pushed a hand through his hair and exhaled a slow breath. Sensing the right words might wear down her defenses, he chose them carefully. "I'm not going to end up like my father, chasing after a woman half my age when I'm pushing seventy. Spending my pension on hair implants and diving trips in the Caribbean because I'm afraid she won't stay with me otherwise. And I won't put my kids through what I went through growing up."

She considered him with narrowed eyes, her posture rigid. "Do you think if your parents had gotten married, they'd still be together now? And supposing they were, would they be happy?"

"I don't know, Ellie. Maybe they would've tried harder. Maybe

Dad would've given it more thought before he left to be with Carla when I was eight years old. And Mom wouldn't have let Ted move into our house when I was ten and had his baby almost immediately, only to toss him out five years later. Maybe I wouldn't have had to move to Dad's house and then back to Mom's half a dozen times because I couldn't get along with their latest partners or whatever kids got dragged in with them. Maybe I would've been a priority to them if they weren't so consumed with pursuing their latest romantic interest."

Ellie gave her head a little shake. "But Spencer, that's *them*. It's not you. You don't have to be like that. I don't think you could be."

"I'm not like Joel, either. But still you couldn't bring yourself to trust me."

"Why would you say that?" she asked, her brow furrowed.

"It's obvious, isn't it? You didn't trust me not to break your heart the way he did."

Her pretty dark eyes widened. "That's not true. I know you wouldn't do that. It's just that…oh, Spence, you didn't invite me for dinner so we could rehash all this, did you?"

"No, I didn't." He raised his hands in a gesture of capitulation. "I'm sorry, Ellie. We don't have to discuss it ever again."

"Well, it's probably good we're talking about it. We never really got a chance to clear the air after—"

"Yeah, I know." Absently, Spencer rolled one of the ornaments between his hands. "It's just too bad we never spent a Christmas together. You didn't give me a chance to change your feelings about the holidays."

One of her eyebrows lifted, along with the edge of her mouth, signaling that she was ready to move past their prickly discussion. "How would you have done that?"

"I would've replaced all those painful memories with warm fuzzy ones. I had a plan, you know, involving some generously spiked eggnog, a sprig of mistletoe, a roaring fire and a whole lot of canoodling on the couch. Of course it unraveled when you flew off to the Dominican." Spencer kept his tone light, but watched her reaction carefully.

"Sorry I spoiled it." Her lips curled up higher, while the

remainder of the tension in her face dissipated. "You're a wonderful man, Spence."

He felt his chest tighten a little, as a sense of everything he'd had with her, and lost, tumbled through him in a rush of mingled gratitude and regret. "It was easy being wonderful with you. Or at least a better man than I'd ever been before. Which is why—"

"Ellie!" someone called.

Twisting in his chair, Spencer spotted Abby Wells approaching with a dark-haired man by her side.

"Hi, Abby," Ellie said, and Spencer glanced back to see something like relief flit through her expression.

"How were your meals?" Abby asked when she and the man reached the table.

"The chicken pot pie was pure heaven." Ellie splayed her hand against her chest. "It might've even rivalled my mom's homemade crust, but don't tell her that."

"I don't think you've met my husband, Jason Brinleigh." Abby motioned toward the man beside her. "Jason, this is Ellie Lynd and her...friend, Spencer Brooks."

"Good to meet you, Ellie and Spencer," Jason said, and after shaking both their hands, he added, "Abby told me you'll be in town over the holidays, Ellie. You should come by the winery for a private tour and tasting."

"I'd love that," Ellie said. "I'm sure I could pry myself away from my laptop for an afternoon."

"Do you like port?" Jason asked. "We've got a tawny port behind the bar that's a perfect aperitif. I'll bring you each a glass, on the house."

"Thanks, I'd like that," Spencer said, though he only wanted to be left alone with Ellie, and restrained himself from making shooing motions with his hand.

Ellie shook her head. "Not for me. Got to keep my wits about me. More writing to do tonight."

"Coffee, then?" Abby suggested.

"Sure. Thank you," Ellie agreed, though when they'd asked for their bills, she'd mentioned that it was getting late and she wanted to head back up to her room to write. Maybe

Abby and Jason dropping by the table was a stroke of luck that would buy him a few more minutes with her.

"I've got some things to discuss with Oscar. We'll chat later, Ellie," Abby said before she drifted away from the table, following her husband toward the bar. Before they parted, Jason leaned in to brush a kiss against her cheek, and she smiled and gripped his hand in affection.

Spencer turned to face Ellie, intent on finishing what he'd begun to say, but with the shift in mood between them he couldn't pick up the thread of their conversation. He didn't have time to gather his thoughts before Jason returned, carrying a glass of port and a mug of coffee.

With Jason watching him expectantly, Spencer sipped the dark red wine. "Excellent," he said with a nod. "From your winery?"

"Yes, new this year. Enjoy. I'll leave you two alone," Jason said and tossed out a wink as he retreated from the table. "Nice meeting you."

Ellie ripped open a creamer and dumped the contents into her coffee. "So can you give me a lift to the party tomorrow?"

"Sure," Spencer said, his spirits bolstered by her confirmation that he'd be seeing her again. "Is a quarter past five all right?"

She nodded, lifting her mug to her lips for a careful sip.

"Thanks for agreeing to help, Ellie. You're an angel," he said. "Not a Christmas angel, per se. Just a regular, any-old-day-of-the-year sort of angel."

Ellie rolled her eyes, and a good-natured smirk tugged at one cheek. "Thanks for getting me out of my room for dinner, but I'd really better get back to my laptop before I lose the will to accomplish anything tonight." She rose from her chair, then picked up her mug and cradled it between her hands. "Guess I can take this with me. Goodnight, Spence."

Disappointment snaked through him, but he smiled and nodded. "It's kinda funny," he said impulsively as she turned to go.

Ellie swung back to face him. "What's funny?"

He lifted his shoulders, raising his glass for another small sip of port. "Just the idea of a woman locking herself in a room all by herself to write about a woman trying to escape from being locked in a room all by herself."

She studied him with an inquisitive gaze and gave a tight smile, as though she couldn't quite tell if he was joking. "See you tomorrow."

He watched her go, and once she'd disappeared into the foyer, he stared into his glass of port and considered how the evening had gone.

She hadn't quite fallen into his arms, but he had to be patient. She'd agreed to go to the Christmas party, and that alone was a major coup. He'd expected to put a lot more effort into persuading her. Even if she wasn't doing it to please him, the important task of getting her there had been accomplished. She might still change her mind, but Spencer was pretty sure she wouldn't. When Ellie Lynd made a commitment, she stuck to her word. He'd known that about her from the first day they met, when she showed up to interview him with swollen eyes and a pink, runny nose. She'd explained that after agreeing to look after her niece's new puppy for the weekend, she'd discovered she was highly allergic, but stuck it out despite the suffering.

That particular facet of Ellie's personality would work against him if he hoped to prod her into reconsidering marriage, but he was willing to do whatever it took to win her back. The more time he spent with her, the more he wanted her—*needed* her—back in his life.

"Is the port all right?"

Spencer looked up to find Jason standing over him again, having evidently noticed the scowl on his face and interpreted it to mean he was unhappy with the aperitif.

"The port's wonderful. It's just..." He paused, exhaling. "If you don't mind what might be an overly personal observation from a complete stranger, when I saw you and Abby together, you looked like newlyweds who can hardly tear their eyes off each another."

A grin spread across Jason's face. "I don't mind an observation like that, from anybody. After six years, we're as tight as ever."

"That's all I want for me and Ellie. What you guys have."

"But you're just friends?" Jason asked with an inquisitive tilt of his brows.

"Now we are, but we used to be much more," Spencer admitted. "We hit an impasse in our relationship. The thing is, I'm pretty sure I could have her back if I agreed to live together, without getting married."

"But that's not what you want?"

"Nope. I'm not interested in settling." Spencer grimaced, realizing he'd said more to this virtual stranger than he'd meant to. "Sorry. You didn't come over here to discuss my personal problems."

"I don't mind," Jason said, folding his arms. "You sound like you need to get a few things off your chest. Wish I could help."

"Know any tricks for changing a woman's mind?" Spencer asked with a half-smile. "Maybe I should just give her what she wants. It's better than losing her. I just feel like it can't work as long as she's holding back from a full commitment."

Jason pulled out the chair across from Spencer and sat down. "I'm no expert on the female mind, but I do know that tricks don't work. And I just might be qualified to speak from the other perspective."

Spencer raised a brow. "How so?"

"I had a commitment phobia, just like Ellie. I got my heart trampled on and I didn't want to let it happen again, so I pulled back from Abby, despite being crazy about her."

Leaning forward, Spencer asked, "So what made you come around?"

"It all came down to one very strange, very frightening night, when I almost lost her." The edges of his mouth twitched upward as he added, "But I found my way, thanks to the guiding hand of our resident ghost."

SEVEN

Ellie glanced around the empty pub, bewildered. What was she doing there in the middle of the night? Or was it morning? Gray light filled the windows, muted by a thick mist, while a low fire glowed in the stone fireplace.

She turned in surprise when a young woman whisked past her, wearing a pale blue dress with a skirt that reached the floor and an apron tied overtop. A few locks of dark hair had slipped from beneath her ruffled bonnet and fluttered about her face. Ellie stared in curiosity at the woman's attire, guessing she might be a historical reenactor from Fort George who had come to The Roses for a meal before her shift.

Except The Roses didn't serve breakfast, and none of the staff were around anyhow. Ellie glanced at her wrist to check the time and saw she wasn't wearing her watch. She also noted with relief that she was dressed in jeans and a long-sleeve shirt rather than the pink flannel nightgown she'd changed into for bed.

"Excuse me, do you have the time?" she asked, but the woman ignored her, lifting the bulk of her skirt off the floor as she hurried toward the door.

Only then did Ellie notice a fair-haired young man, tall and lean with smooth features, standing in the doorway. His deep brown eyes gleamed with reflected firelight.

The woman gripped his hand and tugged him away from the door. "Don't go," she said. "Not yet."

His lips curved into a gentle smile. "We've already said goodbye three times, my love. You have to let me go."

"I'm not ready." Her voice thick with tears, she clung to his shirtsleeve with one hand, while her other hand cupped his cheek. "Just stay a little longer."

"Becca, I can't. I'm expected at the garrison."

Becca.

Rebecca Norris.

Ellie spun around, scanning the pub, noting how drastically

the room had changed since her supper with Spencer. The small tables suited to four or six guests were gone, replaced with long tables that could accommodate up to ten. Lanterns glowed in place of the electric light fixtures. Behind the bar, pewter mugs lined the shelves above stacks of wooden barrels, the beer taps and touch-screen cash register having vanished.

Am I dreaming?

Of course—what else could this be? Relieved to have puzzled out her situation, Ellie marveled at the vivid details her unconscious mind had conjured. The firelight glinting off the mug handles. The grooves and rings marring the wooden tabletops. The damp chill of the room and the earthy, smoky scents.

But the parting lovers fascinated Ellie most of all. She sidled closer to them, wary of interrupting their goodbye, though she didn't think they were aware of her presence.

Rebecca shook her head and her curls bounced off her reddened cheeks. "Jack, I'm afraid... I'm afraid I won't see you again. And the baby—" She splayed her hand across her abdomen. Ellie hadn't noticed its rounded shape beneath the apron.

Tenderness filled the young man's eyes, though his jaw tightened. "I hate leaving you. I have no choice. I'm doing this to protect you and our child. If we don't stop the Americans at Queenston, they'll invade Newark next. I couldn't let anything happen to you. Oh, I almost forgot this." He reached into the pocket of his coat and withdrew an object Ellie couldn't see clearly. He pressed it into Rebecca's palm.

She opened her hand, revealing a small toy soldier carved from wood. A girlish giggle escaped her. She sniffed back her tears and smiled at him. "Jack, the arms are too long. His hands reach his knees. And he doesn't seem to have feet."

A rueful smile played on the young man's lips. "Well, let's hope I'm better at firing a musket than I am at carving. I can fix it—"

"No. It's perfect the way it is." Rebecca gripped the small soldier in her fist and held it against her chest.

Ellie grinned, charmed by the scene unfolding before her. Her imagination was on fire tonight, and she resolved to remember every detail and write it all down when she woke up. Maybe work it into a future novel.

"I haven't had time to paint it," Jack said. "I'll finish it when I get back."

"Why are you giving it to me now?"

His shoulders rose. "In case..."

"In case you don't come back?" She choked out the words in a near-whisper.

"Becca, I've never been in battle before. I don't know what to expect. If anything should happen to me, you can give it to the child to paint when he's old enough."

"You assume it's a boy? Suppose it's a girl?"

Jack looked at her with piercing sadness in his eyes. "She'll keep it close and think of her papa."

Becca shook her head again, more fervently. "Come back to us, Jack. You have to. I couldn't survive without you."

As Ellie's listened, Oscar's words from yesterday slipped into her mind. *Rebecca's husband, Jack, was killed in battle, and she passed away just after their baby was born.*

Ellie's stomach dropped like a chunk of granite. Jack wouldn't be coming back, and though neither he nor Rebecca could have known, her words would prove to be prophetic.

"You'll be all right," Jack said, his tone resolute. "You've got your parents and your sister to take care of you." He cradled her belly between his hands, offering an encouraging smile. "Stay strong, Becca, so I won't have to worry about you and the baby."

"Don't get distracted thinking about me while you're being shot at, Jack Norris," she told him sternly. "Keep your mind on the battlefield and look after yourself."

"But thinking about you is just what I'll need to bolster my courage." One edge of his mouth hiked higher. "I'll have your beautiful eyes and your smile with me in here"—he tapped the side of his head—"and in here"—then spread his hand on his chest.

Jack, you romantic devil. Ellie could easily picture Spencer saying the same kind of thing, and the image raised a smile to her lips. Now that Spencer had entered her thoughts, she half-expected him to materialize at her side. When he didn't, she willed him to appear, to share this moment with her, and when that didn't work, a bleak feeling enveloped her heart.

Rebecca rose onto her toes and pressed her mouth to Jack's. The lovers lingered in each other's arms a moment longer, before he pulled away and turned to slip through the door, disappearing into the mist outside.

Watching the door swing shut behind him, Ellie felt a wrenching sensation in her chest. Her head swam with panic and confusion as the room tilted around her. Then she felt herself flung forward, her body dissolving into Rebecca's.

She looked down at her right hand, still clutching the wooden solider, and then glanced at her left hand, where a slender silver band encircled the ring finger. She touched the firm swell of her belly, awed by the strange awareness of another life inside her. When her thoughts settled on Jack, the man she loved with a fierce ache, overwhelming sorrow and dread crashed over her.

She tried to call out to him, but the air had evaporated from her lungs, and as she attempted to reach for the door, her limbs, suddenly heavy and tingling with numbness, refused to move.

Don't go!

Ellie gasped as her eyes jerked open. Staring up at the shadowy beams in the ceiling, she sucked in a long, harsh breath. When she lifted her head to scan the room, she found herself back upstairs, tucked in bed, the dark shapes of bedroom furniture looming around her.

With one hand, she raked away the strands of hair clinging to her face, and used the other to throw back the sheet and bedspread covering her. Rolling to one side of the bed, she reached for the lamp on the nightstand and switched it on. As light spilled over the bed, she placed her hand against her battering heart. *Calm down, Ellie. It might have felt real, but it wasn't.*

Of course it wasn't. She was a writer, and using the vague details she'd heard of Rebecca Norris's life, her creative imagination had woven a particularly intense dream. Why couldn't she dream so vividly about Lady Elizabeth Hungerford?

That she could use.

Ellie glanced at the clock in the nightstand and saw it was 3:42 a.m. She should go back to sleep, but her throat was parched and her heart kept pummeling her breastbone. She swung her feet over the side of the bed and got to her feet, wavering a moment before she regained her bearings.

Still unsteady and bleary, she padded along the cold floor to the bathroom and switched on the light. She pushed back her tousled hair and squinted at the mirror while her eyes adjusted to the brightness. Locating a glass on the counter, she clumsily held it under the tap, filled it with water and gulped the cold liquid.

After switching off the bathroom light, Ellie shuffled back to the bedroom, figuring she'd be able to fall asleep once she crawled back into bed.

Just as she reached for the bedspread, muffled sounds from outside her room pierced the quiet. She froze, pulling in a breath and holding it for a moment.

The sound echoed through the walls—unmistakably a woman weeping.

Jarred fully awake, Ellie crept closer to the wall beside the bed, listening. She hadn't bumped into the guest staying in the next room, and couldn't know if the woman might be old or young, alone or with someone else. The deep, mournful sobs quivered through Ellie and wrenched her heart.

She stood immobile for several lingering moments, considering. She hated to interfere in a stranger's business, especially at this time of night, but she couldn't ignore someone who might need help.

Finally, she decided to tiptoe into the hall and see if she could get a better idea what might be going on in the next room. From there, she'd determine whether to knock on the door and offer her assistance.

She padded to the door and reached for the knob. The instant her fingers touched the cool metal, the weeping stopped.

In the sudden silence, tingles of apprehension prickled her nape, then scooted down the length of her spine. She began to question whether she'd heard anything at all, or whether her brain had still been tangled up in that odd dream. Or maybe...

She withdrew her hand and pressed her palms together, pulling in a long breath and then blowing it out slowly to ease the knot in her belly. *Get a grip, Ellie. You're being ridiculous.* Whoever had been crying must have fallen asleep. Maybe the woman had woken up from a bad dream, just as Ellie had. Anyway, her help wasn't needed now and she had to get some sleep.

Stepping toward the bed, she stopped when her gaze fell on the trashcan. The wedding invitation still rested at the bottom, and the sight of it yanked her thoughts from the drama of parting lovers in 1812 to the reality of her own life. She bent to pick up the slip and study it for a moment.

Spencer had been right, of course. She should be grateful Joel had pulled the plug on their wedding. Otherwise, she might be married to him now, and she didn't wish to be. Or more likely, he would have left her sometime after they were married—a worse outcome than being jilted before the ceremony. It wasn't that she still wanted Joel. If she wanted anyone, it would be Spencer and no one else. If only...

Ellie crushed the invitation into a ball and tossed it back into the trashcan. Climbing onto the bed, she slid her legs under the covers and switched off the lamp. Rebecca and Jack's tragic story had faded to the back of her mind, but as she closed her eyes, the emotions the dream had churned up began to resurface, weighing on her heart. The paralyzing fear she'd sensed in Rebecca the moment Jack walked out the door had felt more familiar than she'd wanted to admit.

What are you so afraid of, Ellie? Losing Spence? The man who says he wants to spend the rest of his life with you?

No wonder Spencer was confused. Her resistance to marriage didn't seem to make logical sense. But logic had little to do with it, when love wasn't rational, and neither was this fear holding her hostage. She'd pushed Spence away before he had a chance to break her heart. Maybe he'd been right in saying she didn't have enough faith in him. Maybe she'd never find faith in anyone again.

Fear was a funny thing—shivers in the dark of a creepy old inn could steal a night's sleep, but were easy to laugh off once the sun rose. The types of fears that burrowed far deeper into a person's soul had a way of cloaking themselves in pragmatism. If only the morning light could chase away her doubts.

EIGHT

Greenwich Palace, 1527

Elizabeth stepped into formation with the other dancers at the front of the stage, holding her pose as the final notes from the viols and sackbuts in the balcony reverberated through the grand hall. When the music fell silent, the dancers lowered the glittering golden masks from their eyes. The audience erupted in applause, and Elizabeth sank into a deep curtsey, relief sweeping through her. She'd missed no more than a handful of the steps that she'd had little time to rehearse.

She slid a glance toward the king, who had secretly joined the masque among a group of noblemen, all disguised in black satin robes and hoods. Even in his gem-studded mask, King Henry, the tallest and most robust of the men, was easy to pick out.

When the king removed his mask, his generous mouth spread into a broad smile within the sandy-blond strands of his beard, and as the audience roared their approval, Princess Mary and the other young girls encircled him. King Henry grasped his daughter's hand and led her closer to the French envoys seated in the front row. He then loosened the net and released the jeweled bands from her hair, letting her golden curls fall to her shoulders.

The envoys nodded and smiled in admiration, to which the king beamed. If the rumours Elizabeth had heard were true, the betrothal of Mary to King Francis's son, the Duke of Orleans, would be the cornerstone of a new treaty between England and France.

Music filled the hall once more, and the king swept his daughter into a brief few steps of the galliard before passing her into the arms of the French ambassador. Elizabeth and the other ladies followed, capering onto the carpet before the audience and, as they'd been instructed, choosing partners from among the nobles.

Elizabeth scanned the men around her, searching among the throng of embroidered doublets and velvet caps for Lord Throckmorton, her heart thrumming in hope that one of the other ladies hadn't yet claimed him. When she turned, it was Lord Hungerford who approached, his dark, steady gaze fastened on her. Her cheeks heated

Sensing a presence near her in the doorway of the lounge, Ellie glanced up from her laptop screen to find Abby peering down at her, wearing her coat and holding a stack of magazines against her chest.

"Sorry, I don't mean to interrupt." Abby's gaze flitted over Ellie's laptop as she bent to stack the magazines on the coffee table. "I just came by to drop off some fresh reading material. Last year's editions of Chatelaine were getting stale."

Ellie's hands fell away from the keyboard. "No problem. I'm just trying to cram in a bit more writing before I have to leave for this party." She glanced at her jeans and red cowl-neck sweater. "It's an informal thing."

Abby smiled. "You look good. Is a change of scene helping you write?"

"I think so. I've actually made some good progress. But I'm still not quite connecting with the character. And my neck is killing me." Ellie leaned back on the sofa and rubbed her hand across her nape, grimacing.

"You look a little tired today." Abby eyed her with a slight frown creasing her forehead. "Is the bed in your room comfortable?"

"Yes, it's fine. But last night I heard a woman crying briefly in the next room. It was unsettling. She sounded really distressed."

"Interesting. There is a couple in the room next to yours." Abby folded her arms, the edges of her lips twitching into a hint of a smile. "But they're both men."

Ellie threw her a swift glance. "Maybe it was another room."

"Maybe."

Sitting forward, Ellie considered the information for a moment, and decided against mentioning her dream. Judging by the glint in Abby's eyes, she was likely to make something more out of the whole strange incident than Ellie wanted. "I'd better get my coat," she said, glancing at her watch. "My ride will be here any minute."

"I have to go, too. Have a good time at the party," Abby said with a wave, before striding to the door.

Ellie gathered up her laptop and climbed the stairs to her room, where she grabbed her coat and exchanged shoes for boots. She was leaving the room when her cell phone jangled. She pulled it out of her purse, saw Gwen's number on the screen, and tapped the icon to answer.

"I got your message," Gwen said. "Did Spencer really show up there?"

Ellie headed downstairs while she talked. "I ran into him in one of the shops. How did you know it was Spence? I didn't tell you."

Gwen paused before replying in a subdued tone, "I guessed it was him because I'm the one who told him where you were staying."

At the foot of the stairs, Ellie froze. "You what?"

Behind the front desk, Oscar's shoulders jerked when he heard her tone, and he glanced over at her, averting his gaze when he saw her talking on the phone.

"He dropped by the apartment, looking for you," Gwen said. "I let it slip that you were staying at The Roses. I'm sorry," she added quickly. "I didn't think he'd actually follow you there. Are you mad?"

"Not at you." Clenching her jaw, Ellie blew out a sharp breath through her nose. "I should've known it was too much of a coincidence that we both happened to be here."

"He said that?"

"Yes." Her hand balled into a fist as she remembered his cool demeanour when they'd supposedly met by chance at the gourmet shop. "But don't worry. I'll be seeing him in a few minutes. I'll give him a piece of my mind."

"You're seeing him?" Gwen asked, a hopeful lift in her voice.

"Not seeing him. It's just a thing he wanted help with. Probably another ruse," Ellie grumbled.

"How's the writing going?"

"Fine. Well, the words haven't quite been flowing as I'd hoped, but I'm plugging away at it."

"It happens. Every writer struggles through periods like that, right?"

"I suppose." But this was something new for Ellie. In comparison, The Last Prince of York had seemingly flowed through her fingers from beginning to end. Or at least she remembered it that way, maybe because she'd enjoyed the experience of writing her first novel so much more.

After disconnecting the call, she paced across the vestibule several times, quietly fuming, while Oscar eyed her with a wary expression. Had Spence's story of Gino asking him to play Santa at the Helping Hands party been another fabrication? Well, she had to presume that the party was real, unless he was planning to drive her into the woods and tie her to a tree until she agreed to marry him.

The entrance door swung open and Abby stepped into the vestibule, a funny smile tugging at her rosy cheeks. "Ellie, there's someone outside waiting for you."

"Spencer?" Ellie huffed in indignation. "Why doesn't he come in?"

Abby's puzzling grin widened. "I think you should just go out there."

"Why?"

"Trust me."

"It's not you I can't trust," Ellie groused as she clomped toward the door. She shoved it open with force and marched out onto the front step, barely aware of the cold evening air nipping her heated cheeks.

She stopped abruptly on the sidewalk. Her jaw sagged in astonishment at the sight of a sleek white horse standing by the curb. A pair of long poles extended from its harness to an elegant open-top carriage. Next to the carriage door, Spencer stood with his hands clasped behind his back and a grin stretched across his face.

NINE

Ellie's focus swung back to the horse. She skimmed an appreciative gaze over its graceful profile and iridescent pale coat, contrasted by dark leather tack studded with brass bells that jingled as the animal tossed its mane. She then studied the carriage, gleaming white with and elegantly curved body and sumptuous red leather seats. A brass lantern glowed above each of the front spoked wheels. The driver, donning a nineteenth-century wool cloak, sat perched on a high bench, holding the reins. He touched his gloved fingers to the brim of his top hat and smiled down.

By the time Ellie's gaze returned to Spencer, her grin matched his. "What's all this for?" she asked.

"I said I'd pick you up at five-fifteen, didn't I?"

"Silly me, I was expecting your Honda Civic."

His shoulders lifted. "How dull would that be? Besides, the best way to write about history is to immerse yourself in it. This was luxury transportation in a past era."

"True. I've been in horse-drawn hay wagons before, but this is much more romantic," she said, thinking better of the word only after it had slipped from her lips.

Spencer proffered his hand. "Your carriage awaits, m'lady."

Despite her best efforts, her annoyance at him had melted into the snow beneath her feet. She hesitated only a moment before sliding her fingers into his to let him help her up the step into the carriage.

As she settled into the plush seat, Spencer climbed in beside her. When the driver flicked the reins, the horse ambled forward and the carriage lurched into motion. Ellie gripped a bar beside her, a giddy laugh escaping her. Exhilaration swept through her as they moved along the street at an easy pace, bells jangling pleasantly.

"You crazy man," she said. "This is wonderful."

Pleasure shone in Spencer's eyes. "Glad you like it. You

once mentioned to me that if you ever came to Niagara-on-the-Lake, a horse-drawn carriage ride would be at the top of your to-do list."

"I did? I don't remember, but it sounds right. Although this is about the last thing I pictured myself doing when I arranged to spend the week holed up at the inn. I'll admit, this isn't a bad diversion."

"I realize you weren't exactly thrilled when I showed up in town and threw a wrench in your plans," he said, his smile contrite.

"Well, I…" Ellie bit her lip. His deception edged back into her thoughts, but she tucked it away. She's discuss it with him later, when they were alone. For now, she'd enjoy this moment. "Maybe a night out is just what I need. I never have been able to write in a vacuum, anyhow."

When the carriage turned onto Queen Street, she straightened and pulled in a sharp breath. Hundreds of tiny coloured lights glistened along shop windows, around street lamps, and among the limbs of the trees lining the road. She twisted in her seat to catch a glimpse of the clock at the top of the cenotaph, glowing white against the indigo sky. Elation zipped through her chest before she had a chance to suppress it.

"Breathtaking, isn't it?" Spencer asked.

"The lights are pretty," Ellie admitted. She settled her gaze on him, studying the pink hue of his cheeks and nose, his full lips parted into a gentle smile, those sea-blue eyes that seemed to draw in every trace of light around him. Forget the holiday decorations—it was Spencer who stole her breath.

"You look happy," he said. "Good. That's all I wanted."

She arched an eyebrow. "That's all you want?"

Spencer nodded. "The way you were when we were together. With or without me in your life, I want nothing but happiness for you, Ellie. I hope you know that."

The long, tender look he gave her stirred a warm quiver in her belly. She didn't protest when his fingers grazed the shoulder of her coat, then laced through the locks of hair resting there, letting the strands slip through.

His touch pulled her back in time to evenings spent in her

apartment or at his house, when they'd sat glued to one another, talking, touching, kissing. Never imagining a future where they'd be apart.

Her heart pounded with a dull ache, yearning for those moments when she'd felt safe and thoroughly loved. Truly happy. Moments that had receded into memories.

Spencer dropped his hand to her arm, then her hand, wrapping his gloved fingers around hers. "Ellie, I've got to ask you something you might not want me to ask, but I have to."

She stiffened, her gaze darting down to their clasped hands and then back to his face, trying to read his expression. She should've known. A man didn't make a grand, romantic gesture like this for no reason. More likely it was the culmination of a plan that had begun yesterday when he stalked her through the streets of Niagara-on-the-Lake. A spark of anger tinged with apprehension tightened her insides.

"Yes?" she said quietly, steeling herself.

He drew a quick breath and asked with a hopeful tone, "Do you think you could open your heart to Christmas, just a crack?"

Ellie stared at him, her lips parting, though it took her a moment to form a reply. "That's what you wanted to ask?"

Spencer nodded. "I think it's time you let go of your grudge against the holidays, don't you? I know you used to love Christmas when you were a kid. I never got to see that joy in your face. I figured I'd take one more shot at drawing it out of you."

Rather than relief, inexplicable disappointment stole through Ellie, leaving a hollow void in her chest. "I did love Christmas. That's why I wanted a Christmastime wedding. Then a week before Christmas, Joel...well, you know what he did. I guess the magic of the season fell victim to it as well." She held his gaze, her eyes pleading for understanding. "I'm over Joel. I really am. But—"

Releasing her hand, Spencer touched the sleeve of her coat. "You don't need to explain, Ellie. Just try to keep an open mind, all right? That's all I ask."

She bobbed her head. "All right."

He turned away then, his gaze shifting to the grand Victorian building on the corner, the Prince of Wales Hotel, its white pillars and balconies strung with pine garlands and red bows.

Ellie fought to keep her smile from slipping, battling to hide the surge of muddled emotions that made the edges of her lips wobble. No proposal was coming. Of course not. He'd kept his promise not to bring up marriage again.

Confusion tumbled through her, mixed with anger turned on herself, squeezing the knot in her gut. She should be relieved rather than troubled. A dreamy carriage ride along a pretty street changed nothing between them. It only meant that Spencer still cared about her happiness—not that he still wanted her as his wife.

That was good.

Wasn't it?

So why was her heart throbbing so heavily that her chest ached?

Spencer adjusted the white beard fastened to his face, carefully smoothing the flyaway strands away from his lips. He glanced around the little storage room where he'd been sent to change into costume, but couldn't find a mirror. Hoping his suit was on straight, he patted down the red velvet coat, already sweating within its bulk. A padded panel sewn into the front gave him a round belly but restricted his movements. Worse, the stitching in the hat irritated his scalp and the black boots pinched his toes, but he supposed he could endure the discomfort for the sake of a roomful of underprivileged kids in need of Christmas cheer.

And with any luck, he'd bring some cheer to Ellie as well. The carriage ride had already lifted her spirits. She'd been uptight around him the night before, but the rigid set of her shoulders had eased the moment she settled into the carriage seat. And despite her efforts to appear indifferent, her face had transformed with childlike wonder the moment she caught sight of the holiday lights on Queen Street. He'd do anything to see that same glow in her eyes again.

Jason had said that tricks didn't work with women, but it seemed a little nudge here and there could do wonders. With her heart opening to Christmas, maybe those deeper barriers would become a little easier to knock down.

He was sliding the white gloves onto his hands when rapping sounded on the other side of the door, followed by a muffled female voice. "Are you ready, Spencer?"

He opened the door to a cacophony of children's voices, laughter, and music that flooded in around the diminutive figure of Glenna Harvey, facing him in the doorway, the bell at the tip of her conical felt hat reaching the level of his eyes.

"I think I'm all set. How do I look?" he asked, fighting down a chuckle at the sight of the eighty-year-old decked out in an elf costume, complete with striped tights and curly red shoes.

Glenna squinted up at him through thick gold-rimmed glasses. "You look fine. Come on. The little hooligans are getting restless." She hooked her hand under his elbow and tugged him toward the sleigh-shaped bench set up in the corner of the community centre's main hall. The squeals in the room multiplied the instant he appeared, and the children who had lined up to see Santa rushed forward, their eyes shining and their little bodies vibrating in anticipation.

The place was packed with kids of all ages, with parents in tow, darting among the various booths. Next to Santa's station, little girls crowded around two volunteers dressed as Elsa and Anna from *Frozen,* who were painting faces with Christmas designs. On the other side, a magician stood performing illusion for a circle of rapt onlookers. A fishing game and a basketball hoop had been set up along the far wall, offering prizes, and in some location Spencer couldn't see, a local church choir sang Christmas carols, barely audible above the commotion. Tantalizing aromas of pizza and hot chocolate wafted in from the kitchen at the back of the hall.

Spencer searched for Ellie at the ice cream bar outside the kitchen, but his view was obscured by a group headed toward a smaller room across the corridor, where a photo booth had been set up, with silly hats and glasses provided. Once the crowd thinned out, he finally spotted her, an apron wrapped around her waist, her hair tied into a hastily fashioned ponytail. She chatted with Sonia while she scooped ice cream into a cone for a waiting little girl.

Glenna spread her arms to stop the kids from pouncing on Spencer all at once. "One at a time, now. If you want to see Santa, get back in line!" she barked, a deep frown settling between her brows. She didn't strike Spencer as the grandmotherly type, though according to Gino, she'd been a dedicated Helping Hands volunteer for decades.

Lowering himself into the sleigh, Spencer clutched his padded belly and bellowed his best deep "Ho, ho, ho!"

The boy who was first in line scurried around Glenna and crawled into Spencer's lap. He shook away unruly dark bangs and gazed up with serious brown eyes.

"Merry Christmas," Spencer said with a touch of apprehension. "What's your name?"

"Lucas." The boy tilted his head, giving Spencer a speculative look. "I had a cold last year so I couldn't come see you. I guess that's why you brought me a teddy bear. You forgot I'm too old for teddies now. I'm seven, by the way. So this year I want either some Lego or a remote control car like my friend Michael got last year. You know the one, right? It's red with stripes on the side."

Nodding as he listened, Spencer found his attention wandering back toward the ice cream bar. This time he caught Ellie's gaze. She straightened and smiled, lifting her hand in a small wave. Already overheating in the suit, he felt a deeper warmth spread through his chest.

A small hand fluttered in front of his face. "Santa, are you paying attention?"

Spencer jerked his gaze back to the boy perched on his lap. "Yes. Of course, Lucas. My elf assistant will find something in my sack that I'm sure will be just right for you." He motioned for Glenna, and she turned to the gifts stacked behind the sleigh, arranged by age and gender. Selecting a medium-sized package wrapped in superhero paper, she passed it to Spencer, who then handed it to the boy.

A smile lit up Lucas's face for the first time. He shook the box, listening to the shifting contents. "Thanks, Santa. Do I have to wait until tomorrow to open it?"

"Certainly you do," Spencer said with a wink. "No peeking, now. Have a wonderful Christmas, Lucas."

After Lucas hopped down and dashed toward his mother, who'd been waiting off to the side, Glenna leaned close and whispered in Spencer's ear, "Robotic dinosaur. I wrapped it myself this morning." She shrugged her thin shoulders. "Best I could do. The little fiend will have to like it or lump it."

Sometime later, once the lineup of kids thinned out, Glenna posted a sign on the sleigh indicating Santa would be back in half an hour.

"Go get something to eat while you can," she told Spencer. "I don't know about you, but I'm starving."

"Me too," he said. "And I need to stretch my legs. You should get off your feet, Glenna. I'm sure you're exhausted."

"Why, because I'm old?" Pressing her lips tight, she straightened her bowed back as best she could. "I volunteered for this gig because it keeps me active. Keeps the blood flowing to my limbs. See you back here at seven-thirty."

As she turned and shuffled away, Spencer moved to stand up. He stopped when Ellie approached, and instead he patted his knee, inviting her to sit.

She shook her head, grinning. "No way, Santa. What kind of a ho, ho, ho do you think I am?"

Spencer smiled wide beneath his moustache. "Are you sorry now you didn't put on the elf costume?" He tilted his head toward Glenna's retreating back.

"Not a bit. I'm having too much fun doling out ice cream."

"You're having a good time?"

"I am." Ellie stepped closer and leaned her hip against the edge of the sleigh. "This is a wonderful organization. Sonia

370

told me they're distributing warm coats in one of the other rooms, and they've put together food hampers and gifts that volunteers are going to deliver to families later tonight."

Spencer got to his feet, pressing his hands against the small of his back and jutting out his padded belly as he stretched. "I know. I spent my afternoon curling ribbons with a pair of scissors. I didn't even know that was a thing before today."

"And I spent my morning feeling sorry for myself because my writing hasn't been flowing quite as well as I'd like. I'm ashamed I never thought about volunteering for this sort of event before. It feels good."

"This is my first time, too," he admitted. "It's a nice change to realize it's not all about you."

Ellie smiled. She looked lovely, despite the wisps of hair falling loose from her ponytail and the ice cream smudges on her apron. "Are you hungry?"

"Are you kidding? The smell of that pizza has been torturing me for the last hour. Gino made it, so it's got to be incredible."

"I'm starving too." Ellie eyed him briefly, a small smile lingering on her lips. "You might want to eat somewhere out of sight. You'll have to take the beard off if you don't want sauce and cheese all over it."

"Will you join me?"

"Sure. I've got a short break from my post."

While they crossed the hall, side by side, Spencer suppressed an urge to reach for her hand. She'd let him hold her hand in the carriage, but a public display of affection might be pushing his luck—and besides, she'd have to be dressed as Mrs. Claus to maintain the illusion. He grinned to himself, enjoying the image of her in a white wig and half-moon glasses. Not just because it amused him, but because it warmed him to picture the two of them fifty years from now, strolling with their hands clasped. He would never grow tired of her soft skin or the gentle grip of her fingers entwined with his.

"Do you know where Gino went?" he asked, realizing he hadn't seen his friend in some time.

"I spoke to him a few minutes ago," Ellie said. "He and Sonia are working on the hampers. I didn't realize Sonia was Russian until I heard her accent. She's very sweet. They both are. Gino told me he got involved with Helping Hands because his family went through some rough times when he was young, after his father got sick and couldn't work."

"Yeah, those were tough years for him," Spencer replied. "When we were in high school, I made a point to invite him over for dinner a couple of times a week, to make sure he ate properly. He got his first job at fifteen so he could help out with the bills. All the other guys were working to pay for a car or maybe save up for university, but Gino just wanted to buy new shoes for his little sisters."

"Wow, that's heartbreaking." Ellie looked at him with a concerned crease in her brow.

"At least his early experience working in restaurants set him on the path to a career he loves."

"How are his parents now?"

"Mr. Rossi died a few years ago, but Mrs. Rossi is doing well. I'll be seeing his whole family when they come down for Christmas dinner. I have to admit—" He stopped speaking at the door to the kitchen, as they stepped into the pizza line and a dozen pairs of young eyes turned to Spencer.

"Admit what?" Ellie asked.

He bent closer to her ear so he could finish his thought privately. Warmth rising from her skin and the floral scent of her hair tangled into his senses, making him pause a moment before replying. She looked up at him with expectant eyes.

"Back then I was kind of jealous of Gino's tightknit family," he said. "At Christmas, they didn't have much to go around, but they pulled together and made the best of their situation. We had plenty of food and presents at my place, but Gino had the one thing I wanted more than anything—a real home, with people who would do anything for him, like he would for them. I never felt like I had that." With his gaze locked onto Ellie's, his chest expanded with an almost painful swell of feeling for her. "Until I had you."

Ten

The clock on the dashboard of Spencer's Honda Civic showed 10:52 when he pulled up by the curb outside The Roses. Ellie glanced out the passenger side window at the looming inn, a foreboding dark shape whose upper floor seemed to meld into the inky sky.

"Thanks for driving me back." She slid her gaze to Spencer beside her. The temperature had dropped over the course of the evening, making her grateful he'd left his car at the community centre for the ride back.

"No problem. Thank you for helping out tonight, especially with the clean-up. I think it went really well."

"It did. I'm glad you talked me into it."

"Me too." A few beats of silence passed before Spencer cleared his throat and added, "You must be tired."

"I'm not tired," Ellie blurted, though her back and feet ached from standing for hours. Her heart felt lighter than it had it ages, and she wasn't quite ready to go to bed. Or say goodnight to Spencer. "Would you like to come in for a drink?"

Though his brows arched in surprise, he barely hesitated. "Sure."

"Follow me." Ellie opened the car door and stepped out into the cold night air. She hurried into the warmth of the pub, with Spencer close behind her.

With only a handful of patrons lingering over drinks at the tables closest to the fireplace, the pub was quiet enough for soft Christmas music to be heard. When Ellie's gaze fell on the modern fixtures behind the bar, her steps faltered, as images of nineteenth-century wooden barrels and pewter mugs flickered into her mind's eye.

Spencer's voice jarred her back to the present. "Where would you like to sit? The bar's free."

"Sounds good." She slid onto a stool and smiled at the bartender. "Could I please have a martini?"

The man was tall and slight, sporting a close-cropped beard and blond bangs combed across his forehead. "Sure thing. What can I get you, sir?"

"Same for me." Settling onto the stool next to Ellie, Spencer leaned his elbow on the polished oak bar, and observed her with a steady gaze as his mouth angled into a thoughtful smile.

Ellie darted a glance at her drab jeans and sweater, wishing now that she'd worn something a little more elegant. "What are you staring at?"

"You, looking relaxed and happy."

"I am relaxed and happy. The party was a lot more fun than I expected."

"Glad to hear it. The kids enjoyed it, too." Spencer reached into his pocket for his wallet when the bartender set the drinks in front of them.

Ellie sipped her martini and set it back on the coaster. "It felt kind of amazing, seeing the big smiles on those kids. My part was just serving ice cream, but with everyone pulling together, I think we created a really special evening that they'll remember for a long time."

"I agree." His drink in hand, Spencer twisted his stool to face her. "I'd do it again, even though playing Santa had its difficult moments. One little girl asked if I could get her dad out of prison for Christmas. And a boy told me he didn't need any toys—he just wanted me to bring something for his mom to cheer her up. Hard to know what to say to those requests."

"Oh, wow. That is hard." Ellie sighed and propped her chin on her fist. "I guess embracing the season means forgetting about yourself and your own problems, and finding pleasure in lifting whatever burden you can from those who have too much on their shoulders. I'm sure those kids and their parents have gone through a lot worse than a canceled wedding."

Spencer's smile widened into a sly grin. "Why, Ms. Scrooge, I do believe you have discovered the true meaning of Christmas. God bless us, every one!" He clinked his martini glass against hers before lifting it to his lips.

Ellie rolled her eyes. "Let's not go overboard. My mission this week is still to focus on my novel. Not making merry."

"Fine, I get it. I'm just honoured that I was here to see your heart grow three sizes today."

"Spence, quit teasing me." She swallowed more of her drink, averting her gaze from his to avoid letting him see just how right he was. As she studied the festive green and gold garlands strung above the bar, it dawned on her how different she felt about the season tonight. As though a truth she'd tried to banish from her heart had resurfaced, nudging out the dark emotions that had festered there for two years. Thinking back on her childhood, she remembered how the coloured lights, pretty baubles and stacks of presents had felt like magic. But even as Joel's desertion had tainted those traditions for her, Christmas had a deeper power he could never touch.

"So how is the writing coming?" Spencer asked. "Making progress?"

Ellie nodded, though she didn't feel much like discussing her work. "I used your suggestion. It's—*oh.*"

Her thoughts froze when her gaze fell on a small framed portrait hung on one of the posts behind the bar. Setting down her glass, she leaned closer for a better look at the painting.

The pretty young woman in the portrait wore a blue ruffled gown. Her dark hair was fastened atop her head with a spray of white flowers. She stared back from the canvas with wide blue eyes, her pink bow lips curved into a gentle smile.

A funny tingling sensation crept across Ellie's scalp and down her spine.

"Excuse me," she called to the bartender, who was pouring a beer for another customer at the far end of the bar. "That portrait. I didn't notice it here before."

The bartender glanced over his shoulder at the painting. "It's been here for years. The owner took it down last week to replace the frame. It went back up just this afternoon."

"It's Rebecca," Ellie mumbled.

"Right. Seen her around?" the bartender asked with a teasing smile as he set the beer glass on the bar.

"No, of course not," Ellie said, though she was sure she *had* seen the woman's face—or at least dreamed it. Fairly sure, anyhow. Maybe her brain was playing tricks on her, filling in foggy bits in her memory simply because the woman in the portrait had a similar style of clothes and hair to the one in her dream.

"Still a skeptic?" Spencer asked. "Jason sounded pretty convincing when he told me about his encounter with the ghost the night of the fire six years ago. Did Abby tell you about it?"

Tearing her focus from the portrait, Ellie gulped a mouthful of martini before answering. "She told me that when Jason ran into the burning building looking for her, he thought he saw and apparition on the stairs who gestured to the room where he found her. But he could have easily imagined a human shape in the heavy smoke, or hallucinated it. When did you talk to Jason?"

"We had a little chat last night after you went back to your room. Did you also know about his dream?"

Ellie stared at him, debating with herself whether she really wanted to know as fresh goose bumps sprouted on her skin. "What dream?"

"The only reason Jason came rushing to the inn in the middle of the night was because he'd dreamed about Rebecca Norris and her husband, about their deaths. He woke with an overwhelming sense that Abby was in danger, and went looking for her. Ellie, are you all right?" Spencer eyed her with concern as she choked on her mouthful of martini, spewing droplets across the gleaming wood surface of the bar.

Ellie bobbed her head, struggling to speak through a fit of coughing.

"Would you like some water?"

She dragged in a few breaths, regaining control. "Another martini," she managed to croak.

Spencer signaled to the bartender. "Two more, please." He reached for a napkin to mop up the spill on the bar.

Ellie glanced at the portrait again. She blinked a few times, bracing herself against a strange sensation of the room tilting to one side, then the other. The first martini was already muddling her brain. She shouldn't have another. But at the moment, a little muddle in her brain felt like just what she needed.

Spencer pulled out his wallet to pay for the drinks. While he extracted a couple of bills, a slip of paper tucked into one of the card slots caught Ellie's eye. She read the letters printed along the edge of the slip—*Molière*—and knew at once what it was.

"You still have it?" she asked, astonished.

He looked at her, his brow furrowed in question.

"The ticket stub. For *The Hypochondriac,* the play we saw at the Stratford Festival in the summer."

Glancing at the stub, Spencer gave a half-smile and a shrug before snapping his wallet shut. "All kinds of old junk accumulates in there. I never think to clean it out."

"It was a good play," Ellie said. "A good night overall." She paused, remembering how she's laughed so hard her stomach had ached. And after leaving the theatre, they'd strolled along the Avon River, unwinding into blissful contentment as they admired the lights along the riverbank reflecting on the still, dark water.

Later still, in their room at that Victorian bed and breakfast, they hadn't bothered to switch on the lights. In the murky dark, once they'd undressed each other, he'd carried her to the bed and explored her body with exquisite, slow caresses, dropping tantalizing kisses along every inch of her skin.

"A *great* night," she added, her words a near-whisper carried on her breath, her mind awash with sensual memories. She looked at Spencer and saw his expression had changed, as though his thoughts mirrored hers. She shifted a little on her stool, hesitant but at the same time enthralled by his warm and intimate gaze fastened on her.

"The best," he said. The rich timbre of his voice caressed her nerves and sent a quiver of excitement through her limbs.

Rather than fight the feeling, Ellie let it flow through her. Losing herself in Spencer's enticing sea-blue eyes felt so much nicer than the angst she'd been tussling with the last few days. Forget about the minefield of emotions surrounding Christmas, weird dreams and strange noises in the hallway, and the troubles she was having with her novel. Most of all, forget about guarding her heart—just for tonight.

Ellie reached for her drink and swallowed several mouthfuls, while Spencer did the same.

"Is Gino expecting you back at his place?" She wasn't sure what she meant by the question, and judging by the quizzical look on his face, Spencer wasn't either. "I mean, will he wonder what's happened to you?"

Spencer shrugged. "Eventually, I suppose. I'm sure he and Sonia won't be waiting up. So I'm in no rush."

Ellie contemplated the small amount of clear liquor left in her glass. She didn't want Spencer to go. They could talk longer. They used to talk for hours. She cast about for something to discuss, came up empty, and ended up saying, "I might just go up to my room."

"All right." He drained his glass and set it on the bar. "I'll walk you to the stairs."

"Okay." Ellie got to her feet, keeping her hand on the stool for a moment to steady herself against the whirling in her head.

"Shall we?" Spencer placed his hand on her back and walked with her through the doors leading to the deserted, dimly lit vestibule.

At the foot of the stairs, she turned to face him.

"Well, goodnight," he said, though he didn't move. His eyes raked over her, a slow and tender journey that heated her flesh as though his hands and not his gaze had caressed her.

Ellie stepped closer, leaving little space between them, and placed her palms on his chest. It had been too long since she'd touched him, and as she breathed in his male scent, so familiar and comforting, longing swept through her. "Thank you for convincing me to come to the party. It really did soften my feelings toward Christmas...to a certain degree."

A smile played on his lips while his arms wrapped around her waist. "Mission accomplished, then."

"To a certain degree," Ellie repeated softly. She relaxed

against him, tipping her head back so that his mouth hovered above hers, his warm breath fanning her lips. Desire heated his gaze. Her body responded, pulsing with awareness, fueled by a combination of alcohol and titillating memories.

This was a bad idea. Friends didn't kiss each other. Former lovers really shouldn't. But she pushed aside the rational voice nattering inside her head and, closing her eyes, she brushed her mouth against his. His lips molded to hers, their caress soft and tender. The shape and taste of his mouth exhilarated her senses, pulling her back in time six weeks, as though nothing had happened to tear them apart.

Without thought, she deepened the kiss, delighting in the fervent strokes of his mouth on hers.

A soft whimper escaped her. Angling her head back, she broke the kiss, "Spencer, we shouldn't."

"I know." He blew out a breath, ragged with longing. "But I need you, Ellie." He bent his head to trail his lips along her jaw, and glided lower to trace the curve of her neck.

She shuddered, clutching his shoulders, her nerves throbbing with need for him.

"Come upstairs," she blurted.

Spencer didn't hesitate. Backing away a few inches, he curled his hand around hers. "Let's go."

ELEVEN

Ellie kicked the door shut and left the lights off. She sank into Spencer's arms, welcoming his insistent kisses. They tore at each other's clothes, removing the garments haphazardly and tossing them aside.

The filmy curtains allowed in enough light from the street to outline his masculine form. Her hands roamed over his familiar shape, her palm molding to his sturdy shoulders and smooth chest. Overwhelmed, Ellie blinked back tears that prickled her eyes. Her body had suffered from his absence as keenly as her soul.

Spencer's large, warm hands slid down her spine and came to rest on her hips. He sank to his knees and pressed his mouth to her belly, searing her sensitive flesh with delicate kisses, in just the way he knew would rouse her. Delicious heat jolted to her core. Closing her eyes, Ellie laced her fingers into his hair, her knees weakening until she feared they might buckle.

Her breath came faster as he moved upward, his lips tracing a slow path along her skin, while his fingers curled between her thighs. Anticipation raced like fire through her veins. Her heart pounded against his roaming mouth as sensation rocked her body. She groaned in protest when he climbed to his feet.

"God I've missed you," Spencer muttered, his mouth finding hers. "Every inch of you."

She smoothed her hands down the long muscles of his back and held him close. His body fit with hers as it always had, his chest heaving against her breasts. She skimmed kisses along his shoulders and throat, delighting in the hungry moans rumbling beneath her lips.

"I need you now," he said, his voice thick with longing.

"Then let's not waste any more time." Gripping his arms, Ellie tugged him to the bed.

He crawled onto the covers and she followed, prodding him backward to lie against the pillow. As she slid her body over his, he reached up to smooth her hair away from her face and over her shoulders, before his hands traveled downward to tease and explore.

Hovering above him, Ellie closed her eyes and let his caresses warm and rouse her.

"I still love you, Ellie," he said, his tone steady and serious. "I never stopped. I couldn't imagine not loving you."

Ellie opened her eyes, her breath catching on the steady pulsing of her heart in her throat. She couldn't speak, so instead lowered herself onto him, taking him inside her. He gripped her thighs and rolled his hips forward, filling her.

Ellie sighed with pleasure. Relaxing into the rhythm of their lovemaking, she drew a breath and at last let her reply spill from her lips.

"Spence, I love you too."

She closed the door softly. Soft, flickering light threw wavering shadows against the wall of the inn's second-floor hallway. Ellie looked along the wall to her right and found the light's source, a plain tin sconce that held a pair of slender candles. Funny, she hadn't noticed it there before. Come to think of it, candles left to burn unattended in the middle of the night had to be an egregious fire hazard. Someone had been careless in forgetting to blow them out. She thought about doing so herself, once she located the wall switch. But there didn't seem to be a switch anywhere.

Creeek. Creeek. Creeek.

Stiffening, she pulled in a sharp breath. She didn't turn around, but stood frozen, recognizing the unmistakable moan of a rocking chair rolling back and forth against old floorboards. Not in the next room this time, but directly behind her, in the corner where she'd seen the antique chair.

Ellie turned her head just slightly, and the knot in her

stomach pulled tighter when another sound joined the creak of the chair. A woman's quiet weeping. The soul-wrenching sobs quivered along Ellie's backbone.

She closed her eyes a moment to steel herself before slowly turning around.

In its usual spot in the corner, the chair swayed in long, smooth motions. Its occupant, a woman wearing a white cotton shift and a ruffled cap, sat with her head forward so that her long dark hair, loose from the cap, draped over her face. Clutching something to her chest, she rocked herself forward and back with her bare feet pressed against the wood-plank floor. Her shoulders shuddered with the force of her desperate sobs.

Ellie tried to speak, but couldn't find her voice. Her gaze skittered over the billowy shift molded to a rounded belly. She knew without seeing the woman's face that she was Rebecca. She also recognized the wooden object in Rebecca's hands as the toy solder Jack had given her the day he left for battle.

This was another dream. It had to be. Yet the raw pain in Rebecca's weeping tore at Ellie's heart, and she fought to contain a hitch in her own chest. She supposed Rebecca must have just learned of her husband's death, and she couldn't imagine the young woman's anguish. The man she cherished dead on a battlefield. With war raging around her, she'd been left on her own to give birth. Expecting to raise the baby alone, she didn't yet realize her own life would end before she had the chance to know her child.

Crazy as it was, Ellie had the sense that she'd known Rebecca all her life, and the young woman's fear and grief gripped her soul. An impulse to comfort her propelled Ellie forward, and she reached out to touch Rebecca's quivering shoulder.

Just as her hand fell upon the white cotton sleeve, Ellie jerked awake. Tangled in bed sheets, she stared at the morning light glowing against the curtains drawn across the window. For a moment Rebecca's desperate sobs echoed in her ears, but they swiftly faded. The rapid thumping of Ellie's own heart took their place.

TWELVE

She turned her head and found Spencer asleep beside her, his back facing her. Sunlight gilded the smooth skin of his arm and shoulder.

Overwhelmed with a need to hold him, she rolled onto her side and scooted closer to wrap her arms around his torso. She buried her face in his shoulder, breathing in his warm scent, and waited for her pounding heart to slow its pace.

Within moments, Spencer stirred. He rolled onto his back and met her gaze with hooded eyes and a drowsy smile.

"Morning," he said, his voice rough from sleep. He kissed her temple and slid his arm around her back. He then angled his head back to observe her face more closely. His hand came to rest between her breasts. "Your heart's racing. What's wrong?"

"Nothing. Just a bad dream."

Spencer pulled her closer, pressing the length of his body against her. His warmth and strength calmed her.

"I woke up earlier," he said, "and for a moment I was afraid that what happened between us last night was just a dream. Then I turned over and saw you sleeping beside me." A blissful smile curved his lips. "I don't think I've ever experienced a moment of purer happiness in my entire life."

Ellie grinned, letting the last shreds of unease from her dream fall away. She bent her head and brushed her mouth over his. He responded with a slow, tantalizing kiss that left her breathless.

Breaking the kiss, she moaned and fell back against her pillow. "Spencer, I'm starving. Hold that thought, and let's go get some breakfast."

"In a minute." He threaded his fingers into her disheveled hair, holding her gaze with his mesmerizing blue eyes, and she found she really didn't want to go anywhere. "I want to say something."

"Okay."

Spencer didn't speak right away, but trailed his fingers along her arm, tickling her skin. "I still love you, Ellie," he said at last. "I've never stopped loving you."

Her heart swelled with joy, though her body went rigid. She could tell he was leading up to something more. She recognized the tender, determined look in his eyes from the day he'd dropped to one knee at the park and asked her to marry him.

"You said that last night," she said apprehensively.

A slow smile curved his lips. "Ellie, relax. I'm not about to propose. I'm not such a masochist that I'd put myself through that again."

"Oh." She drew a long breath. "All right. Go ahead."

"I'm ready to compromise." With feather-light strokes, his fingertips traced her jaw, then cupped her chin. "Since I can't live without you, it looks like you hold all the cards. We'll live together—no wedding. But I *do* want a commitment. We can buy each other rings. We'll be life partners. Whether you want to be called 'wife' or not, that's what you'll be to me."

Ellie raised herself onto her elbow, gaping at him in astonishment. She hadn't thought beyond today. Or even beyond last night. And here he was, handing her everything she'd asked for.

"Ellie, please say something." Spencer studied her with a worried frown pinching his brows.

"Will you let me think about it?"

"Yeah. Sure." He leaned in and kissed her mouth lightly. "For how long?"

"I don't know, Spence. Long enough to have a cup of coffee in me, at least." She offered a soft smile, letting him know his suggestion hadn't sent her into a panic.

"I suppose that's reasonable. You should never make a major decision before your morning caffeine hits your system." He shifted into a sitting position, stretching his arms. "I had kind of a disturbing dream too. I saw a woman crying. She was sitting in that old rocking chair in the hallway, wearing a nightgown, but I couldn't see her face. She was holding something. Don't know what it was." He shook his head. "It's weird, since I don't usually remember my dreams."

Ellie blinked at him. She opened her lips to ask if he was teasing her, then snapped her mouth shut.

She hadn't told him a single detail about her dream. How could he know?

Swinging his legs over the side of the bed, Spencer got to his feet and headed to the bathroom. "Mind if I use the shower first?"

"Go ahead." Ellie lay still and watched him close the door. Her heart pounding, thoughts whirling, she listened as the toilet flushed, then water drummed in the shower.

Her mind reeled, unable to settle on which bewildering development to latch onto—Spencer's proposal to live together, or the identical dream they'd apparently both had. For the moment, the dream won out.

Just a weird coincidence?

Yet is seemed impossible.

Throwing the covers back, Ellie pulled on her nightgown and climbed out of bed. She picked up her cell phone from the table and hesitated, considering whether it was too early to call Abby. She went ahead and selected the number.

After three rings, Abby answered. "Morning, Ellie. What's up?"

"Sorry to call so early," Ellie began.

"No problem. I'm up making breakfast. Is something wrong?"

"Nothing's wrong. I'm just curious to know more about Rebecca Norris. And her husband, Jack. I know he was killed in the War of 1812."

"Yes, he died at the Battle of Queenston Heights."

Ellie sank onto the bed, her pulse thundering. *Queenston.* In her first dream, Jack had mentioned he was headed there to join the troops repelling the American invasion. She couldn't have known that...but then again, it was a famous battle that she knew a little about, easily retrievable by her subconscious mind.

"You've been to the park and seen the big memorial for General Brock?" Abby asked.

Ellie cleared her throat. "I've been there on school trips." She'd climbed the steps to the top of the monument's limestone column, and gazed out over the bluff toward the Niagara River where the American militia had crossed in hopes of establishing a foothold on the Canadian side.

"Even though the British army won that battle, they lost a number of regular soldiers and militia, as well as Brock, of course," Abby added.

"So what happened to Rebecca's baby?"

"She had a little girl named Emma. According to Jason's family records, Rebecca's sister raised her. I believe they moved to a nearby town when Emma was young."

Ellie mumbled her reply more to herself than to Abby. "So if Rebecca's spirit is still hanging around the inn, maybe she's been looking for her baby all this time. Maybe she intended to watch over her daughter as she grew up, and she's been in distress, not knowing what became of her child."

"Ellie, did something happen?" Abby asked. "Did you see something strange?"

"No... not exactly. Just a dream. It's nothing," Ellie said, though she realized that there had to be something more to these strange occurrences than she'd wanted to admit. She needed time to sort things out in her own mind.

Abby seemed to grasp the finality in Ellie's tone and didn't press the question. "So how was the party last night?"

"Good. I enjoyed it." Ellie glanced toward the bathroom, where muffled singing mingled with the steady drumming of water in the shower. "I think Spence and I might be getting back together."

Abby gasped. "Really? That's great. I could see a real spark between the two of you."

"You could?"

"Sure. I didn't think I should say anything, but I got a sense that you belonged together. Sometimes it's just obvious that two people are meant for one another."

A warm glow suffused Ellie's chest. "You and Jason have that, too."

"Do we?" Abby said, a smile evident in her voice.

Hearing the shower shut off, Ellie added quickly, "One more thing, Abby. I noticed the rocking chair in the hallway. Is it a family heirloom?"

"Probably. No one's really sure where it came from originally. I found it with a bunch of old stuff in the cellar when I had the inn restored. Thankfully I'd taken it out to have it repaired before the fire. It's better off at the inn than at home, where Becca could get her sticky little hands on it."

"Did you name your daughter after Rebecca?"

"Yes. It seemed appropriate since, at the time, I thought Rebecca's spirit might've had something to do with getting Jason and me together. I know it sounds silly—"

"Not at all. I hope you'll bring Becca by the inn sometime while I'm here so I can meet her."

"I'll try, but she usually resists coming to the inn. Five-year-olds have active imaginations, and she's heard the stories. She claims the ghost has touched her."

"Really?" Ellie said.

"She said she felt a hand stroke her hair, affectionately the way I do, but when she turned around, no one was there. Which doesn't seem too scary, but I guess it creeped her out. Being a mother herself," Abby added with a chuckle, "I suppose Rebecca must have a soft spot in her heart for little girls."

THIRTEEN

Spencer watched Ellie across the table while she sipped her coffee. He couldn't help staring at her, maybe to convince himself she really was there eating breakfast with him after a passionate night of lovemaking—the very thing he'd hoped for but hadn't dared to expect. Asking her to live together had never been part of his plan, but he'd been overcome, waking from that troubling dream to find himself in Ellie's arms with her warm, supple shape pressed against him.

He couldn't regret his decision when looking into her eyes, knowing she still loved him, made him as giddy with happiness now as it had then.

Spencer slid his hand past the bowl of sugar packets between them and clasped her free hand, drawing a contented smile to her lips.

"Are you happy?" he asked, and trepidation clenched his chest as he waited for her answer.

Ellie set her coffee cup on its saucer and threw a glance toward the café's wide window. Bright morning sunshine glinted off the cars traveling along Queen Street and spilled through the window to burnish the golden strands in her hair.

"Of course," she said, squeezing his fingers. "I didn't expect any of this to happen, but I'm glad you came. I missed you more than I was willing to admit, even to myself."

"Then I'm sorry I waited so long to barge back into your life."

Ellie pushed aside her plate, which was empty other than a few smears of strawberry jam and a dusting of crumbs from her toast. "I should move into your place, don't you think? It's larger than mine. But not until Gwen can find a new roommate."

Spencer's heart struck his ribs with a blow that halted his breath. "So that's a yes?"

"It's a yes." An ecstatic smile slid across Ellie's face.

Elated, he lifted her hand to his lips and kissed it several times, before clasping it between his palms. "Good. Great. I can't wait to do this."

"Me neither."

"Meanwhile, we need to make up for lost time. Spend the day with me."

"I'm really getting behind in my writing." She picked up her cup and swirled the dregs of her coffee.

"Do you want some help?"

"I'd love it. Could we work on it later today?"

"Sure."

Ellie's phone on the table warbled. She glanced at the screen. "It's Abby."

"Go ahead and answer."

She swiped the screen and lifted the phone to her ear. "Hi, Abby." Ellie paused to listen. "Really? That's so nice of you, but I'm sure you're busy today. It's Christmas Eve." Pausing again, she cut a glance at Spencer. "Well, okay. Thanks. Yes, we're just finishing breakfast. See you later. Bye."

"Exciting news?" Spencer asked as she ended the call.

"Sort of. Earlier I was asking Abby about Rebecca Norris's daughter, Emma. She told Jason, and he dug around and found a picture of Emma. Abby said she's got a laser printer and a spare frame at home, so she'd scan the portrait and print a copy to hang up in the inn later today."

Spencer cocked an eyebrow. "I didn't realize you were so interested."

"I would've thought you'd be intrigued, too, being a historian. And considering that dream you told me about."

"What about it?"

"It was Rebecca, wasn't it?" Ellie slid her phone into her purse, keeping her searching gaze firmly fastened on his face.

"I don't know. It was just a dream. It didn't have to be anyone in particular." Spencer remembered a woman in a rocking chair, but the details had faded, and he struggled to coax a more distinct picture of her from his memory. He recalled more vividly the gut-wrenching misery in her sobs, which still made the hairs on his arms bristle when he thought of it.

Ellie paused to swallow the last of her coffee. "Should we

get a refill or be on our way?"

"We should go, but not back to the inn yet. There's a jewellery store across the street. I meant what I said about commitment rings."

"You mean right now? Well, why not?" When he reached for his wallet, she stopped him. "I'm buying breakfast. Wait here. I'll be right back."

While Ellie grabbed her purse and headed to the service counter to pay, Spencer finished his own neglected coffee and watched her. Admiring the feminine sway of her hips and the bounce of her hair on her shoulders, he almost succeeded in ignoring the unsettled feeling that nettled him. His sudden decision to live together had been easy to make in the moment, and the rings had been his idea—but still, the notion of buying something less than an engagement ring didn't sit quite right.

Never mind. Over time, he was sure he could shed his reluctance and focus on appreciating what he had. Even an informal commitment from Ellie was something she'd take seriously. Maybe he was the one who had to stop demanding guarantees where there could be none. He needed to put his faith in her, as well as trust his own heart.

Outside the jewellery store, Spencer gripped Ellie's hand and pulled her to the side of the door.

"I have to tell you something," he said. "I can't do this without being honest with you."

She threw him a cautious look. "Go ahead."

"I lied to you."

Her eyes widened. "About what?"

"I told you the ticket stub in my wallet was just garbage I hadn't gotten rid of. But I kept it on purpose, as a memento. A reminder of you every time I open my wallet."

Ellie smiled, folding her gloved hands around his bare hands. "That's sweet, Spence. Buy why didn't you keep a picture of me instead?"

"Photos are static. That stub puts a picture in my mind of your face while you were watching the play. Smiling and laughing. You glanced at me and your eyes were shining. I wanted to keep that moment with me."

"Really?" Her gentle gaze rested on his. Draping an arm around her back, he drew her a little closer. With his fingers, he traced slow circles on the warm, silky skin of her throat, feeling the flutter of her pulse.

"When you reached across the seats and took my hand," he went on, "I felt like my heart was crammed full of more hope and joy than I'd thought it could possibly hold. Whenever I open my wallet and catch a glimpse of that tattered ticket stub, it brings me back to that feeling."

Pressing her lips tight, Ellie blinked several times, as though tears threatened. "I don't keep a memento on me, but I remember it the same as you. I'm yours now, Spence, and we'll have many more special nights together. Now let's go look at rings."

She tried to tug him toward the door, but he held her back, hoping he wouldn't regret what he was about to tell her.

"I'm not quite done with the honesty bit. I hope you won't be angry." He paused to gather his resolve. "I wasn't exactly truthful about my reason for coming to Niagara-on-the-Lake. It wasn't a coincidence we ran into each other. I knew you were here. Gino provided a good cover story, but really I came for you."

"I know," she said with a soft smile. "Gwen told me. I was mad at you at first," she gave his arm a gentle punch, "but then you showed up with that horse-drawn carriage and spoiled my bad mood. Let's go get those rings."

FOURTEEN

They returned to The Roses just as the sun was sinking behind the inn's sloped roof. At the front desk, Oscar stood from his chair when Ellie and Spencer walked in the door.

"Welcome back, Ellie. I've got something here for you." He handed her a pewter frame that held a copy of a vintage photograph. "Abby asked me to give you this when you came in."

Ellie pulled off her gloves before taking the portrait. The woman in the photo bore a remarkable resemblance to Rebecca Norris but looked older, perhaps sixty, with her silver-threaded dark hair arranged in a neat coil atop her head. In her high ruffled collar, a brooch pinned at her throat, she looked like a staid and proper Victorian lady, though she had a slight curve to her feminine lips that hinted at a smile and lively, striking dark eyes.

"This is Emma Norris?" Spencer asked over her shoulder.

"Emma Wood was her married name," Oscar said. "That's about 1875, according to Abby."

"She looks happy," Ellie said.

"Survived the births of seven children. I suppose that was something to be happy about in those days."

"Rebecca would be comforted to know her daughter lived a full life, don't you think?" A funny thrill quivered through Ellie as she studied the photo. "Doesn't Abby intend to hang it in the pub?"

"I believe so," Oscar said, "but she didn't have time. She'll do it after Christmas."

"May I keep it in my room until then?"

"I don't see why not."

"Thanks. I'll take good care of it."

Upstairs in her room, Ellie set the portrait carefully on the dresser before unwinding her scarf from her neck and sliding off her coat. "It's almost suppertime," she said to Spencer, "but maybe there's time for you to review a couple chapters of my novel before we eat."

"Absolutely. I've been looking forward to it." Spencer tossed his coat on the bed before reaching for her and enfolding her in his arms. "Sorry I kept you out so long."

Ellie linked her hands behind his neck and smiled up at him. "No, I had fun." After choosing their rings at the jewellery store, they'd perused the shops on Queen Street and eaten lunch at a bistro before touring a small art gallery they discovered. She'd barely noticed the time passing.

His warm gaze settled on her face. "I can't wait to get that ring back on your finger. For good."

"Same here. I wish I didn't have to wait two days for mine to be sized."

"I won't wear mine until you have yours." He dragged his hand slowly up her back and under the drape of her hair, stroking her nape and sending delicious shivers along her skin. "You're glad we did this?"

"Of course." Ellie hadn't thought about wearing another ring since returning the diamond solitaire and matching gold wedding band Joel had given her. But in the three days since she'd arrived at Niagara-on-the-Lake, intent on avoiding both Spencer and the holidays, those plans had fallen to pieces and her future looked much different than she'd imagined. "Are you?"

"Very glad." Spencer brushed a few delicate kisses against her forehead. "As much as I'd like to keep you right here in my arms, you've got a novel to write. What would you like me to read?"

Reluctantly, Ellie eased out of his embrace and took a step toward her laptop. Then she paused, turning to him. "First, I want to talk to you about something. Your dream last night about Rebecca Norris."

He folded his arms, sliding her a quizzical look. "Just an anonymous woman. I told you I couldn't tell who it was. What about it?"

She sank onto the bed and looked up at him. "I had exactly the same dream. A woman crying in that rocking chair out in the hallway, holding a little wooden toy soldier in her hand."

Spencer barked out a laugh. "Come on."

"I did, Spence. She was pregnant in your dream, wasn't she?"

"Maybe. I don't remember that detail."

Ellie blew out a breath in frustration. "Didn't you feel connected to her, as though she was someone close to you? As though her emotions were almost...I don't know, so intense that you could almost feel them as your own."

Spencer stared at her in silence, his brow deeply furrowed.

"You don't believe me?"

"I didn't say that."

"You said that Jason sounded convincing when he told you about his dream that alerted him something was wrong the night of the fire, and then seeing the ghost on the stairwell."

"I'm convinced *he* believes it. That doesn't mean it was anything more than a mixture of coincidence and fantasy."

"Coincides only go so far." Ellie reached for his hand and squeezed it, willing him to accept what she was telling him. "I had another dream the night before, about Rebecca saying goodbye to her husband before he left for battle. And she looked just like her portrait, which I'd never seen before. I woke up and heard sobbing from outside the room. I've heard the chair rocking, too. I know I wasn't dreaming then. I figured it was in my imagination, but when you told me about your dream...I can't deny anymore that something is going on that I can't explain."

Spencer didn't reply at first. Still gripping her hand, he sat beside her on the bed. "I don't know what to say, Ellie. Are you afraid to stay here?"

"No. I'm not afraid at all. If there is a ghost here, she's not the type who would hurt anyone."

His mouth quirked up at one edge, forming a playful smile as he held her gaze. "I was sort of hoping you'd say you're scared and you need me to spend the night with you again."

Ellie let out a sigh. Maybe he thought she'd lost her mind—and maybe she had—but she didn't want to argue about it.

"I do want you to stay tonight," she said. Winding her arms around his shoulders, she slid onto his lap. "But not because

I'm scared. I just want you here. As long as *you're* not afraid of ghosts."

"Are you kidding? Ghosts are a tradition on Christmas Eve." His hand slid between her thighs and traced the inseam of her jeans in a tantalizing motion. "But I don't need any spirit to show me my future. It's with you. That's all I need to know."

Ellie woke in the morning curled in Spencer's arms beneath a mound of bed covers. When she lifted her head to peer into his face, her movement roused him and his eyes cracked open.

"Merry Christmas," she said.

Spencer's eyes widened with a look of exaggerated surprise. "Wow, a genuine yuletide miracle."

"How could I not be happy today?" Her hand emerged from beneath the sheet to caress his cheek. "I think maybe my heart *has* grown three sizes after all. It feels like it might burst."

"I feel the same." Spencer's sea-blue eyes brimmed with joy that mirrored her own. "Any ghostly dreams or visitations last night?"

"None. I slept wonderfully."

"Me too." He shifted upright and the sheet fell away from his bare chest. "It just doesn't feel right waking up Christmas morning without a tree and presents. Oh, wait. I do have something for you." He climbed out of bed, shivering in the morning chill, and picked up the rumpled pullover he'd discarded on the floor last night.

Ellie sat up, hugging the sheet to her chest. "Spence, you didn't. I don't have anything for you."

"Doesn't matter." After pulling on his sweater, Spencer circled the bed to retrieve his coat from the hook on the back of the door. Fishing in a side pocket, he extracted a couple of small items and then, keeping them close to his chest so she wouldn't see them, he brought them back to the bed.

He smoothed out the covers next to Ellie's legs before showing her a miniature pine tree that looked like it was it was meant for a train set or a dollhouse. He balanced it on the bedspread and then placed beside it a small box wrapped in blue paper.

Ellie laughed in delight. "Cute. Now let me open it."

"Go ahead."

She picked up the box and tore the paper off, revealing a velvet box. "It isn't, is it?" She opened the box and gasped at the item sitting inside—the ring she'd chosen, a slender white gold band that had a twist of rose gold through the middle with three embedded diamonds.

"How did you get it sized so quickly?"

"I called the jeweller just after we left, and for a little extra they put a rush on it."

"You must have gone back to pick it up while I was in the gallery, and you told me you had to nip across the road to get a last-minute gift for Gino." Ellie leaned in for a quick kiss. "Thank you. I'm glad to have it today. Which finger does it go on?"

"I guess on your left hand. I haven't exactly read up on the protocol for commitment rings. Shall I?"

"All right." She handed him the ring and held out her left hand for him. A giddy thrill pulsed through her chest as Spencer slid the band onto her finger. "People might mistake us for married," she said, holding up her hand to admire the polished gold glinting in the light.

"I'm sure they will, just like the jeweler assumed we were looking for wedding bands when we came into the store. I don't mind at all if they do." Spencer kissed her shoulder. "It looks perfect on you."

"You can wear yours now." Ellie curled her hand against her chest, letting her skin warm the cool metal.

"Gladly. It's still in my coat." He stood from the bed and headed back to the coat rack, while Ellie reached for her nightgown, rumpled on the floor, and pulled it on over her head.

When she stood, her gaze fell on the portrait on the table beside her computer. She froze, pulling in a sharp breath.

"What's the matter?" Spencer asked.

She spun to stare at him. "Did you move the picture?"

"No. You must have left it there last night."

"I could swear I put it over there." She glanced at the dresser, picturing herself placing the portrait there when she came in. She was certain she hadn't moved it.

"I didn't touch it." Spencer gave her an uneasy look. "Ellie, forget the picture. Come over here. Your turn to do the honours."

He held out his ring, identical to hers but larger and broader, and Ellie took it from him. He proffered his hand and she slipped the band onto his finger, then slid her palm over his hand so their rings lined up side by side.

"Yours is perfect too," she said. "This is perfect." She wondered if they should say something more, exchange some sort of vows, but they hadn't prepared anything and she felt too overwhelmed to say much. Besides, they didn't need formalities to legitimize their promise to one another. They didn't need anything more than this—just the two of them with *forever* etched into their hearts.

Still she felt a funny that little pinch in her gut, a brief twisting sensation that made her smile slip. Somehow the exchange of rings she'd looked forward to felt anticlimactic. Over and done before she had a chance to absorb its significance. She breathed in deep and let the feeling fade. She had everything she wanted and nothing to regret.

Spencer gripped her waist and drew her close. "Ellie, you can't spend the evening alone at a Chinese restaurant. Come to Gino's with me for dinner."

"Okay. If they've got room for one more, I'll come."

A smile spread across his face. "They already asked me to bring you."

Fifteen

On his way to the kitchen, Spencer stepped carefully through mounds of Lego blocks, super-hero figures and stuffed unicorns spread around Gino's three nieces and two nephews who were playing on the carpet. With Gino's mother, his three sisters and their husbands crowded among the kids in the modest bungalow, there was barely a place left to stand in the living room.

Gino had the kitchen to himself, having banished his wife and their guests from his space while he prepared dinner. Spencer found him at the marble-topped isle, dumping herbs and garlic cloves into a food processor.

"Need any help?" Spencer asked, though he knew Gino would turn him down. In the last four days, Gino hadn't let him touch a thing in his pristine kitchen.

"Nope. Got it all under control. You know you'd only slow me down," Gino said, flashing the dimpled grin that had melted many a female heart in high school. "But you can hang out here if you need a break from my family."

"You know I love your family."

Gino added olive oil to his concoction, then reached for a bottle of red wine vinegar. "It's okay. I know they're a lot to take all together in one bunch."

Spencer eyed the glass bowl on the kitchen island, filled with chopped romaine lettuce, peppers, cucumbers and grape tomatoes. "Are you making salad dressing?"

"Yup."

"What's in the oven?" Spencer bent to peer through window on the oven door. "Smells amazing."

"*Cannelloni alla besciamella*," Gino said while he closed the lid on the food processor. "That's just the first course. Save room for the braised beef and porcini mushroom ragu. Sorry, no turkey and yams tonight."

"You won't hear any complaints from me. It all sounds incredible."

Gino pressed the pulse button on the food processor a few times. "Help yourself to a beer. And while you're in there, can you grab the ricotta salata for me?"

"Sure." Spencer opened the fridge door and selected a bottle of beer before hunting down the package of cheese. In the back of the fridge, he spotted a layered dessert topped with strawberries and dusted with cocoa. "Is that your nonna's famous tiramisu?"

"The one and only."

Closing the fridge door, Spencer handed the cheese to Gino. "After stuffing myself with your pasta and ragu and Sonia's appetizers, I might have to save dessert for breakfast."

"If you're here in the morning." Though Gino bent his head over the cutting board as he unwrapped the cheese and cut off a chunk, Spencer caught the suggestive tilt of his eyebrow.

Spencer grabbed a bottle opener from the counter to pop the cap off his beer. "Well, this place will be crowded enough tonight without me taking up a bed."

He would have preferred to asked Ellie to spend the night with him at Gino's, despite the sacrifice of privacy, rather than stay another night at The Roses. Not that he believed anything supernatural was going on, but Ellie seemed to be getting caught up in the ghost legends, letting her imagination trample over her good sense. Her memory must be playing tricks to convince her they'd both had the identical dream in the same night. But she had only one more night at the inn before they'd both be back home, and she could forget her odd fixation on Rebecca Norris.

"I'm happy for you, man, "Gino said. "Ellie's great. I guess playing Santa worked out for you." He nodded toward Spencer's left hand holding his beer bottle. "I noticed the matching rings. Does it mean—?"

"We're not engaged. They're commitment rings." Spencer glanced through the kitchen pass-through to the living room, where Ellie stood chatting with Sonia, a glass of red wine in one hand and a small plate in the other, beside a table laid out with an array of appetizers. "We're going to live together."

"Seriously?" Gino glanced over in surprise while dumping

the cheese onto the salad. "You swore you'd never do that."

"I know." A bitter feeling rolled through Spencer's gut at the reminder that his plan to win Ellie over to marriage had failed. "I guess I'd rather do it her way than not have her at all."

"Maybe in time she'll consider marriage," Gino said with a shrug.

"I hope so. But it'll have to be her idea. I won't push her."

"Suppose you decide to have kids?"

"I want kids. I think she does, too." The idea of starting a family excited him, but he wasn't sure when or how to broach the subject with Ellie. Things had been progressing so nicely, he was afraid to push his luck.

Gino turned to the sink and ran his hands under the faucet. "You're both over thirty. Something to start thinking about."

"Are you and Sonia thinking about it?"

"Yeah. We're trying." A wide grin dimpled his cheeks again. "Can't wait for it to happen. Of course, for next year's Christmas we might have to rent a hall to squeeze everyone in."

Sonia picked up a pair of tongs from the table and snagged what looked like a boiled dumpling from one of the serving plates. "You want to try the *pelmeni*? It's my mother's recipe, stuffed with ground beef and pork," she said, depositing the morsel onto Ellie's plate without waiting for a reply.

"I had so many of those potato *pampushki* already," Ellie said. "I'll try just one. I'm afraid I'll spoil my appetite for dinner."

Sonia placed several of the dumplings on her own plate. "Don't worry. We take hours to eat. You will have time to try everything." Lifting her hand close to her face, she frowned at a bandage wrapped around one of her perfectly manicured nails. "*Chyort.* This looks terrible. I cut my finger chopping onions."

"I didn't notice," Ellie assured her. Sonia's nails weren't the first thing one would observe about the statuesque green-eyed blonde whose striking looks complemented her Mediterranean hunk of a husband. Ellie nibbled the savoury dumpling and nodded her approval. "It's good. I don't think I've ever tried traditional Russian food before."

"I make it sometimes," Sonia said, retrieving her wine glass from the table for a sip, "but Gino does most of the cooking. He agreed to let me do the appetizers tonight. Maybe someday he'll let me make the goose with apples and aspic my mother used to make for Christmas dinner."

"Did you celebrate Christmas much differently in Russia?" Ellie wondered.

"Different day. For us, Christmas was January seventh. Of course, when I was a young girl, church holidays were banned under the Soviet Union, but my family still kept the traditions quietly. After the Soviet Union fell, all the old public celebrations returned." A wistful smile curved Sonia's glossy lips. "On Christmas Eve we ate only after the first star appeared in the sky, then we would go to church. Grandfather Frost brought the presents for under the tree. And on Christmas Day, with seven kids in my family, it was very noisy in my house." She nodded toward the children, two of whom were wrestling by the Christmas tree, making the Scotch pine sway and its decorations quiver. "A lot like this."

"You must miss your family during the holidays," Ellie said.

"Very much. But Gino's family makes me feel at home here." She eyed Ellie with sympathy. "I'm sorry you can't be with your family today."

Ellie lifted her shoulders, too embarrassed to admit she could have spent the holidays with her family but had chosen not to. "It wasn't so bad spending a quiet morning at the inn."

Sonia's lips pinched into a frown. "I would not go near that place at night," she said, then set down her wine glass, freeing her right hand to make the sign of the cross on herself. "Ellie, try the *shuba* salad next. It's made with herring and beets." She motioned toward a layered salad with a bright pink glaze.

"I'll have a small taste," Ellie said, though she wasn't a fan of either herring or beets. She reached for the spoon to prevent Sonia from serving her too large a helping.

"Such a beautiful ring," Sonia gasped. "Is it new?"

"Yes. Spencer gave it to me this morning." Ellie felt a rush of pleasure as the light gleamed off the diamonds while she spooned a small portion of the salad onto her plate.

Sonia's eyes rounded and she pressed her palm to her chest. "You're engaged?"

"No, we're not engaged. It's a commitment ring." Ellie tried to inject enthusiasm into her voice, but her amendment just sounded weak.

Sonia eyed her with a puzzled look, before a compassionate smile flitted over her mouth. "Maybe he will propose later. When it comes to marriage, men sometimes have—what is the expression? Cold toes?"

"Cold feet. But it's not that. He wants to get married. It's me that's hesitating."

One of Sonia's elegantly shaped eyebrows lifted. "But why? I can see how much you are both in love. You were meant to be married."

"It's not as simple as that."

"Who says it is simple? It's never simple. Complications, always. I married an Italian man. Romantic and passionate, yes, but stubborn like a mule." Sonia laughed and rolled her eyes. "But when you love the mule, you have patience. Until you understand his view, you will never get him to budge. Eventually you both get where you need to go. Now taste the *zimne nogi*. No one has tried it yet." She sank a serving spoon into a murky grayish jellied salad shaped into a dome. "It's very traditional," she added with a broad grin, "made with jellied pigs' feet."

SIXTEEN

Hours later, Ellie dropped onto the bed in her room and sprawled on her back across the bedspread. "Spencer, I've never eaten so much in my life," she groaned. "Why did I even attempt to stuff in that tiramisu? It just looked so delicious. And it *was*."

"I feel the same." With a grunt, he landed beside her and stretched out his limbs.

Ellie turned her head to look at him. "You can stay again tonight, but just for sleeping. I'm too tired to move."

"Fine by me. I'm not planning on budging an inch until morning."

They lay side by side in silence for a minute, absorbing the quiet stillness after an evening filled with noise and commotion. When she glanced over at Spencer, his eyes were closed.

"Do you think I'm impossibly stubborn?" she asked quietly.

He let out a sharp laugh, then groaned and clutched his stomach. "Stubborn, yes. Exasperatingly so, sometimes. But impossible? Never." Shifting his body slightly, he slid his arm around her shoulder.

Ellie cuddled against him. She let her heavy eyelids fall closed and listened to the steady drumming of his heart against her ear. "I guess not. Somehow you managed to scuttle my plans to spend the holidays sulking all by myself. You actually made me like Christmas again. And here we are making plans for a life together."

"I didn't get quite everything I wanted," Spencer said, his voice low and sluggish. "But what I have, I intend to hold onto. You're worth it, Ellie."

She smiled, feeling warm and secure in his arms. "Merry Christmas," she mumbled, fighting now to push back the drowsiness clouding her brain. "Sorry it was so unconventional."

"Are you serious?" He placed a sleepy kiss on the top of her head. "Best Christmas of my life. Big, loud and chaotic, yes, but it's just what Christmas is supposed to be. I want that for us someday."

"Me too."

Downy snowflakes swirled in a thick curtain through the morning light and clung to the windowpane, as Ellie folded the rest of her clothes and fit each item neatly into her suitcase. Next she slid her laptop into its case and zipped it closed. With Spencer gone, retrieving his things from Gino's place, an eerie quiet had settled over the room. She felt ready to leave, eager to start the next phase of her life with Spencer.

When her phone chimed, she turned and retrieved it from the dresser, finding an incoming text message from Spencer.

I'm downstairs in the pub. Ready for lunch?

She typed a quick answer: *Be there soon. Order me a chicken sandwich and a beer, please.*

Ellie slid her phone into her purse on the bed. She had her hand on the suitcase lid, about to close it, when she spotted the edge of a white card protruding from one of the elasticised pockets.

She pulled out the card and stared in disbelief at the smooth white paper with red lettering and a holly-and-bells motif.

Ellie darted her gaze to the empty trashcan beside the dresser. She was sure she'd tossed the wedding invitation in there. Not just once, but twice. And hadn't she crumpled it into a ball? Had she dreamed or imagined doing it?

But the surprise of finding it back in her suitcase, restored to its original condition, took second place to her amazement at how little emotion the slip of paper aroused in her. Reading the text over silently, she felt absolutely nothing. No anger. No regret or sadness. Only numbness remained.

Gripping the invitation in both hands, she tore it into four pieces and tossed the scraps back into the trashcan with a flourish. *Let's see it reappear now. No way is it going to mend itself now.*

The same couldn't be said of her heart. Once in tatters, with a little stitch here and there, it had slowly knit itself back together. She'd been too busy protecting her heart under lock and key to recognize how resilient she truly was. Spencer could have given up on her, and maybe he should have, but she knew in her soul that he never would.

While shutting the suitcase, she noticed the framed photograph of Emma Norris Wood still lying on the dresser. She'd nearly forgotten she was supposed to return it to Abby. Ellie wasn't entirely sure why she'd asked to see it in the first place. She remembered becoming intensely interested in the inn's history, but why? Maybe as a distraction from the problems she'd been having with her novel. Her reasons, whatever they were, seemed lost in a murky part of her memory.

Looping her laptop case over her shoulder, Ellie picked up her suitcase, slung her coat over her arm and then grabbed the photo with her free hand before leaving the room.

As she closed the door, she glanced to her right and spotted the rocking chair sitting serenely in a pool of soft light from the hallway window. Setting down her suitcase and coat, she approached the chair, urged forward by a sudden compulsion. The antique had stood empty during most of her stay, but hadn't she seen someone sitting in it at some point? She wasn't sure.

A second impulse compelled her to set the framed photo on the chair, leaning it against the cushion. She only briefly questioned the act, deciding it made perfect sense. Abby would find the picture there the next time she came upstairs, and meanwhile, the old chair seemed like just the right place for it. She smiled, a satisfied feeling moving through her, and picked up her cases to head downstairs.

She and Spencer sat by the window in the nearly deserted pub, with just one other couple at a nearby table.

After swallowing the last bite of crust from his slice of apple pie, Spencer tossed his napkin onto his plate. "Better be on my way," he said, pulling his wallet out of his back pocket.

"I wish you could stay and come with me to Abby's for dinner." Ellie set down her fork next to her half-eaten wedge of cheesecake.

"Me too, but my mother sounded really upset when she called. The least I can do is pick her up at the airport. I'll give her a shoulder to cry on and try to restrain myself from saying 'I told you so.' Although I did warn her that online dating has its pitfalls."

"I can imagine she was distraught, finding out the guy spent time in prison for fraud."

"Would've been handy if she'd checked into that *before* flying off to spend Christmas with him," Spencer said dryly, "but at least she didn't go ahead and give him the money when he asked. I hope to God I never get that desperate for companionship."

Ellie reached across the table and gripped his hand. "Of course you won't. You'll just have me asking you for money," she teased.

Spencer laughed. "You'll be the main breadwinner before long when your book takes off. But today, lunch is on me." He opened his wallet and stared at it, his smile fading as he spread one of the pockets wide. "My ticket stub from the play is gone."

"You lost it?"

"Must have fallen out."

"Oh no," Ellie said with genuine dismay. "Maybe you'll need to put a picture of me in there after all."

"It's fine. I'll always have your beautiful eyes and your smile with me in here"—Spencer tapped the side of his head—"and in here"—then spread his hand on his chest.

A funny little quiver zipped down Ellie's spine. His words and gestures echoed in her mind like déjà vu—as though somehow she'd known just what was he was about to say.

She locked her gaze with his, losing herself for a moment in his sea-blue eyes that held an ocean's depth of tenderness and devotion. The tremor in her spine curled lower into her belly.

Spencer dropped some cash onto the table and got to his feet, before snagging his coat from the back of his chair. "Stay and finish your dessert. I'll see you tomorrow." Once he had his coat on, he bent to kiss her mouth lightly before heading to the door.

"Bye." Ellie watched him push the door open. The gust of cold air that swirled in around him made her shudder.

His foot on the threshold, Spencer threw her a parting smile. Love for him swelled through her in such an overwhelming rush that her breath caught.

Then a sudden flutter of panic invaded her chest and she leapt to her feet. "Spence! Don't go yet."

The couple at the next table stopped talking and glanced over. Spencer froze in the doorway, his smile faltering. "What's wrong, Ellie?"

Circling the table, she was slowed for just a moment when her thigh glanced off a chair, sending it banging against the wall. She sprinted to him, her pulse pounding a frenzied rhythm in her ears. He let the door fall closed and caught her as she threw her arms around him.

In his arms, everything she wanted crystalized in her mind. She knew it in her bones, and felt it in her chest like the beat of tiny wings against her heart.

"Marry me!" she said, her voice giddy and breathless.

Spencer's puzzled expression changed, melding surprise with confusion. "What?"

Clinging tight to him, Ellie drew a few deep breaths to calm the frenzied thrumming of her nerves. "I love you, Spence. You're the one I want. But not as some kind of forever boyfriend. As my husband."

Brimming with emotion, his gaze raked over her face. "You said the piece of paper didn't matter."

"I know. But I *do* want the paper, Spence. And the ceremony and the reception and the honeymoon. The whole shebang. I always have wanted it. To think I was willing to share that with Joel and not you—I've been hedging my bets like a coward. I've been so afraid to lose you that I held back from giving all of myself to you. I don't want to do that anymore. So what do you say? Spencer Brooks, will you marry me?"

EPILOGUE

Next December

Spencer climbed the basement stairs, carrying a cardboard box under one arm. Glass balls and brass bells shifted and rattled, cushioned by the glittery garlands, velvet bows and artificial holly boughs jumbled in with them. Two years ago, he'd tossed all his decorations into storage without much care. Now he and Ellie had a job ahead of them untangling everything.

Reaching the top of the stairs, he switched off the basement light and closed the door. When he turned to face the front door, through the sidelight pane he noticed a shape moving outside on the front step.

He set the box on the carpet and went to the door to open it, finding a postman holding a package and a portable scanning device. The postman looked up in surprise, before a smile pulled at his rosy cheeks. "Hey, there. I was just about to ring the bell." He glanced down at the device, shifting from one foot to the other on the doormat, his shoulders hunched against the cold. "I've got a package here for Ellie Lynd."

"I'm her husband. I'll sign for it."

"Sure thing." The postman handed over the device and a stylus.

Spencer scrawled his signature on the screen and took the package. A sticker on the box showed the address of Ellie's publisher. "Thanks. Merry Christmas."

"Have a good one," the postman said as he turned to leave.

Spencer shut the door and carried the package to the living room, pausing in the doorway. In front of the fireplace, Ellie stood with her hands on her hips, frowning at the balsam fir in the corner that was strung with tiny white lights and other decorations. Throwing a quick glance at Spencer, she gestured at the right side of the tree. "I think I put too much tinsel on this side. What do you think? Does it look all right?"

"Looks more than all right from here." He trailed an appreciative gaze over the fitted turtleneck sweater and black leggings snugged to his wife's feminine curves. With her hair plaited into a loose braid and her cheeks flushed from the effort of decorating, she'd never looked more beautiful—except, perhaps, on one particular spring day when she'd worn a white lace wedding gown with tiny white flowers woven into her hair, captured in a photo displayed behind her on the mantel.

"You found the rest of the ornaments?" Ellie asked, observing the box under his arm. "Let's see."

"I did, but this is something that just arrived at the door. Something you've been anxiously waiting for."

An ecstatic grin spread across her face. "My book?"

Spencer nodded. "Want to open it now?"

"Of course!" She squealed and clapped her hands. "I'm so nervous! But so excited, I might just burst."

"Have at it, then."

He placed the box on the coffee table, and she sank onto the couch and set about tearing off the packing tape. In seconds she pulled open the flaps and pushed aside a layer of bubble wrap to reveal a stack of pristine paperbacks.

Gingerly, she lifted out one copy to show Spencer the front cover, where a young woman dressed in a Tudor-style scarlet gown and hood gazed with longing at an open window above her head. *The Lady Tower* in gold script spanned the top of the cover, with Ellie's name below.

Her face glowed with elation as she ran her hand over the smooth image. "It looks wonderful, doesn't it?"

"It does."

"I'm so glad they got here before Christmas. It's the best present I could've wished for."

Spencer sat beside her. He couldn't tear his gaze from her face, and didn't want to. Seeing her so happy brought a warm glow to his chest. "I'm proud of you, Ellie. You've got another bestseller in your hands."

"You think so?"

"I know it."

Ellie blinked a few times as a sheen of moisture gathered in her eyes. Setting the book down on the coffee table, she gripped both his hands and leaned in to kiss his mouth. "I couldn't have done it without you. And it wouldn't mean half as much if I didn't have you here to share it with me. I love you."

"I love you too, Ellie." Spencer didn't think he'd ever grow tired of saying it. He leaned in for another soft kiss. "So how about we finish decorating the tree?"

After Spencer jogged to the hallway and returned carrying a large cardboard box, he placed it on the carpet and Ellie joined him while he opened it.

Kneeling, she dragged out a bedraggled glittery red garland and a few boughs of plastic holly. Underneath, she found mismatched glass balls and crumpled velvet bows, jumbled among an eclectic collection of ornaments. She lifted out a snowman made from foam balls and a reindeer crafted from walnut shells.

"My stuff isn't as nice as yours," Spencer said, with a nod toward the delicate glass angels and snowflakes already adorning the tree. "Some of these I've had since I was a kid."

"Everything's perfect. You should put all of it on the tree." She picked up a small bow and smoothed it between her fingers. Every piece gave her a peek into Spencer's past, and it felt right to see them mingled with her ornaments on the first tree they would share as husband and wife.

While he decorated the tree, Ellie placed the holly on the mantel, on either side of the gingerbread clock she'd bought at an antique shop in Stratford. She added brass bells and candy canes to the plain pine wreath above the fireplace.

"I think that's about it," Spencer said, standing back to admire the tree.

"There are a few more things in here." Ellie bent and sifted through the remaining ornaments in the bottom of the box. She found a few broken candy canes and some glass balls missing their hooks. In the corner, she spotted an object that didn't seem to belong among the others.

She lifted out the item and inspected it, turning it in her hands. The small soldier carved from wood looked like an antique toy that had been well played with. The red and black paint on the coat and cap was faded and scuffed, and the tip of the musket at his side had been broken off. She ran her fingers over the features, so worn that the face was almost smooth. A strange sensation of recognition prickled the back of her brain.

"Is this a family heirloom?" she asked, holding out the figure to show Spencer.

As he glanced it, a puzzled look creased his brow. "You found it in the box? That's strange." He took the little soldier from her and studied it. "I've never seen it before."

"I feel like I've seen it," Ellie said, "but I can't remember where. Looks like something you might've picked up in Niagara-on-the-Lake."

"But I haven't opened this box in nearly two years. Maybe I did buy it years ago and I've forgotten." He handed the soldier back to Ellie. "But it's sort of crudely made. The arms are too long. And he doesn't seem to have feet."

"I think it's sweet. It's been well loved." She placed the little figure on the mantel next to the clock, where it looked right at home. "It's a piece of the past, but obviously someone made this for a child, maybe to pass down through the generations. A symbol of optimism for the future."

Spencer stepped next to her and gathered her in his arms. "Something *we* can pass down to future generations?"

"Plan on it." Ellie linked her hands at his nape and smiled up at him. "What I said before was wrong, Spence. As much as I adore my new book, *you're* the best present I could have wished for."

A grin spread across his face. "Is it spooky that I was thinking the exact same thing?"

"Spooky?" She glanced at the little wooden solider on the mantel, and another familiar twinge in the back of her mind made her flinch.

"What's wrong?"

"What you just said reminded me of something, but the

memory just flitted away." She smiled again, relaxing against him. "Doesn't matter. Maybe it's just a sign that we're meant to be together, and things have turned out exactly as they were supposed to."

WELCOME TO MISTLETOE, TEXAS

Candi Cain
Kisses

Nan O'Berry

CANDI CAIN KISSES
BY NAN O'BERRY

Jonathan Barlow needs a change of pace. When his beloved wife passes away, Jonathan finds himself wallowing in grief and determined to find a new start. Accepting a job with a law firm just a few weeks before the holidays, Jonathan and his young daughter make the move to Mistletoe, Texas. A rented room at an old Victorian Inn is just the place to begin again.

Candi Cain inherited the old Victorian from family. It's a place she can call home, a place where all the worries in the world can be forgotten over a cup of hot chocolate and a homemade pastry. When Felicia Barlow and her father come for a stay, she feels drawn the child—a sense of déjà view, for just like Jonathan's daughter, she experienced the loss of a loved one as a child.

Can the wonders of the season and a little girl's wish to Santa awaken two lonely hearts? Things look promising this holiday season at the Candy Cane Inn.

ONE

Candi Cain stepped from the driver's side of her Chevy S10 and felt the full brunt of the cold air that swirled down Main Street. Tossing her dark hair from her face, she smiled and breathed deeply, relishing in the smell of fresh coffee wafting from the diner down the street. She'd missed her Caramel Latté this morning, and the scent of fresh brewed java made her want it all the more.

"I'll send out for some later," she promised herself as she reached inside and grabbed her larger than life purse. Adjusting it on her shoulder, she tossed the end of her scarf over her shoulder and hurried toward the double red front door of the last grand Victorian situated on Main Street. She paused and looked at the antique, hand blown glass panels and the arch formed by two candy canes intertwined on the etched glass with the words Candy Cane Inn painted in red beneath. The sign always managed to lift her spirits. Yeah, it was a cheesy play on words, but deep down she enjoyed the twist. Her lips curved upwards in a smile. Her grandmother, the last owner of the old home, would have as well. Hand on the doorknob, she gave it a quick twist and entered. "Morning, Liz. How are things?" she called to her assistant.

From behind the counter, a blonde head emerged. "Things are just fine," Liz smiled back, her hands patting the rounding belly beneath her apron. "Elijah Steven Hanson is still hanging in there."

"Marvelous," Candi brightened. Unbuttoning her jacket, she hung it on the hook by the doorway and bent down to be eye level with Liz's tummy. She patted the unborn child. "You just stay in there until it's time. I don't want to lose my best employee before Christmas."

"Best employee?" Liz gave her a skeptical look by raising an eyebrow. "Don't you mean your only employee?"

"Just a minor blip," Candi laughed. "I can't imagine

working with anyone else."

"Thanks," Liz sighed, then placed her hands on the small of her back. "But you're going to have to get someone soon. Doctor Abernathy wants to limit my hours."

Candi grew somber. "Sorry to hear that. But I understand. It's much more important that you have a happy baby. I don't want you working too long, causing any health problems. I'll pull some of the applications and we can review them over lunch. I don't think we have too many customers booked for the tearoom this afternoon."

"That will be great, Candi, thank you for understanding."

"Sure thing," she replied. Before another word could be spoken, the shrill ring of a telephone disrupted the conversation. "I'll get it." Candi made her way toward the antique telephone that hung on the wall near the small cubical she called her office. "Good morning, Candy Cane Inn.

"Candi? Mayor Jones here."

"Morning, Mayor. I trust things are going well at city hall."

She heard Liz try to cover her giggle. Candi turned around and stuck her tongue out at her coworker.

"Lover boy Jones," Liz replied in a hushed whisper.

Candi rolled her eyes and twisted the cord around her index finger. "How can I help you?"

"I was wondering if you have time to cater a party for the staff. I know you're busy with the holidays just around the corner."

Candi glanced down at the December calendar at the kiosk and noted the abundance of red in each box. "We're always busy, Mayor, but for you we'll make an exception."

Liz walked by and whispered yet again. "You're in deep, kiddo."

Candi sighed and turned around looking for a pencil or pen. "So, what's this special assignment?" She drew a red pencil from the cup.

"I want to do something a bit different for our Christmas party. It's going to take a bit of planning."

"Planning ahead is a good idea," Candi murmured. "So what day in December?"

"Put a circle on the twenty-third," he continued.

"Got it," Candi murmured, drawing a circle around the

date and then adding the word 'mayor' below.

"I need a cake, some hot chocolate, and of course we want to book the tearoom."

She heard his chair creak and imagined him leaning back to place his wingtips on the desk. "Do you want a sheet cake or tier cake?"

"I'm thinking tier cake. I'd like to have it reflect the theme."

"Theme?" Candi repeated as a small knot formed in the pit of her tummy.

"I'll ask my secretary to send an email with the memo if you don't have it. My father's tradition was to read *A Visit by Saint Nicholas on Christmas Eve*. I want to continue this tradition. So I thought we could piggyback on the story. You do know the story?"

"Yes, of course I do, Mayor." Looking at the mountain of mail tucked in one of the cubbies, Candi spied a white envelope with the address of city hall. "Yes, we've been so busy, we haven't gotten to the mail today. But I believe we have your letter." She drew it out from the stack and ran her fingers beneath the flap, loosening the glue.

"Oh, good, we are planning on turning the reception area in City Hall into Santa's workshop for the collection of toys for the underprivileged children's party. I'm hoping you'll let Mr. Claus set up his chair in the tearoom and let the kids come in and sit on his knee starting at 3 p.m. on the twenty-third."

"Sounds charming," Candi agreed. She closed her eyes and immediately the poem sprang to mind.

"I'm sure you can come up with some wonderful ideas. Maybe we can talk you into participating as an elf?

"Elf?" Candi echoed.

"Yeah, perhaps we can meet for dinner on Friday night and discuss them?"

"Friday?" Candi shook off the reverie. "This Friday?"

"Yes, say about seven p.m? I'll pick you up."

Candi glanced around, wishing she could think of something that needed to be done. However, nothing came to mind. Because of the upcoming holiday, their bookings at the Inn were slow. Only one person was due to check in later this afternoon. She raked her hand through her hair and sighed. "Sure. But let me meet you. I've got to be home early, Saturday is our busy day."

"Sure, sure, I understand. Meet me at the Brazos Steakhouse."

"Right, Brazos." Candi scribbled down the name and time even though she doubted she'd ever forget. "I'll bring along some ideas."

"Great! I'm looking forward to this already." Mayor Jones paused. "Thanks, Candi, and I mean that."

"Have a good day, Mayor." Hanging up the phone, Candi let out a long groan.

"You walked right into that one," Liz snickered.

"I did, didn't I?" Candi sighed. She reached over and picked the letter off the desk. "The mayor is doing a theme for the holidays."

"Theme?" Liz replied and stepped up to take the letter from Candi's hand. Pulling out the official correspondence, she glanced at the contents. "Oh my, our esteemed Mayor thinks big."

Candi moved away, snatching the letter from her coworker's hands. "Our Mayor must be kin to P. T. Barnum."

"P.T. Barnum?"

"Yeah." Candi paused and turned. Then, shaking the letter at Liz, replied. "There's a sucker born every minute."

Laughing, Liz hurried toward the back of the Inn to begin work on the day's menu.

Jonathan Barlow wiggled his fingers to loosen the vice like grip his five-year-old daughter had on his right hand. She shifted her stance closer and clutched the fullness of his dress trousers. He gave a whimsical smile and extended his hand to his new employer. "Thanks again, Mr. Griffin."

"You're more than welcome" Thomas Griffin replied, returning the warm handshake. "I know this is a big change from Fort Worth, but I think you'll fall in love with Mistletoe.

It has that certain small town warmth."

"I know we will." Jonathan looked down to the upturned face of his adorable daughter. Thankfully, today there was no fear, only a look of contentment. He'd spent the last two weeks with her, as they prepared for their big move south. He smoothed the soft dark curls that covered her head. "A change and a chance to start anew is just what we're looking for, isn't it, Felicia?"

His daughter smiled and bobbed her head.

Mr. Griffin chuckled. "Well, I'm going to let you two get started on your new adventure. My secretary tells me you're planning on buying a home on the Southside."

"Yes, we're off to meet with Karen Darden at Mistletoe Reality. Our furniture is in storage, I don't want to keep it there long."

"I understand. Ms. Darden can find the perfect home. I'm sure it won't take too long. So where are you staying until you find a place?"

"We've booked a room at Candy Cane Inn, on Main."

Mr. Griffin nodded. "Lovely place. A few years ago it was scheduled to be torn down, but the owner's granddaughter returned to Mistletoe and remodeled it into an Inn and tearoom." He focused on Jonathan's young daughter. "Miss Candi makes the greatest cupcakes. You like cupcakes?"

Felicia nodded again.

"Then you'll have a good old time."

"It seems everyone is very helpful." Jonathan agreed. "I've been well pleased with their attention to detail. She asked us what we wanted most," he glanced at his daughter. "And it came down to a swing in the backyard."

"Well," Mr. Griffin chuckled. "You go get settled in your room and we'll look forward to seeing you on Monday."

"Monday it is. Thank you again, Mr. Griffin."

"You're quite welcome. Good luck and welcome aboard at Griffin and Price."

Grasping Felicia's hand, Jonathan walked out of the law office and paused at the corner. While they waited for the light to change, allowing them to cross the street, he took time to examine the town. Quaint came to mind. Main Street sported graceful cast iron streetlights in a shepherd hook design. Dotting the skyline were brick and wood structures built in the nineteen hundred's, their façades lined with plate glass windows which allowed shoppers to view their wares as they traversed the broad sidewalks.

"Not a mall in sight," he sighed with guilty pleasure.

Despite the cool wind, the abundant sunshine lured the townsfolk out and about to do a little holiday shopping. He could hear calls of 'Happy Holidays' and 'Season's Greetings' being bounced up and down the sidewalk as those passing by called out to their friends and neighbors. To his surprise, Jonathan received a few calls and nods of "How do you do?" He had a loose hold of his daughter's hand, swinging it back and forth as she skipped beside him. "Definitely wouldn't hear that in the city."

"I like it here, Daddy."

He gave her hand a squeeze. "So do I."

Felicia tugged her hand free and skipped a few steps ahead of him. "Come on, hurry."

"Don't go too far," he called after her.

Dark curls bouncing, she glanced back over her left shoulder. "I won't."

Jonathan noted her smiled reached all the way up to the twinkle in her eyes.

"I'm going to beat you." Her steps quickened again, she turned to the right and stopped. He watched as she stepped up to the old Victorian and placed her hands on the plate glass window to gaze inside.

Jonathan hurried over to join her. His hand on her shoulder, together they peered into the building. A large entryway greeted them. Behind the desk he could see someone milling about.

"Oh, Daddy, can we go in?"

Then, Jonathan caught a movement at the back of the room. He watched as a woman with dark hair brought out a tray of cupcakes and placed them underneath a glass dome on the counter. The noise around them faded until all he could hear was the sound of his heart beating in his ears.

She was a pixie. No, taller than a pixie, but cute. Her dark hair swirled around her head, the ends curling in an attractive fashion. His gaze focused on her lips, and he was reminded how they resembled the color of a rose. As he watched, she brushed her hands down the red and white striped apron, completely unaware she was being observed.

She straightened. Her glance moved over the top of the counter and widened when she saw them. A soft smile pulled her lips across her face. Jonathan could have sworn a heavy weight boxer had sent a fist spiraling into his solar plexus, and he found himself struggling to breathe.

TWO

Candi didn't have to see anyone. Her sixth sense raised the hairs on the back of her neck and sent shivers down her spine. Refusing to give into the urge to look up, she concentrated on her task and placed the delicate cupcakes with marzipan green holly into the tall cake stand at the edge of the counter. Once done, she let out the breath she held and slowly stood upright. Wiping the dampness from her hands onto the apron, she gazed down at her creations, satisfied their whimsical look would bring customers in to pad the lining of her cash register. She reached up and brushed her bangs from her forehead. Knowing she needed to get on with decorating the tearoom, she gave a sigh and backed away.

Still, the feeling hadn't faded. She'd have to look sooner or later. "Might as well get it over with," she murmured and brought her gaze across the room to the windows along the front of the building. A child stood, her face pressed against the glass, her cheeks tinged pink from the sun while a riot of dark curls framed the angelic pale face. If she'd been asked to describe a cherub, this little girl would have fit the bill.

The face turned. Candi followed her line of sight to the tall man standing next to her. A slight gasp followed as she locked gazes with the most perfect man she'd ever laid eyes upon. His thick brown hair parted on the side and swept over his brow, reminiscent of the fifties. Below his elegant brow, a pair of warm brown eyes held a twinkle of mischief. He lifted the left side of his lips in a captivating smile that revealed a dimple.

Gawd, I'm a sucker for male dimples. Candi swallowed the urge to pull out a business card and tell him to call her anytime. She brushed her hands across her apron in hopes of quelling the riot of butterflies that suddenly took flight. Somehow, she managed to smile back and move her feet toward the door of the Candy Cane Inn. "You can do this," she whispered.

Then grasping the handle, she pushed the door swinging it open and put on the brightest face ever. "Why, hello, won't you come in?"

"Can we, Daddy?"

Daddy. Candi's heart gave a twist as the fluttering romantic thoughts took the flight of a Phoenix. *Of course, anyone that perfect had to be taken.*

"Sure." His voice rolled across her skin like a piece of velvet.

Oh, man, the little voice inside her head sighed. Ignoring it, she fixed a cheerful smile on her face and stepped back so the little girl and her father could enter.

"Thank you," he murmured as he moved past. The scent of cologne lingered in the air, a mix of spice and evergreen. She waited for a moment and inhaled deeply, hoping to create a lasting memory. Turning, she watched as they crossed the floor to stand at the front desk.

Every man should wear a suit, she mused studying him from behind. The dark cut looked expensive from his cuff all the way to the wool camel-colored scarf lazily draped around his neck. She found herself so transfixed, she forgot about the door closing behind her until it gave her backsides a playful slap. Eyes widening, Candi took a quick step forward before turning her head to cast an evil glance at the offending structure.

"These all look good," he remarked. "Do you make them every day for your guests?"

Candi hurried around the corner. "I've been known to, but we are getting ready for afternoon tea. Would you like to join us?"

"Tea?" His brow drew artfully together.

Candi grinned. "Holiday shopping is going on, so The Candi Cane Inn's tearoom opens during the afternoons to treat shoppers to some hot chocolate, tea, coffee, and today, cupcakes."

"I see." He mused.

Candi watched as the little girl's hand moved to her father's sleeve. "Can we have tea?"

"Well, I suppose we had best confirm our reservations."

Candi blinked. "Reservations? Are you staying at the Inn?"

"Yes, I called last week about having a room while we look

for a home in the area."

She blinked, running the list of names across her mind. "Yes of course I do remember, Mr. Barlow. I believe I talked to you on Tuesday?"

He smiled and her toes curled against the soles of her shoes. "Yes."

"Let me get the register." She bent down and pulled a large, green cloth notebook from below the counter. "Here we go." Opening to the correct page, she turned it to face him. "If you will just sign in?" She watched as he reached out and grasped the pen, then wrote his name with elegant penmanship.

"Welcome, Mr. Barlow and Felicia," Candi replied. "If you'll follow me, I'll take you to a table in the tearoom."

Moving through the arched opening, Candi led them into what was once the front parlor of the old Victorian. Instead of a sofa and sitting chairs, there were two-dozen small round tables, each with a pair of bentwood chairs to provide seating. Beside the three long windows along the front of the house stood large flowerpots hosting holly plants and in the center of each were dowel rods painted white with red ribbons twisted around them to resemble candy sticks. "Here we go." She stopped before one small table near a window and held out the chair for Felicia. "May I help you with your jacket?"

"I can get it." Felicia assured her and only fumbled with one button at the top.

Candi waited patiently as Felicia pulled her arms from the sleeves. Then Candi took the coat and hung it across the back of her chair. Candi looked over to Mr. Barlow. "Would you prefer a cup of coffee?"

"Please."

"And Felicia? We also have hot chocolate, or do you prefer tea?"

Felicia looked at her father. "I think some hot chocolate would be just the ticket."

"I won't be but a minute." Leaving them to get settled, Candi hurried toward the back of the tearoom. Rounding the corner, she caught Liz moving toward her.

"Did I hear the doorbell ring?"

"Our new guests, the Barlow's," Candi replied.

"Oh geez, I almost forgot." Liz slapped her forehead. "What room?"

"Put them in the Sugar Plum suite. I think Felicia will like the turret view."

"Felicia?"

"His daughter."

Liz nodded. "Ok, I'll slip up the elevator and make sure the rooms are ready."

"Don't rush. I persuaded them to have tea."

"Good, I have the cart ready." Liz pointed over her shoulder.

"Here we go," Candi murmured as she pushed the rolling cart toward the table where her two guests were seated. Jonathan pressed his napkin into his lap and turned to face her.

"So, what have we here?" he asked.

"Cupcakes, pie, a few cinnamon rolls I baked this morning, or a slice of sheet cake?"

He glanced over to his daughter, who shrugged her shoulders in response.

"Oh, undecided are we?" Candi pursed her lips. "Well, perhaps you'd like to try one of the cupcakes?"

The little cherub glanced at her father and then gave a nod of excitement.

Jonathan caught Candi's grin as he spoke. "A cinnamon roll sounds very enticing. I think Felicia would like to try one of those cupcakes."

As Candi stepped over to the side of the cart and lifted the glass dome from the plate of rolls, the aroma of warm yeast, vanilla, cinnamon, and pecans filled the air."

"Do they taste as good as they smell?" He inquired.

Candi winked. "I think so."

Jonathan and his daughter watched as she slipped on a

pair of plastic gloves and pulled one roll from the display. Placing it on a red and white striped plate, she sliced the treat with a knife. "Here."

Setting the roll on the plate, she went to hand it to him as he reached for it. Their fingers brushed as he took the plate, and a shock of electricity rushed up her arm. Candi's cheeks grew warm. She stared at him and for a moment, and the room seemed like it was filled with only the two of them.

"Daddy?"

Candi blinked. Jonathan pulled his hand back, then gave a short nervous laugh.

"Yes?"

"Can I get a cupcake?"

"Very well, one cupcake." Jonathan agreed.

He could see Candi watching his daughter take her first bite. The little girl dampened her lips in anticipation, then quick as a wink, shoved the slice between her lips. She chewed once. Her glance immediately focused on her father.

"Yum," she said, rubbing her hand on her tummy in a circular motion.

"That good?"

She nodded.

"Here goes," he replied and did the same. His eyes widened. He turned and found Candi watching his every move, her hands clasped together in front of her chest in anticipation. "Oh, my," he murmured past the rich pastry he was still chewing. "This...this is out of this world."

"Told you so." The little girl pulled another slice to her waiting lips. "Yummy." She held out a pinch of her cupcake. "You want to try some, Daddy?"

As she watched, Jonathan leaned over and accepted his daughter's offering. He caught Candi's eye and nodded.

Candi let out the pent-up breath she'd held. "You like it. Awesome."

"These are exceptional. I don't know when I've had a roll this good," he said and put the fork down. "Will you have this tomorrow morning?"

"I think tomorrow we'll be making cinnamon bread."

"The first thing I'm going to have to do is join a gym."

Chuckling, Candi pulled a teapot from the warming dish. "Let me fill your cup. I still have some coffee left." She tilted the china pot over the cup and Jonathan noticed the two candy canes forming a heart.

"Tell me, is everything here decorated with candy canes?"

She blushed. "No." She placed the pot back on the cart. "But, my Grandmother Noelle loved the holidays." Candi glanced around the room. "She lived in this house from the time she was born until the day she died."

He could see her eyes glisten.

"She bought every type of china with holiday designs she could find. She left us with quite a stock."

"She must have been a wonderful woman."

"One of the best," Candi agreed. As he watched, she turned her attention to Felicia and picked up a second teapot. She poured his daughter half a mug of rich hot chocolate. Jonathan breathed in deeply, savoring the scent of the rich aroma.

The sound of voices disrupted their conversation. Candi turned and glanced at the customers waiting to be seated. "Well, I should be going."

"Of course."

"Enjoy."

Jonathan reached for his cup and watched her walk to the archway. All smiles, she greeted the guests and showed them to their tables. Before long, each chair was filled and the conversations filled the room.

"Daddy, I'm full."

He looked over at his daughter who was stifling a yawn. "That's fine. Would you like to go up and see our rooms, maybe take a nap while I make a few phone calls?"

Felicia nodded.

"Okay." He wiped his mouth and stood up, taking time to help his daughter from the chair. Picking up her coat, he tossed it over his arm and took her hand leading her over to the cash register where Candi stood. "Did you get enough?"

"We are full." Jonathan placed his hand on his middle. "I have a feeling until we find our home, having tea will be a daily ritual."

"I look forward to it." She pressed several points on the monitor. "Let's see: a cinnamon roll, cupcake, coffee, and hot chocolate. That will be six dollars and eighty-four cents."

Jonathan reached for his wallet. "Here's a twenty."

She took the bill he handed her. "Let me get your change." Pressing one last button, the cash drawer opened and she pulled out the change. "Here you go."

Her fingers brushed the palm of his hand. Again, the same reaction, just touching his skin sent chills swirling around her arms. Unnerved, Candi's hand trembled.

"If we could get our key?"

"Your key?" She took a deep breath, and then nodded. "Yes, of course, I don't know what I was thinking." She stepped away from the register. "Liz, do you mind taking over?"

Jonathan watched as a very pregnant woman stepped to the register.

"Welcome," she smiled.

"Thank you." He gave a nod and followed Candi to the front desk.

He waited as she moved to the set of mail cubbies built into the wall. Pulling an electronic key from the slot, she handed it to him.

"We've given you the Sugar Plum suite. You take the elevator to the second floor and turn to the right."

"Thank you."

Candi glanced toward him, and once again their eyes locked. The liquid brown of his eyes went from brown to warm velvet. "It's been a pleasure," she whispered in a thick sultry voice that brought a deep smile to his lips. Heat built into her cheeks just hearing the sound of her voice. What was coming over her?

"Just let me know if you need anything."

"Oh, I will. We'll see you at dinner."

"Yes, dinner."

Grasping Felicia's hand, Jonathan moved toward the elevator. Leading his daughter inside, he pressed the button marked two. Candi's face was the last thing he saw as the door closed.

Candi watched as he walked toward the elevator, his daughter's small hand tucked inside his larger one. She swallowed the lump in her throat as the door closed and the light clicked on the second floor.

"Nice."

Liz's voice broke through the fog that clouded Candi's brain.

"Yes, very nice," she murmured in agreement.

"So, did he say why he's here?"

Candi ignored Liz's stare and walked toward the cash register in the tearoom. "No, not really."

"Not really? As in maybe he gave a hint? Come on, level with me." Liz gasped. "A good-looking man like that and you didn't find out why he came to Mistletoe?"

"Good-looking or not, in case you didn't notice, he's married and has a daughter." Candi sighed and picked up the receipts from the meals.

"Are you sure?" Liz glanced back at the door. "I didn't see a ring."

Candi shrugged. "Some men don't wear them."

"True. Oh, man, bummer." Liz sighed. "I was so hoping for Mr. Right to come find you."

"Yeah, bummer," Candi agreed. "I think I'm going to give up on Mr. Right."

Liz poked her with her elbow as she moved toward the kitchen. "Maybe if you sit on Santa's knee, he'll put him in your stocking."

Candi chuckled. *Oh, I could ask, but I don't think it's a stocking I want him in.*

THREE

The fire crackled. Jonathan stared at the flames emanating from the fireplace in the sitting room that separated his bedroom from Felicia's. When Ms. Cain remarked about suites, he assumed she'd offered them one big room. He was very pleased to see that their rooms stretched across the front of the building, even including a nice private bath with a claw tub. Felicia had squealed with delight and splashed until the warmth of the water turned tepid. Now, she lay napping across the double bed in the round turreted room decorated to a little girl's delight with soft pink striped wallpaper and delicate carved woodwork painted white. In front of the windows, a padded cushion served as a window seat from which you could see all of Main Street below.

He sat down in the red overstuffed chair and propped his feet up on the ottoman, then wiggled his toes at the warmth from the gas fireplace. "All I need is a good cup of coffee and I can relax in silence." He glanced over at the coffee pot on the sideboard, but it would require leaving his comfy position. "Maybe later," he sighed and pulled his laptop onto his lap. Flipping the top up, he clicked on the machine and waited for the WIFI to load. Seconds later, he was able to connect.

Jonathan flipped to his inbox. The usual ad for male enhancement went straight to the trash, a welcome from the law firm, and a note from Miss. Darden. He hurried and clicked on the agent's email. Scanning the typed message, his eyes zoned in on the one line, "I found an adorable Craftsman home in a wonderful school zone."

"Oh, please, be available," he murmured and moved the cursor toward the attached cache of pictures. Unfortunately, his cell took that moment to turn on. Eyes focused on the screen page, he managed to grasp his cell and bring it to his ear. "Hello?"

The sound of his mother in law's voice filled his head.

"Jonathan, son, how are you?"

He sighed and closed his email app. "Hi, Mom, I'm just fine."

"Oh good, you made it down to Mistletoe without incident?"

"Yes, we did."

There was a pause. In his mind, he could see her sitting on the edge of her wingback chair, pausing, then summoning up her courage to ask the next question. Of course, he could take her out of her misery and tell her Felicia was fine, but he understood her need to initiate the question.

"How is Felicia taking the move?"

There it was, the long thread firmly attaching his mother to his child. "She's fine," he assured her. "We have a lovely hotel." He paused. "Well, it's not so much a hotel as it is an old Victorian home turned into an Inn."

"Sounds charming."

There was doubt in her voice. "Actually, it is. The place is called Candy Cane Inn. We had tea today in the dining room."

"Tea!" His mother exclaimed. "I didn't think anyone did that anymore."

"Even in Mistletoe, there is culture." He chuckled.

"I didn't mean that, dear. It's just that you're so far. If something were to happen to Felicia, it would take me a while to get down there."

"It's okay, Mom. I don't expect you to drop everything and run the moment you hear our voices. Felicia is okay. We are actually happy. In fact, the agent sent me pictures of a house to look at. Would you like to see?"

"Yes, yes I would. Let me move to the computer."

Jonathan waited. In his mind, he could see her moving past the dining room to his father's study. She had mastered the basics of the computer. She could turn it on, write messages, and hit send. Not too shabby for a sixty-five year old who was much more at home talking on the phone than using text. "In the office?"

"Yes."

He noted the huff in her voice as if she had been in a hurry.

"Oh good, your Dad left it on."

"Where is Dad now?"

This time she sighed. "Down at the club. He's meeting some business partners for dinner."

Her loneliness was evident in the hollowness of her voice. This was one of the reasons he'd decided to leave. Her attachment to Felicia was becoming more of a dependence. "Maybe you should have gone with him."

"No, I can't make heads or tails of all that chatter about supply and demand." She gave a light laugh, but he knew her heart wasn't in it. "Oh, I'm in. Send away."

Jonathan brought his computer back to life and within seconds, the information about the house was winging its way toward his mother's house on the outskirts of Ft. Worth.

"Oh, my, a craftsman," she murmured.

"I figured start small, then once the practice starts moving, I can upgrade if I want to."

"Yes, yes of course. How many bedrooms?"

"Three. One downstairs has its own bathroom, but I'll be upstairs because of Felicia."

"Oh good, if she has any of those bad dreams...."

"Yep, I can get to her."

"Oh, love that kitchen. So light and airy," she said in a wistful tone. "Makes me want to come down and bake cookies."

"Once we are settled, we'll make that a date," he assured her.

"I'd like that."

They talked for several more minutes before Jonathan heard his daughter stirring in the other room. "Hey mom, I got to go. Felicia is getting up, and I want to take her for dinner."

"Yes, you do that. I'll call later tonight before bedtime."

"Sure thing." He paused. It was going to sound stupid, but he did it anyway. "Hey, Mom?"

"Yes?"

"I love you."

Her voice grew raspy. "I love you too, Jonathan. You take care of my baby." She sniffed. "Bye."

"Bye," he murmured and heard the phone click off.

"Daddy, was that Gramma?"

He turned and smiled. "Yes, she wanted to make sure you were okay."

"Can I talk to her?" Felicia took a step toward him, extending her hand.

"Later. She had to go to supper with Poppie."

"Oh." Her soft brown eyes stared at him. "I'm hungry."

Jonathan's lips twitched upward. "I bet you are. So what is it tonight? Hamburgers?"

Felicia grinned.

"Hamburger," he said and shut the top of his laptop. "Okay, let me get my coat. You, go in the bathroom, wash your face, and brush your teeth.

The tearoom had closed. Candi glanced at her watch and wondered how her guests were faring. She hoped that Mr. Barlow and his daughter were enjoying their rooms. She glanced down at the notes she had been making on the mayor's ideas. The sketch of a three tier cake with blue icing and sugar stars filled the paper. She wondered if there was a Santa sleigh she might purchase for the top and have the reindeer running along the sides. "Let's see, there were Dasher, Dancer, Prancer, Vixen, Comet, Cupid, Donner, and Blitzen." Her mouth turned down in a frown. "An awful lot of reindeer on a cake."

"Did you forget Rudolph?"

Candi blinked and looked up. Felicia had her hands holding onto the edge of the counter and her brown eyes gazing down at the image Candi had doodled.

Placing her right elbow on the countertop, Candi leaned her chin on her open palm, putting her at the same level as the little girl. "Did I?"

Felicia nodded. "You did. You got all the other ones, but Santa has to be able to see if there's lots of fog."

Candi straightened. "You are so right. How about if we put Rudolph on the platter, standing next to the cake so it looks like he's leading the team down to the roof tops?"

"I think that's a good idea."

"Why thank you, Felicia, I do too."

"Helping Ms. Candi?"

Jonathan's mellow voice rolled across Candi's skin. She could feel a slight blush creep into her cheeks. "Your daughter was enlightening me to the fact I forgot to include Rudolph," Candi explained.

"Shameful." He teased, giving her a wink.

She noticed their coats. "Going out for dinner?"

He glanced at the overcoat he carried on his arm, then back to her, only to lift his arms in a slight shrug. "We thought we'd grab a burger."

"Oh, sounds good," Candi nodded. "Are you brown bagging or looking to sit down?"

"I think brown bagging. We've got an early day tomorrow. My realtor sent us a house to look at."

Candi's eyes widened. "Nice. Okay, if it were me, I'd drive up Main to Balthazar." She pointed to the right. "Hang a right at the stop light; go down two more streets until you come to Caspar. The Silver Spur is our local version of fast food. They have great burgers and their onion rings are to die for."

"Silver Spur it is." He took Felicia's hand and as Candi watched they took three steps to the door, only to pause.

"Yes?" she questioned as he turned back.

"Would you like to go?"

"Me?"

"Or are you working the front desk?"

She lifted her mouth in a wry grin. "Front desk. Sorry. But thank you for the offer."

"Sure thing." Jonathan said with a nod. "See you in a bit."

Candi took a deep breath as he moved out the door with his daughter in tow. "Great, I just turned down an outing with Mr. Wonderful."

Walking to the front window, she parted the curtains and watched as he helped Felicia into the car. It wasn't a budget car either; she mused as he rounded the hood and climbed in the driver's side.

She heard the roar of the motor as he flicked on the lights, started the car, and eased away from the curb. Instinctively, she crossed over to the doors and flipped on the porch light for their return. Candi turned and gazed at the front counter. "Well, it's just me and a Debra Holland novel for the rest of the evening." She made her way back to the counter and picked up the paperback she'd been reading.

Two hours later, she was still there when the door opened and Felicia came bounding in. Candi put her book down. "Did you have a good time?"

Felicia's chin moved down. "I did, but I think Daddy got bored. He kept looking at his watch."

"Busted," Jonathan's deep low voice met her ears.

Candi looked up and smiled. "Did you enjoy yourself?"

"I did." He brought one hand from behind his back. "We decided since you couldn't come, we'd bring you something back."

Her eyes widened. "Oh, my gosh." She took the bag and breathed deep. "How sweet of you." She closed her eyes. Oh, it smells so good. It's a cheeseburger."

"Yes," Felicia said.

Candi opened her eyes, then raised her brows. "How did you know it was my favorite?" Her comment put a grin on Felicia's face. "I hate to eat alone…"

Jonathan pulled a drink carrier around with his other hand. "We have Sundaes."

Candi winked. "Let's go in the tearoom and eat."

Leading the way, she pushed open the doors and led the little group inside. While Jonathan put the ice cream on the table, she cut on the lights.

"There we go."

He pulled another chair to the table. "Madame?" He bowed and pulled the chair out for her to sit. Felicia giggled.

"Thank you." Candi sat and opened her sack. Reaching in, she plucked a fry and stuck it into her mouth. Her eyes closed in bliss. "Oh, I know it's sad, but why does bad stuff have to taste so good?"

Jonathan grinned. "So true." He stuck his spoon deep into the chocolate syrup that was slathered over his ice cream. "What is there to do in Mistletoe, now that the sun is going down?"

"Well," she swallowed. "There's always a walk around

downtown to the square to marvel at the lights."

"A walk, ey?" Jonathan turned to his daughter. "Felicia, would you like to walk to the square?"

"Oh, yes!"

"All right, let's eat up."

Candi took a bite of her burger and watched as the little girl dipped her spoon into the frozen treat. Really, she shouldn't be going. The man was married after all. Another thought shooed it from her mind. *You're going as a friend, nothing more. Then, when his wife comes to town, you can be the first to welcome her.* She pressed her lips together and stared at the half-eaten sandwich held between her hands. *Right.* She swallowed. However, the thought didn't make her food sit any more comfortably in her stomach.

"Ms. Cain?"

She blinked and shifted her gaze to Jonathan's concerned one. "Huh?"

"I asked if you were ready."

Suddenly, the meal before her seemed unimportant. "Of course," she said brightly and shoved the last two remaining bites of her burger into the sack. "Let me get my coat."

They gathered up the trash and deposited what they couldn't eat. Candi made her way to the counter and picked up her coat.

"Allow me," Jonathan said.

"Sure." Tentatively, she handed him her coat and turned. This was wrong. Her heartbeat increased as Jonathan stepped closer. She could feel the hairs on her arms rise as he held out the coat. Knowing what she needed to do, Candi slipped her arms into the sleeves. Time seemed to slow as he drew the coat up toward her shoulders. His hands drew close to her skin. The silk lining brushed against her arms lending a tentative surge of electricity that caused her to take a deep breath.

The heavy woolen fabric found its home against her shoulders. By all rights, she should move away. Yet, despite the knowledge, her feet seemed rooted in the spot. Jonathan, likewise, seemed in no hurry to turn away. The warmth of his fingers along the shoulder of her jacket seared her skin.

"Daddy, you ready?"

Thank god for children, Candi thought to herself as Jonathan jerked and stepped away.

"Almost, pumpkin."

"Thank you," Candi rushed breathlessly, before stepping away.

"Candi, I...."

She shook her head. "I appreciate your help with my coat." Candi moistened her lips, she brushed her hands through her short locks and tugged at the collar of her jacket. His gaze unnerved her. She needed to keep some distance between them in order to help her think clearly. Then, she made the mistake of locking gazes with him.

How absolutely exquisite his eyes were. His irises were warm brown, the color of the hot chocolate she served and surrounded by a line of deep sable. Hypnotic, they held her fast until the only sound she heard was her breath rushing from her lungs. He must have known the effect he was having on her. As she stared, the corners of his mouth lifted ever so slightly. Candi shoved her hands deep into the pockets of her jacket. It took all the strength she could muster to look away. She managed to squeak out. "Shall we, I think Felicia is ready to go?"

"Of course."

She moved toward his daughter and it seemed only natural for her to grasp Felicia's hand. Holding her hand palm down, without hesitation, the child slipped her hand into Candi's and looked up with an angelic smile that melted her heart.

"This is going to be fun."

Candi squeezed her hand. "Yes." Moving to the door, she opened it and they moved outside.

The cool night air nipped at her nose. She turned to look at Felicia. "Do you have a hat?"

"On the back of my jacket."

Candi let go of her hand and pulled the hood up and over the child's head. "Can't have you getting ill, now can we?"

"Shall I lock the door?" Jonathan questioned.

Candi gazed over at him. "Yes, please. I have my keys."

He nodded and reached around to turn the latch. Giving it a hard tug, he pulled the heavy door to and joined them on the top step. "And off we go."

Letting Candi set the pace, they strolled leisurely down the sidewalk toward the town square. The twilight gained ground, and one by one the automatic sensors triggered the lampposts to turn on. Felicia focused her attention upon the shimmer of light, which danced to imitate the motion of a flame.

"Oh, Daddy, it's so pretty."

"Yes, it is."

Somewhere up ahead, they heard voices singing carols. Jonathan glanced over at Candi.

"The different high schools send their choruses out during the early evening hours. Each group dresses according to a different time period in history. It's always fun to see what they can come up with."

"Look." Felicia pointed.

Around the corner came a group of students dressed in Victorian costumes. The tallest gentleman carried a lantern on a shepherd's hook. The girls wore dresses of red and jackets of deep green. They each wore bonnets and carried white muffs with holly pinned on the sides.

"Dickens has come to life," Jonathan murmured.

Candi couldn't help but agree. The group saw them and paused, breaking into the carol known as Greensleeves. The blend of their voices soon drew others to the corner. The crowd stood quietly, listening to the beauty of the words, thoroughly entertained. When the song came to an end, the crowd broke into applause. As the group moved toward the other end of the street, Candi let go of Felicia's hand. The little girl moved toward the plate glass window storefront.

"Look," Felicia urged them. "It's Santa Claus reading his mail."

Candi pressed her hands into the pockets of her coat and moved to stand behind the child. "Santa has to have lots of elves to help him get the mail. Have you written your letter yet?"

Felicia gazed back at her with a somber face and shook her head.

"Oh, my, we'll have to take care of that."

"Do all the stores have a different theme?" Jonathan inquired.

Candi nodded. "They do."

"What will yours be?"

She took a deep breath. "I'm not quite sure. I've got a few days to think about it. Come on, I'll show you to the square."

Jonathan reached for Felicia's hand and she reluctantly left the splendor of the store window. Rounding the corner, a tall fir tree covered with what seemed like a million twinkling lights, became visible.

Felicia came to a complete stop and stared. "Daddy!"

Candi paused as Jonathan knelt down beside his daughter and put his arms around her. "What do you think?"

"It's so beautiful," she gasped. "Can we get closer?"

Jonathan looked back at Candi and raised a brow.

"Of course we can." Candi lifted her hands from the pockets of her coat. "But we have to cross the street, so it's very important you hold our hands."

Felicia nodded.

They crossed the street and made it to the acre of ground known to the residents of Mistletoe as The Grand Square. In the center, a tall white pine stood decorated with tiny white lights, and perched on the top, a brilliant angel dressed in blue satin. The perimeter of the tree was protected by a century old iron fence, and beyond a field of green grass, holly trees were trimmed to provide an umbrella-like canopy over the cobblestone walkway. They moved to the center where wooden benches offered a place to sit and observe the holiday splendor.

"Can I go up to the tree?" Felicia turned to look at Candi as she spoke.

"Yes, just don't go beyond the candy cane fence."

The little girl nodded and skipped off to join the other children surrounding the base of the tree.

"Let's sit over here." Candi pointed to a bench on the right.

They moved toward the bench and sat down.

"What's over there that's so important?" Jonathan inquired.

A soft smile eased her lips upward. Unable to turn away from the children who stood staring at the base of the tree, Candi answered his question. "The ladies of the children's hospital down on Broad Street set up a Christmas village. All different kinds of houses, businesses, and scenes are placed around the tree, complete with a train. Listen."

They grew quiet and the faint sound of a toy train whistle followed. Behind the sound, a small gasp of delight rose in the air as each child gasped in unison.

"She'll stand there all night," Jonathan mused.

"They all will," Candi whispered. "I remember doing the same thing as a child. But this is what Christmas memories are made of." She turned and looked at Jonathan. "And at Christmas, aren't we all children?"

His gaze met hers and she felt a warm glow move through her. His face softened as he turned to gaze at his child. "Perhaps, Mistletoe will provide just the right magic I need."

Four

Candi stilled. She watched Jonathan's face. For a moment, the lines at the edges of his eyes deepened. She didn't have to follow the line of his sight to know he was watching his daughter. *Mistletoe will provide just the right magic.* The words he spoke echoed in her mind. She could sense the hurt that lay just beneath the surface. Pausing, she opened her mouth to speak.

"It's getting late. I think we need to get back to the Inn."

"Yes, of course."

He rose to his feet. "I'll only be a moment."

Candi said nothing. Instead, she watched as he moved toward the tree and placed his hands on his daughter's shoulders. For a moment it seemed as if all the pain and sorrow the world could hold weighed heavy upon him. He bent low. His lips moved as he spoke to his daughter, who turned and looked up at him. With a nod, she moved back, away from the tree, and took his hand.

Candi sighed and put on a bright face. She wanted to move toward them and sweep the child up into her arms, then promise nothing bad would ever happen.

Jonathan paused. "Shall we?"

"Of course."

The walk back to the hotel was silent, the magic of the moment tainted by the tragedy she could only guess at. Entering the Candy Cane Inn, their faces were tinted from the breeze and chill in the air. Candy pulled off her coat and waited while Jonathan helped his daughter remove hers. Straightening, he turned. The sadness in his eyes lingered, yet he put on a brave face.

"Felicia and I thank you for showing us the holiday sites."

"You're so welcome," Candi replied.

"We'll see you in the morning."

"Have a good night. I hope you enjoy your rooms."

With a nod, Jonathan took his daughter's hand and moved toward the elevator. Candi watched until the door closed. "Poor man," she sighed. Her steps seemed labored as she moved to the back stairs and made her way up to her suite situated in the old servant quarters at the rear of the Inn.

Opening the door, she draped her jacket on the hall tree and slipped off her shoes. Flicking on the light illuminated the large area that once had been the servant's kitchen. After her aunt left the house in her care, she'd worked with a local designer to create a stunning three-room apartment complete with a nice side kitchen, full bath, living room, and bedroom. She'd let the old fireplace stay. Reclaiming the deep cherry had been a labor of love. Standing before it, she reached up and straightened the photos that occupied the mantel, three generations of Cain women. Candi hoped to follow with an offspring of her own. Yet her prospects seemed bleak. "Is it too much to ask to find a man like Dad and Grandpa?"

The faces smiled back at her without comment. Candi sighed and hurried to her bedroom. After changing into something comfortable, she grabbed her novel and curled up on the sofa. "If I can't find a real one, I'll just have to settle for second best."

"Did you have a good time?" Jonathan asked as he pulled the covers beneath Felicia's arms.

"I did. Can we go back tomorrow night?"

"Now, Felicia, I'm not sure. Tomorrow we're going to look at a house. We might be too tired."

"So maybe?" she replied.

Jonathan took a deep breath. "Maybe," he agreed. Leaning down, he pressed his lips to her forehead. "Sleep tight."

Rising, he headed toward the door when her voice stopped him.

"Daddy?"

"Yes, Felicia."

"I'm glad we came to Mistletoe. I like Miss Candi."

Jonathan thought about it for a beat of his heart. "Yeah," he agreed. "I do too."

Moving to his room, he drew the sweater over his head and stripped down to his boxers. Grabbing his p.j.'s, he headed toward the bathroom and turned on the tap. He was glad they came to Mistletoe. Felicia, clearly, was enjoying herself. He squeezed the toothpaste onto his brush and began to brush.

Steam rolled up and fogged the mirror. With a swipe of his hand, it was gone. Brush resting against the side of his jaw, he studied the reflection in the mirror. No reminders of his late wife. Perhaps, finally he could lay Tiffany's memory to rest. For too long, she'd been his crutch for not accepting outings with the last company he was with. If he were honest with himself, he'd admit he was lonely. He stared at the reflection in the mirror.

"Are you really ready?"

The stern version of himself stared back from the mirror. *Am I?*

Jonathan shifted his gaze to the sink. Was he really ready to put Tiffany to rest? Her illness wasn't detected until it was too late. He could still remember the doctor pulling him into the side room, the soft compassion of his voice as he put an arm around his shoulders and said those horrid words. "We've done all that we can. Now, it's up to God."

Jonathan grasped the sides of the sink tight and closed his eyes. His heart thumped painfully in the center of his chest. Oh, how he had trusted God. How he'd bargained as they tried every experimental drug the doctors could find. But it was not enough, the cancer in her lungs proved too aggressive. He took a deep breath and opened his eyes. *Yes, it's time to move on. For Felicia's sake, I need to begin anew.* Straightening his shoulders, Jonathan disrobed and stepped into the warmth of the shower.

The sun slid its fingers between the curtains and stirred Jonathan to life. He hadn't known a time in the past few months where his sleep had been as deep or as rewarding. The long talk he'd had with himself seemed to have dispelled the anguish his heart had been dealt. Stretching, he turned on his back and listened to the sounds around him. There were small birds chirping, a car moving slowly up the street below, and in the other room the soft dialogue from a television. Felicia was up.

One more deep breath and he pushed the covers aside to reach for his robe. Slipping his hands into the sleeves, he brought the material over his shoulders and looped the sash around his middle. He didn't bother with his slippers, the polished wood floors were not as chilly as he expected. He opened the door. Felicia turned her head.

"Hi, Daddy."

He glanced at the cartoon on the screen as he made his way over to the couch. "Morning, princess, did you sleep well?"

Felicia nodded and waited for him to sit down before clambering up into his lap. Her arms encompassed his neck in a tight hug.

"Well, good morning to you, too." He squeezed back.

"What are we going to do today, Daddy? Can we go back to the tree?"

Jonathan brushed the curls from her face. "Nope, not today. Today, we are going to look at a house."

Her face brightened. "A house, just for you and me?"

"Just for me and you, and a room for Grandma and Poppie," he said and swiped a finger down her upturned nose.

Felicia giggled.

"Okay," he said and helped her down. "We'll get dressed and go have breakfast."

Hand in hand, they walked into the room where Felicia slept. While she peeled off her nightgown, Jonathan pulled a pair of blue jeans, a tee, and matching sweater from her suitcase.

"Do I have to make my bed?"

Jonathan glanced over his shoulder. "No, but we can spread the covers up so it looks nice."

Felicia climbed onto the mattress and grabbed her jeans. "I like my bed. Miss Candi gave me the best room." She slipped her legs into her jeans. "Did you know you can watch people come into the hotel from my window?"

"Your window?" Jonathan raised a brow in question.

Felicia shook her head. "My window," she said with certainty. "I hope my new home has a window just like this one."

Jonathan lifted the tee over her head so she could slip her arms inside. "If it doesn't, perhaps we can have one built for you."

He pulled the shirt down and she reached for her sweater.

"I want a pink room, too."

"Noted." He replied. "Now, you get your socks and shoes on. I'm going to get dressed."

Leaving her to finish, Jonathan moved to his own room and donned his own jeans and plaid button-down shirt. Casual, he mused. He was beginning to like this. Grabbing his wallet, he moved back into the living room.

"Ready?"

"Ready," his daughter called back.

She clicked off the television and hurried to join him. They swung their hands as they walked to the elevator, and it was only a short ride down to the first floor. To his surprise, Candi wasn't at the front desk. Instead, it was the smaller petite woman from the previous day.

"Morning," she called out, offering them a brilliant smile.

"Morning."

Felicia let go of his hand and hurried over to the front desk. "Is Candi here?"

The woman gave a shake of her head. "No, sorry. She had an errand to run this morning. You must be Felicia."

"I am!"

The woman nodded. "She said for me to tell you good luck with your home search." The woman reached below the counter and produced a small pink and white striped box. "She made this for you this morning."

Felicia looked back at her father.

"What do you say?" Jonathan coached.

"Thank you." Felicia took the box, admiring it.

"It's Liz, isn't it?" Jonathan asked.

"Yep, I'm Liz, and I hope you're enjoying your stay."

"Thank you, we are," Jonathan remarked, only to be interrupted by a squeal from his daughter.

"Look, my own special cupcake!"

Jonathan peered into the box. Candi had created two cupcakes both with candy houses perched atop the mound of icing in the center of each.

"One for you and one for me." Felicia smiled broadly at her father.

"She's very talented," he remarked.

"Yes, she is," Liz nodded in agreement. "So where are you headed?"

"Miss Darden is taking us out to a home on Evergreen Street," he replied.

"Daddy, can I eat it?" Felicia interrupted.

"No, save it for lunch."

"Yes, Daddy."

Liz grinned. "That's going to be a hard request." She turned her attention back to him. "Evergreen Street is a nice neighborhood. Good families, nice homes, Felicia should be able to find lots of friends to play with."

"That's good to hear." He turned to his daughter. "Shall we?"

Felicia nodded.

"Here we are," Karen Darden called as soon as Jonathan opened the door. "Welcome to your new home."

He stood for a moment and stared at the well-manicured lawn that sloped up to the broad front porch complete with a swing.

"Nice." He nodded and opened the car door for his daughter to join him.

Karen strutted toward him, dressed in her blue jeans and gray cowl neck sweater, clipboard in hand. "Isn't it great? A true craftsman-styled home."

"How many square feet?"

"A little over nineteen hundred," Karen replied. She gazed down at her clipboard. "The home was built in 1916 and remodeled late last year, so all new floors, electrical, and plumbing."

"I like the idea of no renovations."

Jonathan caught Karen's smile.

"What? A strong man like yourself isn't afraid of a little work, are you?" Karen teased.

There was something about the way she looked at him through her dark black lashes. *Is she coming on to me?* He gave a shake of his head.

"No. Not afraid, I'm just a little short on time."

"Ah." Karen brought the clipboard to her chest. "Shall we see the inside?"

"Yes."

She led the way to the front door, then paused long enough to slip her fingers into the pocket of her jeans to fish out the keys. Dangling them between her two fingers, she gave him a coy bat of her eyes.

"Would you like to open the door?"

The hair on the back of his neck itched. She was coming on to him. Granted, he was a single parent, but this was not a game he wanted played right before his daughter's eyes. Ignoring her implications, Jonathan reached out and took the keys, making sure their hands never touched.

"Thanks." He inserted the key and opened the door.

Felicia rushed inside and ran to the middle of the living room.

"Look, Daddy, a real fireplace!"

Jonathan's gaze was drawn to the white painted brick structure that stood on the far wall of the living room.

"We can hang stockings for Santa this year!" Felicia turned, her hands clasped in front of her, beaming at her dad.

"This is just the first house, Felicia, don't count your chickens before they're hatched," he warned.

Yet the little kid inside of him was just as excited.

"There's a kitchen and dining room just beyond the arch." Karen pointed to the double doorway framed by an arch.

Jonathan walked through, noting the windows on the southern side that let in the afternoon light.

"You can have your larger table here," Karen said, then pointed to the other doorway. "In the kitchen there is room for a small table, or you can use some bar stools at the counter."

He stepped into the kitchen area and was pleased to see a

modern kitchen with a beautiful center island. A set of curved windows stood beside the back door. He could see himself putting Felicia's small arts and crafts table in the nook and perhaps adding a window bench like the one in their rooms at the Candy Cane Inn.

"The stove is professional-grade with six burners. The previous owner loved to cook."

"And the bedrooms?"

She gave him a smirk. "I thought you'd never ask."

Walking to the back wall of the kitchen, she pushed back a barn-like door and revealed a laundry room with a staircase leading up.

"You can take the stairs here to the second floor or use the steps in the living room. Follow me."

Upstairs, Karen showed him three bedrooms and a full bath, The most spacious bedroom included a small seating area in front of a double window.

"There is a small bedroom and half bath downstairs," Karen informed him.

Felicia looked over at the smaller bedroom. "Is this mine?"

Karen nodded. "It sure could be."

Jonathan stepped to the doorway as his daughter entered. The room had been painted white and had a small dormer window on the left. Felicia turned her head to stare at him.

"No window seat," she sighed.

Jonathan knelt down. "We could put one in right below that window." He pointed to the left.

Felicia nodded.

"Any other objections?"

"No."

He waited while she took a deep breath.

"What is it, Felicia?"

His heart tugged as she spoke.

"It isn't the Candy Cane Inn."

Jonathan smiled and opened his arms. His daughter rushed toward him and he enclosed her into a massive hug. "Not to worry," he whispered. "We'll be there for a few more days."

He patted her back. "Come on, let's look at the next house

and see if we like it."

Liz saw Candi coming up the walk and hurried over to the kitchen doorway, swinging it wide for her to enter.

"Thanks," she said breathlessly as she juggled the bags to lift them onto the counter. "How goes it?" she asked, removing her coat and lying it across the seat of the barstool.

"Good," Liz replied. "I talked with Mr. Barlow and his daughter today."

"So, did you like them?" Candi tried to keep her facial expression neutral, while pulling bread from the bag and doing her best not to look at Liz.

"Oh, I thought they were cute."

Candi paused. "Cute? Just cute?"

Liz shrugged. "I guess it depends on how you like them...or should I say 'him'?"

Candi gave Liz a hesitant glance. "I'm not sure what you're getting at?"

"Sure you are," Liz laughed. "That man would make a pair of sweat pants look like something from a high-end designer."

Candi gave her a playful swat. "You are so bad."

Liz began to pull things out of the bag. "Blueberries?"

"Muffins," Candi remarked, and took the container from her hands to place them into the refrigerator.

"Crayons?" Liz looked up. "Are you stressed?"

"No, but Felicia has nothing to do. I thought it would be nice for her to have something to do in the evenings."

Candi caught the skeptical glance and ignored it.

"Right. Just doing this out of the goodness of your heart," Liz harrumphed.

"Something like that," Candi admitted. "Hold down the fort for me."

She grabbed the bag of books, crayons, and something a bit more special before Liz had time to object. Hurrying out of the kitchen, she made her way up the back staircase to the second floor where the Barlow's rooms were. Pushing the door at the end of the hallway open, she stepped onto the landing and moved toward the front three rooms. Candi paused at the doorway and stared at the big brass electronic lock.

Should I knock? She stared and pressed her lips together indecisively. She didn't see his car in the parking lot or out front. "Maybe I should." She brought her hand up and rapped against the door.

"Mr. Barlow?"

No answer. Candi dampened her lips with the edge of her tongue and pulled the master lock card from her trouser pocket. Sliding it quickly through the slot, she waited for the lights to flash green. Glancing to the left, then to the right, she opened the door and stepped in.

"Mr. Barlow?" she called out. Of course, there wasn't anyone to answer. Still, she felt a bit silly. "Get a grip on yourself," she scolded and moved toward the smaller room in the turret where she'd spent many a summer.

She pushed the door open and set the bag on the bed. Reaching inside, she pulled out a small cloth angel and placed it on Felicia's pillow.

"There." She smiled down at the figure. "You'll be responsible for taking care of my little friend."

Leaving the rest of the gifts on the bed, she walked back into the main room and paused long enough to sense the smell of his aftershave. "Lord, even when that man's not here, he can still give me goose bumps."

She rubbed her hands along her arms hoping to warm them before hurrying back to the kitchen to help Liz.

FIVE

Jonathan pulled the car around to the parking lot behind the Candy Cane Inn and got out, moving to the passenger side to help Felicia.

His daughter slid from the seat with her head down, then held out her hand without being asked.

"Tired, baby girl?" Jonathan asked.

She nodded.

"Come here," he told her, and as she neared, he swooped her up into his arms.

With Felicia's head on his shoulder, he walked into the rear entrance of the Inn. Walking quietly toward the front desk, he nearly ran into Candi who was coming out from the kitchen.

"Oh, hello," she said.

"Hello," Jonathan called softly.

He could see Candi glance at his daughter. "House hunting got the better of her?"

He nodded.

"I tell you what, take her upstairs and I'll bring you some supper. It will be just soup and sandwiches, but it will be filling."

"You don't mind?" Jonathan asked.

"Not at all. She looks tuckered out."

Jonathan nodded. "She is."

Candi patted his daughter's back. "Go on upstairs. I'll be right up."

"Thanks." Jonathan moved toward the elevator and punched the up button. As he waited, he turned back to see Candi at the kitchen doorway. "Candi?"

She paused and looked back at him. "Yes?"

"Thank you for your kindness. You don't have to do this."

"I know I don't have to, but I want to. I know what it's like to be a new face in the crowd."

The elevator opened and Jonathan gave a quick smile before he stepped inside.

"You've got it bad," Liz murmured.

"Got what?" Candi asked innocently as she pulled a tray from the cabinet.

"A good case of womanly lust," Liz explained.

"I don't know what you are talking about."

"Oh, don't you?" Liz accused as she opened a top cabinet and pulled two bowls down. Placing them on the tray, she narrowed her eyes. "You had supper with the Barlow's. You took them around to see the sights. Today, you even went out and bought that little girl a present."

"And?" Candi demanded, her brow arching.

"And, from where I'm standing it looks like a good, honest case of lust for our guest," Liz replied.

"Oh, hush you." Candi scoffed as she ladled some warm chicken soup into one of the bowls.

Liz just raised a hand. "Don't mind me. I'm just pointing something out."

"Point away," Candi remarked and placed two sandwiches wrapped in plastic wrap beside the bowls. "Are these chicken salad?"

"You know they are," Liz sighed and pulled a stool beside the counter to sit on.

"You're tired. You should go home." Candi said.

"I will, when you come down."

Picking up the tray, she walked to the kitchen door. "Just rest, I won't be long. Then you can go home. Tomorrow is Sunday and I hope you'll spend the day off your feet."

"I love you, too." Liz called out to her as she walked through to the hallway.

Candi couldn't hide the smile as she made her way to the elevator and up to the second floor.

There was no need to use her master key. This time she knocked with the toe of her shoe and waited for Jonathan to answer. She could hear his footsteps and heard the lock turn. Putting a smile on her face, she only had to wait a moment for him to pull the door open.

"Thanks." He backed away from the door and allowed her to enter.

"Felicia asleep?"

He nodded. "Fell asleep as I was putting her gown on."

"Poor thing," Candi tisked. "It's hard work finding a new home."

"That it is," Jonathan agreed.

He picked up some papers on the coffee table and made room for the tray.

"Thank you," Candi murmured as she placed it on the open area. Straightening, she asked, "Did you find one you liked?"

Jonathan took a deep breath. "Yeah, I think we did." He looked at her, then gestured toward the empty chair across from the sofa. "Will you join me?"

Candi looked over her shoulder and nervously rubbed her open palms down the side of her slacks. "I don't want to keep you up."

"No, please. Sit. I could use a sounding board," Jonathan begged.

"Sure."

Candi sat down and waited.

"I think we're going to purchase the house on Evergreen Street," he told her.

"Evergreen. That's a nice neighborhood," Candi remarked. "The yards are big and well kept. I think Felicia will enjoy it."

Jonathan chuckled. "As long as I make her a window seat like she has in that room."

Candi grinned. "It's a great seat. I spent many a summer watching the comings and goings of Mistletoe from that spot."

"Speaking of which," he reached for half of a sandwich, "Did you leave the angel on her bed?"

Candi nodded. "You said you were waiting for your things. I thought she might need someone to watch over her."

"Thank you," Jonathan mumbled as he took a bite. "She was so thrilled with that and the crayons."

"I thought she could use those to make her Santa list," Candi told him.

"She will. I think it will be tomorrow's chore."

Candi gave a nod, "A good thing for a Sunday." She stood. "I need to go down. Liz needs to go home and get off her feet."

"Sure." Jonathan rose. "I need to give Miss. Darden a call and tell her what we've decided."

"I know she'll be thrilled. Oh, before I leave, there will be cinnamon buns on the counter in the morning. I leave them there for guests when I go to church," Candi explained.

Jonathan nodded. "Thank you."

"Well, see you in the morning. Have a great evening."

"Sure, and thank you, Candi, for everything."

Walking down the hallway, Candi couldn't help but feel the pang of hurt beat against her heart. Soon Jonathan and Felicia would be leaving. She pressed the button to go down. "I'm sure going to miss them." Stepping inside the elevator, she let the door close, blocking out the sight of the door to the Sugar Plum suite.

The sky took on the color of gray silk, Candi noted as she hurried past the sign proclaiming the small white clapboard chapel as 'Mistletoe Methodist Church,' As usual, she was late. Plucking a bulletin from the table, she hurried into the chapel and took her usual seat three rows from the entrance. Miss. Clara, all of ninety-two, scooted down the polished pine bench so Candi could slip in.

Candi plopped down and took a deep breath. Her gaze wandered to the stained glass windows depicting different stories of the Bible until it came to rest on the image of Joseph leading the little brown donkey, while Mary, her head bent, cradled the infant Jesus as they fled to Egypt. By far, this was her favorite.

"Don't you love the flowers?" Miss Clara whispered.

Candi smiled. "I do. You ladies did a marvelous job."

"I think the scent of the Christmas tree is very calming."

Candi glanced at the tall fir tree by the choir loft. It was decorated with white ornaments and flocked ribbon wound around its boughs. She took another deep breath and closed her eyes, then replied. "I couldn't agree more."

The opening chords of the familiar carol *Oh Come All Ye Faithful* halted any further conversation as Candi stood and joined the congregation in song.

As they reached the words, "Come and behold him..." a warm voice whispered, "Is there room?"

Her eyes grew wide. She knew that warm vibrant tone. She turned to look and found herself staring once again into that man's familiar brown eyes. Heart thumping, Candi nodded and scooted down so that he could direct his daughter in first. Then he took the last seat near the aisle. Without hesitation, he picked up the words from the carol and sang.

Candi's skin seemed to come alive. Not only was he good-looking, a wonderful dad, but the man could sing. Every eye turned in her direction as the hymn came to a close. Even Miss Clara, who was usually reserved, reached over her and placed a gloved hand upon his jacket sleeve.

"That was simply beautiful," she declared, her eyes misting.

He nodded at Miss Clara. His whispered words were barely audible. "Thank you."

Candi felt herself blush.

"Well, from God's mouth to our hearts, let our blessings flow," Reverend Phelps said. "Now, shall we pray?"

Heads bowed. Candi listened as the minister asked for guidance and understanding for his flock. A chorus of 'amen' followed.

"At this time, let us reach out and greet our neighbors."

Candi shook Mrs. Clara's hand and without thinking, turned to her right only to remember that Jonathan stood waiting.

Her heart skipped a beat as he reached for her hand. The familiar jolt of electricity raced up her arm and made a beeline straight for her middle, where a flock of butterflies rose and took flight.

"I didn't expect to find you here," she said, unable to stop herself from staring.

"Yes, well, we decided to find the closest church to the Inn, since we're about to become part of the community." Jonathan replied. "Lucky for us, you were here."

"Yes, lucky."

He chuckled, and Candi decided then and there that was her favorite sound. Before she could respond, others crowded over the back of the pew, shaking her hand and his. She smiled and nodded at the comments, yet she seemed to have developed her own personal 'Barlow' radar that let her know what he was doing. Finally, when she thought her nerves could stand no more, the organist took pity and began to play. The voices of the congregation dwindled away and heads turned back toward the minister, leaving only God and Candi to know the strain behind the smile on her lips.

As the service ended, Jonathan placed the hymnal back in the shelf behind the pew.

"I have to go speak to someone. I'll be right back," Candi said, and quickly made her way down the bench to the aisle on the other side.

"Sure," Jonathan remarked.

Taking his daughter's hand, he led her out into the center aisle and joined the crowd moving toward the doorway.

"You've got a lovely voice," an elderly lady complemented him. Her husband nodded.

"Perhaps you'd like to join our choir?"

"Thanks," Jonathan replied. "My daughter and I are just moving in and learning our way around town. Perhaps when we get settled."

"The choir is always looking, do keep us in mind." The older man nodded and they moved forward.

"New here are you?" A woman's voice made Jonathan turn. A blonde in her late twenties moved beside him.

"Yes, just signed the papers for a house yesterday."

"Oh, wonderful," she remarked, glancing down only to dismiss his daughter. "Perhaps I could show you and your wife around?"

Jonathan recognized a "fishing" expedition.

"Mistletoe is a friendly little place." She looked around the church. "Is your wife here?"

"My mommy's in heaven," Felicia piped up.

The woman's eyes glittered. "Oh, what a shame."

Still, she never looked at the child. Jonathan couldn't help but dismiss her. A quick glance around the entrance of the church and he spied Candi.

"Jonathan?" The woman was speaking to him again.

"Yes?"

"I was asking if you'd like to have lunch."

He glanced in Candi's direction just as she turned around. Their gazes met and the sun seemed to shine brighter. "Lunch," he mumbled, trying to think of a reason not to join her.

"Candi!" Felicia cried out and pulled from his grasp.

"Felicia, come back." Jonathan called, but his daughter only ran faster.

He watched as Candi paused and knelt down to his daughter as Felicia raised her arms upwards. Candi picked his daughter up and a few words passed between them. Then Candi placed Felicia back on the ground and grasped her hand. The two made their way back to where Jonathan stood.

"Hello." Candi's voice danced across the air to him. She tugged the strap of her purse to a more secure location on her shoulder and offered him a bright smile before turning to the blonde standing across from him. "Hi, Tricia. How are you doing? I didn't realize you were back from your vacation?"

The blonde took a step nearer to his right side and their hands brushed. Jonathan quickly stuffed his into the pocket of his coat so she wouldn't lay claim.

"I'm just fine." She smiled at him and lifting her hand brushed her bangs from her face. "I went to the Keys for a Thanksgiving break. But you know I wouldn't miss Christmas in Mistletoe."

"Of course you wouldn't." Candi nodded, then added, "Tough break up with Gleason, right?"

The woman's glance sent daggers flying in Candi's direction. Standing up straight, Tricia glanced at Jonathan, then back to Candi. "Gleason? Oh, that's ancient history; you really must get out more. But I guess that old Inn has you working day and night just to get by. Such a shame. I was just inviting Mr. Barlow to lunch."

"Oh?" Candi blinked as if taken by surprise. "Really?" She gave a confused look his way.

Jonathan found his face filling with heat.

"That's a surprise. Jonathan asked to go back to the Inn and help me with the Christmas tree."

She made a point of smiling at Tricia and Jonathan wanted to laugh. "Oh, I did, didn't I?"

Candi's eyes seemed to twinkle. "You most certainly did." She leaned toward Tricia. "He did it in the middle of the sermon. I was afraid Miss Clara was going to overhear and whack his knuckles like she used to do when we were children." Her smile broadened. "I know, perhaps you'd like to join us?"

He watched the blonde, now known as Tricia, pout. Then Candi added to her coup de grace by stepping close and sliding her arm through his.

Tricia stepped back and shifted nervously on her feet. Casting a glance around, she gave a half-hearted shrug. "Well I would, but I'm a bit short on time, maybe later."

"Later, yes of course." Jonathan found himself nodding.

Tricia flashed more of a grimace than a smile before she walked away.

When she was out of earshot, Jonathan breathed a sigh of relief.

"It wasn't that bad, was it?" Candi whispered.

"No. Oh no," he lied. "I felt like a deer caught in headlights."

They both laughed. Jonathan's heart paused. He watched Candi reach down, with a tender grasp and take his daughter's hand.

"Well, we can't have that, can we?"

Felicia shook her head no.

"Did you walk?"

Candi nodded. "It was a short distance."

"How about if we ride back together?" He offered.

"I'd like that," Candi smiled.

"Shall we go?"

Jonathan led them through the parking lot to his sedan. After placing Felicia into her car seat, he opened the passenger door for Candi. She paused. "We really don't have to do this, you know."

"Do what?"

"Pretend you're going to help me with the tree." Candi replied.

Jonathan smiled. "No, we don't, but I've got nothing planned. Besides, it might do Felicia good."

"You're sure?"

"Positive," Jonathan assured her. "Unless of course, you mind?"

She shook her head.

"Then Miss Cain, will you do my daughter and me the honor of allowing us to help set up your Christmas tree?"

Candi chuckled. "I'd love to." And with that, she slid into the seat.

"Watch your hands," Jonathan murmured, then closed the door. In a quick few steps, he moved around to the driver's side and took his seat. Inserting the key into the ignition, he turned the motor on. He rested his hand on the back of the seat and went to glance out the back window, only to find Candi's eyes searching his.

"What?"

"Are you always this gallant?"

He shrugged. "Well, I do owe you something for riding in on your white horse and saving me from that dragon."

Her lips twitched and Jonathan felt his smile widen.

"Daddy, there are no dragons," his daughter corrected him.

"If you believe in flying reindeer, I'll believe in dragons."

Still laughing, Jonathan eased his car from the parking space, and with Candi as his co-pilot; they made it through the streets to the Inn.

"Where does this go?" Jonathan asked as he carried in a bright red aluminum washtub.

"Over here by the door," Candi called.

He followed her voice into the tearoom and placed the tub in the cleared space Felicia and Candi made possible.

"There's only one more," Candi said with an apologetic look on her face.

"How many trees do you put up?" he asked.

"Well." Her voice made a cute little squeak. "There's the one near the elevator, the two in the tearoom, and a small one in my rooms upstairs."

Jonathan's hands found their way to his hips and he gave her a macho stare. "Do I have to haul a heavy bucket of water upstairs?"

Candi bit her lips and shook her head no. "That one's artificial."

"Thank goodness," Jonathan groaned.

Felicia giggled. "Aren't you having fun, Daddy?"

"Loads." He exaggerated and reached over to tweak her nose.

"Would you like a cup of coffee?" Candi asked.

"Yes, please."

He followed her over to the counter where the coffee pot sat and watched as she poured him a cup.

"Here you go." She handed the stoneware mug decorated with a reindeer to him.

"More Christmas?"

She shrugged. "We use what we have."

He waited while she poured her own cup. Holding it with both hands, she took a sip. "So, what is the real reason for your move to Mistletoe?"

Jonathan took a deep breath. "It's complicated."

"Life is." She looked past him to where Felicia was admiring the tree. "I was just about her age when I came here to live. My Dad just lost my mom, and Grandma and Aunt Noelle took us in."

She glanced over at him and saw the moisture pool in his eyes. "Jonathan?"

He swallowed the lump in his throat. "My wife." His voice grew raspy. "My wife, Tiffany, passed away last year from cancer."

Out of the corner of his eye, he glimpsed Candi's hand cover her mouth.

"Oh, Jonathan, I'm so sorry. I didn't know. I wouldn't have...." Her words died away.

"We haven't had much of a holiday spirit since then. I allowed my mother and father to take over while I worked through my grief. When this job offer came through, I thought it was a way to make a new start."

"I see." Her words were barely above a whisper. She reached out and touched his sleeve. "I'm sorry, Jonathan. I'm so sorry."

He nodded and placed his cup on the counter. "I should get that other tub. I won't be but a minute."

Six

Candi sat quietly for a moment letting the enormity of his words sink in. *Of course they had that lost look. No wonder she gravitated toward Felicia.* "Poor baby," she murmured and put down her coffee cup. "Well, as long as they are here, I'll give them a Christmas to remember."

She straightened her shoulders and moved to where Felicia stood.

"So, how good are you at putting ornaments on a tree?"

Felicia glanced over at her. "I don't know. Daddy and I never really had a tree of our own. Gramma had a fancy one and I could look but not touch."

"I see." Candi nodded. "Well, I have a box of ornaments I've collected ever since I was a little girl like you. I think you can be trusted with them. Come on," She motioned with her hand, and Felicia fell into step.

In the closet at the rear of the front office, Candi found the box she was looking for. A second one, much smaller, she handed to Felicia.

"Let's go back to the trees."

Felicia followed her to the tearoom where they placed the boxes on a table near the two trees to be decorated. Candi lifted one lip of the cardboard top and a multitude of colored objects came into view.

"Oh, how pretty!" Felicia cried out and reached for one. Halfway there she paused. "May I hold one?"

"Of course," Candi smiled and gave her a painted ballet dancer.

Felicia held it up to the light and the ornament twirled and twinkled.

"I got that ornament when I was ten," Candi told her. "My Daddy thought I should be a ballet dancer because I was so tall."

Jonathan's daughter glanced over her shoulder. "Did you like to dance?"

Candi opened her eyes wide and nodded. "I love to dance.

However, I was born with two left feet."

Felicia gazed down at Candi's toes. "They look okay to me."

Candi giggled. "Sure they do, because I'm not dancing."

Felicia laughed.

"Okay, let's get these out of the box."

Together the two began lifting the ornaments from their packing. Whenever something interesting came along, Felicia would ask for the story. They were so engrossed in the different tales, neither one heard Jonathan enter with the second bucket.

"This goes here?" He nodded toward the second window.

"Yes, please," Candi replied and waited until the tub was on the floor. "Now, we just need to bring in the trees."

"And where might they be?"

She shrugged. "Out back, sitting in buckets of water with a chemical to preserve them while they are in the house."

"Okay," Jonathan dusted off his hands. "Who's going to hold the door open for me?"

"I will!" Felicia squealed and rushed from the room to get the back door.

Moving to the backyard, Jonathan gazed at the large fir trees. "You would pick something that might scrape the ceiling."

"What can I say," Candi defended herself. "I love Christmas."

Jonathan nodded. "Okay, you take the top; I'll grab the bottom and the stand."

"Awesome."

Working together, they brought the two trees into the tearoom and set them in the stands.

"There," he breathed, slightly out of breath. "They're both anchored. All that's left is to put on the bulbs and tinsel."

"You want to help, Daddy?"

He gazed at his daughter, Felicia. "No, not today. I'm going to make a phone call. But you go ahead and help Candi."

"Going to call about the house?" Candi asked as he started to walk away.

"Yes, I won't be long."

She nodded her understanding and turned back to Felicia. "So, let's get these trees decorated."

Candi didn't sleep well. The discussion with Jonathan brought up several memories she thought she'd forgotten.

Lifting her morning cup of coffee, she took a sip. "How could I have been so stupid? Of course it upset him."

Wallowing in self-pity was not her style. With a sigh she put down the coffee and started to gather the ingredients for a sheet cake. Apron on, flour sifted, she swiftly cracked the eggs into a bowl and focused on blending them together. Candi scraped the sides of the bowl and folded the creamy batter back into the eggs and tried to think through her mistake.

"The man's just moved in. You know nothing about him. And there you were, throwing yourself at him, supposedly saving him from Tricia. Maybe he didn't want to be saved?"

With a groan, she shifted the bowl against her hip and set off a furious turn of the whisk. Concentrating on the contents, Candi didn't hear the front door open.

"What did that batter do to you?"

With a squeal, Candi turned. Fumbling the bowl and gasping, she watched the whisk clatter onto the tile floor.

"You scared me to death," she squeaked, and bent down to pick up the metal whisk before giving it a good shake in Liz's smiling face. "Now I have to sanitize this."

"Scared ya, huh?"

Candi leveled her narrow gaze at her friend before walking over to deposit the whisk into the sink. "Don't do that again."

Liz chuckled and slipped her arms out of her coat. "Still doesn't answer my question." She removed her apron from the hook and deposited her heavy woolen jacket in its place. Slipping it over her head, Liz tied the apron strings behind her. "So, what did that batter do to you?"

Candi opened a drawer and reached for a new utensil, tactically avoiding her friend's pensive gaze. "I'm not sure what you mean?"

"Liz gave a deep sigh and eyed the bowl tucked snug in Candi's arm. "First, you were giving that batter quite a beating, like you were fighting off an unwanted suitor. Secondly, you were hand mixing when there's a perfectly good professional grade mixer on the counter. The only time you do this is when you are over thinking a man issue. In this case, is it our star boarder?"

Candi arched a brow. "Your analogy sucks."

Liz laughed. "Hit close to home, did I?"

Candi huffed and began to beat the contents of the bowl once more, only this time at a much more leisured pace. "I'd rather not talk about it, if you don't mind."

Liz pulled two pieces of parchment paper and lined the next two pans from the rack. Ignoring the woman standing across from her, she brushed the paper with butter before speaking. "It's okay, Candi, I probably pushed you too far the other day. It's just..." She shrugged. "If he's the right guy, I'd hate to see you give up."

"What do you mean, give up? And who do you think is Mr. Right?"

Liz turned and raised a brow. "Really, you're going to ask me that? I'm referring to Mr. Barlow upstairs."

"He's not Mr. Right," Candi stated, bringing up her defenses.

"Right," Liz's words were laden with sarcasm. "It's just that every time a man gets close, you pull away."

"I do not."

"Oh? What about our esteemed mayor?

Candi frowned. "Mayor Jones and I are not an item."

Liz gave a lift of her shoulders, brushing off Candi's excuse. "Well, you may not think you're an item, but he is the only man that's asked you out in over eight months."

"Oh, and now who's counting?" Candi challenged. She set the bowl down and reached for the cake pans.

"I'm living vicariously through your romance now that I've got this bun in the oven." Liz patted her growing belly.

Candi shook her head. "Look, we went to the cultural arts center last summer as two friends, not as a dating couple."

Liz lifted one brow. "There's a difference?"

"It was business," Candi growled back.

"If you say so." Liz picked up the metal sifter and popped the sides, letting a light rain of flour cover the bottom of the pan. "I just hate for you to brush away a chance for happiness."

Candi's mouth soured. "Jonathan and I ended up in church."

"Together?"

Candi sighed. "He came in after the service started and asked to join me in the pew. There, satisfied?"

"Maybe? Were you alone?"

"Liz, this was church. Nearly three hundred people where there. As well as his daughter."

"Unique chaperone."

Candi huffed. "You are incorrigible."

Liz shrugged.

"Look, if you must know, he hasn't gotten over his late wife."

Liz eyes rounded. "Oh, Candi, maybe you should walk away."

"I can't. When I look at Felicia, I remember what it was like for me."

"Candi," Liz seemed to breathe her name. She paused for a heartbeat before changing direction.

"Okay, so you don't want to stop. But is he ready to move on? It sounds like he is still holding on to her memory."

"Maybe? Maybe not? Oh, I don't know." Candi sighed.

"Have you asked?"

Candi paused. "No, I haven't. Felicia is always with us. I don't want to bring up any bad memories."

"Okay," Liz gave in. "I can understand that. Just, don't invest your heart until you're sure. Mister Tall Dark and very handsome seems to be the catch of the season."

"Yeah, that's what Tricia Bradshaw seems to think."

"Oh, do tell. You've got hot gossip and haven't been spilling it?" Liz sounded shocked.

Candi gave a soft chuckle. "Well, it's not that big of a secret." While they finished readying the pans , she explained what went on after church services.

"Poor Tricia, she really is working hard to get over Gleason," Liz sighed. "You want me to put these in the oven?"

"I'll do it," Candi replied. Sliding on the oven mitts, she pulled down the door and with care placed the pans inside.

"Look," Liz began. "I know I'm butting in, but nothing would make me happier than to see you head over heels in love. Maybe what you need to do is make a list of what you want in a mate."

"I want Prince Charming," Candi sighed.

Liz lifted her hand and made a dramatic wave. "Oh no dear, he's taken."

Candi laughed.

"Seriously," Liz continued. "What do you want in the 'ideal' man?"

Candi grew serious. "You know, I haven't given it much thought. I suppose he should be kind, gentle, and a good conversationalist."

"Candi, you're not interviewing an employee. Think about it. What do you want your man to be?"

"I don't know. Maybe, to be a man that walks beside me, not over me, someone who respects me and loves me with all his heart."

She saw Liz nod her head. "Now, you're more on track. Keep working on this, and while you're at it, see if you can get him to admit he's ready to move on. If not, don't waste your time."

Candi nodded. "I'll work on it." Rounding the corner of the worktable, Candi put an arm around Liz's shoulders. "Thanks, Liz."

Liz hugged her back. "It's what friends are for. Now, let's get these cakes ready." She turned toward the clipboard they kept on the desk. "Oh, and don't forget you have a meeting with the mayor on Friday."

"Yeah, I need to get to work on those sketches."

Coming out of the kitchen, she caught the opening of the elevator and Jonathan emerging with Felicia by his side. She smiled.

"Good Morning, everyone off to work?"

"Daddy's going to work. I get to go to school," Felicia told her.

"My, that's going to be fun."

"By the way," Jonathan asked. "Do you know of any good

child care facilities?"

"Actually I do. There's a good one at the corner of Mill Street and Swan Avenue called Grandma's Attic. My friend Liz is planning on sending her child there. I'll give you the phone number."

Candi reached for the phonebook and turned to the Yellow Pages. "Here."

She turned the book so that he could insert the number into his cell.

"Great," Jonathan smiled. "Thanks, I'll check them out."

"Good Morning." The cheerful greeting ushered Jonathan and Felicia inside the building labeled "Grandma's Attic". Behind the counter, a woman stood smiling. Her dark hair was pulled away from her face into a ponytail.

"Welcome to Grandma's Attic, how may I help you?" The woman's smile turned to Felicia standing quietly at her father's side.

Jonathan rested his hand upon Felicia's dark curls. He glanced down at her, then back to the woman behind the counter. "I've come to register my daughter for school. Please tell me you have an opening?"

"I do believe we have room. Let me get the paperwork."

She turned to the file cabinet against the wall and opening the top drawer, pulled a manila folder from its depths. "We'll need a few documents such as the young lady's birth certificate, shot records, and a bill showing your legal residence."

Jonathan stepped up to the counter and motioned for Felicia to hand over her backpack. "I think I have everything," he murmured, unzipping the back pocket and pulling a long envelope from inside. Undoing the string that held the flap against the back, he reached inside and pulled a packet of papers and laid them on the counter.

"Great," she smiled. "While you're filling out the information on this sheet, I'll make copies."

"Of course," Jonathan said as they exchanged papers. While he concentrated on filling out the information, the whir of the copier beat out a steady rhythm.

"Looks like we have everything," she said fingering the documents. There was a pause, and she glanced in his direction, "Except the bill showing legal residence."

Jonathan glanced up and gave a 'forgive me' smile. "Yes, about that." The end of the pen twirled between his fingers. "I'm going to sign the papers on the house this morning. It's over on Evergreen. So we haven't received any kind of bill yet."

The woman grimaced.

A shot of alarm curled around his stomach.

"It's important that your residence is verifiable," she began.

"It is or will be. I've just joined the Griffin law firm." He gestured with the end of the pen down the street.

"That's very good, sir." She glanced behind her. "However, we'll need a phone or electric bill."

Jonathan swallowed. "It will be another few weeks before we get one of those."

She placed a hand upon her chest to show her sincerity. "I believe you, Mr. Barlow." She looked to her right. "However, rules are important."

The light caught her nametag and Jonathan pulled out his most persuasive voice. "Look, Miss Linda, I have to report to work." He lifted his right arm to study his watch. "In fifteen minutes to be exact." Then, he lightly placed his hand back on his daughter's head. "Unfortunately, I can't very well take my daughter with me."

"I-I don't know what to say," Miss Linda sighed. "But rules are rules."

The side door cracked and a voice called out. "Miss Linda, is anything amiss?"

Jonathan turned his head and watched as a tall, gray-haired woman approached. He felt his daughter grow close, and he could see the uncomfortable glance Miss Linda gave him.

"Pardon," she whispered. Then holding her head high she stepped over to the older woman. "No, nothing is wrong, Mrs.

Drake, it's just that Mr. Barlow has not yet received a bill. He's just moved into town."

"Yes. People are always on the move." Mrs. Drake smiled and stepped toward Miss Linda holding out her hand. Linda turned the papers over. The situation conjured up images of grade school and being taken to the principal's office. He watched as Mrs. Drake's brows arched and then drew together above the silver cat's eye glasses. He couldn't help it, perspiration popped across his upper lip. Somehow, he stifled the urge to wipe it with his sleeve.

"Your paperwork seems in order," Mrs. Drake agreed.

Jonathan felt a glimmer of hope. She lifted the corners of her lips and handed him the papers.

"And we'll be glad to accept Miss Felicia," Mrs. Drake took a breath and drew her shoulder's back, "just as soon as you have proof of living status here in town."

Jonathan's jaw went slack. When he found the courage to speak, he heard himself sputtering, "But I have to work."

"Yes." Mrs. Drake folded her hands together and smiled. "While I sympathize with you, rules are rules."

Dumbfounded, he stared. "So you're not going to...." He let the sentence hang.

"I'm afraid not, Mr. Barlow," Mrs. Drake said, taking pride in her words as if the speech had been rehearsed many times. "We will keep her entry papers on file for three weeks, until you get a bill...."

"Yes, I know, verifying my address." Jonathan mumbled. "You couldn't use the Inn?"

"No, I'm afraid not. We need your permanent address."

Five minutes later, Jonathan and Felicia stood on the street, wondering what to do.

"Are we going back to the Inn, Daddy?"

Jonathan took a deep breath and glanced in the direction of his new job. His shoulders sagged in defeat. "I don't know," he admitted.

"Daddy?" Felicia's worried voice carried to his ears.

Jonathan put away his worry and glanced down at Felicia's upturned face. "Yes, baby girl?"

"Can we go to Candi's and have another cinnamon roll? Maybe she can help us out?"

Jonathan found himself looking toward Main Street where the Inn was located.

Perhaps, if I'm lucky.

Grasping his daughter's hand, Jonathan smiled. "Why not, I need to take a bribe to make up for being late."

Ushering his daughter back to the car, they took the short drive back to the Inn.

SEVEN

Candi slid the glass coffeepot back on the warmer as the bell over the front door jangled. Turning, her eyes widened as Jonathan Barlow walked through the door with Felicia.

"Candi! Candi!" The little girl cried with glee. "We came back."

"So you did," she grinned, then looked to Jonathan. "To what do I owe this honor?"

"Cinnamon rolls," he grinned and held his head down sheepishly before bringing his gaze back to focus on hers. "I seem to be late for work."

"So," Candi sighed and brought her hands to her hips. "I'm being used as a bribe."

He shrugged.

She couldn't contain the grin that tugged at the corners of her lips. Felicia slipped up to the edge of the glass case and pressed her face against the surface. "Um, they smell so good."

Candi turned away from Jonathan and stepped behind the counter. "They just came out of the oven." She gave him a shy glance. "Do you want one or two?"

"Can I have a dozen, with maybe one for Felicia and myself?"

"A dozen?" She gave him a sidelong glance. "I detect a real problem."

Jonathan shoved his hands into the pockets of his trousers and stared at his daughter. "Well, it seems I don't have a bill showing my address."

Candi's brow furrowed and she glanced from father to daughter. "I'm not sure I'm understanding."

"I can't go to school," Felicia explained.

"Oh," Candi's eyes widened as the situation became clearer, "I forgot what a stickler for details Mrs. Drake can be."

"Yes, that's one way of putting it," Jonathan agreed as he knelt down beside his daughter. "So I have to find something for Felicia to do."

Candi reached behind her and pulled two paper plates

from the stack on the counter. "Here you go." She shifted a bun onto each paper plate, then handed the plates over the top of the case.

"Thanks."

For the briefest of seconds, his fingers touched hers. Candi's heart ramped with an extra beat. She had to remember to breathe.

A rough smile spread across Jonathan's face.

He felt it too! "Go ahead and sit down. I'll go back and get those other buns for you."

All too quick, his fingers slid away and he focused on bringing the plates to the table where his precious daughter was camped.

"Yeah, great," Candi murmured beneath her breath, hurrying around the corner to the workroom and nearly bumping into Liz.

"Is that Mr. tall, dark, and handsome?" she questioned and rose up on her toes, craning her neck to catch a glimpse of Candi's visitor.

"Yes," Candi hissed. "I need a box."

Liz pointed over to the metal table where several flat boxes stood waiting to be filled. Yet her eyes never left the man in question. "I have to admit, his daughter is adorable."

"Yes, she is," Candi admitted as she folded the box together.

"You know, this could be your big chance to see if Mr. Barlow is ready to move on."

Candi's brow wrinkled. "What do you mean?"

"Well," Liz's eyes rounded in innocence "he's got no one for daycare. We were going to bake cookies. I was just thinking, what little girl wouldn't love to bake cookies?"

Candi's mouth formed a small 'O' and she blinked.

"You mean...." She looked over her shoulder at the showroom. "No, I couldn't."

Liz's stare intensified. "Why?"

"Why? Because, it's not right," Candi gasped.

"Who says?" Liz raised one brow. "Emily Post never wrote a book on it. Why can't you?"

Candi's mouth went dry as she swallowed. "Could I?"

"Of course. It would be great to see if you two got along."

Candi gave her a terse glance. "I'm not auditioning to take her mother's place."

"Well, from where you stand now, you don't know if he's ready for a change, maybe she's not either."

Ignoring Liz's glance, she turned and looked back at the two figures, heads bent nearly touching as they devoured their buns.

"Just saying, it's the perfect opportunity."

"All right, if the subject comes up, I'll think about it."

Liz gave a deep huff along with a shake of her head before she returned to work.

Ignoring the jab, Candi walked back to the counter and placed a dozen rolls into the cardboard box before tying it with red and white ribbon. Pouring a cup of coffee for Jonathan, her mind shifted to the conversation with Liz. *It wouldn't be hard. All I'd have to do, is say Hey, why not let Felicia spend the day with me?*

She crossed to the small fridge under the counter and removed an orange juice.

"No, it's just devious," the angel on Candi's shoulder reminded her.

Candi shut the door and shook off the conversation and walked back into the tearoom.

"Here you go," she smiled and placed the drinks on the table.

Jonathan stopped chewing and looked to her. "You don't happen to know if there is a place where I can hire a baby sitter for a day or two."

Candi glanced back at the workroom door and saw Liz's grinning face.

Knowing she was licked, Candi gave a soft sigh and spoke. "Actually, my friend Liz and I were just talking about your problem."

"Oh?"

"Yeah," Candi gave Liz a glance. "We wondered if Felicia would like to stay here?"

"Oh, Daddy," Felicia's voice filled with excitement.

"Now, wait a minute," He cautioned his daughter, then

speaking to Candi, he asked. "Wouldn't she get in the way?"

Candi shook her head. "No, we're doing holiday cookies. She can help us decorate if she'd like."

"Please?" Felicia turned her pleading eyes toward her father. "I'll be good, Daddy, honest."

Not even the strongest man could resist that face.

"I-I wouldn't want to impose," he began.

"It wouldn't be an imposition."

His eyes widened in surprise. "Remember, you don't have children. You don't know how many questions she could ask."

Now, Candi chuckled. "I don't think Felicia would cause trouble."

"You really don't mind?" he asked again.

Candi shook her head. "Not at all."

She gazed down at Felicia's bright face. "I think we'd have a good time."

Jonathan rose from his chair. "If you're sure."

"I am."

"I'm just down the road."

"At Griffin's." Candi finished the sentence for him. "I know. Now, run along." She picked up the box of cinnamon rolls and pressed it into his hands. "Run along and have a good day."

"Yes, Daddy," Felicia said, placing a scowl on her face. "You can't be super late for your first day."

Jonathan's footsteps were lighter as he hurried up the steps to the law offices of Griffin and Price. The image of Felicia, hand in hand with Candi as they waved goodbye, made him feel somewhat giddy. Opening the door, he entered and placed the box on the secretary's desk . The smell of warm cinnamon and vanilla filled the air.

"These have to have come from Candy Cane Inn," Louise Morgan sighed.

Putting down the files she had been carrying, she carefully lifted the lid and inhaled deeply. "Oh my, a slice of heaven."

Jonathan smiled. "Have one. It's a peace offering."

Louise lifted a roll out and licked her fingers where the icing had slid. 'Peace offering?"

"I'm late on my first day."

Louise held up a finger as she munched on the delicious confection. Once her mouth was empty, she spoke. "Mr. Barlow, if you bring these every day you can be late as often as you please. Boy, that Candi knows how to bake!"

Placing the bun on a napkin, Louise slid into her seat and licked her fingers. "So, seriously, why the treat?"

Jonathan shoved his hands in his pockets and rocked on his heels. "It seems I need a favor. In order to get Felicia into a day school, I have to produce a bill with my address."

"What school?"

"Grandma's Attic."

"Ah." Louise took another bite and nodded. "Mrs. Drake is a stickler for rules, but she's fantastic with kids."

"So I found out," Jonathan sighed.

"Louise dabbed the edges of her lips with the napkin. "So where is that sweet little one of yours?"

Jonathan gave a nod toward Main Street. "She's spending the day with Candi, baking cookies."

Louise sighed. "I wish I was your little one. That sounds like a lot more fun than this." She glanced over to the stack of manila folders teetering on the corner of her desk. A mischievous twinkle sprang from her eyes as her grin widened.

"What?" Jonathan asked.

"I think I just found an answer to your problem."

His brow furrowed. "You do?"

She gave a slow and steady nod. "Get Candi to create an order and deliver it to the house. You be there to greet her and sign the ticket. Zap! Problem solved."

His eyes widened. "That would work, wouldn't it?"

"Yep." Louise replied as she latched onto another roll

"Louise! You're a genius!"

Jonathan leaned down and engulfed her into a deep hug. When he released her, Louise had two huge spots of pink in the center of her cheeks.

"W-why Mr. Barlow," she blushed.

Candi pulled the tie of the apron into a bow. "Now, turn around."

Felicia did exactly as she was told. The heart-shaped apron was just under her armpits and nearly covered her down to her knees.

"Beautiful," Candi exclaimed.

"Now, for the hat." Liz grinned.

As Candi watched, Liz placed a paper bag she'd rolled into the shape of a chef's hat onto Felicia's head.

"Perfect," Liz sighed.

"Let's get a selfie," Candi said and grabbed her phone from the counter. "Gather round."

She picked up Felicia and put her on the stool. Liz hurried behind her and Candi leaned in close.

"Serious face," she called out.

"Cheese," Liz said.

They all smiled.

"Silly face!" Liz cried out.

The three made funny faces and Candi snapped the frame. They straightened and she produced the pictures for them all to see.

"Oh, these have to go up on the web," Liz giggled. "Let me have that phone."

Candi turned the phone over to her friend. "While Liz is getting those pictures downloaded, let's bake cookies."

She reached for the two-step folding stool and placed it next to the table so Felicia could climb up and work. Patting the seat, she spoke.

"We're going to wash our hands, then I want you to climb up here very carefully. Okay?"

"Okay."

She led Felicia over to the sink and together they scrubbed their hands. Then Candi slipped a pair of plastic gloves over Felicia's smaller hands and got a pair for herself. She helped the little girl onto the stool.

"Today, your job is to help put on sprinkles. We're going to put red on Santa..."

"For his suit, right?" Felicia replied.

"Right." Candi smiled. "Let me get my gloves on and I'll show you."

Slipping on the gloves, Candi took the small pastry brush and dipped it into a cup of melted butter.

"We spread it over the cookie, like this."

She demonstrated, then put the brush back in the cup.

"Then we sprinkle with the colored sugar. You think you can do this?"

Felicia shook her head in agreement. Candi stepped back and watched. Felicia repeated Candi's steps to perfection. Once Felicia had finished the candy coating, she glanced back over her shoulder. "How is this?"

"Perfect." Candi leaned down and gave her a hug. "I'm going to cut some more cookies out. So I'll be right across from you."

Felicia continued to work as Candi joined her. Suddenly the kitchen was filled with the sounds of holiday music. Liz poked her head around and smiled.

"I thought this might help."

The Rudolph song came on and Candi winked. Soon both she and Felicia were singing and working right along. Time flew by quickly, and soon all the dough had been cut and the last of the cookies were baking in the oven.

"What do we do now?" Felicia asked.

"Well," Candi pulled her apron off and disposed of her gloves. "I guess there is only one thing to do."

"What?"

"We need to sample."

Felicia's eyes grew wide.

"Turn around." Candi demonstrated with her finger, by swirling it around.

Felicia turned and Candi relieved her of her protective covering. "Follow me."

She led Felicia into the tearoom and sat her at a table.

"I'm going to get us something to drink and two cookies.

You wait right here."

"Okay, Miss Candi," Felicia nodded.

Candi moved back to the kitchen and poured two small glasses of cold milk, then placed two of the still-warm cookies on to a tray. Carrying it out, she put the cookies on the center of the table and one glass at each seat.

"There we go."

She sat across from Felicia. "Are you a dunker?"

"Dunker?" Felicia wrinkled her nose.

Candi winked and broke part of her cookie and dipped it into the milk. Felicia followed her example. She waited until the little girl's eyes were on her, then she lifted the cookie and put it into her mouth.

"Yum," she said, crunching down on the sweet treat.

"Yum," said Felicia as she followed Candi's example.

Giggling, the two broke off another piece and began to repeat when suddenly a voice in the doorway stopped them.

"What have we here?"

"Daddy!"

Felicia scrambled up. Jonathan bent low to embrace her.

"Is this a tea party?" he asked, looking over to Candi.

"It might be. Felicia helped me with the cookies. We needed to sample them before this afternoon's opening."

"Well," Jonathan stood up. "May I? We can call it a happy house celebration."

Candi stood. "You got the house!"

He nodded and held up the keys.

"Daddy!" Felicia threw her arms around his knees.

"That's wonderful!" Candi joined in.

Without thinking, she rose from the chair and hurried over to embrace him. Jonathan's arms encircled her waist. She raised her head and found his eyes locked on hers.

"Had I known I was going to get this type of reception, I'd have bought the house on Saturday."

Candi's gaze dropped, as heat filled her cheeks. She stepped back, but allowed her hand to rest on the soft tweed of his jacket sleeve.

"I'm happy for you," Candi murmured.

Her hand slid from his jacket and Jonathan grasped it. She stepped back, but he didn't let go. If anything, he seemed to be staring at her more intently than before.

"I thought it was a great welcome."

Candi's heart flipped. In a split second, something had passed between them. She wasn't sure what, but their budding friendship seemed changed. Longing was replaced by fear. Things were moving a little too fast. She was an old fashioned sort of girl. With a nervous smile, she looked toward Felicia. "Well, let's set another place for your daddy."

"Yes, another place." He echoed her words, yet his eyes didn't let her go. Instead, his gaze traveled over her face, finally settling on her lips.

Kiss me, please, her heart begged, only to have him blink and draw back. The moment was gone.

"Come on, Daddy," Felicia giggled. "You can sit right beside me."

Candi slid her hand out of his grasp and stepped away as the little girl came running back to them.

"Oh wonderful, and can I have another Santa Claus cookie, too?"

"You sure can." She nodded and sent her curls flying.

Good, I need a buffer between this man and me. She gave the little girl a grin and was rewarded with a smile.

"Come on, Candi, sit with us."

"Yes, of course."

Candi moved to the table and sat.

"These cookies are delicious." He glanced to his daughter. "I didn't know you were such a good cook."

Felicia's grin widened. "Candi baked. I did the butter and sprinkles."

"They're delicious!."

"You're back a bit early." Candi observed.

Jonathan nodded. "I need your help with a problem."

"Mine?" Candi cast a doubtful look at him.

Jonathan pushed the plate away and leaned on the table. "I have to have a bill that proves I'm living in the house."

"Okay," Candi murmured. "How can I help with that?"

"Louise pointed out today that if I order another dozen of the cinnamon rolls, you could write a bill with the address and deliver it to the house."

Candi nodded. "Establishing your residence."

"Exactly." He reached out and touched her hand. "Would you do it?"

"Of course," Candi agreed.

"Fantastic, I'll call the shipping company and get our furniture sent down."

He lifted his glass.

"To Evergreen Street and the Barlow estate."

"To Every green," Felicia cried out.

"To Every green," Candi giggled as they all clinked glasses celebrating the moment.

Eight

"So, you're taking cinnamon rolls over to 329 Evergreen Street."

Liz folded her arms over her expanding middle and gave her friend 'that look'. Doing her best to ignore it, Candi folded the top of the box and took a deep breath before turning to Liz "That's right. Once Jonathan shows he has a legal residence, then they can get Felicia in school."

"And you lose your chance on Mr. Right." Liz pointed out.

Candi placed a hand on her hip and stared at her friend. "Liz, this is not about finding Mr. Right, it's about helping a family settle into their new home."

Liz almost seemed to pout. "True, but one can hope."

Candi shook her head. "One day, I'll be married, walk around in sweats, and cuss when I have to put on a bra to go to the grocery store, just like you."

Liz gave her the look that would silence the dead. "I just can't stand things constricting me right now."

Candi chuckled. "You've been practicing that 'Mom' look, I can tell."

"Is it working?"

"Liz, you could scare even me." Candy turned to the worktable and lifted the pan of cinnamon rolls into the box. "There." She closed the lid and tied the string around it. "Now for the bill."

Liz followed her into the lobby and watched as Candi pulled a receipt book from a drawer. Then, she carefully wrote Jonathan's name and the address for the new home. Tearing it from the book, she folded it over.

"I won't be gone long."

Liz smiled. "Take all the time you need."

Candi shook her head. Scooping her keys from the cup beneath the front desk, she walked back to the kitchen and grabbed the box.

"Don't over-exert yourself." Candi warned. "Just sit at the

front desk."

"Yes, mother," Liz sighed. "Now go."

Candi moved toward her car and opening the door, deposited the box on the passenger seat. Climbing into the driver's side, she inserted the key into the ignition, and turned on the motor. Backing away, she pulled into traffic. The drive over to Evergreen took about twenty minutes. Luck seemed to be on her side, because she was only stopped by two of the four traffic lights that lined her route.

Candi pulled up to the curb in front of the house and cut the motor.

"Oh how beautiful," she exclaimed as she leaned over the passenger seat to glimpse the home that Jonathan had purchased.

The front door was open and she could see a broom sitting in the space.

"Must be cleaning," she murmured, grasping the twine that held the box and heading toward the open door.

A cool breeze nipped at her heels as she made her way up the flagstone walkway. Stepping onto the porch, she paused as she heard Felicia's voice echoing down the grand staircase.

"Oh, Daddy, can you make me a swing?

Candi grinned. Now she knew what she could give Felicia for Christmas. Stepping into the dining room, Candi peeked out and saw a huge oak tree. Its massive branches would provide the perfect support for a swing.

"Hello, anyone home?" she called.

Walking back to the dining room, she heard her name being called. Heat soared into her cheeks as she drew her head back as Jonathan's smooth voice swirled around her.

"Well, hello there," Jonathan smiled. "Have any trouble finding the place?"

"No. None." She handed him the box. "Cinnamon rolls per your request."

He reached out and took it. In doing so, a shiver of excitement raced through her.

"Thanks." He motioned for Candi to follow him into the spacious kitchen. He placed the box on the counter before he turned back to her. "So, what is your initial reaction?"

Candi tilted her head. "Well, the word home comes to mind. It's a house that stands for family, hearth, and home. It has a feel of belonging to the continuity of life and community."

"So, you like it?"

"I do," Candi nodded. "I think it is the perfect place to bring up Felicia."

She turned to the kitchen window. "See that huge oak tree?"

"Yes."

She heard his footsteps come closer.

"That's the perfect place for a swing."

"A swing?"

She gave a vigorous nod of her head.

"Little girls need a wishing tree, a place where they can go out and talk to the angels. It's the perfect spot."

He leaned closer. She felt the warmth of his breath against her cheek.

"Talk to the angels, huh?"

"My grandmother swore by it."

She turned her head. He was looking at her. A smile curled the corners of his lips and she felt flattered by his interest.

Her curiosity was piqued. "Why did you buy the house?"

"It reminded me of my grandparent's home."

He walked past her to the window and folded his arms across his chest. I always loved going there in the summer. There was so much warmth in that home. My grandparents were so much in love. Every night, they'd do the dishes together. She would wash and he would dry. I wanted Felicia to feel that."

"I think that's a wonderful reason, Jonathan."

He turned and she could see the tenderness of his gaze. Carried away by the raw emotion of the moment, Candi crossed the distance between them and linked her arm beneath his. Her cheek pressed against his shoulder, she spoke again. "Your daughter is going to feel the love. You are a magnificent parent. How lucky Felicia is."

"You think so?"

She nodded.

"Now all I need to find is the right person to share all this with," Jonathan spoke. His voice grew husky as he gazed at her face.

Suddenly, she grew aware of the strength and warmth of his flesh beneath his sweater. Nearly overwhelmed by his nearness, Candi took a small step back. His hand quickly reached for hers, stopping her from making a full retreat.

"Candi, has anyone ever told you how beautiful you are?"

"Beautiful?" she echoed. Her heart thumped wildly in her chest.

Turning to face her, Jonathan cupped her cheek with his left hand and stroked his thumb across her skin. A delightful shiver ran through her. Eyes locking, their breathing came in unison.

Kiss me, please, just kiss me and get it over with.

He leaned close. His eyes never leaving her face, Jonathan gently tilted her head. The thudding of her heart drowned all other sounds from her ears. Her lashes fluttered against her cheek.

She nearly jumped with the first brush of his lips against hers, as if he were testing the waters. She opened her eyes to his questioning glance. Her lips trembled. She raised her hand and slipped it against his shoulder. There she found the wild thumping of his heart. She stepped closer and moved her hand to clasp the back of his neck. She closed her eyes once more as his lips found hers.

She didn't know how long the kiss lasted, only that the world seemed to tilt on its axis, careening toward the edge of the universe. Her knees grew weak. His arms cradled her back, holding her against his body to absorb his strength. Much too soon, his lips lifted. Her eyes flickered open.

"Candi." Her name tumbled from his lips as he swept her closer to him in a deep embrace. His lips brushed her hairline at her temple.

"I've wanted to do that for a long time."

"So, have I," she murmured against the warmth of his chest.

"This is crazy," he continued as his hands stroked her back. "I've known you for only a short time and yet it feels like forever."

"Daddy?"

Candi's eyes widened. She felt him stiffen.

"Felicia."

"Daddy, is Candi okay?"

They separated. Candi glanced at the little girl standing in the doorway, staring at them. She felt a bit ashamed. Nervously, she fingered the wisps of hair around her face. She glanced at Jonathan and found him staring at his shoes. Thinking fast, Candi spoke.

"I'm fine Felicia. I was just giving your dad a hug. I'm so proud of him for finding you the perfect house."

The little girl beamed. "It is perfect, isn't it? Would you like to see my room?"

"I would," Candi replied.

Felicia held out her hand. Candi moved toward her and grasped it.

"We'll be right back, Daddy," she called as she pulled Candi toward the stairway.

Jonathan turned toward the bar and placed his hands against the marble. His head down, he wondered what had gotten into him.

"I never should have put my hands on her," he murmured.

Yet even as he replayed the scene in his mind, he noted that she had not moved away. The realization made his heart fill with happiness. Could it be that Candi Cain could fill the void in his life? The thought left a tingle in the pit of his stomach.

He wanted to spend more time with her. She seem to enjoy being with Felicia, and for certain Felicia enjoyed being with her. Yet he needed to err on the side of caution. The sound of Felicia's feet pounding the stairs broke the silence.

"Daddy! Daddy! Candi likes my room!"

"That's good, pumpkin."

Pushing away from the bar, he moved to the living room. "Let's give Candi the full tour, okay?"

"Okay."

They led her through the house. And with each room, she ooed and ahhed over each idea they had to transform the house into something of their own.

"I think you have some great thoughts," Candi told them as they made their way out to the backyard. "I know a few contractors when you need them for renovations."

"Thanks." Jonathan put his hands in the pockets of his trousers, hoping to resist the urge to reach for her hand and pull her close.

"I'll probably take you up on that offer." He turned and looked back into the house. "I want to do a bit of work on the bathroom that separates our bedrooms upstairs."

"Not to mention building that window seat," she teased.

Jonathan chuckled. "Yes, she has reminded me of that several times today."

"When will you be moving over?"

He swung his gaze back to her. "I talked to the movers where we have our furniture in storage. They promised me they can deliver first of the week. So, we'll be moving here on Saturday. I want to finish the week at the Inn."

"Sure."

But her voice sounded disappointed.

"Speaking of which," Candi said, rubbing her hands down her jeans. "I need to get back. I don't want Liz overdoing it."

"Of course." He turned to Felicia. "Hey, come say goodbye to Candi, she's got to go back to the Inn and we have to go see Mrs. Drake at Grandma's Attic."

Felicia ran over and threw her arms around Candi's legs. "I'm gonna miss you."

Candi knelt down and returned the hug. "I'm gonna miss you, too. I'll see you tonight. Have fun."

She turned to Jonathan. "Let me know if the billing works."

"I will."

She smiled and gave a wave, then walked toward the front of the house where her car was parked. Climbing in, Candi stared back at the house. It was a beautiful house. One fit for a little princess like Felicia. Her eyes misted over.

"How can one little girl worm her way into my heart so fast?" she whispered.

But no answer came. She brought her hands up and wiped her eyes with the back of her hand. "You're a sentimental old fool, Candi Cain."

She inserted the key and gave a turn of her wrist. The car roared to life, and she pulled away from the curb.

The crowd at the tearoom kept Candi busy for the rest of the afternoon. She glimpsed Felicia and her father coming in as she and Liz were clearing the tables and waved. Jonathan and Felicia waved back before hurrying toward the elevator. Carrying a tub of dishes to the kitchen, Candi set them on the counter next to the sink and began to put them into the hot sudsy water. Behind her, she heard Liz move to the worktable.

"Do you want to slice this last sheet cake for tomorrow?" Liz asked.

"Sure," Candi replied as she reached for another small salad plate.

"I saw Jonathan and Felicia come in."

Candi nodded.

"They went upstairs without stopping."

Candi took a deep breath and tried to ignore the hurt in her chest. "Yes, I guess they are tired."

"I wonder if he was able to get Felicia in to school?"

"Don't know."

The two fell silent as they continued to work. Liz finished putting the slices of sheet cake into a container and moved to the refrigerator to place it inside.

"So, how was your trip to Evergreen?"

"It was okay."

"Just okay?" Liz pressed.

Candi swallowed and pulled the last plate from the water.

"They will be moving out this weekend."

Liz stepped closer and placed a comforting hand on Candi's arm. "You're going to miss them."

Candi shook her head. "It's crazy. I feel as if I've known Jonathan for a lifetime."

A soft smile curved Liz's lips upward.

"Sometimes love happens all at once. Haven't you ever heard of love at first sight?"

Candi gave Liz a skeptical look. "Really, isn't that just for songs?"

Liz shrugged. "Perhaps, but writers couldn't write about it unless it were true."

Candi glanced away and swiped the water droplets from the rim of the sink with her cloth. "It can't be love."

"If you say so," Liz sighed. "I'm going home. You get those drawings done."

"I will," Candi nodded. "Drive safe."

She walked Liz to the door and watched her get into her car. Liz blinked her headlights, a signal between the two that all was well and with a wave, she drove away. Candi walked through the first floor and made sure the doors were locked before retiring.

Tonight, she just wanted to get upstairs and complete her work. She was glad she hadn't told Liz about the kiss. It had unnerved her more than she was willing to admit. Candi entered her apartment and closed the door. She leaned against the wooden doorframe and stared at the twinkling lights beyond the window's pane. "I'm reading more into this than there really is. Jonathan and I were just lost in the moment, nothing more."

She said the words and waited. However, the sorrow didn't dissipate. Deep down in her soul, Candi didn't want Jonathan or Felicia to leave.

"I must be out of my mind." She gave a shake of her head. "Okay, time for you to get real. You've a cake to design."

Pushing away from the door, Candi hurried to her room and changed into her sweats and baggy T-shirt. She padded to her tiny kitchen and brewed a cup of tea, then carried it to the small table. Pulling her notebook from the shelf, she opened it to a blank page and began to doodle.

They had stopped for a burger and chocolate shake at the Silver Spur before returning to the Candy Cane Inn. With Felicia bathed, he planned on working on some papers he'd brought home from the office. Sitting on the sofa, Jonathan had just set out the documents when he heard Felicia's voice.

"Daddy?"

Jonathan looked up and caught sight of his daughter on the doorway. "What's up, cupcake?"

"Come hear my prayers?"

"Of course."

He rose from his seat and moved to her room. Lifting the covers, he allowed Felicia to crawl in and settle down. Bringing the covers up, he tucked the comforter around her shoulders.

"How's this?"

"Good." Felicia yawned. "I'm gonna miss Candi."

Jonathan smoothed the covers and gave a nod of his head.

"I will too. She's turned into a good friend."

"Maybe she can come have supper with us or we can have supper here at the Inn?"

"I'm sure that can be arranged. Now, about those prayers, fold your hands together."

He waited as she followed his directions.

"Are we ready?"

"Yes," Felicia said. "Now I lay me down to sleep," she began reciting the age-old prayer her mother had taught her.

Behind his closed eyes, Jonathan saw the image of his late wife surface. Smiling, her long dark hair brushed behind her shoulder, the same indigo eyes as his daughter's stared back at him. His throat felt raw as he swallowed past the lump that formed there. *Concentrate on her words,* he reminded himself.

"God bless Gramma and Poppie, Uncle Louis, and Aunt Bella. And Jesus, thank you for letting us stay with Candi. Please let her bake some more cinnamon rolls so we can have some for Sunday morning."

"Felicia," Jonathan stern voice brought an end to her prayer.

"Amen," Felicia added.

Shaking his head, Jonathan rose, then leaned over and kissed her forehead.

"Sleep tight, sweetheart."

"You too, Daddy."

Moving to the doorway, he raised his hand and cut off the light switch. "Shall I leave the door open?"

"Yes, please."

"Your wish is my command," he whispered.

Jonathan stepped onto the small hallway and moved toward the bathroom. Cutting the light on there would shed light onto her doorway should she need him. He had moved toward the living room when he heard the creak of her bed. Thinking she might be getting up to speak to him, he paused and listened.

"Jesus, I forgot something." Felicia murmured.

He peeked in and saw her kneeling beside the bed, her hands folded tight.

"Please bless my Daddy and my Momma in heaven. And Jesus, please let my Daddy smile again. Amen."

Tears clouded his eyes as he returned to where he'd been. Instead of sitting down with his papers, Jonathan moved to the window and stared at the street below.

He thought he'd hidden his grief well. Still, his daughter had seen through his charade and picked up on his unhappiness. He had to do better. It was unfair of him to include her in his gloom. With slow measured steps, he moved to the coffeepot and flipped on the heating element.

How was he going to begin a new life with the dark cloud of his wife's untimely death hanging over both their heads? However, never before had the move seemed so right. Back in Fort Worth, he'd been the widower, the man who'd lost his beloved wife to a tragic illness. Every place reminded him of Tiffany. It had been so easy to give in to the self pity, the loathing of God, the anger of her leaving him . Last year, when he'd left the Christmas tree in the attic and the house undecorated, he knew it had gone too far.

To his surprise, Tiffany's mother suggested the move. Four months later, he'd found the job posted here in Mistletoe. The rest, as they say, was history. He'd sold the house, packed up the furniture, and with tearful goodbyes, he'd loaded up the car and driven here to begin a new life.

Beginnings mean change. Jonathan walked to the room's window, placed his hands on the wide molding framing the window and hung his head. Change was hard. How easy it would be to go running back and live the life he knew. Tiffany's parents would be there if Felicia needed anything. Had he compounded his troubles by leaving his lifeline?

Lifting his head, Jonathan stared out the window to the stars flickering overhead. "I've got to do better." Then, he called on the one entity that might show him the way.

"God, help me to find a little bit more Christmas in my heart. Let me move past my grief and give my daughter the life she deserves. Help me find my way."

He closed his eyes and mentally added the 'amen'.

NINE

Candi stared at her packed schedule. No matter how she tried to finagle it, she found herself working longer hours as the weekend grew near. What seemed to loom larger than life was the red-circled Friday. Deep down, she dreaded the meeting with Mayor Jones. Yes, she'd finished the sketch of the cake, but she'd much rather be eating dinner with someone else and discussing events at Grandma's Attic than whether or not Santa should be wearing brushed velvet. The truth was, she'd go to that darn meeting because she wanted to forget that Jonathan and Felicia were leaving and she didn't have the guts to admit it to herself.

She stood at the front desk, looking over the order book, when the elevator door opened. She looked up to see Felicia bouncing out, jacket on, smiling. Candi put down her pencil and moved around to meet her.

"Well, good morning. Someone looks excited."

Felicia grinned. "I'm going to school today."

Candi raised her brow and looked up at Jonathan. "So, it worked?"

He nodded. "It sure did. Of course, I was able to get Miss Darden to give a phone call too and report that we had purchased the house and our furniture would be in Monday."

"Karen and Mrs. Drake are related." Candi explained. "It might have been easier to have gone through her in the first place."

Jonathan shrugged. "The way we did it worked."

They stood staring at one another. Finally, he spoke. "Could I buy a sandwich for Felicia to take to school?"

Candi blinked. "Oh, of course." She looked down at the little girl smiling up at her. "Peanut butter and jelly?"

"Yes, please."

"Wait right here." Candi disappeared into the kitchen. Grabbing a loaf of bread, she began to create the requested sandwich. Turning, she went to the refrigerator to pull out a slice of the sheet cake Liz had cut up the night before. Removing the box, she untied the string and gazed down at it. Then she paused. A soft smile replaced the mounting tension. She closed the lid and retied the box with her fancy ribbons.

"This will be a nice surprise," she murmured.

She placed the sandwich in a bag and added a cup of fruit. Holding the box in one hand and the bag in the other, she hurried back to where Felicia and her father were waiting.

"Okay, one lunch and...." She handed the box to Jonathan, "one snack for the class. There should be fifteen slices of a sheet cake in there and they can be cut in half to make it go further."

"You don't have to..." he began.

"I know. But let's just say I want to."

Crouching down, she got eye level with the little girl. "Now, you remember to be sweet. I'll see you tonight, and I can't wait to hear about your first day at school."

Felicia stepped forward and put her arms around Candi's neck.

"Thank you. I can't wait to come back home."

The word *home* echoed in her ears. Her heart twisted. Putting on a brave smile, Candi hugged the little girl back.

"I'll be waiting."

"Felicia," Jonathan called to his daughter. "We've got to go."

"Bye!"

"Bye." Candi waved, and a piece of her heart chipped as the door closed behind the two.

She was still staring at the front door when Liz's voice brought her out of her daydreams.

"Candi, did you get really hungry last night?"

Candi blinked and turned. "What?"

"I asked if you got really hungry last night," Liz repeated. "Why?"

"My left-over sheet cake is missing from the fridge. I was going to set it up on the cake stand and put it out front, but it's gone."

"Find something else," Candi sighed and gazed with

longing once more at the front door.

"I take it a day school is going to be hyped up on sugar."

Candi faced her friend and gave a little shrug. "What can I say?"

Liz smiled knowingly, "Maybe admit you are smitten and get it over with."

Candi didn't deny, nor did she agree. Instead, she merely sighed and walked back toward the kitchen. "So I'm thinking some butter cookies with lemon pie filling in the center."

Jonathan looked down at the mountain of material he'd completed. Yes, some of it was simple work that a first year lawyer would be able to handle. However, he had to remember he was the junior partner at the moment. There would be time for him to shoulder more responsibility as time wore on. Besides, there was Felicia to think about. The intercom buzzed. He pressed the button on his phone.

"Yes?"

"Mr. Barlow, Karen Darden here to see you."

"Okay, send her in."

He folded the manila folder closed and rose as the door opened and the secretary allowed Karen to enter.

"Well, this is a pleasant surprise," he smiled. "I hope everything is all right?"

"Fine." She smiled back. "In fact, you'll be pleased to hear the bank called early this morning, the money was transferred and legally the house is yours to do whatever you like. I've called the power and gas, so the bills have been changed to your address. But my cousin tells me you have already been able to get Felicia into school."

He nodded. "Yes, she was very excited to get there this morning."

"I'm glad."

An awkward silence followed. He watched Karen stare at his lips. Then, summoning up her courage, she blurted out.

"I know it's rather bold of me, but would you like to have

dinner at Brazos?"

"Brazos?" His brows knitted together.

"It's a nice place down by the river. I thought after a long hard week, we could enjoy dinner…as friends." She quickly added.

"I-I don't know," he stammered.

The feeling of being a fly caught in a spider's web swirled about him.

"I know." Karen shook her head. "It's asking an awful lot. But, with getting ready to move in, I thought maybe you'd like some grown-up time away from your daughter. Sort of adult talk."

"Adult talk?" He echoed blankly.

"I can recommend a few baby sitters, but with you staying at the Candy Cane Inn, I'm sure that Candi or Liz wouldn't mind for a few hours."

"It seems you have it all worked out for me."

Karen shrugged. "So, you'll come?"

Jonathan thought about it. He needed to get out in Mistletoe society. His ventures had all been with Candi so far. He'd talk to Liz, perhaps she knew of a teenager who could supervise Felicia for an hour or two.

"All right, I'll meet you at the Brazos."

"Wonderful," Karen's face brightened. "Let's say about seven?"

He nodded.

"Okay, well, I better let you go."

She walked to the door.

"Miss Darden," he called out.

She paused and looked back, her face shining with excitement. "Yes?"

"It will be just as friends."

Suddenly, her face seemed crestfallen.

"Of course, just friends."

Her smile trembled.

"See you Friday night."

He nodded as she let herself out.

Jonathan moved to the windows behind his desk and stared across the road toward Main Street. His heart surged with disappointment, as if all the happiness had been sucked out of his life.

"Mr. Barlow?"

Louise's voice made him turn.

"Yes?"

"I just wanted to see if you were okay," she said.

"Miss Darden leave?"

The secretary nodded.

He lifted his hand and ran it through his hair.

"Mrs. Morgan?"

"Yes?"

"I feel like I've made my first major mistake at the law firm of Griffin and Price."

Her brow arched.

"I take it the march of the unmarried females of Mistletoe has begun?"

He nodded glumly.

She chuckled. "I'll screen your calls and visitors from now on."

"Please." He couldn't contain the misery that tinged his words.

"You could always beg off?"

Jonathan shook his head. "You and I both know how word spreads when a woman is scorned."

"Ah, so true. Well," Louise sighed. "Soldier through."

He nodded as she shut the door.

He picked up Felicia at five. Her boundless energy had her skipping to the car.

"So, what did you do today?" he asked as he buckled her safely into her car seat.

"We made reindeer out of popsicle sticks. I put a red pom-pom on his nose."

She held up the creature.

"It's beautiful," he agreed.

"I'm gonna put it on our tree." Her eyes shimmered with excitement. "Our tree, Daddy, isn't that so cool?"

"So cool," he agreed and made a mental note to shop for a real fir tree later next week.

Jonathan climbed into the car, and they headed to the Inn.

"Look, there's, Candi."

Jonathan glanced to the right and watched as she pushed a large plastic candy cane down into the ground.

"She's decorating for the holiday parade. That's next weekend. Can we help her?"

"Felicia, I don't know."

Jonathan looked up in the rearview mirror as he spoke to his daughter.

"She may not need our help."

"Candi would love our help. We help her and then she can help us."

"Us?" Jonathan asked as they pulled around back to their parking spot.

"Sure," Felicia continued. "We have to decorate our new house. It's our first Christmas."

"Let's not get ahead of ourselves. We have to get our furniture first."

Jonathan pulled the car to a halt and got out to hurry around and help his daughter out of the seat. Once free, Felicia handed him her reindeer and book bag.

"I'm going to help Candi," she said and skipped toward the Inn's rear entrance.

"Felicia, wait for me!" Jonathan cried and with hurried steps tried to catch up with her.

Candi stepped back and scrutinized the placement of the candy cane decorations. The two tallest had been placed in the center, then graduated sizes filtered down to the smallest, creating a beautiful curve.

"Candi! Candi!" Felicia's cry broke the early evening stillness.

Turning, Candi smiled. "Well, welcome home."

"They loved your cake." Felicia told her. "I knew they would. Jimmy Bowman said he wasn't going to eat a piece, but everyone talked about how good it was and finally, he did."

Candi blinked at the amount of information pouring from her mouth in a short spread of time.

"My gracious, I'm glad he ate some."

"Are you putting up decorations?"

"I am," she replied. Her eyes were drawn to Jonathan hurrying down the steps toward her.

"I couldn't stop her," he explained. "I hope she isn't bothering you."

"Oh no," Candi shook her head. "Not at all."

"Can we help?"

"You sure can," Candi replied. "I've got some garland to hang between the candy canes. But you must be careful, cause there are lights inside. Can you be very careful?"

Felicia's head bobbed.

"Then come here."

Opening a plastic tub, she pulled a string of lights wrapped in tulle from within. Handing the cord with the plug to Jonathan, she asked. "Can you run this over to the socket right beside the steps?"

He nodded.

"Now, Felicia, help me unwind this."

They stretched the tulle out along the sidewalk and when complete, Felicia stood beside Candi, feeding her the garland, while she zip-tied it to the candy canes creating a swag-like appearance.

"Plug it in," Candi called to Jonathan.

The lights sprang on and Felicia cried out in delight, clapping her hands together.

"It's beautiful!"

Candi stepped back admiring her handiwork. "I agree."

Jonathan joined them. "Nice touch," he murmured.

Candi looked over him and winked. "You haven't seen the best yet. Come on."

She led them into the Inn and straight to the tearoom.

"So, Liz's husband is a techno wizard," she began. "After I got the letter about the town decorations, I got Liz to soften him up and work on a light program for me." She stepped over to the wall light socket. "He created a computer program to work with the lights."

She flicked the switch. The room was suddenly awash in

a multitude of miniscule fairies flying around the walls, the ceiling, landing on the tables. Felicia squealed.

"It's like fireflies!"

"Exactly," Candi laughed.

"Sugar Plum Fairies," Jonathan murmured.

Candi nodded. "Just like in the poem, 'A vision of sugar plums danced in their heads' she quoted. "However, mine are Sugar Plum Fairies."

The color changed from white to pink. Felicia moved into the center of the room and twirled.

"I love it!"

"Which is just what you're supposed to do," Candi assured her.

The phone in Jonathan's pocket buzzed.

"Excuse me," he reached for it and stepped into the other room.

Candi moved toward Felicia as she held out her hands trying to capture one of the lights.

"Well, that was the moving company." Jonathan said upon his return.

"And?" Candi asked.

"They wanted to confirm that I would be there first thing Friday morning,"

Candi paused. She spoke calmly, with no light in her eyes or smile on her lips. "You'll be leaving early?"

He nodded.

"Oh." She swallowed. "Well, I guess it's for the best."

"Yes, we'll be able to get into our house and be settled by Monday."

Candi walked to the wall and cut the fairy light off. A deep inner pain squeezed at her heart. She swallowed the lump in her throat and turned. "How wonderful for you. Is there is anything I can do?"

"You've been wonderful," Jonathan replied. "Felicia?"

Quietly, the little girl moved toward her father and took his hand.

"I liked your lights," she said in a sad little tone.

Candi gave a wan smile. "Thank you, Felicia, I'm glad."

"See you tomorrow," Jonathan murmured and as Candi watched, they headed toward the elevator doors.

TEN

Jonathan stowed the last of the boxes into the back of his car and turned to Felicia.

"Time to go," he smiled.

His daughter turned to him, her mouth drawn into a frown.

"I don't want to go," she pouted.

Jonathan bent down on one knee and took her shoulders. "Honey, this is not our home. We can't stay here forever."

"Candi does."

Jonathan nodded. "Yes, sweetie, but this house belongs to her."

Felicia held her head down and refused to look at him. "Don't you like Candi?"

Jonathan's fingers squeezed Felicia's shoulders a bit tighter.

"Baby, you know I enjoy Candi's company."

"Then you could get her to let us stay here." She looked up hopefully. "I like my sugar plum room. I want to dance with the lights. We have nothing at that old house."

Jonathan's brows arched. "That old house, as you put it, is going to be our home. And we are going to make it just as fun as the Candy Cane Inn, you'll see."

Standing, he extended his hand to his daughter. "Come on, I've got a surprise for you at the new house."

Felicia looked up. "A pony?"

Jonathan chuckled. "No, nothing as grand as that. But come, you'll see."

Tucking her into the car, they drove toward Evergreen Street. He pulled into the driveway and turned off the car. Stepping out, he hurried around to the passenger side and helped Felicia out.

"What is it?" she asked. "I don't see anything special."

Just then the door to the house opened and Tiffany's mother stepped out. "Felicia," she cried and opened her arms.

"Gramma!"

Happily, his daughter took off toward the woman waiting on the front porch. Jonathan shut the car door. Maybe, with her Gramma there, Felicia could get over the separation from Candi. His heart, well, that was another matter. Turning to face them, he pasted on a smile and hurried to the front porch.

"See, I told you it was a good surprise."

Felicia glanced over at her father. "Yes, a good surprise. Are you going to stay with us?"

Tiffany's mother gave a shake of her head.

"No, sorry, dearie, your Poppie and I are only here for a few days. We came to help you settle in." She extended her hand to Felicia. "Come in and show me your room while Daddy brings in the boxes before he goes to work."

"Do I have to go to school today?" Felicia asked, glancing over her shoulder at her father.

"No, not if you don't want to."

"I think I want to. I'd like to show off my Gramma."

"Then I will gladly take you to school. We'll be fashionably late," Tiffany's mother replied. "Daddy will leave me directions."

"Of course."

He was just taking the last of the boxes inside when the big yellow van drove to a stop in front of the house. A large beefy-looking man climbed out of the cab holding a clipboard.

"Mr. Barlow?"

Jonathan set the box down and nodded. "Yes."

"We've got your stuff." He pointed over his shoulder at the van. "If you'll sign here, we'll get your goods unloaded."

"Right."

Jonathan took the clipboard and signed.

"My mother-in-law is here to help direct you. I'll be back around one to see if you need anything." He handed the papers back. "She has my number if there is an emergency."

"Thank you."

The man tore the carbon copy from the board and handed it to him.

"We'll get right on it."

Picking the box back up, Jonathan strode into the kitchen where Felicia was perched on a counter talking

505

with her grandmother.

"I heard voices." Tiffany's mother said.

"Movers are here." Jonathan replied and set the box down on the floor.

"Oh good, I'll take Felicia to her school."

"Daddy, we don't have any lunch food."

Jonathan stopped. "I forgot. I tell you what, why don't you drive by the Inn and get Miss Candi to fix you a sandwich one last time."

Felicia's eyes brightened. "Oh good, Gramma can meet her. You'll like Candi. She's wonderful."

Jonathan watched something in his mother-in-law's eyes change. He had the feeling she wasn't too keen on meeting Candi Cane. Then she brightened.

"I'd love to meet the lady who's taken such good care of my granddaughter."

Jonathan let her accusing glance roll over him as the two walked out the door. Perhaps calling Tiffany's mother and inviting them down hadn't been the best idea he'd had.

Clarisse Johnson held her granddaughter Felicia's hand and stared up at the Victorian home. "So this is the Candy Cane Inn you've been talking about."

"Yes. We helped Candi put the garland on the front, and inside you can watch the Sugar Plum Fairies dance."

"How quaint," Clarisse murmured, her distain oblivious to the little girl in her care. "Well, let's go in, shall we?"

Felicia hurried up the stairs and opened the door.

"Candi! I'm back."

"Felicia?"

Candi's voice heralded her entrance into the room. Wiping her hands on a kitchen cloth, she smiled seeing the little girl bobbing at the counter.

"Candi, come meet my Gramma."

Putting the cloth in her apron pocket, Candi fixed a bright

smile on her face and hurried forward.

"Hello," she extended her hand. "I'm Candi Cain."

"Clarisse Johnson."

"Felicia's mother's mom?" Candi asked, making the connection to the different last name.

"Yes. Tiffany was my daughter and Felicia's mother."

Their hands touched. Clarisse's shake was less than lukewarm. She quickly withdrew her hand.

"All the way over, Felicia talked about how wonderful her stay was here. I'm sorry you had to take time from your business to dote on her."

"It wasn't any trouble," Candi murmured.

She tried to ignore the piercing look Clarisse was giving her, as if she were somehow the enemy.

"We always try to make our guests feel at home. With Felicia it was easy."

"Can I turn on the fairy lights?" Felicia asked breathlessly.

Candi smiled. "Sure. Can you reach them?"

Felicia's head bobbed. Disappearing around the edge of the corner, she made for the light switch.

"You know, most women, when they find out Jonathan is a widower, just throw themselves at him. Some of them have even pretended to care for Felicia when all they really want is to latch on to an up and coming lawyer."

"Oh, really?" Candi grew still.

"Yes, it happens all the time," Clarisse continued. "That's one of the reasons I suggested he come down here and get away from those types of entanglements. Jonathan has big plans, you see. He wants to make his name known in the state, then move on to a government position."

She turned and her eyes bore into Candi's.

"My husband works in Austin, for the governor."

"I didn't know." Candi's voice sounded weak.

"Look, Gramma," Felicia called.

Clarisse stepped over to the entrance to the tearoom. She smiled as her granddaughter danced among the fluttering lights.

"Jonathan suggested we come for a bagged lunch. He hasn't had time to go to the market, but I'll take care of it this afternoon after I pick up Felicia. You see, we're staying with Jonathan."

"How nice," Candi murmured.

"Yes, it is. I know how much my granddaughter misses her mother even if Jonathan's blind to it. A man is no substitute for a mother's love, and I can't have anyone taking her place now, can I?"

Candi straightened her shoulders. "No. No, you can't, Mrs. Johnson." She hung her head down and turned away. "I'll get that bagged lunch for you."

"Thank you, Miss Cain."

"She's a witch, I tell you, a witch," Liz hissed as Candi smoothed the peanut butter onto the bread.

"Witch or not, you shouldn't have been listening." Candi shook the knife at her.

Liz brushed it away. "I bet Jonathan doesn't know she's talked to you like this. What made her come on like a bear defending its cub?"

"I don't know," Candi shrugged. "But, I've gotten the message. Mr. Barlow is off limits."

"You know what I think?"

"No," Candi sighed, "But I bet you're going to tell me."

"Darn right, I am. I think she realized Felicia has fallen for you and so has Jonathan."

Candi turned to face her friend. "And how is that happening? Felicia hasn't seen anything."

Liz's eyes narrowed. "And is there something to be seen?"

Candi slapped the other half of the bread over top and cut the sandwich in two. "No!"

She shoved the bread into the plastic bag and placed it in a pink-striped paper one.

"Here, put this cupcake in there," Liz sighed.

Candi slipped it in.

"I guess it's a good thing you found out now."

"Yes, lovely," Candi grumbled and hurried away.

Walking into the entrance, she thought about what Liz referred to. There had been only one instance that Felicia saw, the kiss. Had she mentioned it to her Grandmother?

"Here you go" she said brightly as Clarisse turned around.

"Thank you." She held out a twenty. "This should cover your cost."

Candi looked at the money. "No ma'am, there's no cost for this." She turned to Felicia. "You have the best day ever."

Clarisse gave an icy smile. "Cut the lights dear, we're late for school."

"Bye, Candi, bye." The little girl waved furiously as they hurried out the door.

The sound of the door shutting echoed in the entranceway and made Candi flinch. It was as if all her dreams crumbled. Her chin trembled. It started as a sniff, then quickly turned into a torrent of tears.

"Candi?" Liz's voice was filled with concern.

Her hands tried to cover her face and hide the emotion that poured down her cheeks.

"Oh, Candi," Liz hurried over and embraced her. "Shh, that old biddie isn't worth it."

"No," Candi sobbed, "But Jonathan was."

Pulling into the drive, Jonathan was relieved to see the curtains up and the lights on. Yes, it did look like home. Opening the door, he pulled his briefcase out and moved up the walk. He paused at the door and noticed the topiary fir with a twist of lights. Indeed, Clarisse had been at work. He opened the door.

"I'm home."

"Daddy!" Felicia raced from the kitchen, around the perfectly placed sofa, and into his arms, smothering his cheek with kisses. "I missed you."

"Well, I missed you, too. Did you have fun with Gramma?"

Felicia took a deep breath. "We had a tea party."

"That's nice." He stood.

"I'm going to write my letter to Santa. There's a big mailbox at the square. Molly Wilcox says that everyone puts their letters in there. You'll take me, won't you?"

"Of course I will," Jonathan agreed as they walked toward the kitchen.

Clarisse stood behind the counter with an apron around her waist, the perfect model of Betty Crocker, spoon in hand.

"What's for supper?" He asked, depositing his coat and briefcase on the chair at the table.

"Gramma made dinner from a box," Felicia climbed on the stool at the counter where her crayons were.

"A box?" Jonathan glanced over at her drawing.

In her childish hand, she'd drawn Santa's sleigh flying over a house with his reindeer.

"I haven't finished," Felicia replied without being asked. "I want to get this done as a present to Santa. I want to send it with my letter."

"You go ahead and finish." He kissed the crown of her head as she worked and turned his attention to his mother-in-law. "Mother Johnson, can I ask a favor of you?"

"Sure."

"I have to go out tomorrow evening, business meeting of sorts. Can you watch Felicia for me?"

Clarisse Johnson's smile appeared frozen on her lips. "Of course. Is everything all right, Jonathan?"

"Oh, fine." He smiled back. "The lady who sold me the house wants to turn over the final papers."

"Oh. Well go and enjoy."

"Yes," he glanced over at Felicia and winked. "Get your letter done, we'll mail it tomorrow."

Felicia gave him a smile. Walking back through the living room, Jonathan made his way toward the stairway. Pausing, he looked at the spot beside the fireplace. Yes, a good place for a tree. His heart lighter, Jonathan jogged up the stairs and headed for the shower.

"So, what are you going to wear tonight?" Liz asked, easing down to the chair in the tearoom.

"Wear?"

"It's Friday, Buttercup. Or have you been ignoring the whole week?"

"I've tried," Candi whispered.

Liz laughed. "You're going to be fine. It's just gonna take a while for the heart to heal."

"Guess so," Candi shrugged.

"Have you seen him?"

She shook her head. "No, not since he left. I thought maybe he'd call."

"No doubt the dragon has kept him busy."

Candi snorted. "You hush. Just because your mother-in-law is wonderful, you can't go about hoping everyone has the same."

"True. So have you gotten your drawing ready?"

"All done." Candi glanced over to the front desk. "Sitting in my notebook ready to go."

Liz gave her a critical eye. "So you're not changing?"

Candi looked down. "These are my good slacks."

"Go change." Liz sighed. "Wear that blue number you bought at Dazzles."

"Why blue?" Candi sighed.

"It matches your eyes."

"Oh grow up, Liz." Candi stood and moved toward the elevator.

Liz smirked as she heard Candi's footsteps fade. "Sometimes love just needs a push." She picked up the phone and dialed. "Did you get him to agree?"

"Yes. You owe me a pie a month starting in January," Karen's voice echoed with laughter through the cell.

"Jonathan hasn't a clue?"

"None."

Liz's smile grew. "Talk later."

Candi pulled the silvery-shawl Liz lent her close around her shoulders as she stepped into the Brazos. She was glad she'd gotten Mayor Jones to agree to meet her here rather than have the official I'll-pick-you-up-at-seven date. Walking over to the front kiosk, she waited for Donna Bradley to glance up.

"Oh, hey, Candi," her old friend greeted her. "Meeting Mayor Jones?"

Candi took a deep breath and wondered if everyone knew. "Yes. Is he here?"

"He's been waiting. Follow me."

Donna led her across the old building that once had been a grist mill now turned into a four-star restaurant. As they drew near the table, Mayor Frank Jones rose, a big smile illuminating his face.

"Candi, I'm so glad you could make it." He stepped forward and placed a kiss on her cheek. "You look fabulous." He grinned at Donna. "Good enough to do more than kiss."

"Let's leave it at good enough," Candi smiled and took the seat he offered.

"I'll bring your menus in just a moment," Donna smiled as she left.

Frank took his seat. "So, how's business?"

"Fine," she replied and pulled the napkin into her lap.

"I rode past the Candy Cane, your decorations look wonderful. I hear you have quite a light show inside."

"Something Liz's husband came up with."

"Candi?"

She turned at the sound of another voice. Her smile froze. There stood Karen Darden with her arm linked into Jonathan's.

"Hello, Karen," Frank answered.

"Frank."

Candi's eyes shifted to Jonathan. His eyes softened.

"You look well, Candi."

"So do you," she answered, then lowered her eyes toward the tablecloth.

"Frank, while you're here, can I talk to you about something?" Karen asked.

"Sure. You don't mind, do you, Candi?"

Candi's eyes never strayed. "No, I don't mind."

Jonathan waited until Karen and Frank left, then he moved and took Frank's seat.

"How are you, Candi?"

She looked up. Her heart skipped a beat. Somehow overnight, he'd gotten more handsome. "Fine."

She looked down at the napkin and took a steadying breath. "How's Felicia?"

"She's fine."

His hand found hers. "I thought you'd call or come by?"

She looked up. Her heart fluttering, she pulled her hand back, placing it in her lap, "I've been busy."

He drew back. "I see."

Jonathan glanced around the room. "Take a walk with me?"

"I'm waiting to talk to Frank."

"Please."

The look in his eyes implored her to agree. With a nod of her head, she stood and pulled the shawl up around her shoulders. Jonathan's hand found her elbow, and he led her through Brazos' patio doors and out into the moonlight

"It's so beautiful here." He leaned against the rail of the sidewalk and stared up at the full moon.

"What did you want to talk about, Jonathan?" She pulled the shawl tight around her like a shield.

"You. Us." He turned to face her and stuck his hands in his pockets.

Candi smiled. "There is no us. You were a guest at our Inn. We made your stay comfortable. End of story."

"No, it's not. You know it's not." His hand came free and in frustration he raked his dark hair back from his forehead. "I don't understand."

"There's nothing to understand. You're an up and coming lawyer. I know that women throw themselves at you, and Mistletoe is just a stop before you take on a job for the governor."

He listened to the words coming out of her mouth, words that he had heard before almost verbatim. "Candi, that's not true."

He watched her take a deep breath.

"Enjoy your dinner, Jonathan. Tell Felicia I said hello."

Stunned, he could only watch as she turned and walked away.

Candi could feel the tears swell against her lashes. Entering the Brazos, she spied Frank and Karen at the bar. Opening her pocketbook, she pulled her sketch from her purse.

"Excuse me, Karen." She turned to Frank. "Mayor, I apologize for ruining your evening, but I'm not feeling well. Here is my sketch of the cake. Call if it's not to your liking, I'm going home. I need to get some rest."

"Candi," Frank called her name as she thrust the paper into his hands.

"Have a great evening," she murmured and walked away.

ELEVEN

Jonathan walked into the house and tore the tie from his neck. "Mother Johnson!"

He tossed it across the sofa. "Mother Johnson," he called again, this time louder.

Walking into the kitchen, he looked around and found the letter Felicia had written to Santa alongside her picture. He was still staring at it when Clarisse walked in.

"Jonathan, what's all the shouting about? You realize you could awaken Felicia?"

"What did you do?" he demanded.

Clarisse'seyes grew wide. "I'm not following."

"Oh, I think you are. I sent you to the Candy Cane Inn to get Felicia's lunch and you said something to Candi, didn't you."

"Me?" Her hand fluttered to her chest as his eyes narrowed.

"Indeed, you. I saw Candi tonight."

Clarisse took a deep breath.

"She said some very strange things. She told me that I was only here to get my name out. Then I was going to take a job at the governor's office."

"It might have come out in conversation."

"Might," Jonathan snapped. "I came to Mistletoe to start a new life. I will not start that life with my mother-in-law meddling in my affairs or my love life. What gave you that right?"

"I'm not a witness you can interrogate," Clarisse snapped.

Jonathan folded his arms over his chest. "Why? Just tell me why?"

Clarisse tilted her chin in defiance. "Felicia told me you kissed her. My daughter is not cold in her grave and you're flirting."

Jonathan closed his eyes. "Clarisse, Tiffany has been dead for nearly two years. I cannot be a man in mourning for the rest of my life so that you won't forget your daughter. Felicia is living proof."

"Clarisse, Jonathan," Darren Johnson peeked into the

kitchen. "I heard you all the way in the other room."

"Jonathan has accused me of meddling in his life."

Darren stared at his wife, then looked at his son-in-law. "What'd she do?"

"She told a woman that I was only here until I got my name out there so I could work with you at the governor's office."

"Clarisse!"

"He kissed another woman. My Tiffany has just died, and he wants to bring another woman into this house to replace her."

"I never said that," Jonathan replied. "But my love life is my own. If I want to date someone and marry her, I will. But, Mother Johnson, no one could ever take Tiffany's place. I loved your daughter. But there is room in my heart for someone else, and one day you will have to understand that."

"He's right, Clarisse. Jonathan needs to move on with his life. No one will ever replace Tiffany. Come to bed. We have a big day in the morning," Darren told her.

Clarisse walked toward her husband, then turned. "Jonathan, I am sorry. I only did what I thought was best."

He nodded. "I'm not mad, Clarisse, just frustrated. I'll see you in the morning."

Candi tromped down the staircase at the rear of the house, her head splitting from lack of sleep. She wasn't in the mood to deal with a major migraine when she had to work on the mayor's cake. "I need aspirin."

"Liz? Liz?" She could hear the radio blaring holiday tunes. "Can you turn that thing down?"

No response.

"Liz!" She waited. "Oh, for gosh sakes," Candi stomped into the kitchen and switched off the radio. "Liz, I hope I told you we are working on the mayor's cake. Did you get the marzipan ready? Liz...."

Her eyes widened. Liz was leaning against the sink, her

slacks damp and a groan that sounded like it had rolled up from her toes erupting from her lips.

"It isn't time," she replied.

"Oh honey, "Candi rushed to her side. "It's time."

"I want to push."

Candi's eyes widened. "No, no pushing."

Pulling her phone from her pocket, she hit speed dial not even looking at the number. To her surprise Jonathan's voice answered.

"Jonathan?"

"Candi?"

"Liz," she said. "Labor. Now!"

"Got it. Hang up and have her lie down. I'm calling the rescue squad."

Candi ended the call and tossed her phone on the floor. Collecting a few hand towels, she helped Liz lie down.

"I'm so sorry," Liz replied after another contraction. "The mayor's cake."

"Shh. The mayor can wait. You're bringing a new life into this world, one who evidently likes my Inn."

Liz tried to smile. Her eyes widened.

"Breath! Choo Choo" Candi ordered.

Holding on to Liz's hand, they went through the process together.

"Hang in there," Candi urged as the contraction ended.

The door banged open and Jonathan rushed in with Felicia at his heels.

"Is she all right?"

"She fine. She's having a baby." Candi told him. "Where's the rescue squad?"

"Right behind me."

Candi looked back to see several firemen and medics rolling the stretcher forward. She squeezed Liz's hand.

"It's going to be okay."

She rose from her knees and stepped back to let the paramedics do their job. One of the men looked up.

"I don't think this baby is going to wait. Have any fresh towels?"

"I'll go get them," Candi replied and rushed from the room. Grabbing several from the hall, she brought them back and handed them to the paramedics.

"Hey Candi?"

"Yes."

"You might want to escort your little friend into the other room."

"Right." Candi turned and looked at Felicia. "Why don't we go into the tearoom?"

"Good idea," Jonathan agreed.

They led the little girl into the tearoom.

"Will Miss Liz be okay?" Felicia asked, looking from Candi to her father.

"Yes, sweetheart, she will," Candi replied and brushed Felicia's soft curls.

"It's just that the paramedics don't need all of us standing around watching," Jonathan assured her.

He looked to Candi.

"I was surprised when you called."

Candi shrugged. "I really didn't know who I dialed. Thanks for calling the paramedics."

"No problem."

Candi looked down at Felicia who was holding an envelope. "What do you have there?"

"A letter to Santa." Felicia looked up at her. "All the kids in my class were talking about writing letters to Santa. I wanted to do that too. I'm asking for a very special present."

"Oh my, well, we'll definitely have to mail it," Candi agreed.

Felicia turned the envelope over in her hands. "Do you want to know what it is?"

"If you tell me, then it won't come true," Candi explained.

Felicia stared at her letter, then glanced up with tears in her eyes. "It may not come true anyway."

"Felicia," Jonathan murmured.

"It's true." The little girl pushed the chair back and came to her feet, looking directly at her Daddy. "I heard you and Gramma fussing last night. She was wrong. I want Candi as my mother, not to replace my mother in heaven, but to be my mom on earth." Felicia looked at Candi as a tear escaped her lashes and rolled down her cheek. "You love Candi, but you're afraid to tell her. Then Gramma came here and made both of you sad so you won't speak."

"Felicia," Jonathan began.

"Felicia, no one can make anyone fall in love," Candi murmured.

Jonathan swallowed. "But she's right. My mother-in-law did interfere."

Candi blinked.

"I don't know what will happen in the future, but Candi Cain, my daughter is right. I am falling in love with you. I want you in our life."

"Jonathan, I-I don't know what to say."

"Say yes," Felicia whispered.

"Yes, I want to be in your life," Candi whispered. Her eyes, like Felicia's, brimmed with tears.

Jonathan stepped forward and pulled Candi to him. Their lips met and suddenly everything in the world seemed wonderful. "I love you, Candi Cain. I think I loved you from our first kiss. I want to go on kissing you until we see where this crazy ride leads us."

They kissed again as Felicia moved to the light switch and turned on the fairies.

"I got my wish. Thank you, Santa," she whispered.

Their kiss ended. Jonathan leaned his head against Candi's forehead. "We'll have to decide where to live."

"Your house of course," Candi smiled. "I've always loved it."

"This doesn't have to be a long courtship, does it?"

She shook her head no.

Suddenly the cry of an infant filled the air. Felicia clapped her hands.

"Liz has had her baby!"

Candi and Jonathan moved toward the excited little girl. They each took one of her hands and walked toward the kitchen.

"Is it safe to come in?" Candi called out.

"Safe," one of the paramedics responded.

Candi opened the door. Liz was now on the gurney holding her special bundle. They walked over and peered down at the little boy.

"Welcome, Elijah," Candi whispered.

"Hello, Elijah," Felicia said. "Candi, will I be Elijah's big sister?"

"You sure can," Candi smiled back. "Liz is part of the family, just like you're going to be."

Liz's grin grew. "So, you've finally found Mr. Right."

Candi nodded. "Forever and always."

With Jonathan's arm around her, Candi watched as the paramedics wheeled Liz and her new baby out to the waiting ambulance.

"You know, I think I'm going to need another dozen cinnamon buns."

"Oh?" Candi gazed at him. "And why?"

"I'm gonna be very late for work." And he leaned in for another Candi Cain kiss.

ABOUT THE AUTHORS

Visit the Authors of Main Street Blog

E. AYERS

Born and raised with wealth, E. Ayers turned away from all of it and married a few days after turning eighteen, to the shock and dismay of family and friends.

A firm believer in love conquering everything, there was never cause to look back. The newlyweds' life-long love became the springboard for many future novels.

Fascinated with the way people deal with everyday problems, E. Ayers has always been an observer and a listener. A simple problem for one person is a mountain for another. Utilizing those common predicaments, the subsequent novels have touched many lives.

Today finds E. Ayers writing while living in a pre-Civil War home with a dog and a cat. Rattling around in an old money pit provides one's muse with plenty of freedom. A perfect day is spent at the keyboard, coffee in hand, and everything in the house actually working as it should.

As the official matchmaker for all the characters who wander through a mind full of imagination and the need to share, E. Ayers enjoys finding just the right ones to create a story.

Where to Find E. Ayers on the Web

Twitter: @ayersbooks
Website: ayersbooks.com
E. Ayers Blog: http://ayersbooks.wordpress.com/

MORE GREAT BOOKS FROM E. AYERS!

Wedding Vows (boxed set) *
With This Ring (novella) *
I Thee Wed (novella) *
To Have and To Hold (novella) *
Wanting (A River City Novel)
A New Beginning (A River City Novel)
A Challenge (A River City Novel)
Forever (A River City Novel)
A Son (A River City Novel)
A Child's Heart (A River City Novel)
Campaign (A River City Novel)
Coming Out of Hiding (a novel)
A Fine Line (a novella) *
Mariners Cove (a novella) *
Ask Me Again (a novella)
A Skeleton at Her Door (a novella)
Happy Holidays River City (a collection) *

Western Books by E. Ayers

A Snowy Christmas in Wyoming (a novella) *
A Cowboy's Kiss in Wyoming (a novella) *
A Love Song in Wyoming (a novella) *
A Calling in Wyoming (a novella) *

About the Authors

Baby It's Cold Outside (a collection novella) *
A Rancher's Woman (a historical novel) *
A Rancher's Dream (a historical novel) *
Loving Matilda (a historical Kindle World novel) *
Loving Ellen (a historical Kindle World novel) *
Sweetwater Springs Christmas (a historical anthology) *

JILL JAMES

I hope you enjoyed Waking Up For Christmas, my contribution to Christmas at the Inn on Main Street. This story is dedicated to the ladies of Authors of Main Street who, when I threw down the challenge, picked it up so enthusiastically and gracefully. I hope you will let me know what you thought of the story. You can find me at the following places...

Twitter: @Jill_James
Facebook: https://www.facebook.com/Jill.James.author/
Website: http://www.jilljameswrites.com/
Newsletter: http://eepurl.com/hvtn-/

MORE GREAT BOOKS FROM JILL JAMES!

The Lake Willowbee Series
Divorce, Interrupted
Dare To Trust
Defend My Love
The Reluctant Bride – a Lake Willowbee novella

Shifters of San Laura
Dangerous Shift
Stolen Shift – coming 2017

Time of Zombies
Love in the Time of Zombies
The Zombie Hunter's Wife
A Time to Kill Zombies
Zombies in the Grass – coming 2017

CAROL DEVANEY

Carol falls in love with every character she writes in her books. She loves basing them on the good and the bad personalities that make up life. That's what makes them real.

Carol feels as though she's in a movie when visualizing characters and she jumps right onto the page with them.

Often the theme of her books is forgiveness. Whether planned or not, forgiveness sneaks its way into her stories. That's okay, because Carol believes forgiving others is essential. She favors a great story, with slices of twists that cause her to reflect on the problems life throws at us and how we react.

Humor is a big part of her stories and daily routine, and yes, she laughs a lot! Carol believes in happy endings. Travel is one of her favorite things to do. She dabbles in art, always has popcorn and hot chocolate on hand.

Carol is a small-town girl at heart and her stories are peppered with a dose of humor, based on Southern roots. She currently resides in Georgia with her husband and family.

Where to Find Carol DeVaney on the Web

Twitter: @caroldevaney
Facebook: https://www.facebook.com/caroldevaney.author
Website: http://caroldevaney.weebly.com/

MORE GREAT BOOKS FROM CAROL DEVANEY!

A Matter of Taste
Perfect Match
A Smoky Mountain Christmas
Christmas at Apple Lake

SUSAN R. HUGHES

I'm a *USA Today* bestselling author of contemporary and historical romance. I live in Ottawa, Ontario, with my husband and three children. If you'd like to know about my new releases and special offers, you can sign up for my newsletter on my website, listed here.

Where to Find Susan R. Hughes on the Web

Website: http://www.susanrhughes.weebly.com/

MORE GREAT BOOKS FROM SUSAN R. HUGHES!

A Baby for Christmas (Holiday Bundles of Joy Book 1)
A Baby for New Year's (Holiday Bundles of Joy Book 2)
The Christmas Charm
Wine & Roses
Healing Anna's Heart
Secret Vow
Kiss the Bridesmaid
Forever Your Valentine
Halloween Kisses
Divided Hearts
Where the Heart Lies
Sense of Touch
Someone Like You
Heart's Desire
Believe in Me
Mistletoe & Wine

NAN O'BERRY

Home is where the heart lies. Or so Nan O'Berry believes. She grew up on a quiet street in Virginia Beach, Virginia, However, her love of horses led her family to purchase a small farm in the western Tidewater area. She grew up listening to family tales, so it is not surprising that she loves a great story.

Armed with a bachelors degree in Interdisciplinary Studies from Old Dominion University, she loves sharing heroic stories of cowboys, lumberjacks, and small town folks.

Where to Find Nan O'Berry on the Web

Website: http://oberrynan.wixsite.com/nanoberryauthor
Facebook: https://www.facebook.com/Nancy-OBerry-Romance-Author-161753103856411
Twitter: @nanobe1

MORE GREAT BOOKS FROM NAN O'BERRY!

Rebel's Crossroads Series
Contemporary Small Town Romance
Welcome to Rebel's Crossroads. A place where people enjoy a summer afternoon on the front porch with a wave of a hand and a glass of sweet tea. What could be more charming, than finding love in a small town?

Playing With Fire
Random Acts of Kindness

Indigo Spring Series
Contemporary Western Romance
Love comes happily ever after, if you follow your heart's dreams. In Indigo Springs, Texas, that's what awaits the

three Malone brothers. Come meet Logan Malone and his brothers, Jason and Troy, as they navigate true love's often bumpy course.

Prince Charming Wore Spurs
Once Upon a Dream
To Lasso Her Heart

Short Stories
Apple of His Eye
Room at the Inn
Cupid's Beau

Montana Sky Series (Kindle Worlds)
Historical Western Romance

Road to Redemption

www.ingramcontent.com/pod-product-compliance
Lightning Source LLC
Chambersburg PA
CBHW050100120726
47904CB00004B/1161